FIRE
AND
BONE

ALSO BY RACHEL A. MARKS

Winter Rose (novella)

The Dark Cycle

Darkness Brutal
Darkness Fair
Darkness Savage

FIRE
AND
BONE

RACHEL A. MARKS

SKYSCAPE

SKYSCAPE

Published by Skyscape, New York
www.apub.com

Amazon, the Amazon logo, and Skyscape are trademarks of Amazon.com, Inc., or its affiliates.

ISBN-13: 9781503946750
ISBN-10: 1503946754

Cover design by Eileen Carey

Printed in the United States of America

For my bashert, *Joseph, because he knew before I did.*

BEFORE

The flames came without warning at her touch.

She could do nothing. Only watch the fire consume him as her soul splintered.

His long black hair took wing with the blaze, twisting and melting into nothing as his screams filled the forest where they stood. The same forest where she'd kissed his human lips, reveling in his scent. Where she'd let him love her, their secret safe in the arms of the emerald trees. Now all was orange and golden light, eating him away.

She tried to quench the flames with her shawl, her hands, but still his perfect skin blistered and cracked, peeling off in flakes to float away with the sparks above her head. It happened so quickly. The face she'd kissed so many times disappeared in the dancing glow, unveiling a grinning skull.

Her cries of anguish echoed around her as his choked off, his charred body crashing to the ground.

Sweet mother Brighid, no! *What had she done?*

Silver smoke rose in pluming clouds, stinging her eyes, her nostrils, as the burns on her hands healed.

He was hers. Hers. How could the goddess take him?

Her love. Her shadow. But now . . .

Bones in the fire.

Her chest heaved with the weight of it, and she fell to her knees in agony.

No, it wasn't the goddess who'd done this.

She'd done it. She'd killed him.

She'd lost control of the flame.

ONE

SAGE

I have this thing for fire. It terrifies me. Because when I feel the warmth on my skin, or watch the dancing flames, it's as if the pulsing glow is speaking to me. It's only a small whisper, but it's crystal clear in my mind. A voice that merges with the rhythm of the flickering tongues of light: *Touch. Feed. Control.* I'm sure something is very wrong with me, but my crazy isn't my biggest problem right now. It's my lack of a place to crash for the night.

I flick my lighter on and pretend I don't hear the whispers as I hold the flame up to the end of Ziggy's cigarette.

She pulls in a drag and then coughs. She's totally asthmatic, but for some reason she won't quit. "I hope they have some of those blueberry scones left over," she says, leaning on the wall beside the back door of the coffee shop. She twists one of her short dreadlocks around her finger. "They make me feel fancy. And I need to feel fancy on Halloween, like I'm in disguise."

The alley is lit by the small yellow lamp above the door. It casts an odd glow over our surroundings, making the shadows look deep and dangerous. There's even a raven cawing above us, perched on a buzzing power line, rounding off the All Hallows' feel of the night and masking the sporadic rustle of rats behind the dumpster several feet away. This is our routine every other night now, dinner courtesy of Granada Grounds. Apparently, there's some lame law that they have to throw the leftover "spoiled" food away. No donating it to the homeless, just the roaches and rats. But the owner's daughter, Star, made a deal with us that on the nights she's closing she'll put edible leftovers in a sealed container before tossing them out. She usually puts something extra in there, like granola bars or bottles of sparkling water. I guess Ziggy and I are now her charity cases.

Whatever, I'm too hungry to care.

"You need meat, Sage," Ziggy says, looking me up and down. "You're totally bony, girl. Those tits are about to evaporate." She shakes her head in disapproval, takes another drag, and coughs.

I look down at my chest and shrug. I've never been vain. Which is good, because at this point I haven't showered in a week and I had to give myself a haircut with some guy's pocketknife when I got goop in my hair that I couldn't wash out. Ziggy actually cried. My "amazingly bamtastic fiery locks," as she calls them, were ruined.

I'm so over it.

"I thought you liked skinny girls," I say.

"Sorry to break it to you, but you've never been my type, white girl." She winks at me.

I kick a rock her way with my boot. "Heartbreaker."

"Look who's talkin'." She shakes her head. "You've been leavin' puddles of drooling boys behind you for the three months I've known you. When was the last time you let one get up in that?" She motions to my body with her cigarette.

Try never. I don't know why, but the idea of letting a guy get close terrifies me. I haven't even let a boy kiss me since middle school. And that was just a peck—so maybe it wasn't technically a kiss. How pathetic is that? It's not like any guy's ever hurt me; if anything, I think I intimidate them—Ziggy says it's my stoic demeanor. But I don't think

4

that would stop a determined flirt. It's just . . . every time I see a hot guy, someone I'd want to touch and kiss, my skin heats up like I'm a fifty-year-old woman having a hot flash. The urges I get in my head make me flush. So I just back away.

See what I mean about the crazy?

The door beside us squeaks, and Ziggy and I move deeper into the shadows just in case it's not Star.

A blue head of hair peeks out into the alley. "Hey bitches, I got the goods." She spots us and comes out the rest of the way. She's dressed in this tight blue-checkered dress that makes her look like Dorothy from some porno version of *The Wizard of Oz*. "And I have the best idea *ever*."

Uh-oh. Last time Star had an idea, we all nearly ended up in jail.

"We're just hungry for food tonight," I say. "No adventure."

Star frowns, and her fake freckles scrunch up under her eyes. I don't remember Dorothy having freckles, but then her blue dress was also made with a lot more fabric than Star's is.

"There's going to be a ton of food there!" She grins wickedly. "And guys. Loads of guys."

"Chips and beer don't count as food," I say.

"And I'm not into dudes," Ziggy adds, clarifying, even though she doesn't sound as negative as I am about the adventure. "Plus, Miss Sage here is a nun."

"I am not," I say. A nun is holy and pure. That I am definitely not.

"Great!" Star claps. "I've already got the Uber heading our way."

"Are you thick?" Ziggy asks. She takes a casual drag of her cigarette. And coughs.

Star waves at the trailing smoke. "I'm only thinking of *you*. The other night you said you slept in a laundromat. Tonight, you could have a good meal, sleep in a warm house with carpets and couches . . . possibly go in a hot tub!"

And a shower. Oh my God, a shower. "Okay, we'll go," I say.

Ziggy glances sideways at me, then shrugs and throws down her cigarette. "Whatever the nun wants."

Star's face opens in a huge smile and I have no idea what's made her so happy. *Oh goody, two homeless girls are gonna crash a Halloween party with me!* Doesn't she have any real friends? She claps again and makes a small squeal in the back of her throat. "We'll stop by my house and dress you guys up. I have tons more costumes, and—"

"No!" Ziggy and I say in unison.

Star raises her hands in surrender. "Okay, too far. I get it." She tips her head and her blue bangs fall across her eyes. "So, no Halloween? Is it a religious thing?"

"Do we look like we give a shit about holidays?" Ziggy asks.

Star shrugs. "Just checking. I don't want to give you the wrong kinds of cookies for Christmas." She spins in her red stiletto Mary Janes and heads back into the coffeehouse, waving us in after her.

~

The party is in an old Chatsworth neighborhood. The Uber driver pulls up the street, parking in front of a driveway. Ziggy and I get out of the car and follow Star up to the house. It's sort of rocking the 1950s American Dream vibe with a sprawling lawn out front, a curved driveway lined with flowers, and a porch with a swing. It's decorated in the usual Halloween fare: pumpkin lights strung over the garage, huge spider decals in the windows, and a skeleton hanging out in the bushes.

A raven lands on the roof with a sudden flurry of wings as we walk up to the door. It perches on the rain gutter, looking at us sideways. My gut churns. You don't usually see ravens out at night, and this is the second one I've noticed now.

But then I'm distracted by something hanging from the eaves that looks like a blow-up sex doll dressed in a tuxedo.

"That's Jeeves, the butler," Star says when she sees the confused look on my face. "I helped decorate," she adds with pride.

"How do you know these people?" This is probably something I should've asked earlier.

"My cousin lives here. It's his place."

Shit, I don't really know this girl at all. This was an unsafe move on my part. But Ziggy's with me, and no one messes with her. I'll just get my shower, she can get food, and then we'll jet.

"We're early," Star says as she opens the door without knocking. "The real fun won't start for another hour or so. But you should be able to duck into a room and make yourselves at home, no problem."

Ziggy steps inside with Star, and I follow, hesitant. "Will your cousin mind?" I ask. The front room is decorated like a bachelor pad, with beanbag chairs and a pool table. At first glance, I see only half a dozen people, most of them dudes, except one girl. Poor Ziggy.

"Nope, Ben is super chill," Star says, "as long as you don't steal his stuff or punch a hole through a wall."

Not planning on doing either of those things.

"Just lead me to those hamburgers you mentioned in the car," Ziggy says. "I'm famished." Then she turns and points to me. "And skinny'll take two."

"I need to use the bathroom," I say, ignoring her. I can't waste time eating if there's a usable shower in the vicinity.

"There's a guest bedroom and bathroom in the back." Star points to a hall behind her. "Last door on the left. Make yourself at home."

I nod my thanks and zip past a couple of partygoers. The room is small, with an attached bathroom, and it has everything I need. I shut the bathroom door behind me, checking that it locks before stripping down. Then I slide into the shower and let the stream of warm water start peeling off the layers of street and smog.

I grab the soap and scrub more than I need to, mostly because I don't want to get out. I haven't had a hot shower in so long. Too long.

I try not to let myself feel my thin body, my ribs jutting through the skin, my scrawny hips and legs, my knees too sharp and bony, unhealthy, unattractive. It's been a rough year. But I'd rather be here, scrounging for a random shower and a meal, than stuck in a group transition home. I hear those can be even worse than foster homes. I ran away from the last place the system put me in. I've always made sure to get out quick once some bitch or bitch boy gets pissed at my presence, since it inevitably turns into me becoming their personal punching bag. I've always made people nervous. According to my last social worker, I was "difficult to place." I've seen the notes in my file: *Lacks personal connection with peers.* And: *Inability to invest in relationships.*

I'm not really sure why Ziggy puts up with me.

I'm broken, mostly because of the broken woman who spawned me. I swear, adults should have to get a license to make a kid. Prove they've got their shit together before they bring a child into the world. My mom tried, I think. She thought she could piece herself into something resembling a mother by dropping the drugs and dropping the need to feed her overblown selfish streak. But she failed. And so, at age ten, I was released from her forever. I bounced around foster care until it eventually became a blur of angry kids and overworked caregivers. The only place I felt safe was in my own head, where the sneers and fists could be ignored—I must've read a thousand books the first year or two. In the pages of the stories, I could catch killers or kill monsters. My favorites were the legends with angry gods, cursed kings, or castles in the murky fog. Not the romance novels—hell, no. I liked the novels that ended in blood-soaked battlefields best. Which is ironic, I guess, considering I've become a master at conflict avoidance. My default mode is: leave if things get too tense.

I make it on my own now. And while life's gotten more difficult in some ways, it's also much more peaceful. I can sit on the beach and read all day if I want. I can walk for miles and still be home. I'm not tied to anyone or anything. I'm free. I turned eighteen last month, so I could choose to get aid now, or job training, maybe go back to school, but the system can kiss my ass. If I'm going to figure my life out, it won't be under some social worker's microscope. I'm done with being a name on a file.

I get out of the shower and dry off, then fold the towel, placing it exactly how it was before I used it. I look at my pile of dirty clothes on the floor and sigh. I don't want to put those stiff things back on. There's a robe on the back of the door, so I grab it and slip into it, then walk into the bedroom. It drags behind me, way too big for my shrunken frame. The noises of the party seem louder now, but I don't hear anyone in the hallway. I check the closet for clothes and spot a couple of things that might work; there's a white cotton button-up on a hanger and a pair of jeans in a stack of folded pants on the shelf above it. Maybe I could wear them for now. I'm so tired. And I'm dying to have clean clothes on for a second. I'll put my own stuff on again before I leave.

The jeans are too big so I roll them at the waist, then find socks and a wifebeater in what looks like a small laundry basket. I put them on and slide the white dress shirt over the tank. I gather my dirty clothes and throw them into the basket, then shuffle over to the bed and plop down onto the heavenly mattress. I lean back on a pile of pillows so comfortable and soft, I can't keep my eyes open.

I breathe deeply, and sleep pulls me under.

～

Wings rustle as he enters the stone room. The flames in the hearth behind me crackle as I take in the sight of him. At last I see him with my own eyes. My fate.

The King of Ravens.

His black hair is flecked with gold from the firelight, and his shadowed gaze glints with silver. The inking of a black raven is etched over his bare skin. It wraps around the muscles of his broad shoulders and covers his right arm. On his head he wears a silver laurel. Around his neck is the heavy iron torque that holds back his immense power.

He grips the body of a limp winter fox in one fist and a bloody dagger in the other. The white body drips crimson onto the stone floor as the king steps closer to me. I can't look away from the rare fox, its beauty snuffed out by those beastly hands. That will be me very soon if I'm not cautious.

But even in my fear, I stand firm. I cannot cower from him. In spite of all I've done, I'm no craven thing. He is my punishment, my eternal cage. Because of what happened in the arms of the trees . . .

No. I can't let myself think of the human boy I burned in the wood. How with a kiss I pulled life from him until there was nothing left. I was a fool to think I could control it on my own. I deserve punishment. This dark beast's coldness is what I have earned.

The Cast's envoy stands in the corner, watching my first exchange with the king. He's a thin man, a bit hunched in his heavy furs, balding. Not what I expected from the representative of the powerful Cast of Seven, who live in the Otherworld, lording over all of us demis for their maker, the mother goddess, Danu. I would think the Cast would send someone more daunting in size to oversee the initial introduction of this match that they've allowed my mother and the Morrigan to draft.

This is the first time the Cast has permitted a Bond between two Houses, two bloodlines, two separate, very different powers: fire and spirit. Somehow the mistake I made warrants a complete shift in the order just to control me. And so the King of Ravens is my doom.

There is no escape once the vows of the Bond are sealed at the next new moon and I've given myself over fully. This beast is far more powerful than I am. He'll surely eat away at my soul, my powers, a little at a time, until all that's left of me is a mindless shell.

Like the charcoal bones of the boy I killed.

I still see the horror of that day when I close my eyes. The hollow skull smoking on the mossy ground of the forest, the embers of my youthful foolishness.

The king steps closer and drops the body of the fox at my feet. Its golden eyes are glazed over with death, and it wears a glistening ring of blood around its throat.

"For you," the king says, his voice prickling over my skin. "An offering for my future Bonded, the Daughter of Fire."

I give a curt nod and try not to stare at the pool of red spreading along the cracks in the stone floor.

He holds out the dagger. "Would you prefer to do the honors?"

I look at his blood-smeared palm and my mouth goes dry. "Much gratitude, but no. I wouldn't wish to dirty my skirts."

His eyes rake over me. "You must settle yourself into this life, Daughter of Fire. We are not full of youthful whims here in the North. You are now a grown woman, and this is a cold world." He steps closer and takes my chin in his fingers, the sticky blood smearing my skin. "It is a shame that you are so lovely."

I make myself meet his icy, silver-blue gaze. "Why?"

His lips tilt in a sad smile. "Because, my fire creature, nothing beautiful survives my cold touch. I doubt you'll be the first."

TWO

SAGE

"She's definitely not much to look at," a voice says, pulling me from sleep. I was dreaming of . . . I don't know, it's fluttered out of my head already. But I do know I'm not alone in the room.

I sit up in a rush and scramble back against the wall.

Three large males hover over me, all wearing cat ears and holding red Solo cups. Two are blond with pale skin, and the third is super tan with brown eyes and dark brown hair. They study me intently, like I'm some sort of science experiment they're trying to figure out.

"Whoa," blond number one says, his head pulling back.

Blond number two adds, "Skittish thing," like I'm not staring right at him.

The tan guy takes a drink, then says, "You'd be skittish too if you woke up to someone insulting you."

Blondie One looks dubious. "You know I'm flawless, Ben."

"Sure I do," Brown Eyes answers dryly. He must be the cousin.

Star pushes them all aside. "Gods' bones, give the girl space to breathe. I told you to leave her be until Faelan gets here."

"You aren't in charge, Star," Blondie Two says, then chugs his drink. Whatever's in the cup appears to be red; some of it stains his lips before he licks it off.

Star rolls her eyes and throws up her hands. "Far be it from me to make Faelan's job easier."

"What the hell's going on?" I ask, looking from one figure to the other. I've woken up in the twilight zone. Who's Faelan?

"Ignore these beefburgers, Sage," Star says as she sets her cup down on the bedside table. "Go away, all of you. The girl needs to rest."

Ben starts to object. "But what about the spe—"

She smacks her hand over his mouth. "Later, Ben." She shoos at the three muscular guys with her tiny hands.

They bow their heads, looking contrite as they leave the room.

Star sighs dramatically and sits on the bed. "Boys are so annoying."

"Star, what is going on?" I hug one of the pillows to my chest.

"Oh, they just heard about you and were curious."

"You talked to them about me?" Why would she do that? That's weird and creepy. Horror stories of street kids being bought and sold like cattle fill my head.

Her face pinches with concern. "Not like in a stalker way!" she says. "I just told them that I was hoping we could . . . you know, help you. Good karma and all that." She looks at me sheepishly. "Not creepy, I swear."

"A little creepy," I say. But I relax some, seeing open honesty in her eyes. It's not normal for people to be so nice, which is probably why I'm freaking out.

"I'm sorry. I'm just bad with humans," she says in a whisper, like it's a confession. "But I'll scold those boys later for scaring you, I promise."

Humans?

"It's all right," I say. "I'm not used to people giving a shit."

"You poor thing," she says, and her eyes glisten.

I laugh softly and nudge her shoulder. "It's okay, Star."

Her gaze skips to the space between us and her jaw clenches like she's suddenly realizing how close I am to her.

Now we're back to the awkward. I move away and lean on the wall again. "If it's all right, I'd like to try and get some sleep. Then I'll go. Feel free to burn the sheets afterward."

"No rush," she says, not picking up on my sarcasm. She reaches over and grabs her cup, takes a sip, and then holds it out to me. "Here, have this. I'll make myself another one."

I accept the cup. It's filled with brown liquid that smells kind of herbal. "What is it?"

"Spiced tea and vodka, my own special recipe." She smiles in her genuine way again, and I can't help but relax a little. "It's super yummy."

"Thanks for the shower and not freaking out about the clothes." I motion to the white shirt and jeans I borrowed. "And thanks for a place to crash. I wouldn't wanna be out there tonight." Not on Halloween, when all of LA acts like lunatic children.

She blushes a little and nods. "Just sleep. I'll check on you later. And I'll make sure the boys don't come back." Then she slips out into the party and the cloud of laughter and music.

I scoot down in the pillows and sniff the drink. It has a nice nutmeg spark to it, kind of soothing to my nerves. I take a sip and breathe deeply, trying to focus on the moment. I'm safe. I'm warm and clean. It won't be long until all three of those things go back to not being true. I need to enjoy this.

I drink a few more sips of the spiced vodka, then set it aside before curling into a ball and sinking into the soft mattress. Everything in me settles. I don't remember the last time I felt this way. Maybe never. I hope Ziggy is okay. I should probably go check on her . . .

I reach over to take another sip of the drink. It's really good. Like, *really* good.

I down the rest in a single shot, then set the cup on the table.

It falls to the floor.

Oops.

I laugh, then sigh happily and roll over, suddenly fascinated by the textures on the wall. Maybe I don't want to sleep. Sleep is boring. I'm always so boring, always scared to join the fun. I'm tired of being scared.

I sit up and stare at the door. The sound of people and fun and life is so inviting. The beat of the music buzzes against my skin, and the urge to be in the crowd fills me. I should go find Ziggy. Or go dance . . . I stand up, wobbling a little, but I make it to the door. Then I'm down the hall and in the cluster of party madness before I even realize I've made a decision to join in. I scan the faces in the living room for a second, searching for Ziggy, but then my body is swaying and twisting to the electronic pulse of the notes, and my friend is forgotten.

As I move through the crowd, I touch chests and arms and cheeks, and people turn to look as I head for where everyone's dancing. I smile, feeling powerful, feeling the energy in the room shift. I don't normally want attention; I hate people looking at me. But now I wonder why I've never done this before, let people see me.

"This isn't good," I hear someone say behind me. "Look at her." I think it's that Ben guy.

He's hot. I kind of want to let him do things to me.

It's so weird. So not me . . .

"Just go with it, Ben," Star says. "Faelan will be here any second."

I watch her walk past me through the dancers. She's added wings to her slutty Dorothy costume. They're silver and sheer and—wow, they almost look real.

I turn and spot Ben. His eyes grow wide as I move to take his wrist, pulling him into the cluster of dancers, urging him closer. "Yeah, Ben. Listen to Dorothy. Just go with it, dance with me." My voice is soft, so I don't think he can hear me over the music, but his brow knits together.

"You smell really good," he says, looking a little dazed and a lot confused as he begins to move with me. His voice is low too, but I can hear him as clear as day over the pounding beat. He's got these soft brown eyes that are almost copper, and his brown hair is highlighted with red where it falls over his brow. His skin is lovely and tan. The cat ears he had on earlier are gone. As he leans closer, his lips part, and I hesitate.

Are those fangs? I blink at them, confused, but then I realize it must be part of a costume. He's a vampire for Halloween? Such a cliché, but in a lame way it sort of makes him look even more inviting . . .

My gut swirls and tightens as I move my gaze back up to his eyes, and those strange urges rise, the ones I always get when I see someone I want to kiss. Warmth soaks my skin. I *need* something. I'm not sure what. A connection. Touch. Like I haven't touched anyone in my entire life.

I slide my fingers up the muscles of his arm.

The heat in my skin, in his, grows a little and a vibration moves through my chest.

A small gasp escapes my lips. My head fills with the smell of spice, turmeric and nutmeg, and warmth settles in my throat as if I've just taken a bite of something delicious.

I can't help reaching out to touch him again. My hand grazes the hem of his shirt, and I close my eyes. Then I do something completely insane. I slip my hand underneath the cotton, sliding my palm across his stomach.

Ecstasy becomes a second heartbeat in my skin. The smell of nutmeg turns dull and metallic in my head, and the tang in the back of my throat morphs into the taste of blood. Light and fire flicker behind my eyelids, glowing orange and gold, and I'm cloaked in warmth, as if I just stepped into a sauna. It heats my skin, my insides, and I'm suddenly starving—for what, I can't tell. I only know I want more. More touch, more taste, more fire. I want all of it. All of him.

I press my hands firmly against his chest and start to take in a breath—

I'm shoved, hard. My eyes fly open just in time to see that I'm careening into a trio of Wonder Women. They disperse with squeals of surprise, and I land in a beanbag chair, knocking over a bunch of drinks as I slide along the floor.

Before I can get my bearings, a large guy is parting the crowd, coming at me with a strange metal shackle in his gloved hand. "Hold still," he says, his voice low and dangerous, the hint of an accent weaving into his words. It registers that I need to get away from him, but I can't make myself move. There's a click as he hooks the shackle around my neck. Then he barks over his shoulder, "Who thought it was a grand idea to give her the draft and start waking her up before I got here?"

The two blond guys I met earlier step forward and point at Star. She's off to the side, her cheeks beet red.

My attacker releases a growl and frowns down at me with watchful gray-green eyes.

The sight of him stuns me into stillness. He's just a guy, but I know he's not *just* anything as my whole being seems to notice him. The thin scar cutting through his right eyebrow, the odd curve of his ears, the perfection of his bronze skin, the rich dark brown of his hair—half of it tied neatly back with a leather strap, a loose strand tucked behind his ear.

I have an inexplicable urge to pull the strand loose again and watch it slide across his cheek.

Panic rises in a rush. I can't understand anything I'm thinking or feeling as he looms over me.

Then the heavy shackle tingles against my nape, and all my attention quickly shifts to the strange contraption. I smell cooked meat before I feel the searing pain. The metal collar presses deeper into my skin with an audible hiss.

I gasp in shock and start to choke, reaching up to my neck to try and pull the thing off. My hand starts to sizzle, and I jerk it away as it burns, a squeal escaping my throat.

Three inches of the shackle's width are now branded into my palm.

Star rushes forward and kneels at my side. "It's okay, Sage. It won't be so bad once the spell takes hold and you wake up fully. Just breathe."

I try to get away, but everything hurts. "What did you do, Star?" I gasp, shaking now—with rage or pain, I can't tell. The memory of dropping the cup flashes in my head. "The drink. You drugged me." I gape at her and try again to move away, but she just scoots forward.

My muscles tense, and I'm ready to run, to fight, the ache from my burning skin fading as panic takes over. "What is this?" I motion to the shackle.

"It's to protect you, to hold in your power," she says. "The pain will pass in a second."

I was such an idiot to trust anyone. This freak of a girl is completely insane. She's just trussed me up for some creepy kidnapping.

My attacker grabs Star by the arm and yanks her up, shoving her away from me. "Back off, pixie."

I blink at him through the pain and terror clouding my senses. My vision blurs a little, then clears again. He's wearing all black, dressed like some sort of bounty hunter in a tight T-shirt, cargo pants, and heavy boots. Something is strapped to his belt: a knife. The hilt is worn—*because he uses it a lot*. There are green-and-blue tattoos all over his arms and up one side of his neck, curved and swirled Celtic designs and unfamiliar lettering inked onto his copper skin. He has another scar on his jaw. And those metallic green eyes . . . they're so hard, calculating. A hunter's eyes.

He's the kind of guy who would be fine with killing Bambi. Or me.

"Look what she's capable of with only half her strength," he says to the thinned crowd around us. He points to something—no, some*one*— on the floor. It's Ben. He's kneeling a few feet away, hunched over as he grips his head like he's in pain. His skin is ashen. There are angry burns running a thin trail up his arm . . . *where my fingers grazed his muscles. Oh my God, did I . . . ?*

"I just thought this would be faster," Star says, sounding pitiful. Her silver wings shiver a little. "This way her power'll be awake once you get her to Master Marius."

"The Emergence has already started, pixie. I'm not the only one out here tonight sniffing around. Prince Kieran could be aware of her now."

Star goes pale, and the shivering spreads to her whole body. "Really?"

The guy nods slowly. "His sister would have plans for our little doe."

Star's features fill with panic. She turns to the blond guys beside her. "Check to be sure Ben is okay."

They move to obey, helping Ben to his feet and dragging him from sight.

That's when I notice that the music has gone silent; everything has. And the pain that was gripping me has faded to a dull throb. The room is half-empty, and all eyes are on me. And still I don't know why. I only know I need to figure out how to get out of here. I search the figures around us for Ziggy, but I don't see her. I hope she ran away, that she caught a whiff of the weird and bolted before these crazy cult freaks could hurt her.

A ringing fills the strained silence, and the tattooed guy pulls a phone from his pocket. He puts it to his ear. "Faelan here," he says, his accent stronger now. Irish. His hard eyes lock on mine. "Yes. I've got her. Brighid's daughter is ours."

THREE

FAELAN

"You've got the wrong girl!" the demigoddess yells as I lift her out of the beanbag chair and drag her by the arm down the hall to the back room. "Please! My mom's name is Lauren, not Brighid!" She squirms and wriggles like a determined salmon and keeps shouting. "The bitch is probably in jail again. Or in a gutter smoking crack. Whatever you've got going on with her, I'm not a part of it. I haven't seen the woman in years." She's trying to convince me of her humanity, trying to convince herself. But her aura is sparking orange and gold. Can't she feel her Other blood ready to be released? Can't she sense her soul aching for her own kind?

If not, she's about to get a very loud wake-up call.

I drop her on the bed and attempt to think past her screeching. I need to take a breath and come at this more delicately, or we'll lose her and she'll end up in Prince Kieran's clutches, captive to the whim of the House of Morrígan. I don't understand how she doesn't realize what she did to Ben. I know female demis are stronger, but the shade was nearly sucked as dry as a husk by a simple touch. She's lucky he wasn't human or he'd be ash right now.

She keeps yelling at me about kicking my ass. I'm not sure how she plans on doing that. She's a mess of a waif in oversize clothes. Not even remotely attractive at first glance, which is a relief. It's probably why the pompous prince overlooked her. Her strawberry hair is ratty and she's far too thin, her features too sharp. But her eyes . . . they're stunning and vibrant, a golden shimmer already surfacing in the hazel, as the fire of her mother's power begins to boil up inside her.

I steel myself against her energy and lean down, hovering. She shrinks back as she looks up at me. Her tongue stills—praise the holy Danu.

I take a breath in through my nose and try not to let the sharp spice of her power hit me too hard. Then I say, as calmly as I can, "You're going to need to understand something if you plan on making it through tonight: I am not your enemy. I'm your best hope of finding safety."

She gives me a derisive look. "Are you shitting me? You attacked me. You burned me and—"

"It was merely the iron collar. You're fine. The pain is temporary."

She shivers and puts her palm in my face. "I've been branded like you own me, dickhead."

"Look at your hand," I say.

She scowls, so I grab her wrist and turn her palm to face her, showing her the healed skin.

She struggles to break away but then looks at it, her mouth opening in shock.

"You aren't human," I say. She doesn't seem to react to my words, still blinking at her healed skin, so I continue my speech. "Your life has been a lie. Everything you knew until this night is forfeit. Your true blood, your magic, began to surface several weeks ago. Tonight, with the full moon, you'll start opening up to it further. The pixie's potion is speeding up the process, but it was bound to boil to the surface with the lunar pull."

She reaches up to hold her wrist like she doesn't recognize the hand in front of her face. "What in the hell?"

I release her and step back. "I know this is difficult," I say without emotion. Familiar words I've said hundreds of times to hundreds of Otherborn over my centuries as a hunter. Maybe I've been doing this too long, introducing Others to the truth about themselves. I'm hardened to their feelings—if I ever cared to begin with. Marius says he appreciates my cold nature, which is why he sends me out more than the other hunters, like I'm some sort of statement to the rest of the ruling deities of the Penta. But I tire of these creatures and their tantrums and childishness—which is the main reason I requested the job of gatekeeper in the hidden realms for the next century. Long past time for retirement.

The demigods, druids, and underlings I pull from the human world are usually spoiled brats by the time I get to them, having had their way most of their false human lives. This girl, though . . . I don't know, she's not what I expected.

Of course, the normal order's been tossed out the window with her. She's far past the age to be collected, which is usually twelve or thirteen. She appears to have been forgotten somehow. Lost. As if the Penta, even the Cast, were ignoring her existence entirely, letting her live a human life. Unless they didn't sense her Other blood at all, though that seems unlikely.

It's amazing that Marius felt her magic, given how repressed it is. He sent out several of his best spies to find her three moons ago, when he dreamed of her sleeping in an alley. But we had to wait, to be sure she was what we thought before contacting her. It's cutting it very close, with her eighteenth Samhain playing out over the last few days, but it looks as if we caught her in time, before she could hurt anyone.

Somehow she locked away her goddess blood and forged her own way through the grime of earth over the years. I'm not exactly sure how to traverse an introduction to our world with a spirit that's already so strong.

"I just wanted a shower," she mumbles, now cradling her hand in her lap and studying the bedspread.

"You'll never want for anything again after tonight," I say.

She still doesn't seem to hear me. There's no look of fear, no understanding or glee, like I usually get.

"I'm going to take you to a safe place where there's a man who wants to help you," I add. "He's rich, very powerful. Under his protection, you'll learn where you come from and discover where you belong. The dark prince won't be able to control you and—"

She barks out a laugh, interrupting me.

"What's so funny?" I ask.

"Dark prince? Seriously?" She laughs again. "Can you even hear yourself?"

I study her and wonder if the potion that Star gave her was too strong. That pixie is so flighty.

The demi stands from the bed and folds her arms over her chest, looking guarded but determined. "Look, muscleman, I can buy this whole you're-not-who-you-think-you-are thing, since my life has basically sucked ass from the start and I'd love to believe that it was all some huge cosmic error. But you're trying to tell me I'm going to meet Daddy Warbucks, who will explain to me that I'm a weird alien or something? And he'll protect me from a *dark prince*? Pardon me if I don't leap to join your cult so I can get a chance at cushy digs. That's not my style."

"You're not an alien."

She just smirks at me and huffs out another derisive laugh. I move to the door and open it wider, yelling out to the others, who I know are listening, "Bring Ben in here." I turn back to her and slide my knife from its sheath.

FOUR

SAGE

The guy steps closer, his fist clutching a dagger at his side. The glinting silver blade is all I can see. He was babbling about moons and pixies or something, and now he's decided to kill me because I'm not buying his bullshit?

I scramble back, pressing myself against the dresser. "What're you doing?"

"Since you won't listen, I'll show you the truth."

A scream rises in my throat, but all I can do is choke in horror. I can tell by his hard gaze that if this strange guy wants me dead, I'm dead. I could fight, but I'll lose.

He pauses a few feet from me. Instead of attacking, he puts the blade to his own forearm. Then he presses hard and slices deep. I stare in horror as blood bubbles up in a rush of deep red.

Panic jolts through me. But before I can move, the bedroom door opens and one of the pale blond guys comes in, propping up a limp and ashen Ben.

Faelan's arm is dripping with blood now—it pitter-patters as it hits the floor. He points his red-tipped knife at Ben and looks at me. "Do you see what you've done to him?"

I swallow hard and stare at the guy I was dancing with. He looks half-dead. His dark brown hair has even turned gray.

I didn't do that. I couldn't have . . .

Faelan puts the tip of his blade to Ben's shirt and uses it to lift up the hem. There are burn marks all over Ben's abdomen where I was touching him. My throat goes tight. I can't stop staring at the mangled skin.

"Ben's a shade," Faelan says. "Fairly hardy, for the most part. A being created by the goddess of death, the Morrígan, from a human whose life was cut short too soon. I believe he's young, only seventy-five years old. His origin is the reason you didn't kill him with your hunger. You *pulled* Ben's life energy into your own body to feed your cells and keep your magic satiated. If Ben were still a human, he'd be a pile of ash right now."

Faelan holds his dripping arm out like he's presenting it in offering. Ben's breath speeds up a little, his eyes opening more, his pupils dilating, as he sniffs the air. "However, Ben needs blood to survive and heal himself," Faelan continues. "So you've harmed more than the shade with your carelessness." He directs his next words to the limp young man. "You have my permission to feed."

A low growl emerges from Ben's throat.

I grip the edge of the dresser behind me, recalling the fangs I glimpsed in his mouth, knowing what I'm about to see, terrified to watch. But I can't look away. Even with my crazy imagination, I never imagined anything like this.

With a guttural moan, Ben grabs Faelan's bloody arm and chomps down on it. Faelan hisses in pain and leans closer to the guy who's suddenly feeding from him. *A vampire . . .*

My whole body shakes as I watch. Ben's strength becomes a force in the room. His body seems to grow a little with each gulp of Faelan's blood. His skin regains its color. His hair turns silky and shiny again. His burn marks fade, and the twisted flesh perfects itself like I'm watching everything happen in reverse. Until the healing is complete.

"Enough," Faelan grunts out, his voice weaker.

Ben immediately pulls back, dropping Faelan's arm. He looks shocked, unsure of what happened, of what he just did. "Forgive me, hunter," he says, shame filling his eyes. He uses his shirt to wipe the blood from his face. "I was weak." When he glances at me, fear replaces the shame in his gaze. "I should've resisted her."

Faelan cradles his wounded arm against his chest. His words are less formal, his Irish accent very clear, when he says, "Just be sure nothin' gets through the barrier I set up. I'll finish this and then we'll leave you be." I can tell he's in pain, but his voice is steady. He gives Ben a nod and they share a look, like they have some sort of strange camaraderie.

I don't understand any of this. I just watched a guy suck another guy's blood and heal himself because I burned him?

I think of my connection with fire, how it whispers to me, how I saw flames behind my eyelids, felt heat when I touched Ben.

I burned him. How is that even possible?

A soft whimper comes from my chest, and my legs turn liquid.

I sink to the floor, my back scraping against the dresser. "What's happening to me?" I ask, my voice barely a whisper.

Faelan is silent for several seconds as he looks down on me, his blood dripping onto the floor beside my foot. His shirt is soaked with it, the black cotton shimmering in the dark room. "As I said, your origin is Emerging. You're not human. You're what some call a demi, or demigoddess. In this case, your mother was a goddess, and your father was a human."

"But my mother—Lauren, she—"

"That woman wasn't your real mother." He releases a tense breath and moves to sit on the bed, leaning closer to me. He lowers his voice, like he's trying to be gentle. "According to our knowledge, the woman— Lauren Spencer—had a child, yes. She gave birth, and the baby girl lived for three years. But then it died. For some reason, you were put in the child's place, her life given to you. Perhaps your watcher at the time hoped it would ease the woman's pain, hoped it would hide you and your magic. Whatever the reason, the human woman never knew she was raising a holy creature."

"She didn't raise me," I say bitterly. I wonder if that's why she looked at me as if I were a stranger. She knew I wasn't *her* Sage. Her little girl had died. Maybe somehow she saw the truth.

Bile rises in my throat. "Oh, God," I whisper. A wave of memories floods through me. So many times people seemed like they couldn't stand being around me, seemed to fear me. I was never able to connect with anyone. They always pulled away. Always. Like they could tell I was *wrong*. Everyone except—

"Ziggy!" I say.

"What?" Faelan's brow pinches in confusion.

"I came here with her. I need to be sure she's okay."

He studies me for a second. "She's human?"

"Yes, she's . . . well, she's my only friend." *And if something happened to her in this mess, it's my fault.*

"If I ensure her safety, will you surrender, demi? Will you come with me willingly?"

"Don't call me that. My name is Sage." *At least I think it is.*

"You're willing to come with me, then?"

My skin prickles in fear at the thought of giving in and going with this guy. But knowing what I did to Ben, and what Ben did to this Faelan guy . . . I need to figure this out—whatever it is. God, could I really hurt someone that badly? Maybe kill them?

"I'll come with you, yes," I say, defeated.

He stands, and I notice the blood on his arm is sticky, nearly dried. He's not bleeding anymore because there's no wound now. He's completely healed too.

"Very good," he says. "Stay close to my side until we can get you someplace safe."

"But Ziggy—"

"I'll show you she's fine." He moves to the door and looks at me with stern emerald eyes. "If she's the human you came with, then she's right out here."

My heart beats faster at the layers of meaning in his words. I stand, and the strange metal ring around my neck shifts, the ache in my skin flaring again for a second. But I grit my teeth at the pain and follow him into the hall.

Star pops her head around the corner, her blue hair bright in the poorly lit space, her face a glowing mask of concern. "Oh, sweetie, you okay?"

The urge to kick her fills me. I'm so pissed, so horrified at what she's done to me. I would've been perfectly happy never knowing any of this. And I felt fine until I drank that potion she gave me. I don't care if she's some sort of magical freak. She's a traitor. A liar. And if she comes any closer, I'm going to stab her with one of her red stilettos.

She must see the intensity of the emotions on my face because the brightness in her eyes dulls, and she backs up a few steps when I walk past.

And then I spot a familiar figure emerging from the kitchen into the living room, shoving a cheeseburger into her mouth.

"Ziggy?" I say, confused.

She's fine. She's . . . eating? Hasn't she been paying attention? Did she miss me being thrown across the room by the commando freak, Faelan?

Ziggy pauses midbite and mutters around her meat. "Aw shit." Her eyes turn sheepish. "Hey, girl. How's the tits?" When I don't move, she adds, "I would've told you about all of this, but . . . well, I'm not exactly in charge. I was just watching you for the big man, Marius. But now that it's all out in the open . . ." She shrugs and takes another bite of cheeseburger, then says with her mouth full, "we can chill for reals."

My body goes cold. She knew this party was a trap. She's with these creeps. She's a part of the con. "Ziggy, what the fuck?" My voice cracks, as every belief I've had over the three months that I've known her crumbles into dust. My one friend in the whole world. She's a lie too.

I cross the room in silence until I'm standing right in front of her. And I punch her in the face.

FIVE

FAELAN

The demigoddess has been silent the whole drive into the city. The only clue that lets me know she hasn't gone catatonic from shock is the way she keeps shaking out her hand and flexing her fingers, likely because of pain from striking the human girl's jaw.

She doesn't hit very hard. I'll have to be sure her tutor works with her on self-defense during her transition. Still, I'm fairly sure that the human, Ziggy, will have a bruise on her jaw for a few days.

It's odd, but the demi seems more disturbed by the human's betrayal of her than by the revelation of her origin. Her energy went a thick dark gray when she walked across the room to slug the girl. It's resting in a heavy fog on her shoulders right now.

"The human was sworn to secrecy," I say, feeling the need to dampen the swirling cloud as it starts to roll down her arms and fill the car. "She was only following orders. She's what we call a watcher. Her job was to keep a close eye on you for us, and it would have meant her death if she'd spoken a word of the truth."

"I don't care," the demi says through her teeth.

I shrug and go back to focusing on the road. I didn't see any signs of Prince Kieran or his minion wraiths when we were leaving the safety of the house, but that doesn't mean he isn't watching. The prince is crafty and determined. Since this demigoddess is the daughter of his mother's rival, she—along with her possible power—would be a great prize. All he'd have to do is convince her to ally herself with the House of Morrígan rather than Brighid at the Emergence ceremony. History is pretty clear: another Bond between Morrígan and Brighid kin would be deadly. But Kieran likely doesn't care. And he's well known for his dark and effective ways of *persuasion*.

The idea of this reed of a girl in his talons stirs an unusual amount of unease in my gut.

But I'm guessing Marius plans to earn this girl's allegiance at any cost, especially with our ranks in the House of Brighid being so depleted. There's no way he'll allow her to be cajoled away from her origin, where she belongs—not this gem. She'll need to be contained, controlled by whoever helps her transition.

A task I wouldn't wish on anyone.

Marius was right when he said we should be cautious. We're far outside of normal right now, thanks to the rarity of her blood along with her late arrival. We aren't even sure how much power she'll possess or how it might sway her soul as it bubbles up. And after what her sister became, the danger of her following suit and going mad is very real for everyone.

I pull the car into the parking garage and up to the valet booth. The young man, a shade who's been working the night shift at Marius's building for a few weeks—I think his name is Samuel—opens the door for the demi.

No, not "the demi." She wants me to think of her as *Sage*. I need to get used to that. I'm not normally on a first-name basis with the demi elite, but this is the deal I made with Marius: to open myself to her a little upon meeting her, to help gain her loyalty for our House from the very start. I need to help her feel comfortable and safe while she's with me—get her to trust me.

I *may* have allowed that part of the plan to go a bit sideways back at the house. I don't like her energy, the way it makes me unsure and uneasy. It'll be a relief to hand her over to Marius so he can match her with whoever ends up picking the short straw. I heard it was my old teacher, Cias. Poor bastard.

I toss Samuel the keys to the Audi and point Sage toward the elevator. "We're this way."

She follows. When we're inside and the doors close, I feel her emotions shift a little, her nerves going from smoky anger to a slight chill of fear. "Who exactly is this guy we're going to meet?"

"His name is Marius. He's the leader of the House of Brighid—though he's a child of Lyr, the god of the sea. Marius has chosen to give his allegiance to the goddess of fire instead. At times a demi will choose a House that isn't their origin after they Emerge. There's a lot that goes into it all, but you'll learn."

Sage gives me a sideways glance and hugs her middle. Ice crystals form on the wall behind her from her fear. She's more vulnerable than I expected her to be. A delicate waif being sent to the gallows. I need to say something to calm her.

I clear my throat. "Your new clothes will have already been sent for. And you'll likely have all-new electronics, a computer, a phone. You won't have to worry about anything you left behind."

She releases a shaky laugh.

"Once you're settled, Marius will go over the daily schedule with you, and you can discuss any changes or preferences with him."

She gives me an odd look. "Schedule?" she asks.

"Training, meals, tutoring—both practical and spiritual. You'll be busy during the next few days as you ready for your Emergence, but you'll get used to it."

She asks casually, "So, are you Irish or something?"

I blink at her, unsure why she's asking or why it's relevant. I thought my accent had faded since I came to live in the States sixty years ago. "Yes. Born in the north."

"Hmm . . ." She nods. "So you'd get the whole living-under-tyranny thing."

I bite the inside of my lip to keep from smiling. "Marius will be sure you're comfortable with the daily rhythm."

"Wow," she says in a dead tone. "I feel so much better."

"You may find you enjoy your time of Emerging. You'll certainly be doted on."

"And maybe Ebola will prove to cure cancer. Who knows."

My eye twitches. Just a few more minutes, and she'll no longer be my responsibility.

We arrive on the fifteenth floor, and the elevator doors open to the lobby.

Sage doesn't move. She just stares at the receptionist behind the tall desk across the room. "What is this place?"

I put a hand on the door to hold it open. "This is Marius's firm. He's working, but he wanted to talk to you before I take you to the house."

"He's a lawyer?" She doesn't seem to like that idea.

"An architect."

"It's the middle of the night. Why's he at work?" She shakes her head, shrinking back. She won't look at me. "No way, this is too weird."

I bite back a groan and let the doors close again, then push the hold button, turning to face her. "Look, Marius is a demigod. If he chooses not to rest, he doesn't have to. The world of business never sleeps, so Marius rarely does either. He likes work, and he likes being productive; meeting him here at this time of night is the usual. It would only be weird to a human." I lower my voice. "And you're not a human, Sage."

Her gaze skips to mine, and pain sparks in her hazel eyes. "You're an ass," she says under her breath. But her back straightens.

I push the hold button again. "An ass who tells you the truth. Sounds grand to me." This time, when the doors open, I take her by the arm and pull her from the box, not giving her a chance to argue.

SIX

SAGE

I try to shake off Faelan's hand, but he just grips me harder and tugs me along like I'm a child.

"Is everything all right?" the receptionist asks, looking from me to Faelan with a frown.

"Right as rain, Dana," he answers with his annoying accent.

I mouth the word *help* at her, but she doesn't move; she just watches us with wide eyes behind thick-rimmed glasses. Her shiny red lips purse in curiosity as we turn left and head down a long hallway.

"Nice try," Faelan says to me. "She's a pixie. And she was gawking because she knows whose daughter you are, not because I was dragging you out of an elevator."

I deflate and study the surroundings as I'm pulled along. The décor is stark—black and white and gray. Gray wooden floors, and white glass walls that have odd black lines and shapes on them for decoration. Not a speck of color in sight.

As I try to make sense of the designs on the walls, I realize I'm looking at oversize replicas of pencil drawings. Sketches of buildings. And I recognize some of the structures. Did this guy Marius design them?

We turn at the end of the hall and come to a set of large double doors. They're a deep crimson.

Like the blood Ben took from Faelan.

I glance down at his arm. There's still dried blood on the tattooed skin, but not a scar in sight. How is this even possible? I can't wrap my head around it. I'm some sort of goddess's child? It's laughably insane. And yet I just watched a vampire I nearly *killed* with my touch suck the blood from my new tour guide—who is totally fine.

Faelan knocks. "It's me, sir."

The door on the right side opens. A tall, pale white-haired man in a white suit is standing there like a sentinel. He bows his head as we pass him, so I'm guessing he's not Marius.

The room is all white, as sparse as a doctor's office, except for a single splash of red-orange—a huge painting of a blossoming rose made of fire that takes up the entire wall opposite us. There's a white wooden desk in the center of the whitewashed cement floor, and sitting behind it is a large black man with silver hair, wearing a fitted charcoal-gray cotton V-neck. His broad shoulder muscles flex as he hunches over his work, moving a pencil across paper. At this angle, he appears perfectly normal, just focused on whatever he's doodling.

He moves aside a ruler as we step closer, studies his drawing for another two seconds, and looks up.

I swallow a gasp. His eyes, they're . . . teal. His gaze moves to my face and holds, then skims over my body, up and down, pausing on my hair.

He must have grayed early because his features look young. He can't be much older than midthirties, lean and muscular, with a small pale scar running along his temple, beside his right eye. His left arm is dotted in a circular pattern with more thick ball-like scars. They look like they were placed there on purpose, to mark him.

"Well, well," he says, sounding a little British. "Look at this creature." He stands and sets his pencil down, then walks around to the front of his desk. He leans back on it casually and folds his muscular arms over his chest. "She's lovely." A small grin tilts his lips. "Isn't she lovely, Faelan?"

Does he need glasses? I'm a total mess.

My captor grunts like he doesn't agree with the assessment of my beauty either.

"Any signs of Kieran following her?" Marius asks.

Faelan shakes his head. "No, sir."

"Very good." Then, directing his words at me, he says, "I am Marius. Forgive my informality. I've been caught up in the realms of imagination. I'm completely enraptured by this theater I'm working on." He motions to the large paper lying across his desk. "The acoustics must be just right. We cannot have Mozart's *Requiem* sounding any less than perfect when it fills the cracks and crevices of the design." His smile grows whimsical and I find it's contagious, like it's trying to sneak onto my own lips. I have to clench my jaw to keep it back. But before I can stop the full effect, my insides melt a little, like when I had that crush on my art teacher in tenth grade.

"Now that you're here," he says, snapping me back to reality, "we must take care of you properly so that you can feel right at home with us. I wouldn't wish for you to worry or find yourself too overcome by—"

A door clicks open behind him, and he cuts off his words as a thin woman with similar teal eyes, long white hair, and very pale skin emerges from a door hidden in the wall. She's strikingly odd looking, not to mention half-naked, wearing only underwear and a light gray dress shirt that isn't buttoned. Something tells me the shirt belongs to Marius, my new Daddy Warbucks.

"We're bored," she whines. "Come back to us, *macushla*. It's nearly morning, and Korinna is growing famished."

"Yes, yes." Marius motions in dismissal. "I'll be there in a moment."

She whimpers, obviously impatient, and goes back into the room, shutting the door behind her.

My anxiety cranks back up to a hundred. What sort of guy *is* this? He hides women in his office to use at his whim? I mean, he's hot and all, for an older guy, but . . .

I study him more closely, trying to figure out if I can trust him. Then I glance at Faelan to gauge his reaction to what just happened.

The commando's eyes are locked on the floor as if his life depended on it.

Wow. Obviously not a gawker—not even when the girl's half-naked. Maybe he's gay?

"So. Where were we?" Marius asks, like we just got interrupted by his secretary. He looks me over again, and this time I stiffen. His gaze stops at my neck. "We really must get you a new torque; that one is archaic. Truly, Faelan. It's no longer the Dark Ages, as much as you may miss them." He laughs softly and goes back around his desk to open a drawer, and then he pulls out a large red velvet box. He opens it and picks up a delicate gold necklace. There's a charm on the end—a Celtic knot with three loops tucked inside a circle—and in the center of the charm sparkles a yellow-orange stone.

Marius holds it out in offering. "You do the honors, Faelan."

Faelan runs a nervous hand through his hair before he leaves my side to walk over and take the chain from his boss. He comes back toward me, holding it awkwardly in his left hand. He pauses in front of me, hesitant, like he's not wanting to get close. But after several awkward seconds, he reaches around my neck to unlock the heavy metal ring resting on my nape.

His chest envelops me, warm against my cheek. I hear a click, and the heavy weight of the shackle falls away as he sets it aside. But he doesn't move back. He stays. Close. And then he begins to place the delicate necklace.

The smell of fresh-cut grass fills my head, and the taste of peppermint blossoms in my mouth, tingling in my nose. And I know it's him, his scent surrounding me.

I close my eyes and take a deep breath.

My skin warms as prickles work their way through my insides—

"Stop," Faelan growls, cutting through the rush. "No feeding." He steps away a little so we're not touching.

My eyes fly open as he moves back. But he only allows a few inches between us as he finishes clasping the necklace into place. "I can feel when you begin to take from me," he says. "Try not to feed without someone's permission."

"You taste like peppermint," I say before my brain can stop my mouth.

Marius chuckles, and a chill runs over me as I realize what I did. I just *fed* off Faelan? I didn't even realize that I was doing anything. How could I take something as monumental as *life* from someone without meaning to—my God, this is insanity.

"I'm sorry," I say, weakly. Shame fills me, like I got caught doing something perverted. "I didn't mean to."

"You'll learn," Faelan says, his tone losing its edge a little. "It's a matter of control."

"According to Faelan, control is everything, and hunger is a demi's weakness," Marius says. "I've always felt his strict ways were unfortunate, especially with all that hidden beauty he carries. I was truly disappointed that he wasn't more liberal when he came into our House. But over the centuries, I've come to appreciate my stoic, unaffected friend. And in your case, Daughter of Fire, it will serve us well. Since you're so . . . full of possibility."

The words seem to be important, but I don't know what they mean. The thin necklace tingles against my skin, distracting me. It warms but it doesn't burn like the heavy collar did. My nerves settle too. It's a sudden and real shift, as if I've taken one of the antianxiety meds the psychiatrist prescribed for me after I got kicked out of my third foster home—like maybe the necklace is working to somehow mask my emotions or something? The idea of an inanimate object muffling my senses would normally terrify me, but I can't seem to work up the fear with the cloud of stillness settling in, crowding it out. Mostly, I just feel relief. I can breathe steadily again, and I don't want to punch something. I'd say, on the whole, it's a huge improvement.

"I believe your potential can be harnessed, though," Marius continues, bringing me back. "And Faelan's sure to be adept at that. His strength will have to be above average to guard against that blossom of power that will emerge as he helps you with your transition over the next few days."

Faelan's gaze snaps to Marius. "What are you talking about? I brought her to you. My part in this is done. I was to return home after this task. I'm meant to guard the doorways to the hidden realms now."

"No, I think not. You're far too young to retire. And the City of Angels needs you. Your House needs you, my friend."

Faelan's skin goes sallow. He looks like he's going to be sick. "Marius," he says, his voice beginning to shake with emotion, "it's not right. I thought you called up Cias. Even if I wasn't meant to leave, I'm a hunter, not a tutor. I collect them, I bring them in. That's it. And we had a deal."

"Cias isn't even close to being strong enough for this," Marius says, seemingly oblivious to Faelan's frustration. "Look at her." He steps closer to me. Before I realize what he's doing, he reaches out, running a finger gently over my temple. A strange buzzing fills my skin as he whispers, "So much hidden there. Why else would she have been tucked away with the humans for so long? Something has kept her locked out—perhaps the Cast. We must discover why. I don't trust anyone more than you."

"No, Marius," Faelan says through his teeth. "You will not get me mixed up with the Cast. I've had enough of this madness you're always planning."

Marius releases a tired sigh. "Foolish boy. So faithless." He turns away from us and walks back over to his desk. He picks up something—a knife, or a very large letter opener—and taps the tip against his chin. "You shall aid in this demi's Emergence, offering yourself as her chosen protector. As your House master, I call you to this task, Faelan Ua Cleirigh. Until it is fulfilled or until you have perished from this plane."

Marius rests the blade against his palm, then slides it across, opening the skin. Thick crimson blood begins to seep from the wound as he holds his hand out in offering. "Come now," he urges Faelan, that lazy grin tilting his lips again.

"Fuck all, Marius," Faelan growls. But he pulls out his own dagger and cuts his palm the same way. He looks pissed as he reaches out and takes Marius's bloody offering.

Marius laughs and pulls Faelan into his chest, giving him a hug, slapping his back like he's congratulating him. "Now *this* will be a contest. Wait until the Introduction tomorrow, you'll see I'm right."

I find myself pitying Faelan, but I'm not sure why. He's acting like Marius just asked him to donate a kidney. The guy looks seriously annoyed as Marius releases him and steps away.

"Take her to the Cottages in Malibu," Marius says. "My wife, Barbara, will happily see she's given every amenity, and you can stay in the east forest bungalow while our guest stays in the west."

"What about Aelia?" Faelan asks. "She's going to be trouble."

"She will obey. I'm her father, after all."

Faelan seems dubious.

Marius turns his attention back to me. "Be gentle with our hunter, kind Sage."

I nod, though I'm not really sure what I'm agreeing to. The only thing I know for sure is that the guy who's supposed to show me everything about myself, about what I am, is completely miserable about it. I should probably be offended, but I'm not. I don't blame him at all. Apparently, I'm deadly.

"Sorry," I whisper as Faelan starts pacing in front of the desk. He glares at me. I wave my hand like I'm trying to explain. "I mean . . . that you're stuck with me." I don't understand what's in my head right now. Why am I apologizing for something I have no control over? Everything in me feels so weird.

"Good morrow, children," Marius says as he heads for the door in the back of the office. "I'll check in at the Cottages this evening to hear the progress report. We'll have supper together." And then he slips into the room where the white-haired woman and someone who's *famished* are waiting for him.

Morbid curiosity fills me. How does all of this hunger/feeding stuff work, anyway? Is it through touching, like I did to Ben? Or drinking blood, like Ben did to Faelan? Or, like, could there also be actual chewing? Does it depend on who's doing the *eating*?

A shiver of revulsion runs through me, along with something else. Something that makes it a bit tougher to breathe.

I look over to Faelan and immediately regret it. He's leaning his hip on the desk, pinching the bridge of his nose, eyes closed. The blue-green tattoos running over his arms seem more obvious now; they shape his muscles like a work of art. He's still got dried blood on his shirt from earlier. The smell of it fills the air around me for a second as I study him.

Peppermint tingles in my nose.

And an ache fills my skin as weird urges tease the back of my mind, to step closer, to touch him. But it's not a normal desire to be close to someone. It's an intense need. A hollow pang. It starts to claw its way out of the darkness inside me just like it did when I touched Ben. Like it does when I look into the flame. *Touch. Feed. Control.*

I reach up to the charm necklace at my chest like it can calm the feeling. And new terror fills me. Because I know. I know now.

It's hunger that's been calling to me in the fire.

SEVEN

SAGE

Faelan leads me back to the car in silence. This time he doesn't tug me along like I'm a fussy preschooler. Actually, he doesn't seem to want to touch me at all. Which is good. I think if he did, I'd freak out in a major way, with this mess inside me.

He's obviously pissed. He practically punched the elevator button into the panel to get the doors to close faster. It's hard to care, though, with my own nerves on fire. I'm trying to take deep breaths and get this heat in my skin to pass. It's so overwhelming, it's actually starting to hurt. I don't know what to do with it.

I hardly notice the wait for the valet to bring the car around. I barely register getting in the Audi or driving through the city. I'm focused so intensely on shoving down this crazy storm inside me that the rest of the world has become a blur of muffled noise and color.

My mind can't seem to think past the embers in my skin, the need. I must be some kind of monster to feel like this about a guy I just met. About anyone. I need to get away from this thing. Somehow. But how? How do you get away from a feeling? For the first time, I understand why people jump off bridges. Everything is just too fucking loud.

I cover my face with my hands and try not to lose it.

A sharp zing fills my chest and something grips the back of my neck.

My eyes fly open and I jerk sideways, pressing my body into the passenger door. Faelan pulls his arm away—his fingers were wrapped around my nape.

"What the hell?" I say, rubbing the spot where he grabbed me. "Don't touch me."

He gives me a sideways glance, staying focused on the road. "I could barely breathe with all your turmoil filling the car. I just dampened your mood a bit with some of my own energy."

"Yeah, next time don't." I'm not sure how he'd be able to calm me down with his own energy, considering how pissed he obviously is about me being dumped on him. But even as the thought comes, I realize the heat in my skin's faded and he's not as tense anymore. We're on a curvy road through what looks like Malibu Canyon. How long have we been driving?

"The last thing I want is your hands on me," I add, trying to make it clear how much I don't want to be around him right now.

"Well, now. You seem spunky again," he says, his tone wry.

"What's that supposed to mean?"

"In Marius's office, you were a mouse. Now you're back to biting my head off."

I squeeze my lips shut to hold back a retort. I close my eyes for a second and then say, "I have no idea what's going on."

"Aye."

That's all he says. Just "aye."

I need to distract myself so I don't hit him. I look out the window. "Where is this cottage?"

"It's about three miles up this road, deeper in the canyon. There's an ocean view."

"I didn't know there were houses out this far."

"There aren't. Marius never does anything the usual way."

"Oh. Kay." Now I'm nervous again.

"It'll be better than a laundromat."

I stare at him. How does he know where I've been sleeping the last few nights? Is he psychic or something?

He seems to sense my surprise. "Star and Ziggy, they were sending Marius information."

Right. I'd almost forgotten about my traitor friends. So glad to be reminded.

"You're clouding up the car again," he says, sounding annoyed. "How in the hell are your emotions so pushy already?"

"Pardon me for having a feeling." I fold my arms across my chest and lean away from him.

The necklace's ability to smother things has apparently passed already. Maybe it was short-lived, like the burning agony of the thick metal torque. But what do I know? I have no clue what's going on. Or where I'm being taken, what it'll mean. I've always done things my own way, on my own. I don't depend on anyone. And now—because I'm freaked out—I'm letting these creepy men push me around? It could be a huge mistake to go along with all of this. How can I be sure they're telling me the truth? So far they haven't explained much of anything at all.

I decide there's no point in holding off on questions anymore, so I ask, "So, if I'm a mini-goddess or whatever—"

"Demigoddess."

"Whatever. I'm a freak of nature. What are *you*?"

"It's not polite to ask that question."

"Seriously? You basically kidnap me and I'm supposed to act like Miss Manners now?"

"I haven't kidnapped you. You've come of your own free will. And if you'd like to go back to that gutter in the Valley, I can drop you on the way back into Downtown tomorrow." His voice has a slight edge to it, though I think he's trying to sound casual.

I consider his offer and wonder if that's the better plan, just having him take me back to my life—what there is of it. If that's seriously an option. My feet are already burning to run, and I haven't even gotten to this "cottage" yet. But if I am some sort of mutant, if I can really hurt people like I hurt Ben . . .

No, this is too volatile. Whatever I feel, I need to see where this goes.

I'll give it a day. If I'm still not buying into the crazy by tomorrow night, then I'll find a way out.

For now, though, I need to push for some answers. "You could at least tell me what a demigoddess actually *is*," I say. "Like, does it mean I'll be able to shoot fire out of my eyes or smite my enemies or get things half off on Rodeo Drive? It's not like there's recent data for this sort of thing, not since the fall of Rome, anyway. Is there literature, a pamphlet? A how-to manual?"

"Do you always talk this much?"

"Aren't you supposed to explain things? Marius said I get whatever I want, right?" I give him a pointed look. "I want information."

He sighs. "I wasn't planning on keeping you in the dark forever, just until you get some sleep, so we could start the transition after a good rest."

With the way I feel right now, I will *not* be sleeping.

We drive in silence for a few minutes before I try again. "You said Marius is a demi, like me, right?"

Faelan nods. "The son of Lyr, the god of the sea."

Lyr . . . that's not a god I recognize from World Civ. There was Poseidon, the Greek sea god. I get an image in my head of the Little Mermaid's dad, the cartoon guy with the pitchfork. Not super awe-inspiring. And it definitely doesn't fit the man I saw back in the skyscraper, other than the white hair.

His parentage doesn't matter right now, though. Mine does. "My mother, you said she was . . ." I remember him saying the name Brighid.

But all he told me was that she was a goddess—not much information, as explanations of deity parents go. "Who was she?"

He shifts in his seat, uncomfortable.

My gut sinks at his reaction to my question, worst-case scenarios running through my head. "Oh crap." I squeeze my eyes shut, like I'm bracing for a hit. "She's the Queen of the Damned or something, isn't she?" Then I mutter to myself, "The lake of fire and Hades, that all fits with my life so far."

When only silence answers, I squint my eyes open to look at him. He's actually smirking.

"Nice. Enjoy my torment, that's helpful."

"I'm Irish. Love of torment's in the blood." He sobers again, his voice becoming reverent. "Your mother . . . she is the graceful Brighid, goddess of fire and hearth, first daughter of the holy Danu."

My skin tingles. The sound of her name coming from his lips seems to hum in the air for an extra second or two this time. I do recognize it from the Catholic group home I was in when I was little. "Isn't Brighid a saint?"

"Actually, some say the worship of the Virgin Mary was the absorption of our great Brighid into Catholicism; others say the Virgin was meant to embody Isis. Either way, neither had anything to do with the rabbi, Yeshua of the East, that the Romans adopted as their own. Your mother is one of the Western deities. The people of Erin—Ireland—sprung from them, namely the *Tuath Dé Danann*, the children of the holy Danu."

"Is any of that even English?"

He shoots me an exasperated glance.

"What?" I hold my hands up in defense. "All I heard was *blah, blah, Virgin, blah, blah, Romans.*"

He squeezes the steering wheel, and it squeaks like it might snap in his grip. He continues as if I didn't say anything, his jaw a bit clenched. "The *Tuath Dé Danann* were the children of our holy Danu. She came

across from the Otherworld and birthed several powerful beings who
became the gods and goddesses of old. Five of them now rule the
Otherworld: Lyr of the sea, as I've mentioned, Arwen of air, Cernunnos
of the earth, Brighid of fire, and the Morrígan of spirit. These were her
five firstborn children, the Penta. The holy Danu eventually took them
back with her to her world, but they return now and then to—"

"Wait," I interrupt. "I've heard of this Morrígan goddess, I think.
Wasn't she the witch who was Arthur's sister and, like, tricked him
into doing the nasty dance with her? I think I saw that in a movie or
something."

He blows out a long breath. "No."

"Oh." I chew on my lip, thinking. "But if they're from Ireland, are
they, like, leprechauns?"

"No."

"But they're not aliens?"

This time his answer is masked in a growl. "No."

"You've gotta help the Yankee here, Paddy. You're only giving me
so much to work with—"

"Fine," he clips out. "I have books. Several hundred books. With
pictures and everything. I will pass them to you as soon as we arrive at
the house."

"I'm just asking questions," I mutter, but secretly I'm thrilled,
thinking about how many shelves several hundred books would fill.

"You don't have even the simplest grasp of history or literature.
What sort of education did you get?"

"An American one," I say. I thought I had a grip on history, but
apparently not—I'm annoyed at myself for reading so much fiction and
not getting my butt to school consistently. My defenses rise as he gives
me a look like I'm stupid. "Pardon me if I was too busy being dragged
around town by social services to retain any pagan prowess. Maybe if
my mom hadn't been shooting shit in her veins and forgetting to take
me to school. Or if the group homes I was shoved in didn't have mass

chaos twenty-four seven so I could actually fucking absorb what I tried to study. If only." My ire rises with each word until I've turned in my seat. I poke him in the shoulder. "Which, by the way, is your alien leaders' fault. Even according to you. That 'cast' of people who traded me with some junkie's baby. How sick *is* that? Who thinks that's *ever* a good idea?"

"The Cast, or whoever left you with that human woman, likely didn't know of her affliction."

I snort in disbelief. "And you want me to trust them?"

"No," he says quickly. "Never trust anyone from here on out."

"Excuse me? But you said—"

"I said you should trust Marius because his first loyalty is always to your mother. And you can trust me. Every other soul, keep at a distance. They may not have your best interests at heart."

I raise an eyebrow. "And you do?"

"I'm pledged to your mother."

"That's not real encouraging from where I'm sitting."

The car slows to turn onto a dirt road, approaching what looks like a large construction site. In the dim morning light, I see the outline of a building's skeleton but nothing that looks remotely like a place to live. I grip the door handle, in case Faelan's about to bury me in concrete or something. "What is this place?"

"I told you, we're—" He stops talking and studies me. "Oh, you're seeing the glamour. This is the Cottages. It only appears to be a construction site to hide it from the humans. Things can get a bit . . . *odd* around places where Otherborn reside. And the demis appreciate privacy. So they cloak some locations in a sort of false imaging. Give it a second."

As he's saying that, everything I'm looking at—the naked metal beams of the skeletal construction, the stacks of pipes and brick— begins to melt, dripping down around me like weird industrial rain on the window, leaving in its wake a curved cobblestone driveway and a three-story mansion that looks like something out of *Gone with the Wind*.

That's a *cottage*?

Large pillars coated in ivy and morning glory vines frame the front porch. There are countless arched windows and French doors on the face, as well as two levels of wraparound porches speckled with potted greenery. Surrounding the house is a whimsical sort of rolling lawn, like an ocean of grass. That's a crazy amount of watering, but even in the low light I can see how green it all is. There are trees and mossy rocks, flowers sprouting everywhere. There's even a babbling brook off to the side, ending in a small pond near the edge of the circular driveway.

Holy shit, it looks like freaking Disneyland.

We park in a carport at the end of the long drive, and I open the door slowly. I get out in a sort of trance, surveying it all in the rising sunlight. I step onto the illuminated stone pathway, expecting a rabbit to hop up to me while birds start chirping happily in the distance, singing about the new day or something equally ridiculous.

"Yes, I know, it's excessive," Faelan says in a tired voice. "This way." He leads me down a side pathway along the small brook, through some thin trees, to an iron gate. He opens it and motions for me to walk in front of him. Dim white-blue lights mark the path we follow, through more trees and over flat mossy stepping-stones. It's like a miniforest on the side yard. I'm stunned by the fresh smells and the feel of the dewy morning air. Then I step past the last few trees and take in the sight of what has to be a dream.

It's just a swimming pool—I know that as I'm looking at it—but it looks like a lagoon. The six-foot waterfall from the raised spa on the third tier of the yard is surreal, frogs croaking over the sound of the rushing water.

Wow.

The rest of the yard is expansive, tall trees surrounding the pool, like a cove in the middle of a forest. Stone and clover and soft curling ferns create the perfect natural look around the pool. And as we step farther into the space, I notice several wooden lounge chairs and dark wood cabanas that are covered with drooping vines and grapes. Torches illuminate the pathway and create deep shadows, while pale green and blue lights among the trees give it a resort vibe. A forest resort.

"The main house is there," Faelan says, breaking through my awe. He points behind us, and I turn back to see the large white house looming. It's just as stunning from this angle—maybe more so. "And the bungalows are this way"—he motions ahead—"up those steps, at the top of the waterfall." He moves in front of me and walks along the water's edge. I follow him up a stone staircase to the level of the steaming spa. There are a ton of trees up here too, and another stone pathway that leads into the shadows.

"I'm in the east and you're in the west," he says, then adds, "for now."

He points toward the right to a small structure that's more like a cottage than the massive thing behind us. It's something out of a faerie tale, vines growing up the face, and tiny shuttered windows on the facade. A glass-walled patio is attached to the side. It looks like a greenhouse; plants are pressing at the windows and growing out of the top, as if the foliage is bursting through the roof and spilling down the sides.

"How am I supposed to sleep in there?" I ask. "It looks like it's full of plants."

"No, that'll be my bungalow. It's facing east, see?" He motions to the door, then to the direction it's facing.

"Oh. How can you even tell?"

"The sunrise?"

And I feel like an idiot. "Right." I glance at the glow rising over the hills, my eyelids getting heavy. "So which one's mine?" I'm about to fall over after being awake all night.

"Here." He starts walking, and I follow him past the greenhouse, around the side. "Your bungalow will face the sunset and the ocean."

We pause at an archway made of pink climbing roses, and I realize the thick tendrils are framing a blue door. This bungalow is in the Spanish style, with a red-tiled roof and peach stucco walls. There's a bay window, and just underneath a box planter is overflowing with pansies and morning glories that haven't opened to the rising sun yet.

"I'll be sleeping in there?" I ask, suddenly doubting my luck. "It's so pretty."

"It's unlocked," he says when I don't move. "You can just go on in."

I reach out to the doorknob. But before I open the door, I turn back to him. "I need you to make sure Ziggy is okay."

"The human?"

I nod, thinking of my friend, of her sitting beside me in the orange laundromat chairs the other night and putting Cheetos up her nose to make me laugh. She was a lie. A total lie. But I can't stop caring that she's all right.

"Sure," Faelan says, studying me. "I can check on her."

"Thanks," I mutter, exhaustion finally taking over.

"Just get some sleep," he says quietly. He reaches over and wraps his hand around mine as it grips the doorknob, then he turns it for me. The door swings open with a soft creak. "Things will seem less overwhelming after some rest."

I pull away, unsure how to feel about him touching me.

He gives me a small smirk and turns, saying over his shoulder as he heads for the east bungalow, "I'll be next door if you need anything. And I'll be fetching you for our first lesson in four hours."

EIGHT

SAGE

Sleep. It's barely happening. There was a moment of stillness, when the warmth and comfort of my new surroundings wrapped around me, the poolside waterfall lulling me with its calming rhythm, allowing me to nearly drift off. But then I remembered the last time I fell asleep and woke to three guys gawking at me. And the way I was trapped. And lied to. My whole life.

Eventually, I sit up and scan my new living quarters, which I didn't bother to look at when I walked in a few hours earlier. I just made a beeline to the couch and collapsed on it, curling myself into the throw blanket tossed over the back.

Now I notice that the couch is purple velvet, soft against my skin. The blanket I was wrapped up in is a pale blue angora, and the throw pillow I rested my head on is delicately embroidered, fit for a queen; it was obviously made by hand. I run a finger over the faded threads and marvel at the detail of the design. Like something out of one of those ancient manuscripts I saw on our school field trip to the museum last year.

I dozed off on that thing. I probably drooled on it.

On the wall across from the couch, where you'd expect a TV, there's a large painting of a forest with the sun setting behind it—it looks old, some of the paint cracking. The rug that's covering the dark wood floor under my feet is white and furry. I really hope it wasn't ever hopping around or anything.

This must be the living room. To my left is the front door; to my right is what looks like a small kitchen nook and two other doors. I assume one of them leads to a bedroom.

I stand and wander over to the closest one, cracking it open. A bathroom. It's old-fashioned in style, but the fixtures look new. I move to the other door and peek inside.

My breath catches in my throat. It's like something out of a dream, where a princess would live. A large canopy bed sits in the center, draped with sheer yellow fabric and covered with a ton of pillows. There's a large window rimmed by built-in bookshelves—look at all those books!—and a puffy yellow chair set off to the side just so. The floor is covered in more fur rugs. A desk and more bookshelves are set into the wall on the other side of the bed, and a hand-painted screen with knotted designs is to my left, in front of what looks like another door. I'm assuming that's the closet.

I'd go look inside, but I don't think I can take in any more lavish surprises right now. I feel so out of place, like my surroundings just highlight how lost I am. This can't possibly be where I belong.

My gaze trails back to the bed. All those pillows. I think of the orange plastic chairs I slept in several nights last week, and I step closer. I reach out and run my palm over the puffy surface of the comforter. It feels like satin, but it looks like simple cotton. I marvel at the sensation of it against my skin, and before I know it I'm climbing up and crawling over the thing, falling into the mountain of pillows until I'm cradled by them.

I don't think I've ever been this comfortable in my entire life.

This. This is heaven.

I close my eyes, and the weight of the last twelve hours lifts from my mind for a fleeting moment. Just long enough for me to fall asleep.

~

I try to hide my shivering as I wait before the altar, in my position as the Bonding begins. Around me, shadows dance over the cairn walls from the restless flames licking up the ram's body—the sacrifice on the pyre behind me—and the smell of sweat and burnt flesh smother the smoky air.

The King of Ravens paints an alarming image, standing almost naked across from me on the other side of the blood circle. He wears the corona radiata, *the golden laurel-leafed crown, on his head of onyx hair. His short beard is neatly trimmed, combed with lavender oil for the ceremony. His sharp silver eyes study me beneath a heavy brow.*

I try not to think about the past. Or future. I try not to think about what those hard hands will feel like on my skin when he seals this Bond.

I study the stone floor rather than look in those metallic eyes. I feel them on me, though, the same way they have been for the fortnight I've been here preparing for the ceremony. He hasn't touched me; he's only brought me gifts and insisted I sit with him beside the greatfire in the evening before he goes out for his hunt. Sometimes I smell him in the hallway outside my rooms. But he never comes in, thank the goddess. The scent of blood is heavy on him in those moments. I'm not sure what I would've done if he'd attempted anything.

After this is done, it won't matter. My bed will be his. As will my life.

A druid walks back and forth behind me, tossing rosemary and lavender onto the pyre after each stanza of his spell. He calls to the wind from the east, he calls to the waters in the west, and he pulls the spirit of flame and earth into the cairn with us, asking the Penta to approve the Bond set to be made between the two most powerful Houses, as he pleads for a blessing from our mothers, Brighid and Morrígan, and thanks the Cast for their permission to seal the Bond between the two very different powers.

A female druid comes to my side with bowl and brush, beginning to paint my skin in blue woad, tracing patterns of knots and runes across my back, then baring my chest and continuing.

The king's gaze follows the woman's strokes, and when she's finished, he raises his chin at me in approval but says nothing. What does he see when he looks at me? My wild copper hair? My simple features? The awkward birthmark just above my heart? I'm round of cheek and hips and not much of a beauty. But however I look to him, I will belong to him.

Determination is set in hard lines on his face, and I wonder if the torque on his neck is working properly. I can see his dark energy lifting in silver and black curls over his shoulders now. It should be tight inside his skin, as mine is. The iron shackle should be holding it in place so that we don't harm each other in the first merging, before we can get used to the feel of each other's powers.

The female druid moves to the king next and begins painting the woad in circles over his torso. The druid chanting behind me recites the final section of his spell, walking the ram's-blood circle painted on the floor. He holds a rowan stick aloft, flicking rosewater over the king and then me as he passes by, mumbling, "A price paid, a covenant sealed, in earth and blood and ash, in spirit and flesh and fire."

The price is my will, my soul, in payment for the life of the human prince that I took.

In the center of the circle, between the king and me, is an altar with two bowls set atop, one full of salt, one full of rye.

The iron union dagger rests between them.

I stare at it, imagining the blade cutting into my flesh. And I can't help when my gaze moves to the king. I want to blink and make this moment a dream, perhaps find myself in the thicket with Lailoken, among the bluebells in the Caledonian wood.

I should run from this son of Morrígan, deny him, deny our mothers, and let the world burn. But my heart twists at the thought. I was running from duty when fate took my heart from me, when the prince succumbed to my fire's will. It was the childish notion of freedom that tore him from me.

Now it's time to accept my punishment for allowing the humans to glimpse our world. Time to atone.

The druid's voice fills the room again. "When moon gives birth to stars," he says, in a droning hum, flicking more rosewater over us with the rowan stick, "let this Bond be sealed in blood."

My skin prickles with fear as the king takes the cue, reaching out to pick up the ceremonial dagger by the leather-wrapped hilt. I focus on not moving, not making a sound, as I watch him bring the blade to his chest, tip pricking his left breast. A drop of crimson pearls up at the spot.

With a slow hiss of breath, he cuts across.

Dark blood slides down his abdomen in a thick swath of red. "My blood with yours," he says. And he turns the knife, holding out the hilt for me.

My hands clench into fists at my side, and I force my shaking limbs to still.

I breathe in slowly again. Then I reach out, taking the ceremonial dagger from him, careful not to touch his fingers.

I pretend not to care about the cage I'm about to be locked in. About the pain in my soul from loss, from the goddess Brighid abandoning me to this darkness, pain from the reality of everything in front of me.

I press the tip of the blade to the center of my chest, the point breaking the skin. I look into the silver eyes of the king in front of me. And consider my fate.

One deep plunge to the heart and the pain will end.

One plunge.

One.

NINE

FAELAN

I rise from sleep quickly, my new task weighing heavily on my mind. I climb down from the nest in the center of my new room. The dirt floor of the bungalow is cool under my feet. My arm brushes against one of the ropes of ivy hanging from the ceiling, and a few leaves wilt as I unintentionally take in a thread of life. My head is still a mess from earlier. I need to shed this if I'm going to do what Marius wants and assist this new demi with her transition. I need to focus.

Once I got settled in here this morning, I managed to fall into a light sleep for a few hours, but the stillness was fleeting. I kept seeing the fear in the demi's eyes, kept smelling her shock. The cloud of her misery seemed to follow me after we parted ways, and it's still sticking to my skin.

I'm not sure how to cleanse myself of it. I consider feeding more, but I already took some energy from the growth around me as I slept, and it hasn't done any good.

Instead, I make my way into the attached greenhouse and splash water on my face from the small fountain near the entrance. I need to clear my head. Ready myself for the task ahead of me.

I told the demi I'd wake her in four hours, and it's been five, so I should probably make sure she's all right with her new living space. We need to get started with this transition.

Damn, I can't believe I'm the one with my neck in the noose. Marius is a bastard. He's obviously known all of this time that he would tap me for the task, if this cottage is any indication. It was clearly created in preparation for my arrival. It's almost an exact replica of my house in upstate New York.

The main room has been converted into a makeshift thicket, with a huge raised nest at the center—a weaving of young, flexible branches, coated in live moss and grasses and vines, and covered in pillows, blankets, and more pillows. As I sleep, I can feed slowly off the life around me. I'll be awake long enough that the life should be able to rejuvenate itself before my next rest.

The greenhouse will make a good training room for the demi. It has an open grassy area in the center surrounded by heavily packed-in life, all growing from the dirt floor, up the walls, tendrils of plants spilling from the ceiling like leafy stalactites. No cement, no metal, just wood walls around me and mossy river rocks and soil beneath my feet.

Not bad for being so close to the city. One of the reasons I rarely come to LA is because it's too tough to find places to sleep, the forests are thinned and dry, and the beaches don't have enough rich life. Looks like Marius has been listening to my complaints over the years.

Yes, he definitely knew that I'd be the one given this job.

Why didn't he tell me when he called me up for the hunt?

Because he knew I'd figure out a way to free myself from the task. Instead, he sprang it on me, and I gave in. Now I'm stuck.

If he wasn't the master, I'd gut him and enjoy it.

I find the closet and pull out a change of clothes, then head into the bathroom to clean up. After a shower and shave I feel a little clearer.

But then I step out into the sunlight and hear a familiar giggle. And my stomach clenches.

Aelia.

I'd hoped to avoid her while I was in LA. But now that I'm staying here, in her father's house . . . feckin' shite.

I consider going back into the cottage and staying inside all day, hiding like a bloody coward. I don't need one more thing to make me nuts. But getting the transition started with the new demi is vital, since she was brought in just under the wire. If I'm responsible for this process, I'm going to be sure it's swift.

So I shore up my sanity and step out of the shadows.

"Well, well," Aelia says as I emerge onto the walkway. Her voice is silk against the air.

And nails against my skin.

"There you are," she says. "I was wondering if you'd hide from us all day." She cuts a lithe figure of perfection, sitting in a lounge chair under a small aspen growing at the edge of the pool, her chestnut hair spilling free over her shoulders, skin a shimmering bronze in the sunlight, long legs delicately bent to show the curves off just right. She slides her sunglasses down her nose and smirks at me. Her ocean eyes glow just a little, showing me she likes what she sees. One of her lemmings is beside her in another chair—Niamh is her name, I think. A pixie with very little intelligence or will of her own. A perfect companion for the witch.

I ignore my boss's daughter and pull a leather strap from around my wrist, then tie back my hair as I walk the path to the opposite cottage.

"I heard a rumor you were living with us again," Aelia says. "I thought Daddy was teasing me. Aren't you going to come give me a kiss before you run off? Has your affection faded since last spring at Beltane?"

Her companion giggles.

I pretend not to hear the gibe and knock on the demi's door with a little more force than I mean to. I swallow the curse I want to throw at Aelia. Me telling the offspring of one of the most powerful demigods in western America to fuck right off probably wouldn't be the best way to begin this new task.

I've made enough mistakes with the witch already.

"Oh, Faelan," Aelia says, "you're always such a cold bastard."

The pixie, Niamh, adds in a dreamy voice, "And it's so hot."

I knock again, even harder this time. Why isn't the demi coming to the door? She better not be ignoring me.

"He won't escape us forever, Niamh," Aelia says. "The truth of his nature will find him eventually."

"Mmm," Niamh says, "I can't wait. The son of sin itself."

My jaw clenches hard enough to crack my teeth. Where the hell is this godsdamn demi?

I try the handle, but it's locked. I'm pissed enough, though, that the metal bends and the doorjamb cracks with a loud snap. I curse under my breath as the door swings open.

Then the smell of smoke hits me, stopping every other thought.

Fire.

I rush inside, looking around, but all I see are gray plumes. I reach out with my energy, feeling for power, for death, for anything that could be connected to the demi. Could she have turned herself to ash already? Why the hell did I leave her alone? I'm meant to be her mentor, her protector. Marius will be sure her death means my own.

I find the couch, but it's vacant. The smoke is coming from under the bedroom door.

The handle is glowing orange, the edges of the door singed.

Holy goddess.

I kick below the latch and break the jamb, then hold my breath as I slip inside. The air singes my skin instantly. My vision blurs, but not before I catch a glimpse of the demi's naked form curled in a cocoon of flames in the center of the embers of the bed. Glowing cracks have formed over her charred skin, her clothes burned completely away. Her power isn't awake enough to let her feel what she's doing to herself and the room.

I flick my own energy to life, trying to cool the air around me, to get a better look, but I don't have enough in me to protect myself so that I can reach her. The flames roar as they consume the fluttering curtains, lick up the bedposts and up the wall, then begin rolling across the ceiling toward me. She's burning the building down around her as she immolates herself. She'll have us all writhing in flames within minutes. When it's done, *she'll* be fine, but she'll also have burned down the entire Santa Monica mountain range.

I close my eyes and focus, searching my surroundings for something that I can siphon power from. There's a stirring beneath my feet, a pace or so away. The earth under the structure sighs and begins to vibrate at my prodding. I won't be able to get my skin on it for the initial surge, but I can pull it toward me, I think. If I don't give a shit about being useful for the next few days, that is.

I can't weave a spell because that would mean breathing and burning my lungs to a crisp. So I release an answering groan of my own and call to the life under me.

The concrete foundation moans in response, fissures popping open in the wood floor. My chest aches with the effort of tugging the life closer, my skin beginning to blister as my energy fades and the air I cooled heats again. An avalanche of thoughts tumbles through my head. I consider running, consider my own demise, consider how little my existence has meant to this world, and how little my death will change anything. It's always this way when the next world calls. But something powerful is swirling deep in my gut, and even as I realize that stopping this is likely a lost cause and I need to run, I can't make my feet move. I can't manage to work up the will to leave the girl's side.

It's a shock to my system, wholly unfamiliar. And it sends a renewed surge of my energy through the air. The pain in my skin blinks out for a flash as the air cools a little.

The floor bursts open. A thick tree root surges up, reaching for my foot, sprouting several saplings as it slides up my leg. I grab hold of it like a lifeline, my body weakening. And before the darkness can claim me, I focus everything I have left on the root, on tugging out the thin threads of life in a steady stream, collecting the energy into my skin as quickly as I can, pleading with it to coat me. Then I push out every ounce I have, every spark I can manage, praying it'll be enough to douse the flames, praying it's not already too late.

But before I can be sure we're all safe, blackness replaces the glow of the hungry flames, and I fall.

TEN

SAGE

Who turned up the heat? It's so warm. Like, *really* warm.

A vague memory of fire and the smell of rosewater drift away as I become more aware of my surroundings. Sweat pearls on my temples. My lungs ache like they've been singed from the inside. As I open my eyes, they sting like mad, my vision blurring. What's with all the fog in the room?

No, not fog. Smoke.

My nerves spark, and I sit up in a rush, every muscle in my body screaming. I feel like I raced an Ironman or something. What the hell?

A cough rips from my chest, raspy and thick with phlegm. And then another. I wipe the tears from my eyes and wave a hand in front of my face to attempt to move the smoke. But when my surroundings become a little clearer, the heat against my skin dulls.

And icy threads of fear weave through me.

Everything around me is black, burned, charred into rubble. The bed I'm sitting on is only coal and sticks now, the ceiling above my head full of smoldering holes. And the cushy chair near the window is glowing embers, the shelves of books framing it . . . the books are all completely destroyed.

What the hell happened?

I was dreaming of fire, wasn't I? No. It was . . . I don't remember. And I'm . . . I'm naked?

My God, did I do this? Panic fills me; new tears spring to my eyes. I scrape them from my cheeks, though, anger instantly following the panic and confusion. Anger at myself, at my situation. At my helplessness. How did this suddenly become my life?

Then I see a form on the floor.

The fear surges again, and I scramble to the body. I'm scared to touch it. The clothes are burned away in places, revealing blisters. The face is hidden, covered by a protective hand, the skin red and disfigured there too. The arms . . . are coated in markings.

Faelan!

Don't be dead, oh, God, don't be dead. But I can't say the words; I can't breathe.

I don't think I should touch him. I don't know what to do.

"What happened?" says a strangely calm voice from the doorway. I register that it's a female, that it's young. But I don't look up. I can't look away from Faelan's still-smoking body.

A second voice whispers, "Goddess below."

"Help," I choke out. *I have to do something! What have I done?*

Something moves in my peripheral vision, and the first girl kneels beside me, wrapping a towel around my body. I think I'm hallucinating. She's glowing. "Go get some of the vine near the door, Niamh," she says to the other girl. Is this person an angel? Her cascading hair seems to have its own light, and her teal eyes and earthy skin emanate some sort of energy. But do angels usually wear bathing suits? Then she says, "Oh, Faelan, you silly asshole."

Okay, I'm thinking she's not an angel.

She places a hand on the twisted skin on his arm, closes her eyes, and whispers something rhythmic and soft, like a song in another language.

The air stirs, raising the hairs on the back of my neck, and her glow slinks over his arm where she's touching him.

The other girl comes back in and tosses a bunch of leaves down. A vine. The glowing girl begins wrapping it around Faelan's arm and his torso, still whispering the same strange words.

I watch in confusion as the emerald leaves turn yellow, then copper, then wilt completely, curling in on themselves.

"It's not much, he might need more," the glowing girl says to the other, who runs back out.

A moan comes from Faelan, and I gasp in relief. He's not dead. "Oh, God, thank God."

"My name's Aelia," the glowing girl says. When I glance up at her in confusion, she's smirking at me. "Not God."

I don't know how to respond so I focus on Faelan again. "We need to call an ambulance. His burns—"

"He'll be fine," Aelia says in a tired voice. "We need to move him to his nest."

"What? He needs a doctor!" His skin is still blistered and singed, his breathing labored.

Aelia just laughs and turns to the girl, Niamh, who's come in with more vines. "Can you text the others and tell them we'll need to add one more to the list for tonight? We have some introductions to make, I think. And go find James—he's still asleep in my room."

She's obviously not listening to me. Is she nuts?

I tuck the towel tighter around my torso and reach down, trying to turn Faelan over to get a better look at his face.

"Uh," Aelia says, "you may not want to do that."

And just as she's warning me, Faelan's eyes fly open. His fingers reach out and grip me by the throat, a guttural noise coming from his chest as he flips me onto my back, climbing over me. All in half a second.

"See," I hear Aelia say through my pulse thundering through my head, "he hates being woken up."

I blink and gag, tugging at his arm, trying to squirm to get him off me, but his grip is ironclad around my neck, his weight pressing down on me.

Aelia slides a finger over his cheek, saying in a seductive voice, "Hey, Faelan. Don't kill the newblood."

He snarls down at me, a total stranger. A monster. His gaze is blank and milky white; his face and neck are burned, skin twisted on the left side. My vision blurs as he squeezes out my life, pressing me into the floor.

And then suddenly he's gone and I'm gasping, choking on the burned air again. As I sit up, I realize he's slumped against another male figure. "Well, hello there," the new guy says. "You're that girl who was a lost dove, aren't you?" he asks, like I'm more interesting than Faelan's burned body. He's got a British accent, and as my vision clears I see he's only wearing boxers. With heart-eyed emojis on them. He's smiling that same sardonic smile that Aelia had on her face a second ago.

"Name's James," he says. "I'd shake your hand, but mine are a bit full. And I hear from Ben that your touch has some side effects. As we can see." He nods to the wounded guy in his arms, then winks like he's cute, and I feel like kicking him. What is so freaking funny about this situation right now? I nearly killed Faelan!

"Let's get our resident wet blanket back to bed," Aelia says, "where he can recoup a bit." She and Niamh help James carry the large and limp Faelan out of the room.

I manage to get to my feet and follow them. But once we're outside, in front of the door to Faelan's cottage, James pauses and glances at me, then at Aelia, like he's worried about something.

"Wait out here," Aelia says. Then they all disappear into the small house.

I stand in a daze, staring at the green door. And as the stillness of the morning falls over me, the soothing sound of the waterfall in the background and the smell of sea air in my nose, the events of the last several minutes start to flick through my head in a panicked rush: the smoke-filled room, the charred surroundings, Faelan's burned body on my floor, his milky eyes when he attacked me.

I feel like someone punched me in the face repeatedly. What just happened? Was it my fault? What did I do to burn it all? How am I not *dead*? None of it feels real.

Aelia and James emerge from the cottage before I can make sense of anything. That Niamh girl isn't with them.

"It's been a laugh, ladies," James says, "but breakfast is calling, and I need to get to the set before they start the gossip about Rihanna's new haircut without me. Plus, I've got lines to memorize for today's shoot." He flashes a quick grin at me, then moves in to give Aelia a blush-worthy kiss before he slips away.

"Your boyfriend works in Hollywood?" I ask her.

She just giggles. "He's not my boyfriend, sweetie. James is a shade. They never reach status around here. Just keep it zipped to my dad that you saw the plebe with me."

I'm not sure what she means, but it sounds vaguely racist. She kissed the guy right back, tongue and all. Is she telling me she French kisses all the peasants for fun?

"Let's get you cleaned up, shall we?" she says in a bright voice as she hooks her arm through mine. She hugs me to her side, leading me toward the main house. "You poor thing. You must be so hungry after all that."

"Is Faelan going to be all right?" Cold fear seeps through me again as the question slips out. And embarrassment is tangled with it. The charred skin, the white eyes—if I did that to him . . . me . . . I must be a monster.

"Oh, he'll be fine. He just needs a nap." She pats my arm. "He's a downer, anyway. He'd probably have you on lockdown until he's sure you're not like the last female offspring from Brighid's tree."

What the hell's that supposed to mean? I start to ask her to explain, but she keeps on talking.

"But bitches need to stick together, right? Can't let the men push us around or they might get the idea that they're in charge." Then she winks and starts talking about some blog post on feminism she read this morning.

I tuck the information in the back of my mind and make a note to ask Faelan about this other "female offspring." If I ever see the guy again.

~

The house is like a museum. There are artifacts from various eras and cultures in large glass cases along the halls and filling whole rooms. There's even a room that looks like it's entirely populated with old stone sarcophagi. I wonder if people really live in this house or if it's just a place where they keep a collection of old stuff, like the Getty Villa. But then we finally pass what could be a den and walk through a real kitchen where a uniformed woman is chopping vegetables.

Aelia ignores the woman and leads me upstairs and down a long hall to her room—a vast space, the walls covered in images of . . . uh, herself: photographs, paintings, even mosaics. I have to bite my lip to keep back a derisive laugh. I don't like to jump to conclusions about people, but this girl *might* be a narcissist. There's a single eight-by-ten-inch watercolor of a pug near the window, the one sign she hasn't reached Code Blue levels of navel-gazing.

The only piece of furniture in the room is a huge bed that looks larger than a king-size. Several of the throw pillows have her likeness on them too: her profile, a close-up of her wide eyes, even one of her lying half-naked on a golden couch on the beach, with the waves behind her. Wow.

She takes me through to a bathroom that could be a Roman bathhouse and shoves me into a large shower stall without ceremony. I toss the towel she gave me over the frosted-glass door, turn on the water, and wash off the soot and ash. It's hard to believe I don't have a single burn on me.

Once I'm done, Aelia hands me a slinky robe and takes me to what she says is her closet, but it looks more like a tiny mall. She studies my silk-covered body for a second—she's obviously annoyed when I won't disrobe and let her gawk at my naked self, but I need to retain at least a shred of dignity—then dresses me in ridiculously expensive-looking clothes from her nine-hundred-square-foot closet as she comments on my thin figure being great for movie roles and how she knows a guy who hires for body work if I'm interested.

I consider telling her I'd rather just find a way to get regular healthy meals so I don't feel like a stick figure. But when she looks in the mirror and complains about her large hips and "massive ass," I decide there's no winning this discussion. Of course, there's nothing massive about her. And considering all the images of herself in her room, I have to wonder if she's fishing for compliments more than actually believing her own propaganda—in fact, I suspect she's secretly insulting me, the way she keeps mentioning how she can see my bones. I just busy myself pretending to be amazed at a pair of pink sunglasses that are inlaid with what I think are real diamonds.

Aelia barely pauses to take a breath as she finishes dressing me and then takes me to a mirror, painting my face with layers of gunk before draping me in garish accessories. The whole time we're at the vanity she's chattering at me about a million pointless pieces of information. My favorite is how some girl named Astrid from the House of Cernunnos—which is apparently *not* a band but the name of another god's family—was dating Faelan until she was adopted by the demi leader of that other House. And from what I can tell, Aelia really doesn't like the girl. She claims Astrid is *so* full of herself because the girl thinks she's some amazing style queen and badass hunter, but really she's just an underling poser. Then Aelia proceeds to describe every dress that this Astrid has ever worn to every event, down to the last thread. She also goes on and on about some guy the girl's dating, named Duncan, who apparently has "very big-name people in the music industry" on his payroll, and Astrid has him wrapped around her finger even though she's totally just using him for his yacht.

Whoever this Astrid girl is, Aelia is obviously jealous.

"I mean, she's an alfar, for Danu's sake, right?" she asks me, as if I know what she's talking about. "Who wants to suck face with a girl that tastes like a kale cleanse? I don't know how Faelan did it all those years. *Blech*."

I start to wonder if I've really entered a world of gods and goddesses or a live broadcast of *TMZ*.

The whole process lasts several hours, and I'm a little shocked when I see her fuzzy pink clock reading 5:00 p.m.

"Maybe we should go check on Faelan," I say as she hands me a purple bag that matches my shoes. "I'm worried he's not—"

"He's fine," she snaps. "Gods. If you're hoping for some kind of romantic thing with the guy, you're gonna be super disappointed."

I just blink at her, feeling like she slapped me. The last thing I need is for this gossip queen rich bitch to hate me. "Okay, well, thanks for the clothes and all," I say, trying to sound cheery, but I'm likely coming off as shrill. "I should probably go back to my room and, uh, start to clean up the place or something. I made a bit of a mess." I think. I have no idea what I did, or if I did anything.

I *do* know that Astrid from the House of Cernunnos—not a band— gets her pubes waxed at Urban Blue in West Hollywood, though. So there's that.

"Don't be silly," Aelia says, back to her casual voice. "My father will be here for dinner in an hour, and I'm sure your cottage is already fixed. No doubt it was finished hours ago."

Fixed? What? "Are you joking?"

"You are slow, aren't you? You slept in a furnace of your own making this morning, for goddess's sake, and you didn't get singed. Doesn't that open your mind a little to the impossible being possible?"

She's a bitch, but she's got a point. And there goes that excuse to covertly check on Faelan. I smile at her and rack my brain for a replacement. "Cool. I'm, just, you know . . . it's all very strange here, but you're being so nice and all"—I clear my throat—"and I'm new, possibly a bit dense, so—can I, uh, go see it? In case it doesn't meet my expectations." I look in the mirror and play with my hair, topping the act off with a duck face. Just in case she thinks I can't be shallow.

"Oh, totally," she says, not looking suspicious. "Go take a peek, but be back for dinner in an hour. Daddy doesn't like having to wait."

The sound of this girl—who's stunningly beautiful, almost unreal—calling the man I remember from last night *Daddy* . . . I have to force myself not to wince.

Instead I run my tongue over my teeth, like I'm checking for lipstick. "Totes." And then I make my escape, slipping out from under her guardianship. As I work my way back through the massive house, I find myself thanking the universe for my horrible hopscotch journey through the foster system. Because if it did anything, it taught me how to become a chameleon and blend in with my surroundings—a gift that, I can tell, will be very handy in my current predicament.

ELEVEN

Sage

I knock on Faelan's door, but only silence echoes back. Unconscious people tend not to answer doors.

When I glance across the walkway to my cottage, I don't see any sign of a fire. The air smells a bit tangy still, but the smoke damage on the outer wall is gone. I'm guessing Aelia is right, and the repairs have already been completed. Do they just move real speedy, like the Flash? Or does time just sorta stand still whenever they need to get stuff done quickly?

I knock on Faelan's door again. Still no answer.

After standing on the welcome mat for a few seconds and absently watching a blue jay hop around on a nearby branch, I decide that things are way too wacky in this place to give a crap about decorum. So I try the knob, and when it won't give, I pull one of the bobby pins from my hair that Aelia used to make it look like I had a stylist instead of a pocketknife. I bend the thin metal and wriggle it into the keyhole. The lock's got pretty old guts so it clicks almost immediately and creaks open a little.

I slip inside and softly shut the door behind me. When I look up, my breath clogs in my throat.

It's a forest. I'm in a forest—or at least it feels that way. Green drips from the ceiling and the curling arms of ferns crowd around my legs. Tree trunks act like natural pillars, the bowers creating a canopy above, the roots nubby under my feet. The air smells like damp green things. Like rain.

"Faelan?" I whisper, searching the thick shadows. My pulse picks up speed at the strangeness.

I step deeper into the room, hearing nothing but the slight shifting of plants around me as I move. But then I push aside some drooping vines, and the leaves above my head rustle loudly. I look up, hoping it's just a bird or something. In the house. Or the forest. I don't know what to call this place. I don't see anything, so I keep going farther. As I move aside a branch blocking my view, it gets even weirder.

A circular structure made of sticks appears in front of me. It's a foot taller than me and rimmed in chunks of brown grass at the top. Dead grass. Moss and mushrooms coat the woven white birch branches, dark earth crumbling out of the crevices along the base.

I stare in confusion for a minute, and then I walk around it, looking for rhyme or reason to the thing.

A soft sigh fills the air, and I freeze, looking up. "Faelan?" But the noise sounds too feminine to have come from the burly Faelan.

No answer comes. I should probably just walk away, leave whatever this is alone. Poking around in the unknown is usually a horrible idea— I've seen enough curious ditzes die in horror movies to know that. But, apparently, I've become a curious ditz.

I slip off Aelia's ridiculous purple heels and prop my foot on one of the branches woven into the body of the structure. I grab a chunk of dead grass along the top and pull myself up to peek over the edge.

My nails dig into the bristly roots, and my breath catches in my throat.

Faelan's head is beside my fingers. He's lying on a bed of browning grass—asleep or dead, I can't tell. But I know where the sigh came from. Aelia's friend, Niamh, is wrapped around him, her delicate fingers splayed on his bare stomach. The two are coated in a thin silver-white substance that looks like it's made of spiderwebs.

I can't stop staring. The girl's head is tucked into the dip of Faelan's shoulder muscle, her long blond hair covering her obviously naked body. His arm is wrapped around her waist to hold her close, and his breath is rustling the hair at her brow. They're like something out of a faerie story, lovers frozen in time, so beautiful it almost hurts to look at them.

And the skin on Faelan's face isn't twisted and charred anymore. Just like when Ben drank Faelan's blood, the burns are completely healed, and only a tinge of pink is left behind on his cheek and neck. There's a little smudge of soot there, on his temple—

His eyes fly open and instantly lock on mine. They're glowing green.

I gasp and jerk back. My fingers slip through the dead grass roots with the sudden movement, and I fall, landing on a fern with an *oomph*.

The air whooshes from my lungs, and I have to focus on trying to breathe as threads of the silver webbing float down. A creak sounds from above, and Faelan appears in shadow, his predatory form crawling over the edge of the structure. He perches there for a second, searching with glowing eyes, then he spots me. He hops down, landing in a crouch like a bronze Tarzan.

I gape at his body as he stands.

Yep. He's naked. Nay. Kid.

Heat washes through me as the vision of him sears my brain. I'm torn between wanting to scrub my memory of the sight and wanting to drool over it for the rest of my life. Why did I have to be the curious ditz?

A growl reverberates from him, and the branches above fill with the sound of leaves rustling and birds screeching.

I look up and spot several bright blue jays fluttering over my head, squawking and cawing like mad. They swoop down one at a time, like they're trying to scare me.

One of them zips closer in a rush, beating its wings at my face.

I scramble away and swing at it, but another one pecks my shoulder, drawing blood. Still another gets its talons into my hair, yanking.

My palm smacks the tiny body as I swat at the air, sending it reeling. I growl right back at the birds, at Faelan who's stepping closer—but before he can reach me, I stagger to my feet, stumbling for the door, flinging it open, tumbling out, and slamming it behind me.

Something hits the wood with a *thunk*, and I find myself hoping one of the blue jays just gave itself a concussion.

I lean against the door and slide to the ground, trying to catch my breath.

Maybe I should be worried that naked Faelan will come after me, but I can't seem to focus on anything but oxygen right now.

Note to self: the safest Faelan is an unconscious Faelan.

The sound of someone clearing their throat interrupts my thoughts. I look up and see Aelia leaning against a tree several feet away.

"So, are you happy with everything you've seen?" she asks, obviously annoyed.

I give a jerky nod.

She breathes out a tired sigh and steps closer. "And now you're a mess again."

"What the hell *was* all that in there?" I ask, done with her weirdness. "I think he made birds attack me. And he was naked! And covered in these spiderwebs, sleeping in some sort of—" I move my hands, searching for the right word to describe it.

"A nest," she fills in, giving me an irritated look.

"Yes! A nest." The idea sends a shiver through me, the vision of him cocooned with that girl, curled up with her, then his body crawling over the edge . . . "What kind of thing *is* that guy?"

"It's super rude to ask that, you know," she says.

So I've heard.

"I really can't believe you interrupted his hibernation—*not* cool. Now I'll have to put him and Niamh back under, and that will cost me. And you."

"Cost what?"

"Power? Energy? Gods, girl, keep up."

Is she kidding? None of this makes any sense.

She steps closer and points at me as she steps over my legs to get to the door. "You're going to owe me some juice."

I shake my head. "I have no clue what that means."

She rolls her eyes and then bends so she's more at my level. "Look, sweetie, this is *so* not my job, but I'll lend you a hand, okay? You burned our resident hunter nearly to a crisp." She points at Faelan's door and raises an accusing brow at me. "You got that?"

When I nod, she continues, "Well, that mess forced his mind—or consciousness or whatever—to retreat, to protect itself and his power, which is why he nearly ripped your head off back in your cottage, and probably sent a few sharp beaks your way a second ago. Right?" She pauses again, like she wants me to agree or something, so I nod once more. "Okay, so then, in order for him to heal and allow his power to fully restore itself, he has to be all dormant and whatnot for a period of time near a power source—Faelan gets his energy from life, things that grow, and Niamh is a pixie who grows things. Got it?"

When I frown, still not fully wrapping my head around the crazy, she closes her eyes and rubs her temple like she's getting a headache. "Oh, my freaking gods," she mutters. And then she says, "So, like, when a creature of Faelan's ilk goes under, they have to pair with a compatible underling. Niamh, as a pixie, is the closest thing we have to an earth faerie. Therefore she's the chick who picked the short straw—even though an alfar would've been better. *Buuuut,*" she draws out the word, "now I've gotta go in there and use a spell to put him back to sleep so he can finish healing—*and* so he doesn't do anything too deadly in his subconscious state." She stands again and combs her fingers through her hair. "Is that all simplistic enough for you?"

It's funny, but she actually used a few big words in that explanation. From the conversation we had in her room, I wouldn't have thought the girl owned a book. I assumed she was about as deep as a desert puddle.

I nod at her again, even though I'm pretty clueless. Will I ever understand this strange world I've been pulled into? The thought of running away from it all rolls through my mind again, but where would I go? And apparently I'm not safe around people—regular people who can't heal by wrapping themselves up with pixies or drinking blood. If I burned down half a house in only minutes, in this supposedly protected place, who knows what I'd do out there. I need to get this under control. I need to understand what I am. Either that or I need to go hide in a mountain cave, like a monk, so I can't hurt anyone.

For now, I'll just steer clear of Faelan. Which leaves the vapid Aelia as my companion and clarifier. And she's even less helpful than Faelan was. I can only hope that Marius will have actual answers when he comes to dinner tonight. That can't happen soon enough.

TWELVE

SAGE

We're sitting on the couch in the den, within sight of the dining room and the entry hall, waiting for Marius to come home. Aelia is looking at her nails like the secret of the universe might reside in her cuticles. I'm trying not to let the avalanche of questions in my head crush my brain. The uniformed maids are going back and forth between the kitchen and the dining room to set the table.

I'm more than a little relieved when I hear footsteps echo from the back hall. Marius enters the room, and Aelia leaps from the couch and tackles him in a hug.

"Daddy!" she squeals like a little girl. She leans away to look at him and asks, in all seriousness, "What'd you bring me?"

He pulls her close again and kisses the top of her head. "Well, my Lia, I found some lovely Russian nesting dolls."

She droops. "I wanted Prada."

"They belonged to the last czar's daughter. A secret note was hidden inside, written in his own hand."

She pulls from his arms. "I still say lame."

He chuckles. "Of course you do. Perhaps next time I'll find something satisfactory."

"How long will you stay with us?" she asks.

"Only for dinner. I have work to do." He looks up at me. "How are you settling in, young Sage?"

Aelia answers for me. "She's fine."

Before Marius can ask me to elaborate, a woman enters the room, and he turns to smile at her. I'm a bit surprised—I didn't realize anyone else was in the house, besides the cook and maids. She walks over to his side and presses into him, kissing his cheek softly. "My love, we've missed you." Her hair is long and golden blond, and her dress is like something out of a glamorous nineteen-fifties style magazine, tightly fitted and glittery with a slit on the side that reaches nearly to her hip. Is she having dinner or going to a casino? "Do you really have to go so soon?"

"I'm afraid so," Marius says, then he motions to me. "Have you met our new arrival, my dear?"

The blond woman flashes me a glance but doesn't fully look at me. Instead, she turns and searches the space behind Marius like she's expecting someone to come in after him. "Well, sure, but where is that young man you said would be joining us? The one with the blue tattoos?"

Aelia rolls her eyes. "Gods, Mom."

Marius frowns at the blond woman—his wife?—like he doesn't understand. Then he looks to me again. "Is Faelan not here for dinner?"

I consider how to explain. "Well, he—"

Aelia cuts me off. "He's resting. Big day with the newborn and all. Training and whatnot." She hooks her arm into his. "Let's eat, Daddy. I'm starving."

I glance sideways at Aelia and try to figure out what's going on. Why is she lying? And should I let her? Aelia is the last person on earth I want to side with, but Marius seems pretty powerful—I don't want him to think I'm against him in any way.

When we're all sitting around the table and I see the family together, my stomach turns sour. I've seen a lot of different family dynamics over the years, living in too many foster homes, some with legitimate kids mixed in with the loaners, and some with a full gaggle of bastards and orphans clustered together in less space than these people would probably give to a dog. But this trio takes the cake with the tension and weirdness.

Obviously, the blond woman is Marius's wife and Aelia's mother, but the only life or awareness she's shown was when she perked up about Faelan. Since then, she's defaulted into some sort of Stepford woman. It's a lot creepy. Those vacant eyes and perfectly curved smile—it's like someone told her to grin three weeks ago, and it's still there, stuck on her face.

Her name is Barbara, and there is a resemblance in Aelia—the same nose and cheekbones. And perfectly glossy hair.

Marius is at the head of the table. He's wearing a white dress shirt and gray slacks, like he just came out of a business meeting. Over the past several minutes he's made small talk with Aelia and let her chat his ear off about some event she's planning. I have to give the man credit: he seems genuinely interested. A careless observer might think he's pleased with his fake wife and vapid daughter, but my guess is he's only got that stoic look on his face because he knows that he'll be leaving us all behind in a half hour or so.

At one point he clears his throat and directs his words to me. "How are you settling in so far?" he asks. He cuts into the thick steak on his plate, the center of it a bloody red. He glances up at me as he takes a dripping bite, waiting for an answer.

I push a piece of lettuce with my fork and try to think of a way to answer him and not lie. Luckily, I'm practiced in half-truths. "I've been resting, mostly. And hanging out with Aelia."

"You two seem to be getting on well," he says, surprise in his voice.

"Well, of course, Daddy," Aelia says. "She's beyond special. A real princess." It's an odd thing to say. And she gives me a look that has some sort of hidden message in it, but I can't tell what it is. *Don't dime me out*, maybe? Is she bribing me with flattery? She's picked the wrong girl for that.

"I have a lot of questions," I say. "When will I get them answered?"

He takes another bite of steak, and his brow dips a little in confusion. "Faelan is here for such things, to teach you and guide you. And once the arrangement is final, he'll also be your protector."

"Final? What arrangement?"

The corner of his mouth turns down on one side. "Has he spoken to you at all about the ceremony?"

My head pulls back. Not liking the sound of that. "Ceremony? What the hell's that mean?"

Marius turns to his daughter and asks in a low voice, "Where is Faelan, Aelia?"

She coughs, choking on her sip of wine. "I told you, he's sleeping."

His gaze narrows.

She does a very convincing shrug, making it all seem like none of her business. "As if I know anything, Daddy. You and your brigade of men are the ones who fix all this stuff." She takes another sip of wine and focuses on her plate.

He draws in a breath, then asks me, "What have you and the hunter spoken of?"

"I, uh . . ." The vision of Faelan's naked body climbing over the rim of the nest flashes through my head again. I swallow hard and try to blink it away. Have we even talked at all? But then I remember: the car. We talked in the car. "He, well, he told me about you. How you're the son of, um . . . a sea god." And I already forgot the name. Great. This is why I should've paid attention in World Civ. "And he explained how your world and the human world overlap. How my mother was the goddess Brighid. My whole life's been a lie. And all that stuff."

Marius waits, like he's thinking I'll say more, but I've given him everything I can remember. That I can tell him.

"I see," is all he says. And I swear that the air chills, the hair on my arms prickling.

"Did you know that an avocado has fat in it?" Barbara pipes up.

Every eye at the table moves to her—she hasn't said a word since we sat down.

"Why would the trainer order me to add one to my shakes? I'm telling you, that's the extra three hip pounds. I just can't peel them off." She shakes her head, the strange faux smile clinging to her lips. Maybe the plastic face is because of Botox or something.

"Enough with the *three hip pounds*, Barb," Aelia mutters.

Barbara reaches out and places a hand on Marius's arm. "I only wish you would help me, dear. Can't you do one of your manipulation spells or whatever it is? I know you've done it for your other wives, I've seen the pictures of—"

Aelia drops her fork on her plate. "The cursed three pounds aren't going anywhere, Barb, because they're in your head."

Barb's stiff features shift into an offended slant. "You'll live three hundred years without a blemish, Aelia. The least you could do is have a little pity on your mortal mother."

"Enough," Marius says, his voice low with warning. "Both of you."

The women give a silent response to each other, squinting their eyes and pinching their lips together, then they return to their plates.

Marius waits an extra beat before taking another bite of steak. He chews for a few tense seconds and then focuses on me again. "Faelan has disappointed me. He's told you very little."

"No, he's done fine," I say, quickly. It's my fault the guy's out of it. "I never did that good in school. The student role isn't my best look. I've got crap focus." Which isn't really true; I actually managed a tolerable 3.0 most of the time, in spite of how rarely I made it to class, but he doesn't have to know that.

Marius raises an eyebrow. "His task for the day was not complicated. All he needed to do was inform you of the ceremony. Apparently this never came up?"

"We've barely seen each—" I start to say before I realize I'm officially a snitch. First I put him in a coma, and now I'm throwing him under the bus. "I mean . . . there was so much talking. He said some stuff, lots of stuff, but maybe I didn't hear it."

"It's good that you're loyal to him," Marius says. "But there's no need for excuses."

Aelia stares into the golden wine she's swirling around her glass. "My dad's talking about the ceremony of Emergence. It's like a creepy birthday party. But with chanting."

"Thank you, Aelia," Marius says. "However, that's not helpful."

"Whatever. She's not going to understand it." She rolls her eyes. "The newblood's been in blind-ville too long. And our resident hunter has a huge stick up his ass, so he's not going to be straight with her."

Barb bobs her fork in the air, a dreamy look filling her eyes at the mention of Faelan. "Last time I saw him, he seemed like a smart young man."

"He's not *young*, Mom," Aelia says. "He's, like, nine million years old."

I drop my fork. "What?"

"That's ludicrous hyperbole," Marius says. "He was born in the fourteenth century."

"Same thing," Aelia says.

The fourteenth century . . . that was . . . a long time ago.

Barb almost lets the spot above her nose crinkle. "I'd say he's quite young compared to your father."

My gaze snaps to Marius again. I study him more closely, scrutinizing his perfect, unblemished skin. I think of Faelan . . . He's more than *seven hundred* years old? He doesn't look a day over twenty-three. How old is Marius if he looks thirty? And how does it work—are they immortal or something? Oh wow, does that mean I'm going to live hundreds of years too?

Even as the thought comes, my brain rejects it. Because if that is my reality now . . . what do I do with something like that?

"The point is that you need to understand what's expected of you as a demi," Marius says, breaking through my amazement. "There's much you've yet to learn, and the hour is late."

Aelia says with a smirk, "Like, three or four years late."

"Excuse me?" What's *that* mean?

"She will do fine," Marius says. "Once the Introduction is done tomorrow evening, she'll have a little time to learn."

I lean forward, gripping the table. "How am I three or four *years* late? Late to *what?*"

"You're a demigoddess," Marius says.

Like I don't know that already! "We covered that."

"Normally you'd have been brought in when your magic began to surface," he continues. "Around your thirteenth or fourteenth year is when that usually occurs. Another demi would have felt your Emergence beginning—a process that takes several years to fulfill itself—but it appears that you were cloaked or muffled in some way. I felt your magic begin to spark only three months ago. I sent the pixie and the human to watch you for a time, to see if I was sensing correctly. It was clear fairly quickly to Star what you were. And so an Emergence ceremony was requested for the next new moon. Unfortunately, that leaves very little time to prepare you. Less than I thought, if a whole day was wasted."

That explanation certainly clarifies the last few months of my life some. But an ache blossoms in my chest when I think of the moment I met Ziggy—how I saved her from that dealer off Chatsworth. Was he a fake too? He nearly shot me—or I thought he was going to. But it was all a ploy to endear me to her. How could I have been so blind? I'm supposed to be the liar. I'm the manipulator, the survivor.

Now I'm the one who's been duped—my whole life.

"When?" I ask.

"The initial Introduction ceremony will be tomorrow night," Marius says. "And until then, things are delicate. Your energies will be confused and unfocused. There is a small amount of danger for you until the official protective bonds can be done by the druids. Then you'll train with your protector until the final Emergence ceremony, which will occur at the next new moon."

Danger. From me or for me? I already know I'm combustible. That I can burn the shit out of things. And people.

I feel like I'm being smothered by the questions piling up inside of me.

I swallow, then clear my throat. "What happens at this thing tomorrow?" The word *ceremony* makes me think of some secret society or fraternity. I imagine chickens being slaughtered on an altar or a potion I'll be forced to drink—something with eye of newt in it.

"It's merely a formality, but it's vital for your safety as you come into your powers," Marius says, his voice gentle, like he can sense my anxiety. "The Introduction ceremony tomorrow will present you to the Otherworld, as well as seal an interim protector for you. That protector's House will shield you until you choose a permanent loyalty to a deity at the Emergence ceremony on the new moon. I'm hoping you will officially choose Faelan to be this protector tomorrow so the House of your mother, Brighid, will have the privilege of giving you safe haven."

"Why can't it just be you who protects me?" I ask.

His brow pinches. "Do you not approve of Faelan?"

"He's fine," I say. Except he makes me feel too many things I shouldn't be feeling. He makes that voice too loud in my head. The one that tells me to take. "But you're, like, in charge, right?" Which probably means Marius is really powerful. Maybe powerful enough to protect himself from me better than Faelan can.

"I'm not usually one to take on such a role." He gives me a troubled look. "It is your choice, but I would strongly suggest you choose Faelan. He's best suited for you, more so than I would be."

Something about his statement worries me. "What's this protector supposed to do exactly?"

Aelia leans back in her chair. "Teach you how to feed." She smirks and takes another sip of wine. "It can get a little . . . weird."

"Enough, Lia," Marius scolds. "A protector will teach you how to control and manipulate the goddess energy in your blood properly." He picks the linen napkin up from his lap and wipes the sides of his mouth, then sets the white cloth on his plate, signaling he's finished. "This isn't a game to us, young Sage, as Aelia may make it seem. Consider what I've said, and we'll finish this later. If you'll excuse me."

"Where are you going?" Aelia asks, sitting up straight again, all her flippancy gone.

Marius stands. "I need to speak with Faelan."

She shoots me a worried glance, and I realize I'm a coconspirator in covering up for nearly burning down the cottage. Not good. But if Aelia thinks it would be bad for her dad to know what happened, then I'll just have to go with it, even though she's annoying.

Right now, I'm more worried about this whole protector thing. There's so much I don't understand about this place, about what's happening to me, and what I am. And after the fire today, it seems even more crucial that I find out.

"I'll say goodbye now," Marius says, "since I'll be leaving straight away through the passage to meet the Cast after I see Faelan." He walks over to Aelia and kisses the top of her head. "You'd do well to keep a low profile, daughter, until tomorrow night, at least."

"Of course, Daddy," she says.

But it's clear by the look on Marius's face that he knows she's not about to heed his warnings. He walks over to Barbara and she stands, letting him kiss her. Their embrace is oddly sterile, and I have to wonder what the story is between them, why he's with a simple human—or why he's married at all—when he's obviously so powerful. And super old. And with what I saw at his office, that half-naked woman hidden away, it's even more strange.

Marius focuses on me. He steps closer and touches my hair gently, almost absently. "You, my rare child, are going to be brilliant." His gaze shifts to mine, and I swear a tingle of electricity runs down my spine. "I know you're desperate for answers, that this must all seem very foreign to you, but your birth House is here for your safety and your comfort. I will ensure that Faelan treats you with the deference you deserve. Just know you are going to be sought. You are the gem in a sea of coal, and once daylight hits you, once the reality of who and what you are sinks into your heart, your world will completely shift." He hesitates and then adds, "And perhaps ours will as well."

I want to ask him what he means, why I can feel the weight of his words in my gut. But before I can get my tongue unstuck, he's slipped out of the room.

THIRTEEN

FAELAN

I open my eyes to a dim haze. I blink, trying to clear my vision, and my eyelashes catch on gauzy coating. A hibernation cocoon? Why am I in—?

There's a soft sigh in my ear, and something slides across my chest and down my bare torso.

I turn my head. My cheek brushes against silk—no, it's hair, smelling like sweetened jasmine. It's a pixie; I can tell from the sugary scent. Her hair is long and reflects the low light with a slow, pulsing glow. Her small fingers play against my abdomen, her leg sliding against mine.

"You're awake," she says in a dreamy voice.

My pulse picks up, my skin heating. "You need to stop that hand from moving any lower, pixie."

I can't see clearly, but I think it's Aelia's friend, Niamh.

She giggles and her body presses into mine as she kisses my neck and whispers close to my ear, "Don't be silly. This isn't my first time coming out of hibernation with a son of Cernunnos. Your brother Finbar's requested me three times."

The sound of *that* name makes my blood boil. "Back off," I say through my teeth. "Now."

Her touch slips away, and she lifts her head from my shoulder. "You can't be serious."

"I can." I reach out and tear open the webbing of the cocoon over my face. "Get out." The realization that this girl's been one of Finbar's ready playthings has snapped me back to reality. Why am I even in here with her?

I sit up, taking a pull of fresh green air into my lungs, trying to clear my head. I haven't had an underling share the process of hibernation in a very long time—several hundred years, I think. I've made a practice of independence in that area because of the weakened state it puts me in. I don't always have full control once the spell is cast.

This pixie in my nest is likely Aelia's doing. Since our run-in last spring, she's lived to torment me.

"Aelia said you might need a nudge but you'd be into me," Niamh says, obviously hurt by my rejection. She'll get over it. She moves beside me, rising from the silver webbing. "Is it because of my huge ears?" She covers her breasts with her hands, her dull eyes looking lost. Her sweet scent dims a bit. She's upset—hurt. Because I'm being a prick.

My pissy mood darkens even more. "What the feck are you on about, woman?" I yank the rest of the gauzy fabric aside, and tufts of grass come with it.

"Finbar says my ears are ridiculous, that my jawline is subpar compared to other girls he's fed with." She reaches up and runs her finger down her chin.

I look away from her, irritated. Because she's actually very pretty. Not a flaw in sight. Just a whole lot of warm, soft skin. "Finbar's an ass," I say. He is an ass. But so am I. "You're fine enough. I'm just not in the mood. And I've got stuff I should be doing. So get yourself covered and get out."

"But Aelia said—"

"Hang the witch. She needs to keep her druid ass out of my business." I climb out of the nest, ignoring my tense muscles, the way my skin stings from the movement, like it's too tight over my right side. As my feet touch the dirt floor, a memory of smoke and heat flashes in my mind.

Sage. Holy shit, the fire. I attempt to keep the urgency from my voice, asking, "What happened with the demi? Is she all right?" Marius is going to rip my throat out if any harm's come to his new jewel.

The pixie tips her head. "Maybe? I'm not sure, I . . ."

I move to the closet, not listening to the rest of what she says. I need to figure out what the hell happened. I put on a pair of jeans and grab a T-shirt. "How long have I been out?" Damn, she won't know the answer to that either.

I'm pulling the shirt over my head when the door opens, and in the blink of an eye Marius is standing three feet away from me. He looms a few inches taller than me. He turns his seal ring round and round on his finger as he stares at me, his lips thin, his normally blue-green eyes a dark navy blue.

Brilliant. I'm fucked.

"Are you enjoying your vacation?" he asks, his voice casual in contrast to the flint in his eyes. I can't tell from his face if we've lost the demi. But my guess is he'd have already carved a few pounds of flesh from my body if we had. Could he know I made a mistake? I'm still not clear on what happened.

His gaze trails up to the edge of my nest where the naked pixie is peering down at us. Then he looks back at me, his irritation blooming into anger. "Breaking two vows in one day? Industrious for you, my stoic friend."

"Sir, I—"

"I knew you'd be resistant to this task, but after all these centuries of obedience I didn't think you had it in you to rebel outright. You were commissioned to watch the demi and begin instructing her on her transition. You are not. She says you haven't even told her of the Introduction that's happening tomorrow night. But somehow you have time to spend with this?" He points up at the pixie. "You led me to believe you had made a vow to the holy Danu, to fast until your soul has worked through your darker notions. It's one of the reasons I chose you for this, your control. So what is *that* doing here?"

The pixie has the good sense to remain still and silent.

"She was merely . . ." My words disappear as I realize that I don't know how to answer. I was in hibernation. But the reason is still foggy. I don't know what I allowed to happen between the pixie and me while I was wrapped up with her. And I'm unsure what happened with the demi. I'm not clear on where my failure falls in the moment, and I don't want to dig this hole any deeper than I already have. Which is worse? That the demi's magic broke through the wards of the torque necklace and she nearly turned me to ash, or that I may have dallied with a pixie in a moment of weakness?

"This is a foolish time to break a soul vow, Faelan. There's too much at stake, and if the Cast were to find out—"

"He didn't touch me," the pixie squeaks. "He refused."

My muscles relax as relief fills me. My vow to Danu is secure. Unless Niamh is lying. But it's against the order for an underling to lie to a lead consort, and she's young, simpleminded. I don't see her sacrificing her place in the House of Brighid for me.

Marius gives her a searching look.

"He was really tired," she adds. "I was just resting with him to refresh the life. That's it. I tried to offer myself to him as more, but he didn't . . ." She pinches her lips together and shakes her head like she can't bear the idea of being rejected.

"Very well," Marius says. "Come speak with me in private, Faelan." He turns and leaves the cottage.

I glance up at Niamh and nod a thank-you before following Marius out into the yard. We walk to the rose garden and are soon surrounded by the sound of splashing water, coming from the fountain just behind us. Mist sprays in the air, clinging to my skin. Marius touches a pink bud, lifting three fat drops of water off the petal. They rise and hover for a second until he moves past and the drops fall, plopping onto a lower leaf.

"I'm leaving to formally meet with the Cast's envoy about our new acquisition," he says. "My plan is to present her at the council tribunal tomorrow night, so that you can take your place as her protector. I'll then present the Cast with an official request for her Emergence after the Introduction's been completed and we know she's more protected. Once the Penta gets wind of her, we won't be able to hide who she is from the masses. The reoccurrence of a Brighid female offspring will tip the balance again. And we have her in our hands; you know what this means."

"Our House could have a place at the table again."

He leans forward and whispers, "If she is truly the second daughter of Brighid, then we hold in our hands a way to push back into the ranks. No more being brushed off as a powerless House, no more sneers. We will be vying for a far higher position again, putting the House of Cernunnos on guard."

That sounds like a good thing to me. Anything to kick my brother Finbar sideways. The bastard has been far too powerful as the leader of our father's House since the Black Death, since Brighid's reign ended. The god Cernunnos held the position of third in the Penta until Brighid slunk into the shadows, relinquishing her place as first in line. The House of Morrígan rose into the void left behind, and the House of Cernunnos followed on her coattails.

Sage could shift the power structure in very real ways. I knew that, but I didn't think Marius would care. He's not one to crave power. However, if history has taught us anything about the Brighid female line, it has shown us the need to be cautious.

"The girl is volatile," I say. I consider elaborating, recalling the fire, but I'm still not sure what happened to put me in hibernation. I do know it was the demi's fault, though. "She could go in any direction. And what if she doesn't choose to give her allegiance to us?"

"That's why I've chosen you, my friend." He rests a fatherly hand on my shoulder. "You're trustworthy. You know how to control your urges, so you can teach her and keep her away from Kieran. You won't fail me."

I swallow hard, the weight of responsibility he's putting on me finally sinking in. He wants to regain the power of our House that was lost all those centuries ago when the first daughter fell and Brighid's power faded. That's no small order. And it all rests on me to convince the demi to choose us. Getting her to trust us. To trust me. "Yes, sir."

"Keep her here, under wraps. Instruct her in what's expected of her, test her powers. But be gentle." He moves closer, whispering again, "And perhaps, if reason doesn't work, other methods can be applied. You are very handsome, hunter, and I've seen her notice." His brow goes up in silent suggestion. "She is young and innocent. It would take only a small nudge in the right direction, no need to cross any lines or break your vow."

"Sir, I—"

"For the House of your goddess, Faelan. You'll find a way, I know you will. She'll bring us back from the brink. This means everything—it could be our last chance." Concern fills his features. "Talks of a shift in the Penta are beginning within the ranks. The Cast are considering the request to push Brighid aside permanently for another—and you know they have no affection for us."

That gets my attention. "What? That can't be right."

"There are whispers that the Cast wish to give our Brighid's position to a lesser of Danu's female offspring. Likely Branwen or Ainé—they've both been vying for favor at the lower tables in the Otherworld."

"That's heresy," I say, feeling the shadow of a horrible possibility fall over us. Could the great fire goddess really lose her place in the power structure?

"Brighid has been silent for so long," Marius says. "And we don't know why. Even the gatekeepers say she's abandoned us. Her envoys left no mark when they crossed over from the Otherworld to bring Sage here after her birth. There were no markers of the goddess's power left behind anywhere. It's as if she didn't plant the child."

I don't see how that could be true. It must have just been missed. No demi born of a goddess arrives here on this plane without leaving trails behind them. "But, obviously, that's false. This demi is proof the goddess hasn't totally abandoned us, no matter what evidence is or isn't left of her envoy's crossing."

"My hope as well. And tomorrow night we can solidify it in the minds of the Cast, along with all of the Penta's children, when we introduce her." He rests a hand on my shoulder, his tone becoming fatherly. "You've always been loyal, Faelan. Since you came to us as that broken young man. I know what you gave up, leaving your father's House. I see your strength. And I know you won't fail me."

If only I had that much faith. "I'll do my best, sir."

"Excellent." He steps away, closer to the fountain, bending the stream of water with a wave of his hand. "I feel the tide turning, friend. We'll find a way back to the power of the old order. Perhaps this girl is a sign that we're nearly there."

FOURTEEN

SAGE

"The shoes you have on aren't perfect, but they'll do," Aelia says, setting her wineglass on the table with a determined clink. "We should go before Daddy sends Faelan the Downer in to start you on your energy diet."

"What? Go where?" I lean back in my chair.

"You need to mingle a little, I think. A few drinks at The Fitz and some time with the girls sounds about right. Maybe we can even get you laid before the boring stuff takes over." She stands. "If you're going to make a splash, you may as well jump."

"Your dad said we need to be careful. Going out to party isn't careful." Though it might be a chance to sneak away from her for a second, get space, which sounds great—but I could hurt someone, which isn't good.

"Oh brother, don't be such a pixie," Aelia says, coming around the table. She takes me by the arm and pulls me up.

I jerk away. "What the hell's that supposed to mean?"

"You're apparently some important demi and you're acting like a pixie—who are sniveling narcs. It's sad. And annoying."

"I couldn't care less if I annoy you." I peer through the windows along the hallway, looking for Marius to come back toward the house.

Even if I wanted to get out of here, this vapid girl is the *last* person I'd go anywhere with.

"The coast is clear," she says. "He won't come back this way. He leaves through the waterfall."

My eyes snap to hers—traveling through water?

"He's the son of Lyr. Think about it." She folds her arms across her chest and looks me over. "Listen, I just want this to go right for my dad. The whole Introduction thing tomorrow night is going to go a lot better for our House if the Otherborn catch scent of you ahead of time. The rumor mill will spread word of your presence, and it won't be business as usual at the ceremony. Just think of the attention, the crowds. It'll be that much more epic when you're presented. The House of Brighid really needs this."

I'm surprised to hear an edge of vulnerability in her tone; she actually sounds like she cares about helping. I don't, though. I've got to do what's best for me, not some power structure I have no stake in. "No way. You're nuts."

"I'm practical. My father's worked really hard to make the House stable again. I want to do what I can to help."

With as much conviction as I can manage, I say, "I'm not going anywhere with you, Aelia."

She purses her lips, sizing me up again. A couple of tense seconds tick by, and then she smirks. "Oh, you're going. Either that or I tell my dad you had sex with Faelan last night and that's why you're acting cagey."

My pulse skips. "What? That's ridiculous." I step back. "And who cares?" Even though for some crazy reason I do care if people think that. Which is stupid.

Her features shift suddenly, fear filling them as her hand rests delicately on her chest. *"Daddy, I'm so mortified,"* she says dramatically. *"I didn't mean to keep it from you, but I can't lie anymore. That girl totally betrayed us. After we brought her here to protect her and comfort her—I caught her . . . feeding off your hunter. She nearly killed him! She would've if I hadn't stopped her."* Her voice wavers, and a shiver runs through me. *"What I saw her doing to him . . . the way she was wrapped around him. He was so helpless, so pale and close to death. And her anger . . . oh gods, Daddy, she got so angry she nearly burned the cottage down. I could've been killed."* She sniffs. *"I didn't want to tell you. I couldn't believe the treachery, how she hurt Faelan was so—"*

"Enough," I finally say, my whole body turned to ice.

A satisfied grin slides across her face.

"Why are you pushing this? I could hurt someone out there. You know that."

She waves away my caution. "Not as long as I'm with you. I can place a temporary protection spell around you that'll last a few hours. You won't attract a wink of trouble. Except maybe the fun kind."

"This can't be good for you if it goes shitways."

"The sooner the general masses see you, the better." She shrugs. "And if you make your debut with me, no one will mess with you—no one who counts, anyway."

God, she's so full of herself. But she might also have a point. I have no idea who to trust—I definitely don't trust this bitch, with her willingness to blather to Marius that I'm some evil creeper who was trying to burn down his property and suck the life out of his employee.

Basically, I'm screwed either way. I may as well take the road I can at least *try* to have some control over. Once we're out of this house, maybe I can get some space, get my head clear, even if it's only for a minute.

"You're sure this spell can keep me from doing anything horrible?" I ask.

"Of course. I wouldn't let you melt any of my friends."

If she can really do that with a spell, why didn't Marius put something like that on me sooner? All I got was this necklace, and it's apparently useless.

I reach up and touch the gold trinket, my finger brushing the orange stone in the center of the design. "What's this thing for, then?"

"It's a torque. Some demis wear them in one form or another."

"Marius said it would help hold back the worst of my powers. It's obviously not working."

She seems to be confused by that idea too. "Weirdly, no. Not if the charred cottage is any indication."

"Well, why? And how are you sure this spell will work if this torque thing won't?"

"It uses a different kind of magic—every torque is spelled with blood magic by a druid from the House of Morrígan. But my spell would use gravity magic instead."

"What's that *mean*?"

She releases a long-suffering sigh. "Look, new girl, *I'm* a druid, I know what I'm doing, okay?"

A druid? This girl? I thought druids looked more like Gandalf than Chanel models.

"Maybe your torque is faulty or something," she adds. "I can look at the spellwork later. I'm getting much better at reading blood magic. But," she says, moving a little closer, whispering, "continuing to push back at me isn't recommended." Then she begins to sing quietly. *"Faelan and Sage nesting in a tree, F-U-C-K-I-N—"*

"Whatever!" I'm so done with this insanity.

She smiles her slinky smile again. "Such a smart new girl." Then she takes my hand, leading me out the side door, into the evening air.

~

The spell she supposedly puts on me as we're riding in the back of the Lincoln Town Car seems pretty lame. She does a little chanting—glowing again—and then tosses this dried green plant in my face. After all of that, she grabs my chin and looks in my eyes before declaring it done.

I'm fairly sure she's bullshitting me. I just wish I knew why. Is she up to something underhanded, or is this really some misguided attempt to help her dad? I'm going to have to be more than a little careful. And on the off chance the spell is real, it's still only going to help protect people from me for a few hours, so I'll try to use every available second to get a break from the crazy.

We drive quite a ways down the Pacific Coast Highway to the 10, then head into Downtown. Our driver doesn't seem to mind Aelia's weird chanting, so it makes me think he's used to the freaky. Maybe he's a vampire? Or a pixie?

"Are there male pixies?" I ask.

Aelia gives me a tired look. "Tonight isn't a factoid mission. It's meant to be fun. But yes, there are guy pixies, though they tend to be rare."

"What other kinds of creature things are there?"

"Are you serious? You're going to ruin my night, aren't you?"

"You're ruining mine, so fair's fair."

"So rude." She pulls a compact from her clutch and opens it, examining her makeup in the tiny mirror. "Our world isn't some show on TeenNick. It doesn't fit in a Hollywood box."

She could've fooled me. "Fine, we'll talk about how you're a psycho manipulator who may be trying to get me killed, then."

She glances at the driver like she's worried. "Whatever, let's not." She pauses, then says, "It's not that complex. I hear you already met Ben, a shade, so the bloodsuckers are checked off. And then you met Niamh, and she's a pixie—though pixies are thick on the ground in LA, so you've probably met a few of those. There are also alfar, wraiths, and selkies—which are like mermaids, except they don't have fins."

I'm suddenly ten years old again. *Part of your world . . .* plays in my head. "Mermaids are real?"

"Don't get too excited. Selkies aren't anything like Ariel. Unless Ariel bit off people's tongues."

A shiver runs through me. Okay, I don't really want to know more on that score, and she's probably just trying to shock me, so I pretend I didn't hear and ask, "What are alfar?" I've never even heard the word before.

"They're earth-based beings, sort of like pixies—which are actually air based—but alfar are way more rare and a whole lot smarter. Tricky little bastards, usually. I guess you could say they're similar to those elves from *Lord of the Rings*. They're warriors and guards for the demi lines."

"And wraiths are like ghosts?"

"No, ghosts are from human spirits. Wraiths were never human. They're where humans got their legend of demons from, and alfar are sorta how they got angels. But trust me, *you* don't want to run into either of them. Not while you're so unaware. If you see one, just walk— or run—in the other direction."

Nice. I want to tell her I don't have a freaking clue what either look like, but realize it's pointless. "So, where are we going exactly?"

"The Fitzgerald. Super exclusive."

"I have no idea what that is."

"It's a club." She makes a *duh* face. "Humans don't end up there much—or, I should say, not many are let in. Just enough so it'll feel real. And the blood attracts the shades, which is good for business because shades tend to be . . . pretty."

"That James guy is a shade," I say, trying to link it all together.

She looks uncomfortable. "Yes, but remember, you never saw him at my house."

Well, looks like I've got dirt on her too. Not murder dirt, but something to hold on to for later, in case I need ammo.

The car pulls up in front of a building, and I realize I've been so focused on getting information from Aelia that I didn't even notice we were smack-dab in the middle of the city. It's only nine o'clock, but there's already a line down the street along the building; the figures are lit by the sign above, which in large cursive letters reads "The Fitz." It looks like something from old Hollywood. And then it dawns on me—the club is named after F. Scott Fitzgerald, the author of *The Great Gatsby*. I assumed she'd be taking me to some gaudy neon palace of techno, but this place actually seems classy.

The structure is old—it looks like it might've been a municipal building, with white stone walls and a large metal door about ten feet high that's etched with an Art Nouveau design. There are actual silk ropes marking off the waiting area and a red carpet leading from the sidewalk to the entrance.

Our driver puts the car in park and gets out, then comes around to open the door on Aelia's side. She slides out gracefully, obviously practiced at presentation. She looks like she's posing for paparazzi, but I don't see any—just a couple of girls with their cell phones out, filming. I'm not so delicate when I emerge, feeling like a lobster escaping a trap as I scoot across the seat. My skirt ends up awkwardly hiked to my thighs by the time I finally get free of the car, and I have to straighten myself out with the whole line of club bunnies looking on. More phones lift to document.

I ignore the gawkers and follow Aelia as she heads for the entrance as if she owns the place. I'm a little wobbly in the heels on the red carpet behind her. One of the large men flanking the entrance nods to her like he knows her and opens the heavy door, ushering us inside. The guy with the clipboard gets on a walkie-talkie and says something, but I don't hear what it is.

A strange combo of big band and electric music fills the air around us in the entryway. My skin tingles as the pulse of the notes crawls over me, and the smell of clove cigarettes and new paint fills my head.

The inside of the club isn't what I expected from the grand exterior. It feels intimate. Maybe because of the oddly gray light or the low ceiling. The life-size images along the walls catch my eye as I trail behind

Aelia—scenes from the nineteen twenties of sly-eyed flappers with bright lipstick and broody-looking men with fedoras, cigarettes hanging lazily from the corners of their mouths. They almost seem alive, a part of the small crowd in the entry, the past mingling with the present.

We walk by a couple of clusters of people as we move through the passage. Heads turn to look at us, at Aelia. It's clear people know her. Of course, she acts oblivious to it all, an air of confidence in her straight shoulders, her lifted chin.

A silver-haired man appears in the opening to the main floor in front of us. He looks a little like a flashy butler from the turn of the century. "Miss Aelia," he says, his tone a bit too airy to be genuine. "It's so lovely to see you here tonight. We weren't expecting you until after the tribunal tomorrow." His blue eyes dart to me, then away again. "Are you bringing in a candidate for the feeding rooms?"

"No, Leaman, this is a new arrival to the fold. Still unclaimed."

"An unclaimed, you say?" He looks over his thin spectacles, studying me intently.

She puts a thin finger on the center of his chest. "Now, now, don't get any ideas for your mistress, Princess Mara. The House of Morrígan isn't going to be in the running for this one. She's all ours."

"Yes, ma'am." He gives a slight bow, glancing at me again before saying, "May I take you to your section?"

She nods and we follow him onto the main floor and through a cocktail area. Waitresses in short skirts walk around carrying trays of drinks, the loud music vibrating the glasses a little. The patrons sit in high booths, looking smug. Some are in small cubbies with privacy curtains, and everyone looks as if their wardrobes and jewelry could solve the LA homeless problem for a week. I think I spot three or four Hollywood stars. I recognize a guy from a reality TV show about making your marriage work sitting in a booth, a drink in each hand, surrounded by fawning females.

It's like they took every LA cliché and brought them all together into one room.

We come to a staircase that's blocked off by a black velvet rope. Another beefy guy is standing to the side. He unhooks the rope and the butler, Leaman, bows again, before telling Aelia to let him know if we need anything.

I follow her up the stairs to a loft area that's enclosed by walls made of mesh material. Silhouetted figures move inside the gauzy tent. Myriad lights speckle the silver netting, casting colors over it—pink and blue and yellow and green—and as the song shifts, the lights shift too.

We pause on the landing, and one of the silhouettes, a young woman, emerges from the rainbow mesh. She has big eyes and long light pink hair that seems almost opal in the lighting. She also has gossamer wings hanging between her shoulder blades, like Star did at the party. I'm pretty sure this one's another pixie. But they must not all have wings—I didn't see any on Niamh.

The woman nods to Aelia and me, a curious look on her face when her overly large eyes meet mine.

But she doesn't comment; she just pulls aside the fabric for us to enter. "May your cups and hearts be full, ladies."

I don't want to go inside the tented area. I'll feel even more trapped than I already do.

But Aelia grabs me and pulls me inside just as a swiftly approaching girl squeals, "Lia!" The girl's delight is needles in my ears, even with the loud music. "I can't believe you made it." She kisses both of Aelia's cheeks, a painted smile on her face. "We were so totally sure you'd get stuck at home with Beast Barb." She turns and yells at a cluster of females in the far corner. "Bitches, get your asses over here and kiss the priestess." But then her attention falls on me, and her grin stiffens. Her eyes scrape over me like she's noting every blemish and flaw. "Who's this?" she asks Aelia.

"This is the new arrival, V," Aelia says, chin tipping up.

I bet she gets that same proud look on her face when she's showing off a new purse. She takes me by the arm and leads me toward the group of females, and I feel like I'm being brought to my judges at the Inquisition. But there's nowhere to go.

"Ladies," Aelia says, "this is Sage." She adds in a whisper, "The new fire demi."

They all frown in silence and study me with skepticism. But then the first girl, V, sneers, dismissing me with a flippant hand gesture. "Give me a break. Your games are so transparent now, Lia," she says with a soft laugh. "She's obviously a street leech. She's got a zit. And look at that scar on her shoulder."

One of the other girls leans in and crinkles her nose. "She smells like an alley cat. Are you force-feeding her to James as a joke?"

I lean away. "Excuse me? No one's feeding anyone to anyone."

The first girl, the one worried about my zit, acts like she didn't hear me, directing her words to Aelia. "James would *never* eat that. I mean, she's painful to look at. Even he wouldn't be desperate enough—"

"James has nothing to do with this," Aelia says. "Why would I waste my time worrying about him?"

"Well, because you're screwing him on a daily basis, obviously," the zit critic says.

Another girl shrugs. "And letting him feed off you."

Aelia looks baffled. "So? He gets me backstage when Coldplay is in town."

"That was one time," a girl says.

"Ugh," Aelia grunts. "Enough about the shade. I came for you to see this." She points at my face and whispers again. "She's the second daughter."

All the girls go back to frowning at me.

"What the hell's a *second daughter*?" I ask, a bit dizzy from all the dumb in the room.

Still no one seems to hear me. The girl on my left reaches out and touches my hair, picking up a strand between her fingers. "It's like a troll chewed off her hair. Look at those split ends."

"It's weird," the quieter girl behind the zit critic pipes up. "She looks totally human."

"No," Aelia says, "that's the cloaking spell I put on her in the car on the way here. She's freaking bursting with juice underneath it."

"Ah," the one examining my hair says in understanding. She stands straight again and points at my face. "So she's not really that ugly."

"Actually, she is," Aelia says. "Isn't it fascinating?"

And we're back to them all frowning at me. Wow.

"Look," I say, "while this brilliant debate over my mutant face is super entertaining, I'm feeling a little dehydrated." I take a small step back from the group. "And claustrophobic."

Aelia pinches my sleeve and pulls me to a table. "Where do you think you're going?"

"I have to pee," I say, jerking my arm out of her grip. My anger sparks, and I grit my teeth as heat begins to coil in my chest. The smell of smoke stings my nostrils. I clench my hands into fists, hoping I'm not about to accidentally set anything on fire. If I don't get away from her and these other bitches, something very bad is going to happen. I can feel it. I need air. Now.

Breathe, Sage, just breathe.

"She's sure spicy," the zit critic says. She flips her curly brown hair. "But I'm tired of her already. Enough about the ugly girl. I think we should talk Diamond Ball. Which designer are we going with for the tiaras?"

"I can take the human to pee," the hair groper says. "I'll swat away the shades."

Aelia rolls her eyes. "She's not human, Freya. But whatever. Just bring her right back. She's not supposed to be wandering around."

They all nod like they're agreeing, even though they don't seem to get what Aelia's talking about. I think my IQ just dropped a hundred points breathing the same air as these girls.

The hair groper, Freya, slips her arm through mine and grins at me before wrinkling her nose. "You sure do smell funny," she says. "I had a human grandma who loved garlic—she smelled better than you." She smiles like she just paid me a compliment.

Lovely.

I consider pushing her away and leaving unattended, but I'm thinking Aelia will just use some weird spell to keep me here. It'll be easier to get away from this Freya girl. So I let her tug me along, out of the loft and down the steps.

FIFTEEN

FAELAN

After Marius leaves, I stay in the rose garden for a minute, trying to figure out how to go about getting Sage to trust us. There's more at stake here than I realized, and I started on the wrong note with the demi. I should have considered that she'd be volatile and treated her more carefully. I knew she was a daughter of Brighid, and I should have known she'd have weaknesses from being left so long among the humans without her magic, without her own kind.

But it's like I haven't seen sense since I met the girl.

I'll pull her aside tonight. Maybe I can go over some of the lore with her, cover some basics so she feels more grounded, more familiar with her new reality before the Introduction.

As I cross the yard, heading for the French doors at the back of the main house, I consider what needs to happen. I'll have to get her to open up to me somehow. I'll need to get her to feel a connection with me in some way that can dispel this tension between us and soften her to our kind. Maybe then she'll feel less vulnerable. Settling into this new life is the only way she'll be able to learn to control her gifts.

I step into the house and look around, searching the air for the sugary spice of her fire energy. The living room is empty, and I feel only simple souls. I do smell something baking, though—a fresh herbal scent. I move deeper into the house and see one of the human maids wiping down the kitchen counter. She glances up at me and her body tenses, the hand on the dishcloth turning into a fist.

"I'm looking for the redhead," I say gently. It's obvious my presence is spooking her. "Her name is Sage. Is she around?"

The maid shakes her head. I can't tell if it's a *No, she's not around* or a *I have no idea who or what you're talking about.* Marius's service crew appears to be all human, so they may have had their memories wiped a few times, which would allow them to be more easily manipulated to keep secrets, but would also leave them a bit on the dim side. Over time, it can make them more skittish too. I nod at the woman. Something behind me catches her eye and she averts her gaze, moving quickly to leave the room.

"Oh, there you are," says a sultry voice behind me. The wife. Gods' bones.

I don't want to turn around.

The scent of pungent licorice seeps off her skin, reaching for me—the smell of human excitement. I feel her hand press into my back and I try not to cringe visibly as it slides up, cupping my nape.

My muscles tense, and I step away before I turn to face her. "I need to speak with Sage. Where is she?"

The wife—I can't remember her name—is tall and slender, her hair long and blond, and her features tight with artificial youth. Her breasts appear to be fake, as does her nose, and the pink tracksuit she's wearing is tight enough to stop blood flow to her brain.

Why would Marius choose her for his new human breeder? Maybe the original version, before the knives and plastics were applied, was more enticing? Aelia is naturally beautiful, and she's retained a class that her mother appears to lack. This modern woman doesn't fit with the house's décor at all—the mosaics that Roman leaders once walked on hanging on Marius's walls, and the ancient vases that held the sacrificial blood of human kings set on pillars along the hallway. It all makes her seem small and insignificant. Marius hasn't let go of much since his emigration to the American colonies, but it seems he's lowered his standards in the department of procreation.

It's a constant subject of debate why the great goddess Danu created her children and their descendants to be incapable of procreating with one another. A deity or a demi can only have offspring with humans. This was Danu's fail-safe: all new births are less powerful than those that came before. No soul will ever be more powerful than our great mother goddess.

However, this means Otherborn have to mingle in the human world if they want their lineage to survive. That creates complications, such as human lovers who age when the demis don't. This usually means the Otherborn parent won't stick around, and most children are left to figure out their bloodline when a hunter like me comes to fetch them. Some Otherborn, like Marius, keep their breeder close for a time, but that's rare.

Especially when the breeder is as tiresome as this human is.

"We missed you at dinner, you know," the wife says, ignoring my question about Sage. Her stiff lips pucker like she's taking a selfie. "Are you hungry? I could find you something to nibble on." Her fingers slide suggestively along her clavicle, like she thinks I'm a shade and she's offering herself up for a taste. I notice several shiny dotted scars on her neck. She tilts her hips and steps toward me. "Whatever you want, I'm happy to help."

I tell myself she's Marius's wife and I should be polite. I should *not* back away in disgust. "No. No, thank you." I'm not thankful. I feel a little ill. "I need to speak with the demi, with Sage."

"The girls went out somewhere," she says absently. "But I'm here." She makes that weird pinched-lip face again.

"Wait, what do you mean? Where did they go?" She can't be serious. Wasn't Marius just with them before he spoke to me?

"Who knows," she says with a sigh. "Aelia is exhausting. I can't keep track of that girl." She frowns a little. "You're not feeding off her, are you? That's against the rules, isn't it? I'm human, so it's fine."

Danu save me. "When did they leave? Did the driver take them?" They couldn't be too far ahead of me. I was only in the rose garden for a minute or two after Marius left.

"How am I supposed to know?"

I turn and head into the kitchen, making a mental list of items I'll need for the location spell. Salt, ash, rose oil, and crushed cloves—no, not cloves, it's cinnamon for a fire-based Otherborn. Cloves are for finding an earth-based Other. I start opening cupboards, looking for salt. I can get rose oil from crushing some of the buds outside in a little olive oil. And cinnamon must be around here somewhere . . .

The wife comes up behind me, peering over my shoulder as I pull a bowl from a shelf. "What in heaven are you doing?"

"Do you know where the cinnamon is?" I ask. It'll mimic the scent of Sage's energy.

The woman laughs. "Of course not. This is a kitchen." She says it like I didn't know.

I find the spice rack in one of the cupboards and collect what I need. I grab the virgin olive oil beside it, then I go to the sink and run a little water into my bowl before tucking everything under my arm and heading for the back doors.

Unfortunately, the wife follows me. I walk through the yard, along the winding stone pathway, back to the rose garden, where I nestle the bowl in the moss. I set the rest of the ingredients next to it. I rip two handfuls of petals off a bush and place them into the bowl. Once I drizzle olive oil over them, I grab a rock and crush the concoction into the water, and the scent of roses spills out around me.

"What are you doing?" the wife asks, sounding fascinated. I wonder if I should be hiding the spellwork from her. Marius never warned me to be cautious with her, but I should probably be doing this in private. Bloody hell. Too late now.

"I'm cooking," I say, picking up the salt and pouring it into my palm before sprinkling it over the rose petals. I follow with the cinnamon as I whisper a few words to begin the spell, but they're in Gaelic so she won't understand them. *"Earth forgets, water's breath,"* I begin, still crushing the roses—my representation of the earth element—into the water. Then I reach down to my boot and pull out my small dagger, prick my finger, and let the blood drip three times into the bowl, continuing, *"Blood in part, as tongues of fire, lead me to your beating heart."*

On the last word, the smell of charred air flicks to life in my nostrils and a spark births over the bowl, a flame licking at the air as the contents are quickly consumed. I watch and wait for the embers to fade a little, smoke rising, and then I lean over and inhale deeply, closing my eyes, focusing every molecule I can on Sage.

Instantly I smell alcohol. I taste the tang of underlings in the air, and a distant beat vibrates in my head. Music.

I wait, worrying that the visual won't filter through as clearly as the other senses. But then I see: she's walking up a metal staircase. Ahead, there's a small loft, curtained with sheer silver fabric. Aelia is in front of her, high heels clicking on the steps.

They're obviously at a club or a bar of some kind. I need to see more, to look around, but that's not how the spell works. I get clues and sort of see/feel/smell through the torque necklace Sage is wearing. There's a woman emerging from the gauzy curtain, a pixie with pale pink hair. She scans Sage and my nerves spark with realization. *People will feel who and what she is.*

Feckin' shite, Aelia, what the bloody hell are you on?

I keep my eyes closed and ask Marius's wife, "Where does Aelia usually hang out?" I hope this human is nosy enough about her daughter's life to know the answer. "Like clubs, with dancing, a place to meet friends?"

"Why?" she asks.

I feel her kneel beside me. She better not touch me or I'll lose the connection. I struggle to hold the spell tight around me. "I need to be sure Aelia's safe. She might be in danger." *Mostly because of the demi she's with.*

"My Aelia is in danger?" Her worry blossoms in the space between us. "I don't know . . . maybe she'd go the Oyster Club? She likes it there—or the Baja Lounge? Oh my, I'm not sure . . ."

The girls are inside a small room now, more figures are in the background, someone else in the room is a witch, maybe two or three—I can sense their energy slinking over Sage's skin. Then I realize that this is Aelia's coven. Why is she bringing Sage to them? They have very little power, and no say among the older druids. Is she really so petty that she thinks the new demi will help her gain standing in the druid ranks?

The music comes through a little clearer. I ask the human, "Is there a club with a big band theme, maybe?"

"Oh, that's The Fitzgerald."

I open my eyes and stand, leaving the spell bowl in the moss, and head for the cottage to grab a few things. Sharp things.

"Where are you going?" the wife calls after me.

Gods, her memory must've been screwed with too. *Nice, Marius.*

"I thought we were going to hang out," she whines. "Don't go."

"I'm getting your daughter. You'll thank me later." And I slip into my cottage to find my daggers.

SIXTEEN

SAGE

There's a line for the bathroom, even though the crowds are still thin. It's early, and the nightlife in LA doesn't usually get pulsing seriously until after eleven. I settle into formation behind a girl who's sucking on a blue lollipop. Her lips and tongue are stained purple. The white-blond ponytails on either side of her head flick at the air when she bobs to the music. She glances at me and gives me a quick grin, then goes back to her lollipop.

It's so weird to think that most of these people in here aren't really *people* at all. Like, what's this girl? A pixie? Her eyes seem teal, though, and her skin is sort of sparkly.

My babysitter, Freya, settles in beside me and leans against the wall. She shoots a sneer at the girl next to me. "Wow, the dregs are out tonight."

Lollipop Girl tips her head in an endearing way. "And apparently so are the petri dishes," she says in a giddy voice. "How is the bottom-feeding Shade Brigade these days?"

Freya looks like she's about to scratch off Lollipop Girl's face.

I clear my throat and try to divert her attention. I consider asking if she knows that the lead actor in that new superhero movie is drinking a cosmo at the bar, but I decide to focus my distraction on her super-red hair instead, since she seemed pretty obsessed with mine. "Hey, so, can you give me some tips on—"

Freya shoves me aside and gets in the other girl's face. "You seem to be forgetting last solstice, little thief. We have video. You and your pet male amoeba are *so* going viral, selkie." She sneers.

"Sure, Aelia clone. Whatever." She tilts her head. "I hear you failed Cast finals, poor baby. Sucks not having a mind of your own." She rubs her fingers together in front of Freya's face, then flicks.

Small drops of water sprinkle Freya's cheeks and forehead. She doesn't seem to know what to say. She just blinks and makes weird noises as her mouth moves.

As much as I'm enjoying watching Lollipop Girl make Freya squirm, I decide to take the opportunity to find some sorely needed space.

I walk farther down a hall, away from the main room and the dance floor that's beginning to fill up. Eventually, I pause in a corner. It's just me and a tangled couple who are sucking face while leaning against the wall. Both have lit cigarettes between their fingers.

They don't seem to know or care that I'm here. Which is nice. But the show they're putting on, groping with their cig-free hands, isn't super enjoyable. The craving for my own cigarette bubbles up as the trails of smoke slink around me, and I kick my traitorous brain when an ache follows; I miss Ziggy so much my chest hurts. How pathetic. I can't believe I let my guard down with anyone. I should've known better.

I push the fake friendship out of my mind and head for the "Exit" sign.

The door swings open, and I take in a lungful of fresh air.

Scratch that, I take in a lungful of *alley* air. The rot and smog hit me, and I cough and cover my nose, surprised at how strong the smell is. The pounding music is a low drone in the background now, and the temperature is less smothering without all the bodies. It's a huge relief to be away from the otherweirdly.

I step over an oily puddle and pause once I get to a spot where I can see the opening of the alley. I search the street, watching the cars pass. People walk by, laughing and twisted up in each other, totally oblivious to what's inside the building they're passing. I wish I was oblivious.

Maybe I should just walk away from this. I could run from these freaks right now, if I wanted to.

But I . . . I can't run from myself. No matter how far away I get from Aelia or Faelan or any of this, I'll still have this *thing* inside me. This thing that starts fires, a thing that can burn with a touch. Or kill. If I left, who knows what it might do. I have no idea how to control it.

I linger in the shadows, my stomach churning as I move to the wall and lean on a drainpipe. I'm completely stuck.

Out of the corner of my eye I spot a dark shape at the other end of the alley, and an odd sound, like water moving, slinks through the air.

The back of my neck prickles, a chill sliding down my spine.

But when I turn, I can't see anything.

I need to calm down. I'm just on edge. My sanity's been through a paper shredder the last twenty-four hours. I try to let the traffic humming in the background calm me, like the sound of the tide, as I focus on the light from a billboard reflecting in marbled blue and pink on the surface of an oily puddle beside my foot.

My God, these heels I'm wearing are ridiculous. *Sequined, Aelia? Really?* They probably cost more than the average person makes in a week.

A rustle of feathers comes from above, and I look up, spotting a small shadow flying overhead from one building to the other. Then the strange water sounds come again, like a slurp, echoing down the alley.

My gaze shifts quickly back to the darker shadows, tingles sliding up my legs as I step out and search the shapes around me. It's probably just a rat—

It comes again. An odd slush and sloop. Louder. Closer.

Movement catches my eye again. And I see it, a shadow on the wall across the alley, shifting, sliding upward like a snake slinking from its coil, while the sound of something fighting to emerge from a drain fills the air.

My pulse jumps as I watch the dark shape glide across the wall.

I stumble sideways, pressing into the bricks at my back as the ground under me tilts.

And then I realize. The shadow is from something coming out of the ground.

Beside me.

Ice fills my veins as I look down at the puddle.

But what I see doesn't make sense: a long tentacle of oily water is sliding up, like gravity is reversing in just that spot. Swirls of light reflect off the surface as it stretches out. But, no—I can't be seeing it right. Because it's impossible.

Suddenly the tentacle shifts, bending sideways, the tip growing claws, and a second tentacle emerges beside it. Both become arms. The sucking grows louder. The talons dig into the asphalt with a crunch as a skeletal face surfaces, a writhing body pulling free of an unseen trap.

I quake, rooted to the spot only a few feet away, watching a dark creature take shape, dripping oily water from its body: a hooded figure, black as pitch, bone thin, with overlong limbs.

The slurping shifts into a moan, and I realize the puddle down the alley is moving too, more shapes climbing from the water.

"Child," comes a low growl. "Fire child."

I stumble back, tripping over a pipe sticking out of the wall. My butt hits the ground, and I scramble along the asphalt to get away, my palms scraping against it. The black ooze creature breaks free of the puddle and crawls toward me, its eyes vacant, two silver voids ready to swallow me.

A claw reaches out and grabs for my ankle. "Mine," the creature moans.

I kick with a scream, losing one of my shoes. A smear of goop stains the thousand-dollar heel.

The thing hisses in rage, mouth agape, revealing dripping fangs.

Every nerve in my body lights, and I lurch to my feet, stumbling toward the mouth of the alley, focused on the streetlights ahead and the cars buzzing past. Safety.

Something bursts into my path, wings flapping wildly, screeching at me, forcing me back into the shadows again. A raven. It caws and beats at the air between me and the road. But as I turn to get away, it flies past and dives for the oily creature.

The dripping shadow shrinks from the bird with a cry of fear. A second dark shape that's scuttling along the wall pauses. Both watch the bird for a second, then bow their heads.

I retreat, shaking, muscles tensed to run again. But I freeze when my vision of the bird shifts. I stare in confusion as smoke begins to seep from the raven's back, spilling out in plumes. It billows from the black body, growing with each quick beat of its wings, taking shape. Until the raven is gone and there's a man standing in front of me. His back is only three feet away.

A man who was a bird a second ago.

Smoke still trails from his shoulders and down his sides.

He speaks—I don't recognize the words, but the tone is commanding, and the two dripping black creatures respond by cowering more. They mew, hunkering down to settle a few feet in front of him as if they were seeking his approval.

The raven man turns, and his metallic eyes fall on me.

The world tips again. My breath falters. I know him . . . I—

Where have I seen him before?

His features are young, etched and severe in their beauty, hair blacker than night, skin so pale it almost appears lit from the inside. But it's his eyes that cut into me—a sharp silver, inhuman, unreal. "You shouldn't be alone, little doe." His voice is a warning as he looks around, like he's searching to see if anyone is nearby.

I can't seem to form words. I still can't process the dripping shadows behind him, their slick bodies, their hollow eyes. Eyes that turn to stare hungrily at me again.

"Don't worry about the wraiths," he says. "They belong to me. As do you, by rights." His lips tilt in a slight grin.

The words jar me. I recoil, shivering, and glance at the waiting shadows. "Those creepy things are with you?"

The raven man steps toward me, taller than I realized, his movement sly like a cat's.

I falter. "Don't touch me."

His hands lift in surrender. "Forgive my clumsy approach, but I wanted to see you up close, to speak to you. Before the water can be muddied too much by others."

"Stay away." I have no idea who or *what* he is, but it's obvious he's not Team Marius. I should've asked more questions at dinner. Marius said there was a danger, but I assumed he was talking about me being the threat to people, not nightmarish creatures like this guy.

"Who are you?" I ask, trying to sound demanding. As if I have any power here. Bluffing is my only weapon right now. I could try to run, but it's clear that I wouldn't make it very far.

He tilts his head like he's surprised I don't know him. "I am your protector, if you wish it. Second son of the Morrígan, Prince of Shadows. My name is Kieran, brother to the King of Ravens. My sister leads the House of Morrígan as the Princess of Bones. We wish to offer you shelter." He bows in a regal way, as if we were in a castle instead of an alley.

Then it dawns on me: *this is the dark prince Faelan was talking about.* Holy shit.

I almost burst into hysterical giggles as the realization settles in. Because this has to be a joke. God is playing a joke on me, right? This guy totally fits the title, now that the dots in my head are connecting. The high cheekbones and proud chin, the oddly formal speech. And that thick dark hair shadowing his eyes. Those eyes . . . you could get lost in them . . . you could . . .

A foggy memory surfaces: a flash of those eyes over me, his hands gripping my naked hips, his body pressing me into the cool clover beneath us.

Heat fills me in a rush. *Where the hell did that come from?*

I have to focus on breathing as the images, vivid and overwhelming, filter through me. It can't be real, it can't. I swear on my life I've never met this freak before, let alone gotten naked with him. I think I'd remember if I had, especially with that raven trick. But his eyes are so familiar.

"You shouldn't fear me," he says, breaking through the images clouding my senses. "I can give you your heart's desire."

I step back again. "Right now I'd like a one-way ticket to Tahiti."

Confusion fills his features. "We don't rule in the south."

"Sounds perfect, then."

He studies me. "You're not what I expected. Not at all." He pauses and then adds, "I pictured dark stoicism. I pictured assurance. But you . . . you're so different than she was. I find it . . . intriguing."

Prickles of awareness crawl over my skin at his words. "Different than who?"

"Your sister, Queen Lily."

I remember what Aelia said about Faelan hoping I wasn't *like the last female offspring from Brighid's tree.* Could she have been talking about the same person? A sister . . .

"You have a strange vibration in your spirit," he continues, moving his gaze over my body. "Almost as if you were at war inside. Why has it taken you so long to surface in our world?"

I shake my head, not understanding.

His expression turns dark, his voice becoming unsettled when he adds, "And your power is . . . wrong."

He knows something about me. And I have the feeling it's something vital. It almost makes me blurt out the questions still crowding my head, but I bite my lip. I have no clue if I can trust this guy. Letting him know how ignorant I am could give him the upper hand. So I keep bluffing, pretending not to be completely freaked out.

"What can I say," I mutter, "I'm a rebel." I dare to turn away, feigning a casual air, and reach down to pick up the heel I lost when I stumbled. "And, uh . . . even though this has been invigorating and all, people are waiting for me, and I can't—"

He re-forms in front of me again in a blink, blocking my path. He steps forward, forcing me to move away.

My back hits the brick wall of the building. And I'm trapped. Those silver eyes locked on mine.

My mind registers that he's too close, that I should strike out and stop him, but I can't seem to figure out how to squirm away. And then I feel his fingers slide over my neck, gripping it delicately. But I still can't look away from those eyes.

His long thumbnail scrapes over my skin, and a shiver rakes through me.

"No, no, little doe," he whispers. "You mustn't rush off before our agreement can be made. I'm meant to protect you. To be your covering."

"I told you not to touch me," I say, breathless. My insides twist into knots. The barrage of emotions that fill my chest make me want to scream—confusion, fear, rage at my vulnerability.

He reaches up with his other hand and touches a strand of my hair that's come loose. "But in this world, you're mine, fire creature. And soon I will be yours."

Raw terror rises to first place.

"Why are you shivering?" he asks, annoyance edging his voice. "What have they done to you?"

They? He's the one pinning me to a wall. "Please don't touch me" is still all I can manage to say.

"You *plead* with me? Are you really so weak? Where is your fire? I feel it in your spirit, why hold back?"

For the life of me, I have no response.

"I see the spell that was placed on you by the druid, Aelia—that is only a glamour, an illusion. You could pluck it away in an instant if you wished." He searches my face. "And I know you can push past the blood magic on this torque. You have enough fire burning within you to raze our whole world if you willed it." His hand presses against my throat, squeezing harder.

I feel the tip of his sharp thumbnail prick the skin on the side of my neck.

A small gasp of pain fills my throat, but his tightening fingers won't let it escape.

"Let me see you, fire child."

I can only shake my head as I begin to choke in his grip.

My pulse gallops faster, and pain throbs in my temples. Splotches of color dance across my vision. I can't react. I can't breathe. I can't think.

Shock freezes my limbs. I should kick him in the nuts. I know how to defend myself. This isn't the first time I've been pinned. But his eyes are all I see, and some traitorous part of me finds familiarity there. It wants full surrender.

Where are the flames I used to burn down the cottage? That I used to almost kill that vampire?

The power won't come.

He presses closer, leaning in, the tip of his nose sliding over my cheek as he draws a breath. "Choose me," he whispers. "I will show you the truth of your birthright." When I stay frozen, he releases a disappointed sigh. "Well, I hate to mar the canvas, but a flower must be allowed to blossom. And it seems you need a little nudge." He pulls back so he can meet my gaze again. "Forgive me for having to do this to you, my love. But I can't bear to see you so trapped. You should be allowed to shine. To be free. Don't you agree?"

I nod frantically.

His grip on my neck loosens.

I gasp, trying to find air, shifting my weight, about to run. At last, my arms lift in defense, ready to strike, to scratch and fight back.

But before I can do anything, his sharp thumbnail digs into the side of my neck.

In a slow, steady move, he slices into my artery.

Searing pain rakes across my skin. I gasp, staring in confusion as crimson sprays his pale features. Red freckles appear on his cheeks, his forehead. My blood? *What just . . . what?*

He keeps his fingers at my neck, sliding them over the wound like he's slowing the bleeding a bit. "Come now, little doe, heal yourself. Open your spirit, release the fire." His familiar silver eyes fill with anticipation.

Warm blood washes over my chest and my breasts, soaking my dress in seconds. I reach up with shaking hands and try to touch my neck. My head pounds with my crashing heartbeat, and my muscles throb, my own skin weighing a hundred pounds as everything blurs.

I open my mouth. But I can't speak, I can't . . .

A loud buzz fills my ears. My lungs tighten and stutter. Warmth seeps over my palm as I cover the gash, trying to hold myself together.

His fingers move to brush across my knuckles.

He steps back, a dark cloud moving over his features. "Where are you, Daughter of Fire? Why do you not heal?"

I fall to my knees. I stare at the oily ground, at my blood dripping onto the asphalt, smearing the reflection of the neon lights.

Faelan's words the other night at the Halloween party echo in my head like a curse: *the dark prince won't be able to control you now . . .*

There's a loud click somewhere to my right. "Oh my gods." A small screech of anger as a door slams. "What the fuck, Kieran? This is *so* unfair. You can't just *feed* from her. Daddy will be enraged!"

Kieran bows to the approaching white blur. "Druid Aelia, I wasn't feeding. Forgive me for rushing the process, but your people have her bound too tight. She needed to be nudged."

"I bound her because she's deadly, idiot. Shit! Look at the mess you're making." Someone grabs my arm and shakes me. "Heal yourself, dummy! My spell was totally lame. It only works because you bought in. So *snap out of it*!"

I fall limp on the ground, light dancing in front of my eyes. My cheek presses onto cool asphalt. Everything hurts. The air weighs too much.

Frantic voices blend with the buzz of the streetlamp. Somewhere in my head I understand that I'm pouring my life out in an alley that smells like an old lady's feet. I know that in only minutes I'm about to stop existing. About to die. Forever.

And I can't fight it. It's not a fist or a nightmare. It's not . . .

My heart slows to a crawl, the waning beat becoming a whooshing thud, the only sound, until I hear nothing at all. I see nothing. The pain is gone, and I just want to sleep.

I wonder if I'll meet the real Sage now. I wonder if that other baby, the human one, is mad that I stole her life.

It was sort of a shitty life.

It won't be mourned. And neither will I . . .

~

I watch the flames snapping in the hearth, wishing for a sign, but the golden fire remains silent.

Even now, after I've obeyed, Mother still shuns me. Three moons have passed since my Bonding to the King of Ravens, and my punishment is complete, my captivity in this bitterly cold place now etched into the annals. I would have thought the goddess would be pleased with my submission—it's so unlike me. But, instead, I feel farther from her than ever before.

Perhaps it's the dark energy in this place. The Morrígan's powers are thick in the king's shield house, a vast keep perched on the icy edge of Mount Na Ndeor, many leagues from the misty green trees of Caledonia.

And now I belong to the King of Ravens.

He has yet to claim my body since that first time during the Bonding ceremony—a quick joining in the clover to seal the Bond—but he is slowly trying to wear down my soul with each silver glance and attempt at a gift. Since the winter fox, he's brought me many things: doves for my greenhouse, a black steed he calls Spark, and two nights ago ruby beads for the winter pixies to weave into my hair. His steady energy seems always close, a patient and watchful shadow. And his attentive manners are disarming when they surface.

He still frightens me, with his large form, his firm hands—a warrior's hands—but he seems more familiar now. I don't tense as much when he comes close, now that I know he won't push me.

He says I'll come to him in the night when I'm ready, that he'll allow me my stubborn ways and eventually I will succumb. "Only a matter of time," he says every night when we part outside my bedroom door. His battle-roughened fingers brush the line of my jaw. He kisses my cheek, whispering into my ear, "And we have an eternity."

Last night, after his gift, I was weakened enough that I nearly gave in. He presented me with a white owl fledgling, and I was overcome by the beauty and innocence of the bird. I took the cage from him and almost turned my head, letting my lips brush his.

But it's only because I've been lonely. So lonely . . .

Now I shiver and hug my woolen shawl around my shoulders at the memory. Wishing I could understand what's happening to me. I am the Daughter of Fire, and I cannot get this cold to leave my bones. It's been there since the Bonding ceremony. It won't shake off.

My human watcher, Lailoken, says it's the king's energy lingering from the new connection, that it will pass and the worst is over. But it feels as if I'm being taken over. And I'm terrified of what this Bond is doing to me, who it's making me become.

Perhaps I'm being foolish, still the silly girl who thought lust was more fun in secret, only worth pursuing if it was forbidden. And then a boy paid for my folly with his life. The only reason I'd pursued him was because he was the son of the human king in the south. I didn't mean to fall in love. Or to kill him. And now I carry that with me. Always.

But for a time, just after the Bonding, I thought a miracle had happened and a piece of my love had returned to me.

My courses had been absent—each moon I waited, but there was no blood show. At first I thought nothing of it, then my bodice felt as if it were suffocating me, and my cheeks grew plump. My powers became unpredictable—I burned the curtains in the gallery on an afternoon when I accidentally spilled my wine. It was as if I'd become a novice again, in need of a torque. I'd seen this happen in women before. I knew I'd been blind. I denied the reality too long and needed to face it.

I was with child.

I didn't speak of it to Lailoken, not even him. Certainly not to my king—he would surely have had the child ripped from my womb. He would have seen it as a betrayal, even though I would never be able to give him children, no matter how many times I came to his bed, our origins making such a thing impossible between us. But I don't see him as a man to share his playthings. No, he'd wish for my womb to be as cold and dead as this icy keep.

It seems his wish has been granted.

"Where are you, Mother?" I ask the flames, my loneliness threatening to consume me now, thinking of the babe. "Tell me what I should do. I can't let myself surrender to this place." I put my palm to my belly, my throat aching.

Three nights ago, I began to bleed, and the child within me was lost. I feel as if my Bond with the son of death sealed the poor babe's fate. I ensured its demise.

"You warned me of my foolishness," I say to my mother, "how it would lead me to a broken heart. And I didn't listen." Tears fill my eyes. I let them come, as if my lover has died all over again. "But I'm listening now. You are the keeper of the hearth, the home. You know how to help me. Please,

goddess, I wish for the child's life to return to me. I wish for my heart to be mended. What should I do, Mother? I will obey you, I swear it. Just speak to me."

I wait, expectantly. Still, I'm shocked when the embers shift, sparks rising up in a rush.

Surrender to him, *the fire whispers, drawing out the sound with the sizzle of wood.* The fire born within you shall bring rebirth. Surrender, child.

And then it fades. I listen intently but nothing else comes. I couldn't have heard correctly, though. She can't mean for me to give in to this. She'd wish for me to fight, to escape.

No, I couldn't have heard right.

My stomach roils and I stand, wandering over to the cage where my new owl sits with watchful eyes. The bird hoots at my approach and ruffles its feathers. "Are you feeling smothered in there, little one?" I ask, understanding what it is to be caged. I open the latch and reach in, urging the bird onto my hand. "You should come with me to dinner tonight. Perhaps then I'll have someone to talk to. The king barely says two words to me."

It flaps its immature wings and hobbles its way over to perch on my wrist. My heart settles, looking into its wide black eyes. It baffles me that the king would give me a gift of such vulnerability and innocence.

I consider the words from the fire, but they don't make any sense. I can't understand why the goddess would wish for me to accept the darkness into myself. She must know that the king is far stronger than me. He'll take me over. I'll lose myself. Could she truly want to see my heart destroyed? Perhaps I should speak to Lailoken and see what his thoughts are. I'll have to tell him of the child, but I think that would give me relief. I'll go now, before dinner. If anyone asks, I'll tell them I'm planning to show him the bird.

I settle the owl on the arm of my chair, then pull the cord for my ladies to come in. The three winter pixies enter, immediately getting to work dressing me for the evening, their thin fingers chilly against my skin. I ask to wear my sturdy boots and my good furs. None of them comment or ask why;

they merely nod, their icy cheeks sparkling in the firelight. Once they're done tying up my unwieldy hair, tucking the orange curls into the gold netting, they silently slip out, as if they were never here.

The owl wobbles back onto my wrist, and I lift my hand, urging him to perch on my shoulder. He grips the fur of my cloak with his talons and nestles into the crook of my neck.

"What should I name you, sweet one?" I ask. "You look like a Fionn. How does that sound?" The bird clicks its beak.

I leave my rooms and walk down the hallway, through the gallery, and down the back staircase. I'll go through the kitchens and find the owl a piece of meat. This isn't my usual time to visit Lailoken, but I'm sure he'll be in his cave. As a monk, he spends his time focused on the solitary activities of prayer and reading, which keep his old legs weak and his eyes dim.

The goddess never seemed to approve of him, perhaps because he's a human. Most of the underlings sneer at my dependence on him, a Christian monk, which is why he never comes to the keep. But when I was orphaned as a girl, he raised me as if he was my father. I asked him once if he was my human father. He claimed that he'd never been with a woman in that way. Then he kissed my head and said he loved me as much as any natural daughter.

"I see you're enjoying my gift." A deep voice echoes up from the bottom of the staircase. "He suits you."

I pause on the stone and spot my Bonded looking up at me. His thick gray furs cover him like a cloak, a dusting of snow still on his broad shoulders. His raven, Bran, flies in the window and perches on the sill, tipping his head, giving the fledgling a curious look.

"I was taking him for a walk," I say.

"A storm is moving in." The king unhooks his heavy furs from his leathers and drops them to the floor. His shade servant, Eric, appears, picking them up and taking them away as the king starts up the stairs toward me.

My muscles clench instinctually, but I tell myself there's no running.

"*The gates are being closed,*" *he says.* "*You were off to your monk, no doubt?*" *I'm surprised—there's no anger or disapproval in his voice.*

"*Yes,*" *I say, my pulse picking up speed as he comes closer.* "*I was going to show him the bird.*"

His height matches mine even though he's two steps down, his shoulders nearly blocking the passage. His black leathers are muddy, and there's blood on the side of his neck. I realize he must've gone on his hunt early, feeling the storm coming in.

A glint of satisfaction lights his eyes. "*I'm glad you're pleased. You can show the old man the bird tomorrow, once the winds calm. I will have a servant clear the path for you.*"

"*Thank you,*" *I say, wondering why he's helping me visit Lailoken. I assumed he felt the same way about my friend as everyone else in this place does.*

He keeps his gaze locked on mine and continues his slow approach, up one step, then the last. When he's on an even level with me he pauses, looking me over closely. His breath emerges in a quick mist as he leans close and kisses my cheek with his chilled lips. Then he whispers against my skin, "*I'm truly sorry about the babe.*"

My pulse stutters. Before I ask how he knew, he's moved past, already disappearing into the shadows above, leaving me alone in the passage to wonder.

SEVENTEEN

FAELAN

I catch Aelia's scent in the air first, then Sage's, as I approach the building. The smell of the fire demi's energy is strong, her power like a shimmering trail I can't quite catch. I follow it toward the main entrance, where humans stand among several shades, all in line along the wall. There's a selkie chatting with the bouncer at the door, distracting him as she sucks on a lollipop. A thin pixie boy slips past them into the club. I see a whisper of something in the air near the selkie, a thread of gold; I think that's a remnant of Sage's energy, but—

"Faelan?" says a shocked female voice. "Is that really you?" My frayed nerves spark, and I don't want to turn. I can't be hearing right. No way. The goddess wouldn't do that to me, not tonight. My head is already bollocks; I need to find Sage, I—

A soft touch on my arm makes me look. "Astrid," I say as my eyes fall on her. After more than three centuries without seeing her, my breath still catches: her regal stance, the smooth, milky skin of her bare shoulders, her perfect alfar features, the delicate way her brow lifts in surprise as she looks me over.

I'm suddenly filled with the memory of us sleeping too long under the old willow tree—and then not sleeping—the day before my brother adopted her as a ward. *My gods, Astrid.* What the bloody hell is she doing here? She's not wearing her usual hunter gear of gambeson and tight leathers, and her bow and quiver aren't perched on her back, but she's exactly the same, with her ridiculously long golden braid.

"You're in LA?" she asks, shock in her voice. She knows how much I've always hated cities—and that was before concrete and high-rises.

"I'm doing a job for Marius," I say. There's so much I want to ask her. But I blink and wake myself back up. I can't stand here. I can't waste time.

I glance around again, looking for that selkie I spotted a second ago with Sage's energy trailing nearby. My guess is they were standing near each other. Maybe Sage spoke with her. I don't see the selkie now, though.

"Shite," I bite out.

Astrid follows my line of sight. "You're looking for someone?"

"I have to go," I say, beginning to walk away.

She grabs my arm, strong as ever. "Wait, how long are you here for? I want to talk to you, Faelan. It's been so long."

"You could've talked to me three hundred years ago, Astrid." I focus on not noticing how familiar her touch feels. "But you chose to stay with my brother, remember?"

She flinches and releases me. "Faelan . . ."

We had decided to leave that summer—both of us. To break our House vow and swear fealty to Brighid instead of Cernunnos, who I'd been serving since my Emergence. In the end, though, she betrayed me, telling my brother Finbar of our plans. They attempted to keep my loyalty by locking me away for a few years, but I broke out. Knowing Astrid, she's thinking, *What are a few chains between old lovers?*

I want to stand here and stare at her stunning features, to tell her she was the only girl I ever loved and explain how she crushed me with her betrayal. Instead, I say, "I'll see you in another three hundred years.

Send Finbar and Duncan my love." And I walk away. I can feel her pain follow me as I go, and it makes my throat ache.

Until I sense another distinctly powerful presence: Kieran.

My teeth clench. I pull a fresh leaf from my pocket and follow the dark energy of the Morrígan blood, past the line of patrons along the front of the club, to the alley. I rub the green life between my fingers as I come around the corner. The leaf's energy soaks into my hand in delicate threads, the life letting me see into the shadows at the far end, letting me recognize the dark prince—

Recognize Aelia crouched over a body at his feet.

And the blood pooling underneath the body.

Details register in a flash: an angry Aelia, her eyes glowing as she scolds Kieran; her hand gripping a still form on the ground; a figure with red hair, wearing a pink dress that's soaked red at the chest, an upturned palm lined in red scrapes. And that smirk on Kieran's face.

Rage courses through me, and I lunge at him with a growl. "What've you done?"

The prince shifts, leaving me grabbing for smoke. He appears at my side and points at Sage, saying with a sneer, "My, my, she has *you* keyed in like the dog you are, doesn't she?"

But I'm too focused on all the blood, on Sage's cut flesh, her glassy eyes. Dead? No, it can't be. But she's definitely fading. My gods . . .

I kneel at her side and gently pull her into my arms. Her head lolls against my shoulder. "Gods and bones . . . Sage . . . please hear me." I shouldn't have left her with Aelia. I never should've taken my eyes off her.

"Calm down," Kieran says. "She'll come back to us."

Aelia stands in a rush. "And if she doesn't, dumbass?"

"Then she's not worthy of the title Daughter of Fire. Perhaps she's been created from faulty blood, and I saved the Penta two weeks of unnecessary turmoil vying for her affection. Her energy was very odd; something isn't right inside her. Isn't it better to know now?"

I glare at him. "If she dies from your hand—"

"If she does, then she wasn't a true daughter," he says, his voice tight.

His sure words jar me. Fresh rage sparks in my gut. "I'll tear your head from your shoulders for this, you bloody stuck-up shit."

"Empty threats," Kieran bites out. "You rejected your royal blood like a fool, and now you wish to come at me? To take on the role of protector to the second daughter of Brighid? But you believe I'm the prideful one."

Aelia grips my arm. "Faelan, heal her. Come on!"

"He can't," Kieran says, a smirk relighting in his metallic eyes. "He gave up that right, didn't you, bastard?"

"Fuck you, Kieran," I snap. "Just use your power to pull her spirit from the brink before it slips away."

He looks me over. "And in return you will . . . what exactly? Wash my car? You're useless."

"Just do it!" Aelia screeches.

I give up trying to convince him to reverse her fall. He could simply hold her spirit here, but he won't. And her flesh isn't healing, which means her spirit will slip away soon. I have to get her help. Quickly.

I tuck her into my chest, whispering into her ear, "Fight this, Sage. I've seen your power. Come back and melt his face off for what he did to you, or I will. And then we'll both be dead. Come on, Daughter of Fire. Come back. Come back to me." My voice falters, and I realize I'm panicked about more than Marius's reaction. I have no idea if it's because of seeing Astrid or if it's because I'm freshly emerged from hibernation. But I'm raw. I'm actually feeling sorrow for the demi. As if I know her. As if I was a soul who cared for anything other than serving my goddess.

"We need to be very sure she's a true daughter," Kieran says. Disappointment threads through his words. "And this is a bad sign. A true blood wouldn't have allowed me to harm them at all. She would've eviscerated me for touching her, and loved it."

"She thinks she's human," I say, flabbergasted. "She doesn't understand yet. It was too soon to force this." I lift her from the ground. Kieran is ten times more powerful than me since I left my House, but I need to make it clear that I'm not going to let go easily. He better stay out of my way and let me take her.

"You're a faithless one, aren't you, bastard?" he says. "Truth doesn't need time. It merely is."

"What the hell are you babbling about?" Aelia asks. "You couldn't have just stabbed her in the gut or something? It takes less than three minutes to bleed out from a severed artery, and you want her to heal herself that fast when she's never done it before?"

Kieran stares down at Aelia. "I will not take a false blood claim as my Bonded."

"She isn't yours to Bond with," I say through my teeth. "That covenant between our Houses died with your brother."

"Then whose is she?" he asks, obviously sure I'm about as much of a threat as a gnat he can swat away. "You believe she's yours?"

I shift her weight in my arms, cradling her tighter to my chest. "No," I say, determination filling me as I start to walk from the alley. "I'm her guard and her shield. You, on the other hand, are no one to her now. And if I have anything to say about it, that's the way it'll stay."

~

Aelia trails after me, keeping close as we walk back to where I parked. I nestle Sage in the passenger seat and try to decide where to take her for help. There's only one soul I know who can meddle with spirits besides Kieran.

Aelia is horribly nervous, but I can't tell if it's fear of her father or fear for Sage.

"Go tell the driver you're riding with me," I say, and she obeys without her usual snarky comeback.

I get behind the wheel and start the car. Next to me, Sage is soaked in blood, pale as moonlight. And her neck, the flesh is . . . "Don't worry," I say, hoping she can hear me. "This is getting fixed. Right now."

Aelia slides into the back seat and slams the door, the blue mist of her energy trailing behind her, showing her fear. "I can't believe this. Kieran is *such* an asshole."

I look at her in the rearview mirror, then pull out onto the road. "What the fuck were you thinking bringing the demi out in the open before the tribunal tomorrow?"

"I wanted to show off the goods a little. It's going to be embarrassing for my father if no one shows up. I was only going to stay for an hour, and I was keeping an eye on her. It's not my fault she ran off like that."

I shake my head. Sometimes I forget that she's basically just a flighty youth. "There is a way to go about this, Aelia. She needed to be sealed with a protector before running around LA."

"Oh, come on, Faelan, you know that's all just semantics. You already sealed that deal when you saved her in the fire."

"I didn't save her. I was keeping your father's property from burning down."

"And what, exactly, are you doing now, then?"

Very good question. "Aelia, if I can't bring her back, we're both fucked. The Cast will have us sequestered. We could end up in the Pit while Kieran gets off scot-free because of his godsdamn rank. We'll be seen as the no-name bastards who lost an heir. It won't just be brushed aside." But it's not just fear of the Cast that I'm feeling. Seeing Sage like this—I'm shaken. I can't deny it. I actually give a shit about her. And it annoys the hell out of me.

"Daddy wouldn't let anything happen to me," Aelia says, pouting.

"I've worked with your father nearly half a millennium. I think I'd know what he's capable of better than you."

"Whatever, you love being his lapdog." She folds her arms across her chest and leans back with a groan. "Where are we going, anyway?"

"Caledonia."

She barks out a laugh. "Scotland? Are you serious? Nothing safe lives there."

"I'm not looking for safe."

We pull off the freeway and head down a side road. The cemetery is rolling hills on our left, an endless sea of green grass and white tombstones. Its morbid nature makes it oddly perfect for this moment. And I'm fairly sure it's the closest passageway. We don't have time to go to the one in Malibu.

I'll never understand why humans bury their dead, thinking it helps a soul that's already long gone from the empty husk. The reality is that dead flesh soils the spirit of the earth, the rot of decay seeping into the energy of root and grass and tree. It takes decades for the spirit to renew itself. But all that decay and death in one place also cracks a window in time and space. I appreciate how past cultures did things, especially the ones who laid their dead in caves. It makes the travel doors much more powerful and easier to utilize, like the catacombs in Paris: the bones of over six million souls below the city create a sizable doorway that's become well traveled. This is no Paris gateway, but it should work with only three of us going through. I hope.

"I'm really not up for this," Aelia says as we pull up the drive through the fields of the dead. "I don't have the right shoes."

I ignore her and keep driving deeper into the property. The Audi's headlights are the only light now as we come around a turn, and I finally spot the road marker for the crypt up ahead. I've only been here once, about fifty years ago. At the time, the small stone structure was tucked back in the trees at the base of a hill. I can't see it from here, but I recall it being only a few dozen yards from the road.

"Maybe you should just leave me here, and I'll call my father to send a car," Aelia says nervously.

"Hell, no." I pull up along the curb and put the gearshift into park. "Get out."

"Faelan, I'm not supposed to travel the passageways."

"Now." I slide out, head to the other side of the car, and open the door. I give Aelia a look as I gather the demi into my arms. "Seriously. I'm not playing around. Your father can *not* be made aware of this, and you know it."

She looks back at me with steel in her eyes, but her blue misty energy seeps out of her chest, revealing her fear again. "Fine." She gets out and follows me across the lawn, toward the crypt. "But why do we need to go to Scotland to get help? There's gotta be a healer in Reseda or Granada Hills or something. They can help us put her in hibernation."

"A healer isn't what we need, and hibernation will be a wash for someone this far gone. We need a person who deals in spirits and souls." I nod for her to walk in front of me. "So can we just get there? We're running out of time."

Her heel gets stuck in the grass, and she stumbles, then growls, pulling her shoes off and carrying them.

I pause in front of the crypt gate; the iron looks rusted clean through, the vines growing up the face the only thing holding it together. It's obviously been unused for a while. I shift the demi in my arms and step over one of several blossoming wormwood and mugwort plants growing around the small building for protection.

I turn to Aelia. "Open the door."

"Excuse you?" She's on her bare tiptoes, like she's trying not to touch the grass any more than necessary.

"It's simple. You just use an unveiling spell."

She gapes at me, her shoes held high in one hand.

I add, "You're the witch."

"Druid," she snaps. "Ugh. I can't believe I ever let you kiss me. You're *such* a jerk."

More like she jumped my lips with hers. But when Aelia wants something, she usually gets it. Until she wanted me.

She keeps mumbling in protest as she walks over and places her hand on the gate. She takes in a deep breath and begins to whisper the unveiling to unlock the door. A slight glow rims her shoulders as she completes the spell, and the iron latches crackle, then pop loose.

She pulls on the gate and it creaks open, a puff of rust billowing out. She coughs and waves a hand in front of her face. "Happy?"

I step past her into the dark space. Every surface is coated in several inches of dust. The grave plates on the wall are covered in a gray blanket that masks the names.

In the doorway, Aelia slips her heels back on before stepping all the way inside. They click on the cement as she looks around. She pauses, and her eyes fall on me again, on the body in my arms. A new wisp of blue mist emerges from her chest.

"Don't worry," I say, "traveling the passages is painless. Once you get used to it."

She smirks. "I've traveled before. We had to travel through a passage twice last year during studies."

"Grand," I mutter. Traveling from LA to San Francisco with a supervisor for physics studies isn't the same as passing over a full continent and an ocean. But she'll figure that out as soon as we go through.

"We need blood," I say. "Demi blood." It takes a demi to crack the passageway, and I have no hands to reach for my dagger. I motion again to Aelia, turning so my hilt is showing.

She takes hold of it and starts to pull the blade free from the waist of my jeans. But then she changes her mind and takes Sage's wrist instead, lifting it to show me. The hand flops in front of my face. The palm is coated in red, sticky now from the blood beginning to dry. "We have loads of demi blood already. Where do we put it?" She waves the hand at me.

"Enough." This isn't a joke. If we don't hurry, it'll be too late—nothing will bring her back. "Place it on the lintel there." I nod to the frame of the crypt's entrance. "But once it touches, we only have a few seconds to slip through before it closes back up."

She nods. "And you're doing the steering so we don't end up in Oxnard or somewhere else horrible?"

"Yes, just be sure you hold on to me."

She slides her arm through mine, hooking it around my bicep. Then she nudges us closer to the lintel. "Here we go." She directs Sage's palm to the rim and squeezes her eyes shut in anticipation as she presses it down.

A crack of green light appears at the center of the doorway, and the whistle of rushing wind pulls at the air. The fissure fractures until it opens fully, like a shattered mirror. And we step through.

EIGHTEEN

FAELAN

Bending space is never as simple as walking from one location to another. It wreaks havoc on a cellular level for a human, and Aelia's blood is more human than Other. While I manage to land on my feet as the passageway releases me, Sage still in my arms, Aelia collapses on the mossy ground in front of me with a whoosh of breath, gasping and gagging. Then she crawls into a cluster of high ferns and begins to vomit.

I only have to crouch for a moment, holding Sage tight to my chest to keep from dropping her. I breathe through the flip of my gut, the buzzing in my muscles, the fading crackle in my ears, used to the odd sensations after hundreds of years of traveling through passageways.

Aelia, however, continues to throw up.

I steady myself and look around. We're in a small thicket. There won't be any humans this deep in the forest, only animals and the occasional wysp—a small creature made of water that lives in the river just north of here and sometimes hides in the fog.

I try to be patient as Aelia whimpers and releases the contents of her stomach for several minutes, but after a while it becomes a little melodramatic, with her mostly just pressing her head into the moss and complaining to herself.

Eventually, I tell her I'll leave her there alone and move on to my destination if she doesn't suck it up.

"I hate you right now," she mutters. She wipes her mouth and shivers, swallowing, but she stands and follows me through the tree line into the deeper wood.

The energy of the trees wraps around me, the rich life soaking through my skin, settling my nerves better than any drug. The white birch and ash creak; robins and siskins titter in the branches above. I spot a merlin eyeing us from a Scots pine, and a red deer pauses in her feeding, turning her head to watch us pass.

The early-morning air is misty on my skin, smelling of moss and approaching rain clouds. I try to focus on the beauty around me. That way maybe I won't notice the chill of Sage's forehead against my neck. I won't think about how fast she's grown cold. Her death will be final very soon—I can only pray it hasn't happened already.

I have to stop a couple of times to confirm the scent of my path, making sure I'm still heading the right way. The man I'm seeking isn't one who likes to be found. I've met him only once before, in a time I like to forget, but it's been a while, and much of the forest has changed since then. The farther in we go, the more I see how aggressively it's been cut back. I have to wonder if the man's even still here.

He has to be. I need him to be.

We finally find the clearing blanketed in yellow and purple flowers, with the familiar giant of a juniper tree on its far side. I hesitate, not sure I'm seeing right. It's exactly the same as I remember from seven centuries ago, when I was a boy who brought a secret message from Queen Lily into these trees. The juniper is a massive, twisted malformation, the taffy-like trunk and branches tipped with green, reaching several dozen feet into the air. It almost looks like a tormented beast as it grows with its arms stretching and curling around several nearby aspen and birch, like they're huddled together in solidarity.

Something moves out from the line of trees on our right, a figure stumbling along in the underbrush, holding a twisted rowan staff. He too looks exactly the same as he did all those centuries ago—though perhaps a bit more disheveled, if that's possible. He's still wrinkled, with ratty silver hair. He's wearing a hat that looks like a bird's nest and patchwork cloaks of green-and-brown wool, woven together with vines and feathers and bones. The ferns behind him shudder like something low to the ground is following him. His scolding filters over the clearing. "No, no, Atticus, stop teasing Fauna. She's having a tumbly-bumbly time. And we need nuts! Yes, yes. Dinner doesn't sing itself."

I can't see who or what he's talking to. And I need to be careful. The man has quite the reputation for turning intruders into trees if he doesn't like them. Trouble is, I don't have a lot of time to endear myself to him.

Aelia stumbles out of the ferns behind me and whines, "Nature sucks. How much farther?"

"We're here," I say, nodding at the clearing.

Her gaze travels over the expanse of yellow and purple and pauses on the hunched wise man. Her eyes widen. "Him? He's the *help*? But . . ." She squints. "Who *is* that?"

"The wizard of the wood, Lailoken."

"Wait." She turns to me. "Do you mean that human from the old stories? I learned about him in my training; he was supposed to be completely nuts. He turned a whole village into toads because they didn't laugh at his joke."

"Don't believe everything the older druids tell you. That never really happened," I say. "Well, not exactly. He's merely eccentric." But she's right. He's known to be completely bonkers. "He's really old, so it comes off as . . ." I search for the right word.

"Batshit crazy?"

"Just follow my lead," I say, "and keep your mouth shut." I shift Sage in my arms, tightening my hold on her, then I step out of the rim of trees and shout a warning. "Oy! Hello there!"

The wise man stops and turns, back straightening. "Who goes? What's the man with the flower in his hands?"

"It's only me, sir. Faelan Ua Cleirigh, House of Brighid. Do you remember me? I've come for your help—"

"Houses and hovels and Otherborn troubles." He begins to walk toward us through the field, shooing with his hand. "Fay, fay! What you bring here isn't wanted. Enough mess has come from god blood." A herd of small animals appear in the brush, following along, hopping around his feet. Rabbits. A puffy-tailed squirrel scuttles up his leg to his shoulder, perching there with a loud chirp.

"No, I don't bring trouble," I say, even though that may not be true. "If I could just petition you for—"

"Bah!" he croaks. "I see what you have. I see her, that fire thing, get it out of my wood. Out, I tell you!"

"Wow," Aelia mumbles behind me. "This is already going so well."

I dare to step closer to the wise man, trying not to let my urgency show. "She's very important," I say.

"No, no, toes and bones, no!" He shakes his staff and turns to walk away. "Shoo to you and your flames."

The foggy air begins to mist, dampening my clothes, settling on Sage's cheek and her dulled red hair. She's slipping away too fast, the chill of her becoming even more striking against my body. Urgency fills me in a rush, and I take a few steps closer to him.

"Don't turn us away," I say, my voice faltering. "We have nowhere else to go. Please, Lailoken."

He pauses at the sound of his name. His head pulls back a little, and he turns to us again, his wrinkled features scrunched in confusion. Pain filters from his shoulders in thin gray threads. The squirrel on his arm scrambles to hide in his armpit. The rabbits at his feet put their paws on his legs, like they're trying to be sure he's all right.

I step toward him again, and he still doesn't move. "Sir?"

"Perfect," Aelia says. "You broke him."

I move even closer, getting a few feet away before I bow my head and whisper, "Sir Lailoken, I've come for your help. Please. Hear my petition."

"Pishposh!" he barks suddenly, making me jump. "I am that man, you say?"

I nod, not sure exactly why he'd ask who he was. "You are Lailoken, the wise man in the wood."

His furrowed features open, a grin brightening his eyes. "Well, well, I am a man most clever, am I not?"

"Yes, sir."

He laughs. "Let's have this task done, then. The night wanes to day quickly. We all know what that means!" He turns and walks away, toward the large juniper tree on the other side of the clearing.

I don't think we do all know what that means, but I follow him anyway, trying to keep up. For an ancient man, he's nearly as speedy as the rabbits trailing behind him. Aelia grumbles, sporadically complaining about sticks poking her feet.

The hovel the wise man calls home is a perfect shelter that nature carved from the guts of the gigantic juniper. The roots, larger than a man, coil from the earth, forming sturdy pillars that make up the walls, along with river stones and moss-coated earth. The oval door is carved with runes and protections. A small window is carved out too, but a bird's nest is packed into the opening.

He waves his staff at the door, and it creaks open on its own before he slips inside. Aelia and I follow. As I enter the small living space, my chest heats, the intense energy inside the ancient tree beginning to circle my hungry skin. Green grows all over, across every surface—clover, moss, mushroom, thyme, and mint, creating a patchwork quilt of life.

It's perfection, the dream home of every child of Cernunnos, like the alfar once slept in before the forests began to disappear. I wonder if this is one of their old homes. If it is, it looks like the human has made a few additions.

There's a small cluster of yellow crystals in the far corner, their pulsing glow heating the space instead of a fire. A large internal root with a flattened surface seems to be used as a table. Several glass bottles are clustered on it next to three skulls: bird, cat, and canine. A bowl is at the center, steam emerging from the contents, a flat crystal cross section glowing underneath it.

Lailoken hobbles over to the bowl and picks it up. He shoves it at Aelia. "You look hungry, druid girl. Perhaps this will cure you."

Aelia cringes away. "Ugh, no way. It smells like moldy cheese."

I shoot her a glare, but Lailoken just chuckles and tosses the steaming bowl back onto the table. The contents splash over the rim, a goopy brown. "It was poisoned, anyway. Don't need a dead druid cluttering my stoop." He laughs again like he's enjoying Aelia's annoyance. Then he waves me forward. "Bring the fire thing here. Settle her on the clover." He motions to the spot where I should lay Sage.

I kneel in the clover and rest her on the cushion of green. When I let go, my arms ache with the lack of her.

Her head is tipped to the side. My gut clenches again at the sight of her sliced neck, the blood now sticky, nearly dried, smeared all down her chest, her shoulder, her dress soaked through and heavy with it. I've seen a lot of death in my time, watched countless horrors done, but I've rarely felt confused by it. Only once, when I found my mother that dark morning, so long ago, floating like a forgotten toy in the river. I was young, and until that moment death had been a stranger to me.

Now, seeing this broken waif in front of me . . . it's like I'm ten years old all over again.

"There it is," says the wise man. He leans his staff against the wall before he kneels across from me, on the other side of Sage. "This is most definitely flowers growing in winter, do you not think?" He shakes his head, musing at his lunatic words.

"Can you fix her?" I ask, deciding to ignore his crazy. When I met him as a boy, he was the most powerful human I'd ever seen, able to do far more than even the most talented demi. But then, humans have a lot in them that they never tap into, especially in the modern age. I can only hope he still has enough wit to understand what's going on with Sage. After so many years hiding in the wood, he seems much more off. He's kept himself alive, though. Somehow.

Lailoken rubs his palms together, studying Sage. "This flame is still burning, I believe." He touches her hair, then glances at me. "Caution is warranted, though. There's much to swallow us. Much to kill. The blood here is not so common." He clucks his tongue like he's tsking a naughty child. "You see what I mean, I'm sure, Mr. Winter."

I decide not to correct him or ask him why he's calling me Mr. Winter. I don't want to make this moment any more confusing than it already is. "Yes," I say, trying to be agreeable instead. "I know she's dangerous." Even though I'm not sure *how* dangerous. Not yet.

"Truly," he says, "is this a lily growing before us? She is fire and shadow. I've seen her burn before." His tone has shifted a bit, amazement filling his words. "It is a true miracle. She's come back to us."

Aelia settles beside me and leans close, whispering, "Did he just call her *Lily*? Could he think she's the other daughter? The first one?"

I don't know how to answer, so I just watch the old man place his palm over Sage's forehead as he begins muttering a pattern of words in ancient Gaelic. Could he really think she's the first daughter, Lily? Maybe I was foolish to bring her here.

After everything that happened to the Otherborn because of the first daughter, any similarities between the outcast queen and our new demi wouldn't be seen as a good thing.

I met Queen Lily when I was a child. She was a woman of light and beauty then, in her prime, bound to the Morrígan's son, the King of Ravens. They'd ruled together for several centuries over our kind. My only interaction with her was at a feast of Samhain just after the king was killed. She had such a quiet sorrow about her when she called me up to her throne and told me she'd pay me a silver coin for a lock of my hair and two extra if I took a message to the wizard in the wood, Lailoken. I still remember her golden eyes as she looked down on me, the weight of grief around her.

I delivered the message, and on my way home, I stopped in the market and bought oatcakes and sweet meats with the silver. Three days later, the queen met her final punishment—she was taken prisoner by the Cast and tossed into the Pit, where she remains to this day.

She was charged with killing her Bonded, the king. They claimed that, in her madness, she had unleashed a scourge called the Black Death, and that in the end tens of millions of humans would die because of her. Her folly opened up the doorway for the Church to start its deadliest blood hunt of Otherborn and caused many centuries of bloodshed on both sides, human and Otherborn. It was a time marked by horror. But I've never been able to see her as the monster the Cast made her out to be. I'll always see her as the sad beauty I once admired.

I still remember her delicate fingers taking my dirty hand in hers. I can still close my eyes and feel her energy. It was so distinct. So colorful. It smelled like rain and sunlight and sweet greens. She was so beautiful, so magical.

This demi in front of us right now—Sage—bears no resemblance, in power or in form or in any way, really, to her older sister, Lily.

"He's not all there," I remind Aelia. "At least he's got the right bloodline. It would be worse if he was calling for a water spirit or something."

"But that's nuts," she hisses. "We don't want him to bring the wrong thing back, do we?"

Lailoken stops muttering under his breath and barks, "Secrets and whispers! No, no, no."

"We're worried you've got it wrong, sir," I explain. "She's not the first daughter, she's the second. Her name is Sage."

The frown scrunching his face deepens. "What, what? Not Lilybird, you say?" He looks down at Sage. Then he brushes his dirt-stained fingertips against her hair.

"No," Aelia says. "Not Lily."

Lailoken sniffs. "I'm not deaf, you know." He places his palm over Sage's eyes and closes his own before he goes back to his mutters like we never interrupted him. I can only hope his spell is correct. I can't understand everything he's saying because he's talking too fast, his words too jumbled.

Aelia rolls her eyes. "Great plan, Faelan. Take her to the wacky man in the woods." She leans back on her elbows, apparently done caring.

After another several minutes of Aelia and me sitting in silence with Lailoken's voice humming in the background, the wise man finally pauses and sighs heavily. "Well, well, the spirit lingers. But she must be fed. Now or never, whatever the weather."

Aelia groans in annoyance. "What in the name of Danu is he talking about now?"

I ignore her and ask the wise man, "Sage's spirit is anchored again? How can you be sure?" She's not moving, not even breathing. Her wound is still gaping.

"Oh, she was never gone and done with, not this one," he says. "Can't you smell her warmth and roses in the flames? All those breads and hopes are still deep in her gut—I think you got lost coming here. She was fine as rain and sunshine."

Aelia sits up straight. "What?"

"No," I say, panic swirling in my chest again. "She's still dead. Her spirit . . ." I can't smell her spark at all. And I can't take her back like this. I can't leave her broken and lost. Not this girl.

The wise man shakes his head, his odd bird's nest hat flopping to the side. "She's all tucked tight in there, safe and sound. The child she is, it's lovely to have found her at last."

I stare at Sage's cold body. What am I missing? Even in hibernation, a fire elemental carries a sense of life, though it's weak. Heat in the body, color in the skin, a fluttering energy left behind, like dying embers. But Sage is a corpse, her skin now tinged in violet, dark circles rimming her eyes.

"Which one?" Lailoken asks, bringing my attention back to him.

Aelia frowns. "Which what, weirdo?"

I consider warning her away from insulting the powerful man but decide it's useless. I'm getting annoyed in a grand way myself.

"Which one"—the wise man's brow goes up—"will feed the princess?"

NINETEEN

FAELAN

He wants us to feed Sage? He knows it's not safe to feed a demi before she's learned to control her powers—definitely not a demi who manifests fire.

In normal circumstances, it would be a deadly plan, but with Sage being a corpse, I'm not sure what it means. She would have to link in to her prey; she'd have to initiate the connection to pull life. Aelia and I can't just pour our energy over her.

The wise man appears to be considering the two of us, like he's trying to decide whom to toss overboard. "The druid would work, I think," he finally says. "If she's gobbled up in a blink, it won't be much trouble. Useless any day of the week." He shrugs.

"What a gentleman," Aelia says.

I'm dead either way because Marius is going to kill me if I bring back a corpse. "I'll do it," I say. Obviously, it's going to be me. I would never put my leader's daughter in harm's way, even though, at this stage in the death, it would be less dangerous.

Gods, it's been more than an hour since Kieran sliced her open and bled her dry.

Aelia looks nervous but she scoots back, opening up room for me to lie beside the demi's body. I pull off my torque to allow myself to be as open as possible, then I slide off my shirt before settling in the clover. "It's fine, Lia," I say. "It's worth a shot."

She just shakes her head, biting her lip.

"Ah, good, good, Mr. Winter," Lailoken says, standing and moving to the table, plucking up one of the bottles. "A little pinch of devil's bane and thornblood." He pulls out the cork and sprinkles black dust over my chest. "This should spark the flame." He smiles down on me like I'm a loaf of bread he's about to toss in the oven. He motions to Sage. "Now take her hand and place it on your chest."

"Thornblood will make the connection too strong," Aelia says, sounding worried now. "Shouldn't we at least find some wolfsbane for protection? I can form a light ring with it."

Lailoken scoffs. "Foolishness. Nothing counters thornblood except mapleweed. Typical druid."

"Whatever, old fart, if you get my friend killed, I'll turn you into a toad."

"Unless I make you warty and green first." Lailoken grins wickedly.

I reach over and pick up Sage's limp wrist. "Let's just get it over with." I place her arm across my chest, pressing her palm down on my sternum with my other hand.

My pulse speeds up, but I brush away the thought of what I'm doing. I don't think about the danger or the possible uselessness of this whole thing. Because what if nothing happens? Or what if something does? Either way, I'm royally bolloxed.

The chill of Sage's skin is striking, and I have to focus on not feeling it, not feeling her death, as I turn my head to look at her and say the usual invitation, wondering if she can even hear me. "You may take from me if you need to."

Everything is still, silent. Even Lailoken's fingers tapping on the table fade into the background.

"Demi," I say, "don't be afraid, take what you need." I add in a whisper, "It's okay, Sage."

Something pricks the center of my chest, shocking me, and I hiss in a breath.

Did she just pull from me? She must have, she—

Pain shoots again, a needle jabbing my skin under her palm. A slight burn fills the spot before spreading out and coating my torso with a hum of warmth.

It's her. She's alive. My relief is palpable, a lifting of the million pounds that landed on my back the second I walked into that alley tonight.

I close my eyes and make myself breathe through the growing sting, beginning to let my skin receive the life energy under my back and arms, everywhere I'm touching green.

"It's working," I hear Aelia say somewhere in the distance. "Her wounds are healing. She's going to be okay . . ."

Every part of me is suddenly focused on the touch of a hand on my skin as Sage's palm begins to twitch. Her fingers flex against me. Then they slide up my chest, slowly, painfully. I clench my teeth against the sting replacing her touch.

Her body shifts closer. The heat spreads, the stinging becoming a fever that fills my skin, sinking deep in my lungs, sending my heart racing. My pulse thunders in my head until it's all I hear. It pounds and aches in my skull, and the searing fire growing in me seems to echo each beat in my chest. I can't see, can't breathe.

I only feel. Her body at my side, pressing in now, the pain fading into the background.

The spice of her energy fills my nose, and her hand plays at my neck, thumb sliding over my jaw as she turns my face to hers. Her sweet breath hits my cheek, and the rhythm in my chest, the rhythm of my heart, merges with the rhythm of her lungs.

My muscles weaken, my skin blazes, and something inside my mind slips, something in my soul breaks loose, and everything in me wants her lips on mine.

I move to find her, turning my body to match hers. My hands catch her waist, and I slide my palm up her side, smelling blood, smelling her heat. I grip the back of her dress in my fist and pull her into my arms, my mouth tingling to feel her skin, her lips and mine nearly touching as my own energy wraps around us, hers tugging on it, taking it inside herself. And the only thing in my head is how desperately I want to kiss her, and kiss her, and—

I'm yanked back and smacked with a chilled hand. "Snap out of it!" Aelia says. No, she's not cold, she's just not as warm as Sage, she's—

"Sage!" I croak out, opening my clouded eyes, trying to sit up, trying to find her. "Is she all right?" My wits click back into place and I shake my head, clearing it of the muddy energy.

"What were you thinking?"

I can't see right. Sage is a blur beside me. "Answer me!"

"She's fine, dumbass. You, however, look like crap."

"I'm okay," I say, mostly to reassure myself. "But I need food."

A heavy blanket is tossed over me. The smell of earth and grass fills my nose as the soothing energy of life filters through my skin. I blink back the burning pain, and my eyes start working again. I lift a hand to touch my chest, feeling the seared skin as it unwinds and smooths out once more, the life around me healing it, and I realize that the blanket is made of growing things, dirt in the weaving having grown emerald sprouts. Sprouts that are slowly curling in on themselves and dying.

"Holy Dagda, Faelan," Aelia says. She's tucking the blanket around my lap. "You are such a male—you almost sucked face with her! Seriously. She could've melted you to the bone."

"I'm fine," I say again.

"Yes, yes," Lailoken says with a laugh. "Fine indeed, young buck."

"Oh gods, this is nuts," Aelia says. "You could've been killed."

"Mr. Winter can contain the flame just fine," Lailoken says. "It's been written that way from the beginning. Hasn't it, Mr. Winter?"

"Stop calling him that!" Aelia growls.

A groan comes from the demi beside me, and we all focus on her again. She grips her head like she's in pain.

"We need to get her back to the Cottages as soon as possible," I say.

"You should feed more first," Aelia says, eyeing me. "While we're here in the wood."

The wise man starts clanging his bottles, looking for something. "Pishposh, the boy is stone. His bones are solid as iron."

"I'm grand, Aelia," I say. And surprisingly it's true—or at least mostly true. I'm not hurt or drained as much as I should be. "I can rest later, but we need to get the demi to where she can be guarded better." I'm relieved Sage is with us, relieved that she's back, but I want to keep it that way.

She's gone silent, curled in the fetal position on the dead clover where we were just lying side by side. Her chest gently rises and falls; the skin at her neck is scarred a little from Kieran's stupidity. But her cheeks are rosy, and she's peaceful.

My gut tightens, thinking of her body pressed against mine. It was all of ten seconds, but there was something about the moment— something I don't want to think about—that I can't have in my life. I clear my throat and reach for my torque, then my shirt, pulling them back on, trying to distract myself. I need to stay focused.

"But!" the wise man says. "You will bring this flame back to me soon." He sounds surprisingly normal. And while he was irritated by Sage's presence when we first got here, he now seems to be looking at her with a strangely protective eye. I wonder what's changed. He picks up one of the bottles and holds it out to me, shaking it in my face. "Give her this in her tea tomorrow morning, yes, yes, and don't leave her alone when she sleeps. Be ever so very careful with her. It's what you've been called to. And as we know, flames need tending always, to keep them from being snuffed out—or devouring the fields." He laughs like he finds himself hilarious.

I take the bottle from him and slip it into my pants pocket. "Thank you for your help, sir. Truly." I squat down beside the sleeping demi and pick her up, cradling her in my arms again as I rise. She actually feels heavier. Or maybe I'm just more drained than I thought.

"Are you sure you're all right?" Aelia asks me.

"Let's go." I head for the door, shifting Sage in my arms. She's definitely heavier, and her arm feels less bony against my chest.

Lailoken opens the door with a wave of his hand. "Toodle-oo!"

As Aelia and I step back out into the clearing, the door slams behind us.

TWENTY

SAGE

Something moves against my arm. My mind surfaces from sleep in a rush, awareness filtering in. The feel of soft pillows under me, the smell of soil, of damp green things—it's soothing and lovely.

I open my heavy eyelids, but everything is blurry. I can't see right. Am I still in the alley? No, it smelled like soot and smog there, and nothing was comfortable.

Memories appear like cloudy puzzle pieces: the creatures slinking from the puddles, the dark-haired guy, he . . . he—cut my neck!

I sit up in a rush, hand going to my neck where the strange raven guy was gripping me. Am I in a forest? I'm surrounded by trees. And under my fingertips there's a thin bumpy line of skin on my neck—a scar?

Faelan told me about a dark prince, and I laughed, I thought it was so funny, that Faelan was crazy, or I was crazy, someone had to be crazy, because guys called the *Dark Prince* are only in books and movies that nerds like Ziggy talk about. They're vampires or wizards, and that stuff is . . . well, it's totally real apparently, so I'm just—holy shit, how can I be okay after what that raven guy did? My blood was on his face. I died! I know I did, I remember—

Something moves beside me again, stopping my tirade of thoughts.

I turn and blink at a shirtless Faelan, who's lying next to me, his eyes beginning to open. His body is only a foot away. He's so . . . wow. I must've been too panicked yesterday to fully take in all those muscles. And that tan. And, oh my, he has a lot of scars on his chest . . .

He props himself on his elbows, brow furrowed in concern. "Is something wrong?"

I open my mouth, but no words manage to come out. Why am I in bed with him? I look around and realize we're not in a forest; we're in his room. I'm in that nest thing where he was naked and snuggly with Aelia's friend. How did I get here, and why isn't he wearing a shirt?

I look down at myself, relieved to see I'm wearing a tank top and pajama shorts. But how did I get into them? "Where's my dress?" I ask stupidly. I should be asking how I'm alive. I should be asking how I got from the alley to here.

He sits up all the way and moves closer. "Your dress had too much blood on it. I had to toss it in the bin."

"Blood?" I know what he means, but my mind is having trouble processing. I was covered in blood. But I'm still alive.

"Do you remember anything that happened?" He studies me.

His intense green eyes make me shift farther away. Grass tickles my palm as I grip the side of the nest. I shake my head. "I remember a guy—or a raven—he was a raven that turned into a guy? I think he tried to kill me, but . . ." I touch my neck again. "I don't understand what happened."

Faelan's gaze follows my fingers. "You were hurt. I'm sorry about the scarring. The wound was open too long for it to heal properly."

"How am I not dead right now?" Because I know beyond a doubt I should be. But I don't even have stitches or bandages. Just a scar?

"As a demi, your spirit anchors to your flesh more firmly than a human's does. Thankfully, despite your unpredictable nature, your spirit held even after your body gave out, longer than normal. Hopefully, you won't be dying for a dozen centuries or more."

I bark out a laugh. And another. But then my throat clogs and tears spring into my eyes.

"You think I'm joking?" he asks.

"I think this whole thing is insane," I say, my voice cracking. I know I'm about to cry so I turn and scramble over the side of the nest, tumbling into the ferns, attempting to get farther away. I'm going to live for centuries? Me. How does a person let that sink in?

"Whoa, woman, where ya going?"

He jumps down after me, but I back up, hands held out to warn him off. I focus on steadying myself, realizing my legs are weak. The trees around me spin a little.

"You're okay," he says. "There's nothing to get in a tizzy about."

I shake my head and make myself breathe through the tangle of emotions welling up. "A *tizzy*? You just keep throwing stuff at me like I know how to swallow it all. This circus is going to have me drooling into my soup and sipping tea with the Mad Hatter in the hydrangeas." When he just frowns, I add, "You're making me nuts!"

He studies me cautiously for a few seconds before he finally says, "Okay, look. We're good to get started on the training, so let's begin today, going through some preliminary information. You can collect yourself in your room, and then in an hour or so we'll meet back in the greenhouse to begin. You'll get clarity. That's what you're looking for, right?"

I nod and sniff, pretending I don't have tears on my cheeks. I'm not even sure why I'm crying. It's so dumb. And it never does any good, anyway.

"Grand, then we'll meet back—"

"Can you just answer one question?" I interrupt. "Why was I in your bed?"

Confusion fills his features.

"I saw you with that pixie, Niamh," I say, slowly, unsure as a look of realization appears on his face. "I know why you had to be with her, to fix your burns from the fire and everything. So, were you and I in the bed together, because . . . I mean, was that some sort of kinky healing thing you did to me?"

He steps back, and revulsion scrunches his features. "Feck, no!"

I blink at his biting tone. He's definitely disgusted at the idea, grossed out at the thought of me in his bed for anything other than sleep.

My throat clenches again, and all I can do is whisper, "Oh good."

"I would never link with you to that level without your permission," he says. "Hibernation is a private and mutual process. Things can occur that you aren't fully aware of. I wasn't pleased with Aelia putting me under with the pixie without my consent. I wouldn't do something like that to you. To anyone." He pauses and seems to consider before adding, "There was a moment, though, in the wood, when . . . I believe I almost . . . well, I nearly kissed you, I think."

His confession jars through me, and I rack my brain, trying to find the memory. Trying to figure out how we could have gotten into a situation where this beast of a guy would ever in a million years kiss *me*.

I come up empty.

"I wasn't fully in control," he says. "But you needed the energy. And in the moment of a feeding . . . magnetism, attraction, can sometimes happen." He quickly adds, "But it's not real, it's temporary."

"I see," I say, even though I don't. He *fed* himself to me and that's how I healed. I took life from him. It kills me that I can do something so monumental, so bizarre, and have no memory of any of it.

"And the fact that I'm weaker than you," he continues, "while you're ignorant about how to control your subconscious . . . It was bound to happen eventually between us."

"Wait." I roll his words over. "What was bound to happen?"

"A feeding, a moment where your control slipped. The transition eventually requires that the Emergent feeds off the trainer as they learn. Sometimes that can become volatile when only one party is . . . practiced in the process. And, like I said, you're likely stronger than me."

His casual tone seems a bit forced. Obviously, he's not a fan of some of the *requirements* of his task with me.

I decide to try and get him to lay more cards on the table, since he's suddenly being honest. "It seems to bother you," I say, "that we almost kissed." It bothers me too, but mostly because I don't remember.

He waits for a second before responding. "Control is important to me."

I have no idea what to take from that. I suppose it's why he didn't want to do this, train me—the possibility of losing control. But I need to figure myself out, to know what I am and what it means. It doesn't matter how he feels about me, or if we almost kissed. And an *almost* kiss means nothing. Especially one that I have no memory of.

"Why don't you go get dressed," he says. "Be back in an hour, and I'll show you the books I have, and you can ask me whatever you wish. But we need to start the training. Sound good?"

I can tell he wants me to be agreeable, but I'm still not sure I can go along with all of this. It's tough to settle with myself that I need to stay in this madness and fake it, like I'm perfectly fine with what's happening. How can I, especially after last night? A guy tried to *kill* me. He overwhelmed me and trapped me and . . . I was completely useless. I've never felt so vulnerable. Or pissed at myself.

I swallow the pain in my throat and ask, "What is this training, exactly?"

Faelan's at his closet, slipping a shirt over his head, his movement tense. He takes a second, like he's thinking about how to answer. "Things will be different with you," he says finally. "Traditionally, we'd start with focusing techniques, but we're short on time, and your power seems to be overwhelming you, even overwhelming the torque." He motions to my necklace. "We need to skip kindergarten and move right into you learning control. Like I said, control is important. Even more so for you."

I nod absently, not sure how to absorb everything. "Okay, I'll get dressed." But then I remember. "Except I have no clothes."

"Aelia filled your closet earlier. Your wardrobe is more than overstuffed now."

I have a full closet. I'm not sure I've even had a closet of my own before, let alone a full one. "Wow, okay. I wonder what she put in it." Probably the same stuff that was in her own. Ugh.

Faelan looks confused. "She put clothes."

"As long as there's yoga pants," I say.

"Those are the stretchy things, right? That's unlikely."

"Well. Then I quit," I say, dryly.

He blinks but then surprises me with a smile, a small dimple appearing in his upper left cheek.

I didn't even know his mouth tipped that direction. I think I just accomplished the impossible.

I smile back at him, and in a flash his dimple disappears. He looks away. "Try not to take too long getting ready. We've got a lot of ground to cover." And then he walks into the greenhouse, leaving me standing beside his nest, alone.

TWENTY-ONE

SAGE

Amazingly enough, my closet isn't just a smaller version of Aelia's; it's actually got stuff in it that I like. There's edge and grit, and not a pink thread in sight. It's still all completely overpriced label wear, but at least it's not Kardashian chic. I can't let myself get used to it, though. I never stay anywhere long, and I doubt this time'll be any different.

I pull out a bra, a T-shirt, and jeans, and I'm shocked when the jeans fit kind of tight, and so does the bra. I don't even remember the last time my clothes weren't baggy. I check the sizes and they're what I would've thought fit me. But the hips and butt are pretty snug in the jeans, and the elastic on the bra is digging in under my arms.

I move to the full-length mirror.

My face . . . is something wrong with the mirror? My face looks rounder.

My hair is damp from my shower, but it seems longer, thicker at my neck now, and hanging farther past my chin in the front—is that right? I step closer to my reflection, touching my cheek and combing my fingers through my hair. I study the jagged silver scar on the side of my neck, marveling again at the fact that I should be dead. And then my eyes fall to my bra.

Holy B-cups, Batman. I have tits.

Right there, in the mirror, I can see them. They're small, but—oh my freaking God, I almost have cleavage. Actual cleavage. Whoa.

I don't want to put a shirt on. These things are amazing.

But how did they get there?

Could this be an Aelia magic thing? How does a person's body change so much in a day? I doubt the two meals I've eaten since getting here put ten pounds on me. Not normal, and completely weird—but, then again, what hasn't fallen into those two categories in the last two days?

I decide that I must be extra bloated from PMS or something, and pull my shirt over my head as I wander over to look at the bookshelf.

Everything is exactly how it was the first time I came in here—before I turned half of it to ash. The yellow gauzy curtains, the fluffy chair, and the countless books filling the shelves around the window and along the walls. And that bed. It's so comfortable, so dreamy. I'd marry it if I could.

But I'm not even a little tired right now. And I'm actually starving.

I go into my small kitchen and open a few cupboards. There are coffee grounds and spices in one, breakfast stuff in another: a box of steel-cut oats, some dried fruit, and a bag of granola. I grab the granola, take a bottle of water from the fridge, and pluck an apple out of the fruit bowl on my way out the door.

As I walk into the yard again, the late-morning air curls around me, the smell of moss and water and night jasmine tickling my nose. It's so gorgeous here. So alive. And this is where I'm living, with a full closet and a full belly. It's like I won a weekend at a five-star resort. With deadly creatures and mayhem, but still . . . it's pretty.

I close my eyes and take in a long breath through my nose, letting a smile fill my lips.

There's a prickle at the back of my neck. I turn to see Faelan watching me from a side doorway that leads into the greenhouse. His arms are crossed over his chest, and he's leaning on the frame, gaze intense, unnerving.

When he realizes I've caught him staring, he straightens, his hands fidgeting with a leather strap around his neck. "We should start," he says. "We don't have a lot of time." And then he disappears inside.

The greenhouse is cluttered with plants—wisteria in purples and pinks drip from the trellised ceiling, and white roses climb the glass walls. There are several trees crowding the edges of the room too, with twisted branches and bright green leaves. It's a chaotic garden in here, just like his bedroom, but this space is open in the center. Stones and moss carpet the floor, and there's a rough-hewn wood desk on the other side, covered with open books, stacked books, and books lying like fallen dominoes.

Faelan obviously doesn't use the desk much. He shuffles a larger book from the bottom of a pile and opens it to a page in the center, saying, "I guess step one before the Introduction tonight will be helping you connect with your power, to feel it for what it is." He focuses intently on the page in front of him. "This talks about some of the science of it. Maybe it'll help us move through the first stage of training more quickly."

I move to his side. It seems like he's trying to avoid looking at me, so I study his profile as I set the bottle of water down on a clear corner, noticing he's squinting a little and his jaw muscle is twitching. My gaze falls on the small medallion hanging from the leather strap around his neck. It's really intricate, a twisted design of green metal, probably oxidized copper. It could almost be a tree. A piece of amber is embedded at the base. It must have been tucked in his shirt before, because I hadn't noticed him wearing it.

"What's that thing around your neck?" I ask.

He gives me a sideways glance. "It's a torque."

"Really? Don't only demis wear those?"

He doesn't respond; he just turns the page of the large book. I glance down, but the words are all squiggles to me. I'm dying to know what it says, how any of this weirdness fits in with science, but first I want to know why he's so clammed up.

I lean on the table, facing him, my back to the book. I can tell he's uncomfortable, which makes me even more curious.

"So you're not going to answer my question?" I ask. "Why are you wearing a torque?" I'd stopped wondering what Faelan is, but now, after everything that happened this morning, I'm all curiosity again. "You're not a shade," I say. "And I'm fairly sure you're not a pixie." His nostrils flare, and I have to bite back a smile. "What did Aelia say the other ones were? Oh yeah, those gross wraith things. And selkie mermaids—I know you're not either of those."

"It's just *selkie*, and you're forgetting alfar."

"Oh right. Aelia said those were like angels."

"No." A dark tone fills his voice. "No, they're not."

"Is that what you are?" I ask quietly. He doesn't seem to like them. Maybe that's why he won't just come out and say what he is—he's ashamed. I wouldn't know an alfar if I fell over its dead body in the street, so he must know I wouldn't look down on him if that's what he is. I wouldn't be like those girls who were gossiping about James in the club because he wasn't status worthy.

He sighs and finally looks at me. "I'm not an underling, Sage," he says. "All the creatures you mentioned are underlings."

"Oh."

He picks up the medallion hanging around his neck and studies it for a few seconds, then he tucks it in his shirt. "I'm a son of Cernunnos. The third son." He says it like the words are weighing him down.

I've heard that name before. Aelia mentioned it yesterday when she was gossiping about some girl named Astrid who Faelan supposedly used to date or something. The House of Cernunnos—not a band. "He's one of the five gods," I say.

"Yes, one of the Penta."

"So you're a demigod." Why would he hide that? And if he's a demigod, shouldn't he have a more important job than babysitting? It seems like being the child of a deity is a fairly big deal, but he's running around following all of Marius's orders. I reach up and touch my own necklace. "And you wear a torque." Now that I think about it, I don't remember seeing one on Marius. Or on the dark raven guy, Kieran.

"It's not something we advertise," he says. "A demi wears a torque for one of two reasons: either someone placed it on them to control their powers, or they place it to control themselves. Whoever places the torque is the only one who can remove it."

Well, I know why I'm wearing one. "Which is it for you?"

"I placed the torque. It helps me contain things."

"What sort of *things*?"

He hesitates but then says, "My father's blood."

"Cernunnos."

"Yes."

"Because . . ." When he doesn't finish for me, I add, "What kind of god is he?"

"He's the god of the wood, of the hunt, and the horned god of fertility."

Um. Horned god of fertility? That sounds a bit skanky. "And he's your . . . dad?"

"Unfortunately."

The idea that he's not a fan of his godparent sends a wave of relief through me for some reason. "So you're like me."

He releases a tense laugh. "No, I'm not like you," he says. "Not even a little bit. I'm a stray."

"What's that mean?"

"It means I first gave my allegiance to my father's House at my Emergence, but a hundred years later I abandoned my vow, breaking my covenant and casting off my name. The House of Brighid took me in, and I chose to give my allegiance to her instead—what there is left to give, anyway."

I want to ask him why he left the other House, but the conversation seems to be distressing him. It's very clear he doesn't usually talk about all of this. "Whatever you say, it sounds like you *are* like me," I say, quietly. When his brow pinches in question, I add, "I was a stray too—in the human world. No one wanted me."

Without hesitation, he says, "We do."

His response hits me in an odd way, the layers underneath the words making us lock eyes for an extra second. Breathing is suddenly tougher, and the skin along the back of my neck tingles again, like when I caught him watching me a few minutes ago.

"So," I say, trying to break the growing tension. I turn back to the table, tapping on the open book. A small puff of dust rises from the page. "This looks cool. Who wrote it? What's all that say?"

He clears his throat and focuses on the book again. "A monk wrote it in the twelfth century, I believe. It's a study of the bloodlines and how the energies, or powers, work on a cellular level."

I move my hand away from the yellowed paper. "Oh, that's . . . complex. And super old."

"It's been protected by magic and re-bound a few times over the centuries, but yes, it's old. And the theories are definitely complicated, especially for the time." There's a small smile in his voice. "The Otherborn have always been ahead in the sciences. But I think you and I can handle it. Even with your American education."

"Very funny." I smirk.

He almost gives me a real smile.

Warmth fills my skin at the flash of his dimple. "So, what's first on the list?"

Discomfort surfaces in his features again, the light in his eyes fading as quickly as it came. He moves away from the desk to the center of the room. "I think we should begin with the most basic theory," he says.

"Showing you where your power—or your energy—comes from." He motions to the spot in front of him. "Can you stand here?"

I hesitate, but then move toward the spot. For some reason, I'm nervous again, feeling the same caution I did when I woke up this morning beside his sleeping, half-naked body.

I position myself to face him, keeping a good space between us. "Like this?"

"Good." The muscle in his temple shifts. He moves around and comes up behind me. "I'm going to take off your torque."

"Okay." My body tenses involuntarily.

His fingers brush the back of my neck, and a surge of heat fills my cheeks, my chest. As soon as he moves away, it passes.

He sets the necklace aside on the desk and walks over to stand in front of me again, looking lost. "So, uh, like I said, this would normally start slower, but I'm going to push you." When I don't argue, he continues. "I need you to focus. Close your eyes and picture yourself from the outside, standing there. Feel the green life, sense the cool of the air around you. Can you do that?"

I close my eyes, trying to focus and do what he said. It's a little weird, but I need to make this work. One of my foster brothers was into meditating. I try to remember what he used to do. After a second of trying to quiet my mind, I feel the air brushing at my skin and smell the plants filling the greenhouse. "Okay, I got it." I think.

"Your world is no longer what you know with your five human senses," he says. "There's going to be an added layer now. And, eventually, several more—but we'll worry about that later." I hear his shoes scrape the dirt floor like he's shifting position. "Uh, let's see . . . it's been a while since I've seen someone else go through this . . . but it's about sensing your body differently. Deeper, inside. There are parts of you, as a demi, that you haven't tapped into in your human life."

"What's that mean?"

"Like when you're sick and your bones ache with fever. Instead of just knowing you've got an infection, like you would with your human awareness, now you should be able to feel the part of your body causing the illness, the flaw, and draw your energy into that spot to repair it on a cellular level."

"Whoa. Really?"

"It'll take practice, though."

"How did I start a fire when I was sleeping? That's the part I'm worried about."

"We'll get to that." His feet shift again and he begins to pace. "First you have to feel deeper, understand where the energy is coming from in a more practical way. So what you have to do is look inward. Peel your skin back and consider your muscles, your tendons, your bones."

I scrunch up my face.

He ignores my reaction and continues. "But most importantly, you should think about the blood that feeds all of it. The life that weaves the energy through you, with your heartbeat." After a pause, he asks impatiently, "Are you focusing?"

"Yeah, yeah, totally." But I'm not sure I know how. What do my insides really look like? "So, the muscles and stuff, that's what I'm thinking of? Or the blood?"

He grunts, and I squint to peek at him. He's frowning at the floor and shaking his head. "Let's simplify it. Just listen to your heartbeat, okay?"

That I can do. I close my eyes again and go as still as possible.

"Breathe in through your nose," he says, "and listen."

I do what he says, breathing in and out slowly. A bird's song rises into my consciousness, and I hear the distant rush of the waterfall outside, but I make myself block them out and hone in on my own body as I breathe. The feel of my pulse moves to the forefront. It beats slowly in my head, in my neck and my hands, a quiet vibration. "Okay, I'm good."

"Your energy, your power, travels through your blood. It feeds your cells, keeping you young. But when uncontrolled, it can seep from your skin unwittingly, having serious effects on the outer world around you. Like the fire in your cottage. Your power spilled out through your skin—maybe because of a nightmare. You understand?"

I nod. That actually makes sense. "But the torque is supposed to stop that?"

"And yet yours didn't. So you're going to have to focus and learn quickly if you don't want to hurt anyone."

No pressure.

"You're listening to your heart, right?" he asks, his voice coming closer.

My pulse beats a little harder. I nod, keeping my eyes closed.

"Now, think about last night," he says, "when Kieran cornered you. Were you afraid?"

I pause at the reminder of the moment, not sure I want to be honest, but there's no point in playing it off. "Yeah." I was terrified, and yet I did nothing to stop it.

"What else did you feel?"

"Confused," I say quickly, and then I add more quietly, "Powerless." My throat tightens, the vulnerability rushing back in.

"Focus on your pulse and be in that moment again."

I don't want to think about it, but my mind fills with the emotions and sensations. My heart gallops faster as I remember the strange pull I felt toward Kieran, the terror when I realized I wasn't able to defend myself, the warmth of my blood smearing my neck and chest, the chill of the asphalt against my cheek before everything disappeared.

A push of heat fills my chest in a sudden surge, rolling down my arms, along my abdomen and legs—

"Okay, breathe," Faelan says urgently. His voice sounds farther away. "Come back."

I open my eyes and see he's across the room, staring at me. The heat in my body fades as quickly as it came, washing out like the tide. "What happened?"

"Did you feel anything?"

"Heat," I say. "In my chest, then my arms and legs."

He steps closer again, walking over to look at the book, reading something quickly. Then he turns back to me. "Your power washed over you, and flames coated your skin. It's called the cadence, the time between the pulse and the release."

"Excuse me?" I look down at my perfectly normal arms. That warmth was actual flames?

"How much time passed between you feeling the energy spark and the moment it spread through you?"

I shake my head. "I don't know . . . maybe two seconds?"

His lips thin. Obviously, that's bad.

"It's a start," he says. "The more you feel the process, the more you'll be able to control it. Can you try again?"

"I guess." I really just want to take a nap, but I need to figure this out.

"We'll take a quick break," he says, his voice turning gentle. "Drink some water, and we'll start over when you're ready."

TWENTY-TWO

Sage

As he reads over more of the squiggly lines, I drink my water and study his profile. He's less tense, like he's leaning into it all. I'm not sure if that should make me relax too, or put me more on guard.

Once I've had enough of a pause, we move back to our spots, and he has me close my eyes and go over the events in the alley again. And again. He asks me to try to be more aware of my body, my pulse, when the emotions come. Each time we go through it, he asks me to tell him more of what I was feeling last night, more of what happened. I don't tell him everything Kieran said, or how those silver eyes hypnotized me, but I try to be as honest as I can. Each time, the heat wave takes over later than the time before. The cadence, as he called it, stretches out several more seconds until, on the third try, he tells me to open my eyes, and I watch the last of the flames slide over my arms before sinking back into my skin.

"Remember what your energy is, that it's fire," he says. "You need to become familiar with the element, inside and out."

The orange glow crawling over me is surreal. It's impossible to truly process what I'm seeing.

Fire. Coming from my own body.

There's the strangest mix of thrill and terror in my gut.

After the fourth time, I'm totally exhausted. Faelan finally lets me take another break, pulling over a chair for me. As I drink more water and snack on some granola, he picks books out of the stacks on the desk and flips through them, then hands me a couple.

"We can't waste time," he says, "so let's go over some of the hierarchy before tonight. It's going to be too overwhelming at the ceremony without it."

That doesn't make me feel good. I'm already trying to pretend like it's not all happening so I don't have an anxiety attack. Faelan really needs to learn some social skills. I open the first book and see it's in another language, like the big one.

"Can't I just wing it tonight? I need sleep."

"You're fine," he says, completely unsympathetic. He hands me a flat gray stone with a hole in the middle. "Now read."

I look at the stone in my palm. There are swirls etched on the surface. "Is this some sort of riddle?"

He takes it from me and holds it up to his right eye. "Through the stone, read the book."

Oh. Wait . . . what?

He hands it back to me, and I turn the rock in my fingers, then look through the dime-size hole down to the open book in my lap. The unrecognizable language shifts and becomes English. "Whoa, cool."

"It's an adder stone—or a hagstone, depending on who you ask. It reveals hidden things. Eventually you won't need it, but for now it'll help."

I take it away from my face, and the script goes back to gibberish.

"Read as much of that as you can," he says. "It'll go over the power structures and how they work in our world. Basic, but vital."

I start reading, popping a chunk of granola in my mouth every few minutes, and Faelan begins organizing the books on the desk.

Eventually, he pulls up a chair beside mine and digs into one too. We read in silence for an hour or so before I start asking questions. He answers patiently but keeps directing me back to the text.

After another half hour, I think I've figured out the hierarchy of this place a little better. Maybe.

Apparently, there's a high goddess named Danu who had a lot of children, five of whom became her favorites: enter the Penta. There are a bunch of other deities in the pantheon, but none are as powerful as those five. And since the children born of Danu can't have kids with other deities for reasons of power balance, as Faelan explained it, they created their lineages with the humans. And now there are demigods and demigoddesses. Like me. Like Marius and the raven guy, Kieran. And, apparently, Faelan. And even within the demis there are rankings: a firstborn is a king or queen while the subsequent siblings are princes or princesses.

Faelan gets annoyed when I start laughing as I read.

"So . . . am I seriously a princess?" I ask, trying not to fall out of my chair.

"Yes," he mutters. "Perhaps you could consider acting like it?"

That just makes me giggle more.

There's also this group called the Cast who seem very shadowy. If I'm following it right, these beings were created to keep the demigods and demigoddesses in line. It began long, long ago, when the mother goddess, Danu, anointed and made seven humans immortal, choosing them for their mercy and wisdom to watch over her grandchildren and keep the Otherworld and its children hidden from humanity. These seven immortal humans are now known as the Cast. They stay in some sort of parallel universe, rarely crossing over to this side, usually sending envoys to speak their will. They sound a bit like untouchable government officials.

At the very bottom of the pack are the aptly named underlings. These are beings that were created by the Penta. Some were once human but changed, like shades, while others were born as what they are, like selkies, pixies, and alfar. According to this book, wraiths are made from emotions. From the descriptions, they sound a lot like poltergeists. I know firsthand that they're definitely terrifying.

Then there are the children of a union between a demi and a human, like Aelia and her coven. They aren't considered underlings—they're in a sort of side category that some people call witches. I remember Aelia calling herself a druid, which the book says are the priests of the Otherworld.

Hilarious. Aelia, a priest?

After a few more minutes, the words on the page in front of me become vague and too confusing for my foggy brain.

My eyes wander and land on Faelan.

I know I should turn away, but I can't seem to find the energy. He's really nice to look at. It's like being in the presence of a lovely painting or sculpture—you have to admire the artistry. So my gaze trails over the angles of his profile, across the strong curve of his shoulders as he leans over what he's reading, before I become mesmerized by the way that strand of hair stays tucked behind his ear, refusing to fall.

I want to scoot to the edge of my chair, get closer to him so that our shoulders will brush. But I stay where I am, baffled by my thoughts. I can't tell if the urge to touch him is coming from my human side or the side of me that burns down houses.

He looks up, like he senses me watching.

I take the opportunity to ask a question that's been rolling around in my mind since last night with Kieran. "Do I really have a sister?"

He goes still.

"Is that a bad question?" I ask.

He shuts the book with a thwack and sets it aside. "I'm not sure this is the time for that. It's a long story."

"It shouldn't be a story, it should just be yes or no," I say.

"If only it were that simple."

That sounds daunting. Aelia made it sound like this sister was a horror. Kieran made it sound like she was amazing. I don't trust either of them.

"Her name was Lily?" I prod.

His gaze skips to mine. "How did you know that?"

"That dark prince," I say.

Faelan leans back in his chair with a sigh. "Of course Kieran would bring her up." He shakes his head, annoyed. But then he says, "Her name was Líle Ó Braonáin. She was a force. She was . . . stunning," and I think there's affection in his voice.

"Is she dead or something?"

"She's been imprisoned in the Pit for several hundred years."

Unease settles over me. "That sounds bad."

He nods. "It is. It's similar to the legends of the biblical hell."

They sent my sister to goddess hell? How can that be a thing for someone so powerful? "What'd she do?"

He rises to his feet, wandering over to one of the small trees lining the other side of the greenhouse. He runs a finger along one of the larger green leaves, turning it yellow, then orange, then amber. It breaks free and floats to the ground.

I watch, confused for a second before I realize he's feeding.

"I never believed that she was fully to blame," he says, "but her crime was severe. I'm not sure how to talk to you about it. So much of what happened never made sense."

"No secrets, Faelan," I say. "I need to know everything that I can."

He touches another leaf, looking nervous. "Yeah. Agreed."

That's not what I expected him to say. I thought he'd argue.

He moves back to the table and pulls what looks like a scroll from behind a stack of books. "Just know that I wasn't trying to keep it from you. But it's not something I can speak to, not really. Not with clarity. It was the fourteenth century when she was accused of killing the king and was taken by the Cast. I was young at that time, only twelve years old.

I hadn't reached my majority and was still being kept out of the court for the most part—as Otherborn, we age the same as a human until we reach the eighteenth or nineteenth year, and then the usual entropy of aging slows to a crawl."

Again, the idea of being immortal hits me in the gut. I'm not going to die. And I'm eighteen, which means I'm going to stop aging now, basically. Completely nuts.

He continues, unaware of my turmoil. "It was a fluke that my brother allowed me to be present at the queen's feast that year. So what I know firsthand of your sister is from the limited awareness of a boy. And when I met her, she seemed very sad. I would never have thought her capable of murdering her Bonded. But they claim it's what drove her to madness and caused her to poison the earth, creating the seed for the scourge of the Black Death."

My gut twists, realizing what he's saying. She was a killer. A mass murderer. My God, didn't the plague kill tens of millions of people?

"The Cast allowed for only a single verified record of the queen," he says. "There have been theories written, novels, even a collection of poetry, but most of what we know today is hearsay." He pushes aside a couple of books and sets down the scroll he's been holding. He unrolls it a little, glancing over the faded script. He rolls and unrolls it a couple more times, looking for a passage. "The Painted Annals aren't ever the full story—nothing is, really—but they're the only full written account I've found of her birth, with sporadic, pivotal tales that reach into the year she was arrested. Everything else is rumor and stories told over centuries by unreliable mouths. Not many alive today knew her personally, and she was a very private soul. I definitely think you should read all the accounts; I'll give this first one to you so you can see for yourself, without my influence or anyone else's." He rolls up the scroll and hands it to me. "It's set to open at the birth announcement."

I take it from him, not sure what to do with it. I'm pretty positive I won't like what I find inside.

"There's more that we . . . that we need to talk about," he adds, his tone getting tense.

The scroll is heavy in my hands. Looking at it, I'm not sure I can take much more. "I hope you're kidding."

"It's about the Introduction tonight."

I shake my head, standing. "No. Enough's enough." I've definitely reached my limit.

His voice lowers in warning. "It's important."

"Yeah, well, so's my sanity." I tuck the scroll under my arm and snatch my bag of granola from the floor, heading for the door. "I'm done."

"Sage, you need to—" he starts, but he cuts off as I walk past. "Listen." And he grabs at my arm, stopping my escape.

I go still, staring at his fingers gripping my elbow. They're pressing in, insistent. "What're you doing?" Warmth slinks from his touch, spreading to my shoulder. "Let go." My gaze moves up to his face.

His features are tight before realization seems to flood him. He releases me, stepping back. Then he looks away. A few tense seconds tick by, and the memory of Kieran choking me returns full throttle, before Faelan adds again, "This is important."

I should just walk out, but he's obviously nervous because of whatever he's got to tell me. "Spit it out, then."

He hesitates for a second but finally says, "During the ceremony tonight, you'll stand in front of the Houses for the Introduction and choose your protector." He pauses, his feet shifting nervously. "You're meant to pick me. And you're to make it clear to everyone that you trust me, that this was your choice."

That seems like a rich demand at this point. "Is it really my choice?"

His brow furrows. "Of course."

"I asked Marius at dinner if he could do the protecting thing. He didn't act like that was okay."

That seems to knock him sideways a bit. "You asked Marius? Why?"

Because Marius is safer, I want to tell him. *He doesn't make me all fluttery in my chest every time I look at him.* But instead I say, "You didn't seem very . . . relatable. And then last night that dark prince, Kieran, said he was throwing his hat in the ring too. It's all completely confusing. I've got no idea what I'm supposed to do." Before I can stop the honesty, I add in a whisper, "And I think I'm sorta scared of you."

He really doesn't like that. He repeats tightly, "*I* scare you?" His fingers curl into a fist at his side. "I saved your life. Twice. Even though you nearly killed me. But Kieran *did* kill you—and somehow I'm the one who scares you?"

"That's not what I meant," I say. "This whole thing is a mess. I never asked for any of it."

"Neither did I."

I stare up at him. Somehow he's suddenly only inches away. My heart pounds a little louder in my head. I swear he's stealing all the air in the room.

"Can I just get some freaking time to think?" I ask under my breath. There's way too much going on here between him and me right now. With his eyes on me like that, I can't tell if he wants to strangle me or kiss me.

He opens up space between us again, his gaze shifting back to the ground as his shoulders sink a little. "Right. I'll tell Marius that it's possible you'll choose someone else tonight."

Even though he looks stricken by the idea, he's not pushing me into something I don't want. But maybe he's relieved I'm giving him an out; he never wanted this to begin with.

Then why does he look pissed enough to crack bricks with his teeth?

"You should go," he says. It's obvious that any understanding we built during our training today has evaporated. "Aelia will come by your cottage and help you get ready for the ceremony. We'll leave around six. It starts at sunset."

I watch his stiff features for a few more heartbeats and then quietly say, "Okay," before I turn and walk away.

TWENTY-THREE

SAGE

Aelia doesn't even knock—she just comes into the cottage exactly as the clock ticks over to 4:00 p.m. Three girls from the other night at the club follow her in: Freya, the zit critic, and the mousy girl.

"You're early," I grumble, too exhausted to get off the couch.

"We've got work to do!" Aelia says, holding up several makeup bags.

I was enjoying staring at the ceiling and finding animal shapes in the plaster. And not thinking about tonight. Because then I have to think about Faelan. And I really don't want to think about Faelan right now. The training thing was almost going well—he'd barely grunted at me the whole time. But he got so intense when the protector thing was brought up. And everything went wacky.

I left, letting him believe that I didn't trust him. And maybe I don't. I shouldn't. But why the hell did I bring up Kieran? I handled it completely wrong. I made him feel like I was considering dumping him for a creep. I'm not sure what I was thinking.

What a mess.

The scroll he gave me is sitting on the coffee table, and I haven't looked at it. I want to know what all the fuss is about my sister. But then I don't. Isn't it bad enough that my fake human family was screwed up? Does my real supernatural one have to be a mess too? It's not like I have to end up like her.

Maybe not knowing is better.

"Come on, street urchin," Aelia says, walking over to the couch. She waves me up. "We're going to need the full two hours."

I sit up, and Freya appears beside Aelia.

"Does she still have that spell on her?" Freya asks.

Aelia rolls her eyes. "No, Freya, gods. I told you, her energy is weird, okay? That's the whole point."

The zit critic frowns at me. "Seriously, she looks different, though. What'd you do to her since last night? She's, like, almost decent looking."

The mousy girl watches it all from the other side of the room. "Really, Victoria, I think she's sorta pretty."

The zit critic, Victoria, smirks. "You would think that, Rayane."

"And her hair," Freya says, squinting at me, "I wanna borrow her conditioner."

Aelia grunts. "Can we just get her to the vanity, please?" She takes my arm to help me off the couch. I start to squirm, but Victoria takes my other arm, and I'm outnumbered.

We're across the room when Victoria stops tugging me. She turns me around to face her and looks me over. She sniffs the air at my neck. "Do you smell that?" she asks Aelia. "Is she marked?"

"No," Aelia snaps. "Stop smelling her, it's weird."

I think of the new scar on my neck. "What do you mean *marked*?"

Aelia gives me a look to shut up. "Nothing. Let's just get your face fixed."

"She has nice eyebrows," the mousy Rayane says.

"Then marry them. Gods, Ray, you're so obvious," Victoria says. "Stop drooling over the newblood." Then she whispers out the side of her mouth to me. "She has demi envy because her druid blood is weak."

"I do not," Rayane says.

Freya snorts.

"What do you mean by *marked*?" I ask again as they shove me into the vanity chair. I didn't even know this was a vanity; I thought it was a desk. But now I see the thing I thought was a pencil holder is actually holding long lipsticks.

Freya runs her fingers through my hair. "It means a fellow demi has claimed you."

I sit up straighter. "What?" That sounds very, *very* bad.

"No one's claimed her," Aelia says, shooing Freya away from my hair. "Stop being ridiculous." But I can see she's nervous—her hands shiver a little when she waves at Freya.

"She sure smells claimed to me," Victoria says. "And you know I have the nose. But I can't tell who it is."

I stand up from the chair and back away, holding my hands up. "Stop touching me and smelling me and being insane—just tell me what is going on."

Freya leans forward and says slowly, like I'm dumb, "We're putting makeup on you for the Introduction."

"You're going to look so much better," Victoria says.

"Though you already look nice," Rayane adds.

Exasperation fills me as I stare at their ridiculously calm faces. "Everyone out!" They all blink in unison, not moving, so I add, "Now!" A small spark flicks to life on my right, and the tissue box on the vanity bursts into flames.

I gape at the sudden blaze.

Aelia moves her hand over the blackening box a few times, snuffing the fire out with her own magic. "Go on, girls, I'll crack this solo. Just hang by the pool and I'll call you in for shoes." She coughs and waves at the smoke in her face.

They seem all too eager to back off now and quickly slip out, Victoria looking over her shoulder a few times before I hear the front door shut.

Aelia turns to me with a huff. "You seriously need to control yourself. Those girls have very powerful fathers. They can't know that your torque isn't working right."

"Oh great! So why'd you bring them here?"

"You're a project. I can't fix this alone." She motions to my body. She pauses, though, looking at me more closely. "You *do* look different, don't you? Hmm." She pinches my arm fat. "A little Faelan does a body good, I guess." She winks at me.

"What?" I step away and cradle my arm.

"You fed off Faelan last night, and it seems to agree with you. You're a little less praying mantis and more grasshopper."

I look down at my body. Faelan did this?

"But now we may have a bit of a problem," she says. She leans on the vanity and frowns at me.

"What—why?"

"I can glamour you to an extent, but Kieran will see right through it. After what he did to you, and you staying under without healing for so long, you should be pretty dead. But here you'll be. All supple—well, near enough—and wide-eyed. He'll know you have enough power to resist death, and he'll be even more determined to demand his ancient rights to you." She blows at her bangs. "But that's all nonsense, and I'm totally sure the Cast will *never* give that a thumbs-up. I mean, do we really want to relive the thrills of the Dark Ages? I think not."

I can't even ask any of the questions screaming in my head, because I'm too confused. I touch the scar on my neck, running my fingers along the thin rise of flesh. "I'm marked by that raven freak, aren't I?"

"Not the scar, no," Aelia says. "If only. No, the mark of a demi is done with an energy merge, and it's impossible to hide. I put a glamour on your scar this morning, so my girls wouldn't notice it. But I couldn't hide the smell of whoever scent-stamped you."

"It wasn't the raven guy?"

She shrugs. "Maybe, but I doubt it." She leans forward conspiratorially. "My money's on Faelan, but it could've been my dad."

"Ew!"

"It's not for sex, perv. It's a protection. To keep the other demis from getting any ideas about messing with you. I mean, the mark only works if you accept it, so this is sorta on you. Except I can tell you're clueless about it by the fact that you look about to vom." She sighs. "Gods' bones, what did I do to earn you?"

She's right. I'm going to barf. I focus on breathing and ask, "How did they put the mark on me?" It feels like a violation, an invasion, whatever she says about me being a part of it.

"It's subtle, a touch. And don't worry, it'll wear off if you reject it." She takes me into the closet and begins hunting for something.

I stand in the middle of the walk-in, feeling powerless. "So it could be your dad who did it, or . . ."

"Faelan." She smirks. "Is it so tough to imagine?" She turns and grabs something off a hanger. "You hate the guy that much?"

"I don't hate him, I . . ."

"Oh, come on, admit it." She nudges my shoulder playfully. "The guy is sex on an untouchable stick." She holds up a dress in front of me. "And he kisses like thunder rumbling through your body." She closes her eyes, like she's pulling up a memory. "I so wish I'd pushed that further. An eternal regret."

My chest stings. "You've kissed Faelan?"

She laughs, hanging the dress back up and taking out another one. "I know, I stooped. But he's poison, that one. And that celibacy vow makes him all the more yum."

She kissed him. And it sounds like it was mutual. Which is weird since Faelan acts more annoyed with Aelia than anything. And what does she mean, *celibacy vow*? Is the guy a secret monk or something? But if he is, why was he sleeping in the nude with Niamh? The memory of him in Marius's office, looking away from the half-naked woman, comes back to me. And how he seems to go distant when we get remotely close to connecting on any deeper level—wait! Hold on. I'm getting distracted.

"So, it wears off," I blurt out, trying to stop my brain from going further down the Faelan rabbit hole. "The mark, I mean?"

"Oh yeah, no biggie. I'd be way more concerned about Kieran tonight." When she sees the panicked look on my face, she adds, "Not that you should be concerned, that's not what I meant. It'll be fine. This is just an introduction to some of the interested parties. You'll let them all look at you, you'll choose your protector, then it's done." She holds up a second dress and smiles wickedly. "And if I have anything to say about it, you'll look fabulous doing it."

Just the idea of being in the same space as that raven guy terrifies me. Why would I put myself back in his orbit after what he did to me? I mean, the guy *killed* me. Not *dead* dead, but that was just a happy coincidence. And the fact that he nearly succeeded seems not to be even a blip on anyone's radar.

"So people get punished in this world, right?" I ask.

Aelia starts grabbing lacy things from a drawer. "It depends, why?"

"Well, Kieran did almost kill me, so—"

She snorts, interrupting me. "Nothing will happen to our favored prince for a vague accident, trust me—I mean, he wasn't *technically* trying to kill you. Plus, his sister totally has the Cast in her pocket and enough equity with the other Penta that no one would mess with her brother. Maybe if you'd actually died, but . . . well, you're an all-powerful demi and whatnot. No one is going to feel sorry for you."

Her flippant words soak into me, and I'm filled with the urge to run from it all, but I have to stay focused. I need to learn to control this thing. Then maybe I'll be able to reclaim my freedom. In the meantime, with the dark prince's unpredictability, I should probably learn how to defend myself while I'm here.

I wonder how Kieran would look with his hair on fire. I bet he wouldn't be so eager to trap me in an alley after that.

For tonight, Faelan will be with me. And Marius. It kills me that I have to depend on any guy. I've always just depended on myself. But it's sort of life and death at this point; whatever Aelia says about an accident, I'm not sure I buy it. I just have to hope the freak won't try anything in front of the rest of them.

TWENTY-FOUR

FAELAN

After Sage left to get ready, I didn't have the balls to call Marius and tell him what's coming tonight when she's asked who she chooses for her protector—how it's probably not going to be me. How it might even be bloody Kieran at this point for all I know. Because I fucked it up.

Instead I went for a swim and showered, reciting *Beowulf* to quiet the commotion in my head. I'm in an extremely pissy mood by the time I'm ready. I can't stop thinking about how I grabbed her—what the hell was that? And after what Kieran did to her . . . dick move. I know too little about practicing patience. I was never the right one for this task—I'm not sure what Marius was thinking.

I can hear Aelia's coven out by the pool, and I don't want to leave my cottage. So I sit in the greenhouse and wait for the sound of Sage's door opening across the walkway.

Time passes slowly. As it becomes obvious we're going to be late, I consider walking over and banging on Sage's door. But the less time I spend with her right now, the better.

My head is too big of a mess.

But it'll be over now, if she's decided against me. And that should be a relief. I'll just go into retirement like I planned—if Marius doesn't have me sanctioned for my failure in handling this. Somehow, the rocky shores of Erin don't sound as tempting as they did a few days ago, though. Not when I have this bloody compulsion to help her, to be there watching. I need to get my shit together.

I hear her door click open. When I step out on the front porch I spot them, Aelia and Sage, and—my thoughts go still, every part of me focusing on the redhead walking across the patio toward me. She's stunning. Not beautiful in a typical sense: her edges are sharp and something about her clothes doesn't quite match her personality. But she's arresting. Everything in me wants to touch her.

I clench my hands into fists and step back.

"What's wrong, Faelan?" Aelia asks with a smirk. "Don't you think Sage looks nice?"

"Her dress is too short," I say.

"Wow, that face," Victoria says. "You look completely repulsed, hunter." And she giggles, like she's pleased with the idea. "You should've seen her an hour ago."

I didn't mean to feed the sharks. I glare at her before I turn to Sage, ready to apologize. But when I see Sage's expression, my words evaporate. I swallow hard. She's not looking at me, but there are threads of embarrassment and discomfort filtering from her shoulders. It makes me want to tear into the vapid Victoria, and tell her that her lipstick and caked-on eye makeup make her look like one of the trollops who used to stroll around outside the pub in my old village.

Instead I say, "You look nice, Sage." When her eyes move to mine in surprise, I feel the need to add, "You're very put together." And then I clear my throat, because it's either that or I keep digging the hole.

"You did a fabulous job, Aelia," Freya says. "She's amazingly less gross."

"Pretty," Rayane says.

"We need to go," I say a bit too harshly.

"Sage should walk in with us, I think," Aelia says. "They need to know she has more of us than just my father behind her."

I look over at the four girls, Aelia and her coven, and wonder what she thinks they'll prove, walking in with Sage. My guess is she thinks Sage's future status will help raise her own clout. I don't like the idea of Sage being used as a prop by Aelia.

"She comes in with me," I say, "and you can follow."

Aelia gives me an irritated look, but she doesn't argue. "Fine, but only because I think that's what Daddy would want, not because you said so."

"Whatever, woman." I motion for Sage to follow me. "Come on."

Aelia moves into my space, more than irritated now. "Don't call me *woman* in that condescending tone! *Male*." She whooshes past, her hair flicking my arm, saying over her shoulder, "You could've put more effort into that outfit, you know. Off-brand slims, seriously? Should've worn the Calvins I got you. At least leave your hair down for a change."

Her entourage follows her, Freya glancing back at me with a wink. "I think you look yummy," she whispers. "That sweater is super touchable." And then they all flitter away on their designer heels, long hair flowing behind them, leaving Sage and me alone.

Sage watches them go like she wishes she could follow.

"Would you rather go with them?" I ask.

She turns back and gives me a wide-eyed look. "No, it's fine. I'm fine."

"You seem to be getting along with Aelia. It's odd. You're such . . . polar opposites."

She studies me for a second like she's trying to decide if I'm complimenting her, then she relaxes a little, more herself again. "The girl is crazy and exasperating. But she's actually pretty informative." She considers and then adds, "She's explained loads more than you have."

"Is that right?" The spark in her eyes brings a surprised lightness to my chest. "*Loads*, aye?"

"Don't be Irish at me."

I tip my head and give her a taste of the old me. "No choice, *macushla*."

A questioning look passes over her features like I've affected her in some way with my endearment. She starts picking nervously at the front of her dress. "Sometimes you're actually a little British, though. Has Marius rubbed off on you?"

"Aye, maybe." And I can't help being captivated by the soft skin of her shoulder as she shrugs, by the small creases that form when she crinkles her nose, the shiny coral of her glossed lips, full and lovely— *gods, what am I doing?*

No. She's not lovely. She's average. Simple. Practically human. "Let's go," I say quickly and walk away. I have to hope she'll follow me, because I don't want to glance back and see the surprise on her face that I know is there.

~

We arrive at Lunar Hall, in downtown LA, and I'm amazed by how many Otherbloods are crowding around the front, waiting to be let in through the main building into the back courtyard, where the ceremony will take place. It wouldn't be good for Sage and me to wander around in the pack and get noticed. She's meant to make an entrance at the right time—it's what Marius would want. So I lead her through a side door, slipping past the guards.

Once we get through the main lobby and find our way out to the banquet courtyard, I realize how large the crowd really is. This is no small tribunal. Pixies and shades are thick as smoke on the ground floor, gathering in groups by their Houses around the circular courtyard, whispering to each other. And multiple demis from every House are sitting in elaborate seats along the half-moon-shaped balcony. Several would've had to come in from overseas. Word must have gotten around that this would be a more high-profile Introduction. Demi Introductions are rare, but none are as rare as a daughter of Brighid. I assumed Marius would keep that off the public radar, but Aelia's gallivanting all over town likely blew any secrets about our newcomer.

On the half-moon balcony overlooking the torchlit courtyard I see two sons of Lyr and a daughter of Arwen—Queen Beatrix, sneering down at the crowds as always, her hooked nose and crooked teeth worn with pride. I see my father's eldest, Finbar, the first son of Cernunnos. There are several alfar around him. And the Cast's envoy, who Marius invited, is standing close. The bald man appears to be intent on speaking to my brother, his thin body stiff, his feminine features pinched. The sight of the important man talking like that with Finbar fills me with unease. Finbar doesn't need any more power in the demi ranks.

But then I'm distracted, because off to the side I spot Kieran and his sister Princess Mara. My steps slow, and my hand moves to the dagger at my waist before I realize I need to take a breath. I'm too tense. This is not the time or place, even if I do have the urge to stab something.

Mara's looking at us, her silver-blue gaze sharpening as it falls on Sage. She leans over and whispers in her brother's ear, her long nails petting the head of a young shade kneeling at her feet. Kieran turns slightly to look. When he spots me, he nods as if we were meeting in a pub.

I don't bother to nod back. He can go fuck himself with his formality. I'm about to say something to Sage to distract her, so she won't notice him there watching—I can already feel her nerves prickling my skin—but then ahead of us a shade starts to feed from a cocktail waitress, so I steer her away into the crowd.

"Oh crap," she whispers, moving closer to me. "Who are all these people? I thought this wasn't supposed to be a huge deal."

"Apparently, things changed," I say, searching the faces for Marius. "Word must've gotten out."

She shakes her head and starts backing up, away from the masses. I take her by the arm and lead her out of the pack, over to the shadows behind the trees that rim the courtyard. "Don't run off now."

She tries to yank away from my grip and only succeeds in stumbling into a bush. I pull her back to her feet. "Calm down. You'll cause a scene."

"Calm down?" she hisses. "How in the hell can I calm down when I feel like I'm about to walk into a nest of vipers?"

She's not far off. "You have all the power here, Sage. Don't let the unknown scare you away from what you deserve by rights." I notice a few heads turning to watch us, so I take her deeper into the shadows, behind a fountain, where only the sound of splashing water and the flicker of torchlight surround us.

"What do I deserve?" In the moonlight, her eyes are a dark emerald.

"You deserve . . ." I feel my mouth begging to say things I can't say, things I can't mean. "You deserve power, the power your mother goddess would wish for you to have."

"I don't want any power over other people, Faelan. I just want freedom." Her hand goes to her mouth, and she chews on a nail for a second. "All my life, I've been waiting to be free from people who had control over me. From having to depend on people who always screw me over. And now it's all tightening around me again. But worse. This . . ." She looks through the shadows to the torches and the hundreds of souls waiting to meet her. "This is so much worse."

"Then you should take this power, Sage." I let go of her arm and nod to the courtyard. "Take it from them, and make them give you what you want. Those bastards don't deserve any of it." I'm a little shocked by my truthful outburst. I mean every word.

Amazement fills her face too as she looks up at me. The sweet smell of it curls around us—and with the smell comes the memory of her in my arms when she fed from me. She's so close right now, so warm, and gods, I want to touch her more. Danu help me, I want to touch her cheek, to run my thumb over her brow. Slide it over her coral lips . . .

"I think something's wrong with me," she whispers, looking away.

I was just thinking the same thing. "Why?"

"Because I shouldn't feel this stuff that I'm feeling for . . . certain *people*." She puts her fingers to her temple and squeezes her eyes shut. "I've got too much twisted shit going on in here."

"Nothing's wrong with you, Sage." *It's me who's wrong.*

"You don't understand," she says, sounding sure. She starts to pace back and forth. "I've got all these feelings. And I'm not sure how to shake it off or get my head straight now. I nearly died last night and I fed off you and I can't even wrap my head around it. But now I'm here and I have to go out there and fake it, and since my torque isn't working right I'm probably going to accidentally melt off someone's face if they look at me crooked."

"That's not how it works."

She stops pacing and gives me an accusing look. "Aren't you even curious why my torque isn't working?" she asks, her voice rising.

I step a little closer to lower the volume. "Look, we'll bring it to Marius's attention tomorrow, right? For now we just need to get through tonight."

"How do I know I'm not going to do something horrible? All that stuff we did today isn't going to help me stop anything big—I can't control this."

Her desperation is palpable. I want to ease her worry, but I'm not sure what to say. It's not as if this Introduction can be put off now. I've never heard of a torque not working before. I just assumed her power was overwhelming it, not that it was faulty. But with what happened in the alley, it's hard to tell.

"Focus on something calm and soothing," I say.

She glowers at me. "Seriously? You want me to go to my happy place?"

"Isn't there anything in all of this that makes you feel good?" I ask.

Her features soften as she studies me, considering my question, then color rises in her cheeks.

"What?" I ask. "What's wrong?"

"Nothing," she mutters, looking away. "I told you, I'm a mess."

I'm completely lost. "You're making this impossible to fix, Sage. Just talk to me."

"I can't. You of all people I can *not* talk to about this."

"That seems ridiculous."

"Well, that's me. Ridiculous Sage. She burns down guesthouses and wakes up hot naked men who attack her with birds and apparently kiss Aelia."

"What the bloody hell are you on about?"

"Who knows."

I shake my head, exasperated. "You've lost me, woman."

She covers her face with her hands and moans into them. "I'm sorry. I don't mean to make you loony right along with me."

I study her, trying to decide how to calm her. She's been thrown into this, forced to absorb a lot in only days, when most Otherborn have years to get used to our world. She's handled it amazingly well, considering.

I soften my voice. "It's all right, Sage."

She looks up from her hands. "Don't be nice to me when I'm acting nuts."

"I promise not to let it become a habit," I say softly, reaching out to brush a strand of hair from her face before I can stop myself. I shouldn't be touching her.

Her eyes lock on mine and something odd passes between us. There's a tug at the center of my chest, pulling me toward her.

I keep my feet planted, but as I lower my hand, my fingers brush her shoulder, her soft skin warm against mine.

The torch a few feet away hisses, the flame brightening a little.

"It's you," she says, her voice barely audible over the sounds of the fountain.

I frown.

She shifts closer. "You're the only thing that makes me feel like I might belong here."

My pulse picks up.

There's pain reflected in her eyes as she looks up at me. "But you terrify me at the same time," she whispers. And her hand comes up, resting gently on my chest. It shivers against my sweater, revealing her fear.

A twinge pricks just under her palm, and I know she's pulling threads of life from me. For some reason, I don't care. "Why do I terrify you?"

She lowers her arm back to her side and the sensation fades.

"Because," she says, "that part of me that needs, that wants . . . it wants you."

She means her hunger. She feels her hunger spark when she's with me. It must be scaring her. The trouble is, I feel something too. But I have no excuse.

I step back. "It's all right. After you choose your protector tonight, they'll help you learn to control your hunger. It won't feel like this forever." And as I look at her, my own body reacting, I'm really hoping she's about to settle on it not being me. This girl could turn out to be the death of my freedom.

She turns away. "Right."

Pain filters into the air in a soft mist near her shoulders, and an unwelcome spark of guilt hits me.

An idea forms in my mind, and even as I tell myself it's horrible, I decide I want to try it, anyway. Marius said I should make her feel settled. That I should use whatever means necessary to help her stay connected to us. And the appalling bloody truth is, I want to feel her one more time.

So I step closer, ignoring my quickening pulse. "I can show you. Just once."

Her wide eyes shine in the moonlight, full of confusion.

"You can control your hunger, Sage." I let myself reach out again, sliding my palm down her arm, taking her wrist in my hand. "You just have to understand it." I place her palm on the side of my neck, not letting my eyes leave hers. A gold mist filters from her chest as her fingers slide over my nape, and a sting follows as she begins to pull, already feeding. I can tell she's not aware of it, though. "You have to listen to the stirring in your belly and make it bend to your will, instead of the other way around. Can you feel it?"

She nods slowly.

"Tell me what it feels like," I say as the familiar sting grows.

She licks her lips. "Warm and . . . comforting." Her fingers flex against my neck.

"That's the pull. What else do you feel?"

"My body is tingling and I smell . . . you."

"That's my energy filling your skin."

"It is?"

"You're feeding right now."

Her eyes grow and she tries to jerk away, but I hold her hand to the side of my neck.

"Don't be afraid," I say. "Remember how it felt today, your energy in your blood. Just let yourself feel what it's doing a little at a time. And then push it back down. Like you're closing a door inside yourself."

"I don't want to hurt you," she says, threads of panic in her voice.

I move closer until our chests are nearly touching and brush my fingers over her cheek. "Close your eyes and let yourself understand it, Sage. You'll never learn to control it if you don't try."

Her eyes flutter shut. The sting becomes an ache in my head and shoulder as her pull deepens, but I stay focused on her, on her chest rising and falling, her teeth tugging on her bottom lip, and I find her breath echoing mine.

"I feel it," she says, in awe. "I'm pushing it back."

And sure enough, the pain in my neck and shoulder dissipates, only the heat left behind in my skin. Her eyes open, and a smile lights her face. But as she begins to back away, I have the exact opposite of a sane response.

My body leans in. My lips find hers. And every molecule I'm made of sighs with relief.

She gasps into my mouth, her surprise filtering between us, making me grip her neck and pull her closer. I need her closer. My fingers slip into her hair, and a new surge of energy spreads through my chest. But this time it's not from her hungry nature. This time it's mine. As my power surges through me, pushing me, forcing me to want more.

Her body relaxes into mine. My palm skims her bare arm, slides to her shoulder, my thumb playing over her clavicle, her jaw, caressing her neck, deepening our connection. She's warm, soft, beautiful as she falls into it with me. I can't help wishing we were anywhere but here as our labored breathing fills the space around us, the kiss stretching out, my pulse thrashing in my chest, the moment ready to drown me.

In the back of my mind I realize there's no more pull from her, no sense of her feeding from me. And I'm stunned at her control when I have none. She touches my face, her fingertips delicate against my jaw, trembling. I smell her elation. I sense her fear blossom into delicate hope. And it cuts into me, the realization that this is more than a simple kiss to her. This is true affection.

But she can't feel that for me. Not me.

I jerk away, nearly tipping into the fountain in my urgency to get my hands off her.

She stares at me, her mouth open in shock. "Wow," she breathes. Her fingers move to her lips. "That was . . ."

"Not smart," I say, amazed at how calm I sound. My body is pissed that I'm so far away from her. My hands ache.

"Thunder," she says.

"What?"

She shakes her head slowly. "Nothing."

TWENTY-FIVE

SAGE

"I'm sorry," Faelan says in a tight voice. "I never should've . . . that wasn't right." His body is tense enough to crack. He looks ready to bolt.

"I'm fine, Faelan," I say, trying to reassure him. "Everything is fine." But I can hardly believe what we did. Not just the kiss, which was—*wow*. My legs are officially useless and I'm ruined forever.

But I controlled it. I controlled the hunger. I took that thing in me that I felt this afternoon and forced it down deep until it was barely a buzz in my head. He was right: once I understood it better I could manipulate it. And I did.

And then he kissed me.

Oh wow, did he kiss me.

Not that he's happy about it. He's obviously not. I'd be offended by his reaction if I wasn't so relieved that I'd pushed back this *thing* inside me.

"Thank you," I say.

His brow goes up in surprise.

"For helping me." I can't keep a grin from surfacing. "I can't believe I stopped it. I feel so much better."

He watches me like he doesn't believe me, and he's waiting for the other shoe to drop.

But I just smile up at him. "I pictured it like hot coals in a box, and all I had to do was put the lid on top, and poof! It went out. Well, mostly, anyway. It was like the embers in my chest went from a burning ache to simmering." I want to touch him again, but I'm worried he'll pull away, so I just add, "I'm really grateful you let me try. I know how dangerous it is."

"I shouldn't have let that happen," he says, pained.

Irritation begins to surface, and I'm about to ask him what's so wrong with kissing me, and why he looks like he just ran over his neighbor's dog when he should be happy his experiment worked, but a familiar voice breaks in.

"There you two are," Aelia says. "Well done keeping her out of eyesight, Faelan." She looks back and forth between us. "Did I interrupt something?"

"When does this thing start?" I ask.

She smirks at me, not missing my deflection. "Daddy's just arrived. He'd like you both to meet him in the gallery upstairs. The girls and I will be in the crowd, and you'll be presented on the second-floor stage, like a real princess." She touches my arm reassuringly. She's being nice? "Good luck," she says with a wink. And then she turns on her heels and saunters away.

"We should go," Faelan says, his tone heavy. "Are you ready?"

"No, but who cares. Let's get this done."

I follow him across the stone and moss pathway, along the line of amber-colored trees. Neither of us speak. It's a relief not having to look at the panic on his face, since all I can see is the back of his head.

The evening air is full of the sound of hissing torches and gossip coming from the courtyard. It's an unforgettable sight, the soft golden glow flickering over the beautiful people, their expensive clothes shimmering, their perfect features and figures making it seem like a movie set instead of real life.

The location looks like an ancient Roman temple, with tall white pillars holding up a crescent-shaped balcony. The most striking people are sitting up there, looking down as if they're watching from Mount Olympus. My guess is that those are the "royalty," the demis. Like me.

I would laugh at the idea of sitting with them if I didn't feel like hiding in a janitor's closet.

We go through a side door into the main building and then over to the elevator. As we step in and the doors slide closed, I can't help flashing back to the last time we were in an elevator together, a couple of days ago. I was so clueless. It makes me wonder how clueless I am right now. How much more insane will my reality get after tonight?

At least I'm making progress, if only a little. I just have to get this part over with so I can learn how to fully control the madness in me. And then I can get out, knowing I'm not going to accidentally hurt anyone.

This world is never going to be mine. If that horror in the alley last night didn't show me that, nothing will.

Faelan pushes the button for the second floor, then steps to the other side of the elevator, as far away from me as he can get. I want to tell him to calm down, that it was just a kiss. I consider a thousand things to say, but instead I just breathe and try not to look as nervous as I feel. Nervous about myself, about what just happened between him and me, about what we're walking into.

"You'll be fine," he says quietly, surprising me.

The elevator dings, the doors open, and he's stepping out before I can respond. I trail behind him, down a hall and into a wide ballroom. Marius is standing near a pair of French doors that appear to open to the balcony where the regal people are sitting.

Marius turns at the click-click of my heels on the wood floor. A smile of satisfaction curls his lips when he spots us. He holds out a hand, and I find myself taking it.

He's in a well-fitted charcoal blazer and a black dress shirt, strikingly handsome. A beaded necklace is around his neck; it must be his torque, keeping his powers under control. The beads look like tiny seashells, and there's a copper medallion with a milky blue stone at the center of a wave pattern. The design probably represents water—his element? It makes me want to look at my own medallion again, makes me wonder what keeps it from working right, especially now that Faelan seems just as baffled by the whole thing.

Marius holds my hand tightly, comforting. "My, my, don't you look lovely, sweet girl," he says, almost fatherly. He touches my shoulder and then releases me. "Look at our princess, Faelan. How will you survive this transition, boy?" He smiles.

Faelan clears his throat and gives Marius a stiff grin.

My gut clenches.

"Sir," Faelan begins, his voice tense, "some feelings have changed and I need to be clear—"

I break in before Faelan can let his boss think that I might've fired him. "I need to ask you something, Marius," I say, even though I don't want to get Faelan in trouble. I just need to get my head straight. Too much is happening all at once. "It's important."

Faelan glances sideways at me.

Marius raises his brow. "What is it, young Sage?"

I consider what I want to know before walking out into the lion's den. I have a million unanswered questions. So much I don't get yet. But one question rings in my head. "What happens if I don't want to take on any kind of royal thing? Like, in a few weeks when this is all said and done, when I'm supposed to decide which house I want to commit to and all that, could I choose to just, like, be a real estate agent instead?"

His eyes narrow. "Why are you asking this?"

"I don't want to be some sort of princess," I say, trying to be as honest as I can. "I want to just chill and be me. I've always wanted to help people. I thought about going to school to be a psychologist for a while, to work with kids."

Marius doesn't seem to know how to process what I'm saying. *"Chill?"*

Faelan steps forward, like a guard. "She's overwhelmed, sir, that's all."

Marius keeps frowning at me. "You wish to live a human life still. Even knowing what you are? Why?"

"I just want the choice," I say.

"If only it were that simple." He considers for a moment. "There is a sacrifice for your blood, young Sage. The order of the Otherworld is old and carries many benefits, but a demi cannot live a fully human life without a heavy cost. Most Otherborn have tasks in society to keep our fingers on the pulse of culture or creativity, even politics. But no one is ever truly free when they are born of Other."

His words fall like shattering glass in my ears. The understanding of what I've been pulled into hits me full force. *No one is ever truly free . . .* "I can't do this," I say, shaking my head, suddenly very sure.

Faelan gives me a panicked look. "Yes, you can. You've got to."

I meet his gaze.

"You can do this, Sage," he says, sounding sure. "You're strong. You can become iron. Just make them believe you mean it, even if you don't, and you'll find a way to get what you want, just like we talked about. Take the power from them. Use it."

"I'm not strong," I say. All I want to do in this moment is the same thing I always do: run.

Strong people don't run.

"You are," he says. "I've never met anyone like you."

His words filter around us, and I feel them in my bones. It almost makes me believe them.

"Whether you do this tonight or not," Marius says, "your blood will Emerge soon. Either you'll learn to control it here with us or you'll go hide in the human world and end up hurting people. Likely killing them."

My mouth goes dry.

"Listen to Faelan," Marius adds. "Let the journey begin and see where it takes you."

I stare past them both, through the glass doors and out into the night. The crowds are too far away to see, the royal beings out in the veranda unclear through the glass. "I need Faelan with me out there," I say, surprising myself.

"What?" Faelan asks, sounding as shocked as I feel.

"Of course," Marius says. "I will present you, and once that's finished you can claim him as your protector, then he'll come out to stand behind you."

Faelan steps forward, saying under his breath, "But Sage, I thought—"

I cut him off, still talking to Marius. "No. I want him with me the whole time." It suddenly feels important for everyone to see him beside me from the beginning.

Marius doesn't look sure but he nods. "Very well. Are you comfortable with that, Faelan?"

Faelan shakes his head. "That's not what you wanted, Sage."

He's sort of right, but he's been there for me during all of this mess—even after he thought I rejected him, he was there, showing me how to be okay. I'm not used to that, so I don't think I really noticed it until right now. But I'm sure as hell not going to pretend it doesn't mean something to me. "I'm asking you to be my protector, Faelan. Will you?"

He studies my face.

"Yes or no?" I ask.

Marius looks between us, concern filling his eyes. "What's going on, Faelan?"

Faelan shakes his head again. "Things have happened."

"What things?" Marius asks, his voice low.

"He's not sure what to do with me," I say, not looking away from Faelan.

His neck muscles tense. "That isn't right. And you know it."

"Are you backing out of our agreement, Faelan?" Marius asks.

"No, sir," Faelan says.

"I'm asking you to be my protector, Faelan," I say more gently, trying to figure out how to explain better how I feel without saying too much. "I'm not asking because I have to, but because I trust you—I don't know why, I barely know you, but I do: I trust you. Whatever else I feel. Right now, in this moment, in spite of everything, you might be the only person here that I do trust." It's amazing. And terrifying.

The tension slides from his features.

"You've already helped me," I add. "And protected me, and saved me. At least get the credit. Walk out there with me and do what you promised."

"If I go out there with you," Faelan says, "it'll look like we're equals. And we're not."

"It will ruffle feathers," Marius says. "But the House of Brighid doesn't tend to worry about such things."

"I can walk out there alone," I say, "but I'm not above anyone. I won't pretend that I am."

"Come now," Marius says, gripping Faelan's shoulders. "Our princess is asking you to be at her side."

Faelan looks a little ill, but he gives me a nod. "Fine."

"Very good," Marius says, jubilant. "I'll go out and announce you. And you and Faelan can follow as soon as you hear your name. Once we're all out there, they'll ask you a set of questions, and you'll answer simply, then we'll be finished."

"What questions?" I ask, nerves sparking again. I didn't think there'd be a test.

"You'll do fine," he says. He gives me one more smile and takes hold of the door handle. "Are you ready for the chase to begin?" A sparkle of mischief lights his eyes as he opens the door.

Then he walks out into the spotlight.

My stomach churns. I'm about to go out in front of a hugely powerful—and *deadly*—group of people and act like I fit in with them. When I really, *really* don't. And at this point, I hope I never do.

"Why did you change your mind?" Faelan asks.

"I didn't," I say.

He gives me a doubtful look.

I shrug. "You assumed I wouldn't choose you."

He shakes his head, obviously agitated. "The time of Emergence will pass quickly," he says, maybe just as much to himself. "In the end, tonight is a small thing."

"Then why does it feel so monumental?"

"Because you're entering the unknown."

I can see Marius, speaking out into the courtyard. He begins talking about the goddess Brighid. Her powers, her goodness. How she's given them a new gift, how she's my mother.

God help me.

"But things will play out," Faelan says. "One way or the other."

I hear my name, and Marius turns and looks back, nodding at us.

"For good or bad?" I ask.

Faelan faces me, his mouth set in determination. "You'll just have to trust in the good." Then he moves aside to let me go in front of him.

I allow myself to feel the strength in his eyes and step out onto the balcony.

~

It's surreal. The cool night air brushing against my skin, the stunning beauty of the onlookers, the soft torchlight on their upturned faces—so many faces looking at me.

There are at least two dozen regal figures seated along the balcony railing, on either side of the small raised platform that Marius, Faelan, and I are standing on. They crane their necks to look at me.

And then I spot him. Last time I saw him it was in a shadowed alley, and only for a few minutes, but that face is seared into my mind.

The dark prince, Kieran.

Marius is speaking, but my pulse is too loud in my ears to hear what he's saying. Everything around me is going blurry. I can't look away from the silver eyes staring holes through me from several seats away. He doesn't look angry, but his intensity is obvious. Like he wants to pin me against a wall again.

The black-haired woman sitting beside him leans over and whispers in his ear, her dark red lips nearly touching his cheek. A slow, dry smile tips his mouth.

My insides squirm.

Aelia's words flash in my head, how he thinks I belong to him because of some ancient claim. But what does that even mean? After what Marius said about my freedom, or lack of it, it makes the idea of Kieran marking me that much more terrifying. If that's true, then I can't get out of this place fast enough.

I back up a step to get away from his searching eyes, but I find myself pressing into Faelan. His hand grips my arm, and he leans close, whispering in my ear, "Steady now."

My skin warms at his touch. I make myself breathe.

Kieran's jaw tightens. His nails look like they're digging into the wooden arms of his chair.

Marius's voice comes again, and this time I catch my name. ". . . a child lost in the fog of humanity, we're so grateful to our goddess that she's been found—our Princess Sage."

A tempered applause fills the air, like they're all too highbrow to show emotion. I have a sudden fear that I'm supposed to curtsy or something.

But Marius holds out a hand for me to step all the way forward. "Let's begin, shall we?"

I pull my mind from Kieran and slowly move in front of Marius. My feet don't work very well, and I almost trip. Is this balcony stable? It feels like everything around me is shaking. Or maybe I'm shaking. Yep, I'm shaking.

"Have you come of your own free will, Princess Sage?" Marius asks. I nod, and he says under his breath, "You must say it aloud."

I try to project to the audience. "Yes, I'm here of my free will." I'm stunned by how normal my voice sounds.

"Very good," Marius says. He bows as he lifts my hand to his lips, brushing my knuckles with a gentle kiss. He looks up at me and smiles. "Welcome, young one." And then he lets go of me and backs away, moving off the stage.

I start to follow him, but Faelan keeps hold of my arm, whispering, "Not done just yet."

I notice a man moving to stand in Marius's place. He's wearing a green hooded robe that drags on the floor behind him; I'd assume he was a monk if I didn't know better. Instead of a cross around his neck, he's wearing a pentagram, and there's a leather strap across his chest from shoulder to belt. It's holding a dagger. A white stone bowl rests in his palms. He steps in front of me as a woman in similar robes walks up behind him. She holds a thin stick in her hand.

"Have you chosen a protector?" the man asks. His voice is coated with age, and his face is stoic, older features sagging a bit.

"Yes," I say, feeling more sure now.

"Name him," he says. "So that he may be presented."

"It's Faelan," I say.

The priest guy furrows his brow and keeps staring at me like he's waiting for more.

Should I have said Faelan's full name? I don't remember how to pronounce the whole thing. Instead I point behind me to my new shadow and add, "Him."

The priest frowns and the woman behind him bites her lip, like she's holding back a smile.

"Very well," the priest grumbles. He looks at Faelan. "Step forward to take the vow, Faelan Ua Cleirigh. You have been called."

Faelan comes from behind to stand next to me.

The priest holds out the stone bowl. "With blade and sacrifice, let the shield be true."

Without a word, Faelan reaches out and pulls the blade from the sheath strapped to the old man's chest. He holds his other hand over the bowl and slices into his palm like he did when he swore to Marius. Blood runs into the bowl.

My pulse quickens at the sight of the crimson filling the white stone.

A young girl comes from somewhere on our left, a long strip of red silk fabric in her hand. She holds it out to Faelan with wide eyes. She's probably twelve or thirteen, dressed in a flowing white gown, a wreath of tiny white roses in her long braided hair, like a girl in an ancient wedding ceremony. She's the first child I've seen since I got here. It reminds me of what Faelan said about his own childhood in this world. Somehow it seems wrong for someone so innocent to be a part of all of this.

Faelan holds out his wounded hand to her, and she begins wrapping the red silk round and round his palm with her elegant fingers. When she's done, she ties it with a knot at his wrist, and gives a quick kiss to his knuckles before letting go with a giggle. Then she backs away and slips into the rows of onlookers.

Next, the woman holding the stick steps forward, her robes dragging behind her. Faelan moves to stand in front of me. His eyes meet mine, and my insides heat with the intensity in them. The memory of his lips, his taste, grips me, and I have to focus on not hyperventilating.

"You're sure?" he whispers.

I nod. But how can I be sure when I barely know what it all means?

The woman places the stick in his palm, and he shifts it to hold it like a paintbrush, dipping it into the bowl of blood that the priest is holding. He hesitates for a moment, then brings the blood-covered tip toward my head.

I pull back a little.

"It's okay," he whispers. "This is how I'll cover you, protect you."

I go still and he puts the stick to the center of my brow. My skin tingles at the touch of the blood, and with slow, deliberate strokes he begins to paint what feels like a crescent shape on my forehead. Its slick warmth spreads across my face, and the familiar minty smell of Faelan fills my senses.

"My blood covers yours," he says loud enough for everyone to hear.

My pulse speeds up again, shaking me as I watch him. His green eyes seem to glow for a moment and gravity shifts under me, pulling me toward him. But I lock my knees and force my body to stay still.

"May the blade that aims for your heart pierce mine," he says, his voice reverent.

My throat tightens at his sincerity, and the stark reality of it all hits me like a fist to the gut. He's promising his life—his *life* to protect me. A girl he barely knows. I want to say something, to respond, but the only words in me right now are *I'm sorry.*

He gives me a slight tip of his head and steps away.

The priest comes forward again. He faces the audience and asks in a stern voice, "Who is your bloodmother?"

I search my brain. Not Lauren, she was my fake mother. "The goddess Brighid," I manage to get out, trying not to tack a question mark on the end of it.

"What is your primary bloodgift?" the priest asks.

My mind races around the word *bloodgift.* After a few tense seconds, I say, "Fire," hoping it's the right answer. "I start fires." It sounds completely ridiculous. And yet everyone stares at me like it's no big deal.

"Do you have a secondary gift?" he asks.

I could have more than one? I shake my head. "No." Another so-called *gift* is the last thing I need.

There's some whispering in the audience, like they didn't expect me to say that.

The priest is unfazed. He reaches out and places a hand on my temple, closing his eyes. He whispers under his breath for several seconds. My eyes find Faelan again, and the mark on my forehead buzzes.

Suddenly the priest declares, "All is set aright!" so loud I nearly jump out of my skin.

"Blood, spirit, water, fire, and bone, the Balance is kept," he continues. "All is as it should be. She is Otherborn, she is now one of us." He motions to my head, then surveys the audience dramatically for several seconds, both the lower courtyard and the royal figures surrounding us on the balcony, like he's trying to catch every eye in the place. "Her guard holds true," he says. "Anyone may vie for her fealty, but only one House shall win this beauty's honor. May the contest commence!"

TWENTY-SIX

FAELAN

I stand at Sage's side, getting ready for the demis to begin their introductions. The awareness of my blood on her forehead is nearly overwhelming, the small crescent moon showing me as her chosen shadow, tied to her as long as she wishes. And after what I did beside the fountain, that idea is . . . terrifying.

Some of the most powerful demis in the West are here to witness my soul's suicide—even the Cast's envoy is looking on with sharp eyes. It's rare for so many to be present at an Introduction. The Emergence ceremony is where the full court gathers. Tonight, however, there are several representatives from every line in attendance. The curiosity about the newblood is strong. And I have a feeling Marius is about to have serious competition for her loyalty.

Sage is a ruby appearing in an ash heap, and the world's head is turning to see it catch the light.

She's standing tall in spite of the fear I can feel on her. I wait just behind her on the small platform as each House approaches to place their gifts and their intentions on the table.

But first the envoy to the Cast comes forward, the representative of our lords—or, more accurately, our babysitters. He looks Sage over, head to toe, taking stock, and allowing those on the Otherside who are watching through his eyes to take stock as well. The silence of the moment stretches out as he studies her. Then he tips his head, like he's listening to something.

"Our lords wish to welcome you to the fold," he says. "They see you are well settled with a protector and will be watching your Emergence closely. The Balance must be kept." When Sage doesn't respond to his words with the usual "May Danu aid us," he adds, "I'm sure you agree," his tone becoming low. A warning.

Sage doesn't know the meaning of the man's words, but she nods, which seems to be enough for the envoy, thank Dagda.

I should've prepped her to meet an envoy. I just didn't expect one to be here. They usually leave the Introductions to the local powers. This is a clear sign of how seriously the Cast is taking a new female demi from the line of fire: with watchful caution.

The envoy bows his head and mutters the blessing of Danu under his breath in Gaelic, "*All is life, all is death, may the Mother be with you,*" before he turns and walks away, his duty complete.

The weight in the air lifts as he goes, and the head druid priestess moves forward to begin calling out the Houses and demi titles.

They are announced in reverse order of importance, so the lowest House walks up to Sage first, the House of Brighid, with Marius as the master, and two of his druid children: Aelia and the eldest daughter, Riona, who must've come in from Paris. And from behind them appears Sage's brother Sean, that hand-carved pipe perched between his lips as always. He's the only useful or respectable demi of Brighid's line left besides Sage—the others have all been sanctioned, decapitated, or cast into the Pit.

He takes his pipe from his teeth and kneels at her feet, saying his hello quietly. That unusual open smile of his fills his features, and his red curls are as unruly as ever.

Sage barely seems to hear him or see him, focused intently on those at the end of the line.

She's got her attention locked on Kieran and his sister Mara. Their party is last, a larger group made up of half a dozen demis, along with their consort underlings and druids.

Her gaze finds them every few seconds, like she's expecting them to pounce on her. Luckily, Kieran would never risk harming her here.

I lean over and whisper in her ear, in case she's missing the importance of what's happening. "This is your older brother." Then I repeat what the priest just announced: "Prince of Morning and Keeper of Music. He's the third son of Brighid."

Her features open in surprise. "Oh, sorry. Hello."

Several seconds of silence pass while Prince Sean puffs on his pipe. Smoke curls up around his shoulders, and he tilts his head, almost childlike, before finally commenting: "My, aren't you a doe."

She frowns. "What's that mean? People keep calling me that."

"It means you're delicate," I say, trying to help things along. She seems relieved for a second, but then she's frowning again, obviously equating delicate with weak.

"It's good to see you, sir," I say to the prince to fill the awkward space.

"Right, right. Let's hope this one lasts, aye?" He chuckles deep in his chest, then wanders off in a trail of smoke.

Sage watches him go before she turns back to Marius and Aelia.

Aelia winks at me, then curtsies in a mocking way in front of Sage before giving her the signal to text her as she and her older sister, Riona, follow Prince Sean. Marius smiles as he walks up. "Your tribute," he says, holding out a key fob. She takes it, and he adds, "It's parked at the Cottages. The red convertible." When he sees Sage's mouth open in shock, his smile widens. "We'll speak again tomorrow evening. You two just try to have a lovely night."

The next House steps forward, laying large gold-dipped seashells at Sage's feet. The priest begins calling out the titles for the House of Lyr. There are three demis present from Lyr, two male and a female, none known to be very powerful. But Gwyn, the House master and princess, is looking between Sage and her brother, Marius, as he walks away. She likely wouldn't want her brother to gain standing. And with Sage being added to the House that he's the master of, that's sure to happen.

Princess Gwyn bows her head. "Welcome to our community, Princess Sage. The children of Lyr greet you in peace. We ask for your consideration and present this tribute in your honor." She motions to the pixie standing beside her. "Her name is Brea, and she will serve you well."

Sage frowns at the pixie girl and then looks back and forth between her and Princess Gwyn. She asks carefully, "You're giving me a *person?*"

"A pixie, princess. Not a person."

Sage's lips tighten and her cheeks turn pink.

I speak up before she can unload on the clueless woman. "Thank you, Princess Gwyn. The Daughter of Fire is honored by your gift." The princess seems mollified by that and nods her goodbye.

Sage glares straight ahead as the House of Lyr all leave, each bowing or curtsying as they pass. The pixie, Brea, stays behind, kneeling a few feet from Sage.

As soon as the remainder of the House has trailed away, Sage turns to me and hisses through her teeth: "What the hell just happened? Did they just give me a slave? This is completely demented."

I lean close and whisper, "Agreed. But for now, let's focus on getting through the night. We'll cure the injustices of our kind tomorrow."

She doesn't seem happy about that. She sets her jaw and keeps glancing down at the pixie, annoyed. The House of Lyr didn't win any points tonight. They clearly took themselves out of the running.

The next to be announced are the two demis from the House of Arwen—Beatrix, the master, and her very creepy brother Picket, who has black eyes and the pointy ears of a bat. Several shade underlings trail behind them—thankfully, they didn't bring along any wraiths, the House of Arwen's weapon of choice.

They look down their noses at Sage as she fidgets with her torque, obviously uncomfortable. She doesn't seem to want to look at them.

"We have no wish to be considered," Queen Beatrix says, her tone dead. "No tribute will come from the House of Arwen."

Sage nods, her features softening in relief.

This is good. Queen Beatrix is just as twisted as she is disagreeable to look at. Who knows what sort of madness she'd start in a contest like this if she were truly jumping in. And if Sage hated the serving pixie as a gift, there's no telling how horrified she'd be with the typical gift from the dark family of Arwen—like the dismembered waxed corpse of Napoléon Bonaparte that they presented during my younger sister's Emergence in 1834.

The House of Arwen wander off, and Sage releases a heavy breath. "Only two more, right?" she asks, her voice shaking. I know she's worried about the last proposal. About Kieran—her eyes go right to him every time there's a pause.

"How're you feeling?" I ask. I don't see her golden light on her skin—amazingly, she appears to be in control.

She shakes her head. "Who knows."

Before I can ask her to elaborate, two of my own brothers of the House of Cernunnos are announced.

Sage straightens, giving her attention to the approaching party.

Duncan and Finbar step forward, both tall and broad shouldered. There are several alfar and shade with them, along with six of Finbar's druid children in the background. They all strain to get a better look at Sage.

My eldest brother, Finbar, King of Ash and Oak, bows his head. "The House of Cernunnos would like to be considered as a home for you, Princess Sage," he says. "Your beauty, your mind, and your heart would be greatly treasured by all within our House, but especially myself."

She seems captivated by him, her eyes widening a little at his words. She watches him intently as he stands straight, his air of confidence obvious. He's gained a lot of power since the last time I saw him, and it shows. The Cernunnos bloodline is known for its beauty, and my brothers both received a large portion. Hair full and dark brown, features stalwart, and that casual look of strength in their heavy-lashed green eyes. Sage is likely dazzled by them, since most females are.

I have to focus all my energy on not stepping between her and their hungry gazes. I know all too well how their minds work.

"We've brought a small token," Duncan says. He sets a carved wooden box at Sage's feet. I spot Astrid behind him, and my shoulders tense even more. She's holding Duncan's hand. She doesn't even spare me a glance as my brother introduces her to Sage, and I wonder if she told Duncan that she spoke with me last night. He describes her to Sage as his near-Bond, and my teeth clench at the realization of how far gone he is with my old lover. Last I heard, he had merely taken Astrid on as a lead concubine after Finbar cast her off.

But a Bonding?

She's more underhanded than I thought. Either that, or Duncan has finally lost his wits.

He reaches down and opens the box, revealing a small tiara coated in glittering diamonds. It may as well be an old shoe for all the attention Sage gives it. She's too busy studying my ex-lover.

She casually says thanks to Duncan for the gift before asking, "So, you're Astrid?"

Several faces turn our way when Sage speaks.

Duncan beams at the recognition, showing his usual haughtiness. "Yes, she's a warrior, a hunter of great note," he says, as if Astrid can't answer for herself.

Sage pinches her lips like she's thinking, looking back and forth between Duncan and Finbar, then she says, "And you're Faelan's family."

The air goes cool with the sudden chill from everyone's discomfort.

My brothers don't seem to know how to respond. Technically, in the way humans look at it, I would be of their blood, therefore we'd be family. But my brothers would never see it that way. To them, I'm a traitor. I did the unthinkable—I broke my vow to our father and left the House that I'd promised my life to at my Emergence. I'm surprised she'd bring up the connection. I explained to her that I'm an outcast.

Astrid touches Duncan's arm, maybe trying to get him to stay quiet.

Sage smiles sweetly, totally oblivious. "Aren't you all so proud of him?" She glances up at me and gives me a wink, and I realize with surprise that she's teasing them. She hooks her arm through mine and turns back to them, leaning in to whisper, "He saved my life just last night, even though I've nearly killed him twice already," like it's a secret.

Astrid merely studies her, cool as ever, but Duncan begins to cough.

Finbar fidgets with his tie. "Yes, well . . . it was more than lovely meeting you at last, Daughter of Fire. I hope you'll consider the House of Cernunnos as your home."

"You are very lovely," Duncan says, absently. He turns to glare at me, like it's my fault that Sage has no self-control.

Astrid seems reluctant to leave, adding, "Perhaps we could have tea sometime soon." She actually sounds genuine, which I don't see as a good sign. She probably wants to gain Sage's trust to help the House win her.

Sage glances away, like she's considering the idea. She nods. "Sure. That would be nice." And then she grins her street-kid grin. "We'll make it a thing."

Astrid blinks, and it's clear that Sage has caught the hunter off guard. "Yes, all right, then. I'll have my secretary contact yours."

Sage nods but her lips press together. "Sounds good."

Once they're gone she leans over and whispers in my ear, "Did she seriously just say her people would call my people?"

I'm relieved. It seems that she wasn't taken in by my brothers' power or beauty. Not yet, anyway.

The priest begins calling out the titles of the House of Morrígan, and we both go still, the air growing thick with tension. The last and highest House of the Penta walk forward like an unkindness of ravens descending, all black hair and pale skin, Princess Mara's red dress a strike of bloody crimson in the low torchlight.

Kieran stays just behind his sister, his charcoal suit tailored to perfection.

Sage's chin lifts like she's trying to look taller and braver. But her fear bellows out in a thin gold mist that I'm sure Kieran and Mara can see.

Princess Mara nods slightly, looking sideways at Sage. The Princess of Bones is well known for how perfectly she embodies the dark power of her mother. She is the first daughter of blood, her eyes sharp and full of crafty ambition. A smirk twists her crimson lips like she has a secret. She would be a stunning beauty, but her skin is too pale, nearly violet. Thin veins web along her hairline, showing through at her temples and jaw, and dark circles rim her silver-blue eyes. A male shade kneels at her feet on a satin leash.

When Sage notices the rope tied to the thin young man's throat, her head pulls back a little.

"Welcome to the fold, sweet child," Princess Mara says, her voice silky. "The House of Morrígan covets your consideration. The blood of Brighid and Morrígan have a history of affection; our goddess mothers being sisters, your sister having been Bonded to my brother—these things make us sisters as well, I think."

It's difficult for me to accept her words. Words of kindness directed to the sister of the queen who killed their beloved king? But Mara is always hunting for more power. She would likely see Sage as a means to an end. As would Kieran.

Sage's throat moves as she glances between the two of them, her wary gaze landing on Kieran.

"You needn't be afraid, princess," Mara says. "My brother is firmly in hand. He's been properly admonished for his clumsy encounter with you the other night. I can understand why you didn't choose him as your protector. But perhaps in time your thoughts toward him will change." Her secret smile appears again.

Kieran moves forward and bows deeply, playing his role, looking surprisingly contrite. "I ask for mercy, Princess Sage. You shouldn't judge my sister by my actions. It's clear that your power exceeds even my own understanding." He rises and steps a little closer. He takes a moment to study her, his gaze lingering on her neck where he cut her. Then he whispers, "You outshine the moon tonight, little doe."

Sage just stares at him, her chest rising and falling quickly.

It takes every ounce of my control to keep from grabbing him and using my dagger to shut him up. I'd get great satisfaction from cutting out that forked tongue.

He doesn't even allow me the courtesy of checking with me—her protector—before he closes the rest of the distance between them and places a small black velvet bag at her feet. "A humble gift from the past. We hope it will bring you peace."

Sage looks down at it but doesn't move to take it.

"Open it," he orders quietly, locking his eyes to hers.

Her breath catches. And she bends slowly to pick it up.

Ice crawls through my veins as I realize his effect on her. She's spellbound. I can barely believe my eyes, but he's clearly more than a threat to her safety. Is he really willing to go as far as to seduce her? Especially after what her sister did to his brother? It can't possibly work.

Goddess, don't let it work.

She unties the ribbon and opens the bag, then tips it over her palm. A medallion on a chain tumbles out. A necklace. But as she holds it up, I realize it's so much more than that.

It's Queen Lily's torque. The ancient piece of jewelry was forged out of bronze metal, an intricate knotted design for fire woven in the circle, and an amber stone embedded in the center with a small moth preserved inside.

A piece of history that hasn't been seen for centuries.

"It was your sister's, long ago," Kieran says to her.

"Where did you get that?" I ask, my harsh tone breaking the moment. I glare at Kieran, daring him to tell the truth. "That belongs to the House of Brighid." It disappeared from the vault around the time of Queen Lily's imprisonment. Marius assumed the goddess had taken it back, since the legend was that she'd given it to her first daughter personally. What is Kieran playing at?

Kieran ignores my objection. "I hope you're pleased, princess. I know the torque you're wearing is weak, and your power can be . . . unpredictable."

Sage's fingers shake as she drops the necklace back into the black bag. "Thank you," she says, barely audible. She clenches the bag in her fist.

Princess Mara nods in satisfaction, and Kieran bows again. Just before they walk away, he turns to me, his eyes hardening in warning as he says under his breath, "Keep her safe for us, hunter."

I glare back at him, forcing myself not to put a dent in his smug face. He's a pompous ass, thinking Sage is his because of some forgotten ancient right. She's not a toy for him to play with. Fortunately, he leaves, following Mara and the rest of the dark clan.

Sage releases her breath and deflates a little, leaning on me for a second.

"You all right?" I ask, trying to gauge her reaction.

She presses her fingers into her temples, shaking her head. "I feel like I'm gonna be sick."

The pixie, Brea, leaps to her feet, bowing in front of Sage. "May I fetch you some poultice for your ailment, princess?"

Sage cringes back, her mouth open, like she's not sure how to react.

This isn't going to work. "That would be lovely, Brea," I say. "The princess will have the winter mint, though," I add, hoping to be rid of her quickly.

The pixie looks from me to Sage, but when Sage doesn't say anything she must decide her princess is agreeing, because she stands, bowing again, then scuttles off to make her useless poultice. We'll only be able to avoid her for so long, I'm guessing. "That should keep her busy," I say to Sage once the pixie is out of earshot.

She just goes back to massaging her temples and groans.

"You did well," I add, hoping to lift the misty cloud that's filtering from her shoulders.

She shakes her head, looking lost. "I'll never get used to this. It's all so flashy. And proper. And how am I supposed to remember all those names and faces? Prince of *this*, queen of *that*. Holy Moses."

"If it matters to them, they'll make sure you don't forget." I decide not to tell her how much she'll wish she could forget some of them soon. I'm guessing she's already wishing that. Instead I ask, "Would you like to freshen up?"

She gives me a hopeful look. "Oh yes, please. Just make sure the bathroom has a window I can escape through."

TWENTY-SEVEN

SAGE

I lean on the counter in the bathroom, pleading with my panicked insides to calm down.

What is wrong with me? I can't understand why I was so shaken by Kieran *again*. And this time was so much worse. When he whispered to me, I heard a familiar voice. I wanted to do what he said, and I wanted to hear him say my name. It was horrible and wrong, and the things my mind pictured . . .

I reach up and touch the thin scar on my neck, reminding myself what he did to me, how much I hate him. Because I do; I hate him with the power of a thousand suns. Even more than I hated him this morning. He makes me feel vulnerable and weak. He takes away my will.

And even more frightening, I know he can see it. He's doing it on purpose.

I wonder if it's some twisted form of revenge for what my sister did, killing his brother.

I'm still gripping the small black velvet bag in my hand, the medallion on the torque digging into my palm. A torque that belonged to my sister. My sister who's in goddess hell because she killed millions.

But strangely, relief filled me when it fell from the bag into my palm. And in spite of what my sister was, I want to be wearing it right this second, as if it's actually mine—as if it's something I lost, thrilled to have found it again. It's a *bad* feeling. I shouldn't be glad at anything Kieran does.

I look up and study my reflection in the mirror. The painted crescent moon on my brow has dried to a crimson brown.

I have Faelan's blood on my forehead. Someone else's blood is on my skin. And I just let him put it on me.

The sensation of it still buzzes in my temples. The smell of him in my head like new life. Like warm grass and rich earth. Strong and comforting.

I breathe in the scent and let it fill me, pushing all thoughts of Kieran from my mind.

I'm loving the smell of someone's blood. I'm buying into the madness.

But I don't know what else to do.

Just breathe, Sage. Bide your time.

Behind me there's a plush, circular red velvet couch sitting in the middle of the ornate bathroom; I consider curling up on it to take a nap since there's no window to climb out of. Maybe they'll forget about me.

There's a knock on the door. "You all right?" Faelan says from outside.

"Yeah," I call out. Then I whimper to myself, "No." I don't want to go back out there. All those faces, the looks, the attention. I don't know how to process it all. It's wrong, it's all wrong.

How can Faelan and Marius expect me to mingle with these people tonight and act normal? It's a walking nightmare.

The one thing I found out that was actually interesting is that I have a brother. I have no idea what to think about him—he looks like a weird

Scottish farmer—and I'm not sure what to call him, but according to Faelan he's a sibling. Family.

I used to wish for a real family. I wished a million times that my dad would rescue me when my mom—or the woman who I thought was my mom—was on one of her benders. I'd wonder why he never came and found me, why he left me with her. Was it to punish me? Had I done something wrong? I wanted a real family so badly it stung in my lungs. All the kids would draw their moms and dads and sisters and brothers with sunshine in the sky and a tree in the yard, and I'd just ache and draw dragons or fairies.

The irony.

And now I meet my family. And I want to scream.

I wonder how Faelan felt when those smug brothers of his set their wooden box of diamonds at my feet, not even sparing him a glance. His tension was obvious. I couldn't just let them act like he wasn't there. It rankled me, like those jocks in high school who think they're God's gift to womankind. And that Astrid chick wasn't doing her gender any favors, fawning over that Duncan guy. If Astrid was really in a relationship with Faelan a long time ago, like Aelia said, why's she drooling all over his stuck-up brother right in front of him?

I've officially decided I don't like her. If there's some kind of Astrid-Aelia smackdown in the future, I'm Team Aelia all the way.

"Sage, you can't hide forever," Faelan's muffled voice says.

"Why not?"

The door swings open a crack. His head peeks in. "You'll have tongues wagging if we stay missing too long."

"So what?" I groan, plopping down onto the circular couch.

"They'll think we're"—his voice lowers—"*busy.*"

I'm up and out of the bathroom in seconds.

We don't go back out on the balcony. Instead we go downstairs and out into the courtyard, through the crowd. I'm not sure how people do this all the time, small talk. It's freaking exhausting. So many faces, sharp gazes cutting through me like a knife. No one looks at me with openness or even curiosity; it's all cunning and manipulation. I recognize it immediately, the all-too-familiar search for a weakness.

In the foster homes, a lot of the adults or older kids would look at me that way: *What can I get out of you? What can you give to me?*

I was a means to an end, a monthly check, a possible hit, a potential lay. Never just Sage.

And here I am again, a thing.

Faelan stays close, not engaging any of the people who approach. He just hovers right behind me, ever present.

I nod and keep a fake smile on my face until I think my cheeks might crack. It's mostly a lot of those underlings, the demigods and demigoddesses remaining on the edges, as if they're allowing their peasants to take a gander at the newcomer before swooping back in. I can't always tell *what* each person is when they approach me with a humble greeting before scuttling off into the crowd again. Some have wings or overly large eyes, so I'm fairly sure they're pixies, but the selkies and the pixies begin to look very similar as the night wears on. The only way I can tell if it's a shade talking to me is if they grin wide enough for me to see their small fangs. The alfar are impossible to be sure of. Though I do see a couple of taller, more elegant figures with features similar to Astrid's: delicate nose, almond-shaped eyes, prominent cheekbones.

Thankfully, there's not a wraith in sight. Something tells me they wouldn't be hanging around this highbrow place. The two I saw seemed more like henchmen than partiers.

After about an hour of exhausting smiles and nods, I'm more than relieved when Aelia and her vapid coven approach me with cocktails in their hands.

"Wow, you did phenomenal," Aelia says, breathless. "Word is, you're total hot real estate, girl. Seriously. Awesome job."

"Thanks, I guess," I say.

She grabs Faelan's arm, her eyes alight. "Holy Danu, Faelan, you have them talking, brazenly coming out with her onto the balcony. They all think you're vying for rank again." She seems to be enjoying this whole thing a *lot*.

Faelan frowns at her, not a fan.

"It's my fault," I say. "I didn't want people thinking he was my slave or something."

Aelia gives us a giddy look. "Well, it's juicy. The girls and I are going to do one more circle around the room, and this time you're coming, Sage." When I open my mouth to protest, she adds quickly, "You'll be perfectly safe now that the protector bond is set, so no excuses. Faelan will be right here."

I glance at Faelan, hoping for help, but he betrays me, agreeing with her. "Go ahead, I'll be watching."

I glare at him and say, "No, thanks. I'll just stick with Faelan."

"No arguing, this is a thing," Aelia says, kissing my cheek. "I'll be back in ten after a quick makeup refresher." Then she and her coven are lost in the gathering crowd.

"Thanks a lot," I say. "Way to save me."

"May as well just go along for tonight," Faelan says. "Maybe you'll enjoy yourself."

"Wow, some warrior you are. Can't even stand up to a tiny teen girl."

"Aelia?" he asks. "That wee thing is terrifying."

"I bet you don't call her *wee* to her face."

"Gods, no."

~

Not as many heads turn toward me as we wander through the crowd. I seem to blend in better without a large Faelan shadow. Instead, I follow

Aelia and her coven as they filter through the bodies, listening to the snatches of gossip I hear buzzing around us.

There's a pale young woman talking about how she's having trouble with her garden, asking for advice from what looks like a pixie. A guy is getting scolded by an older man for not disposing of his "meal" properly—and I don't think he's talking about a plate of spaghetti. Two females are whispering about how mind-blowing some guy named Finbar is in bed—

Whoa, wait, isn't that Faelan's brother?

I pause, loitering near a tree. Totally not snooping. I'm just taking a break.

Aelia and the other girls keep walking, not realizing that I've stopped. I let them go, sticking to the shadows.

"You know he's bargaining for a Bond," one of the gossiping females says. She's a pixie; her wings have a slight blue tint to them in the light. "Hopefully they won't tame him, whoever they are."

The other female shakes her head like she's disappointed. "I was a little surprised he didn't choose Astrid when he had a chance. She was all over him just after they took her in as a ward. I assumed he was grooming her."

"Word is he tasted from that vine but wasn't willing to take his brother's leftovers on permanently." The first girl raises her brow conspiratorially.

The other girl scoffs. "Apparently the second son doesn't have that problem."

"Well, Prince Duncan is notoriously gullible."

"Obviously."

And they both giggle as they wander away.

Wow, sounds like Faelan dodged a bullet.

I lean on the tree, deciding not to go back into the crowd. It's nice here, just out of the way. People walk by now and then, engrossed in their conversations, but no one seems to notice me. Leaves rustle with the light breeze blowing through the courtyard. The air is a little chilly, but not cold. I fold my arms across my chest, rubbing my upper arms as I look over the crowd and watch the flirting, the glares, the games.

And then I spot Faelan on the other side of the courtyard. I let myself look at him, admiring his tall figure, his shoulders perfectly shaped in that black sweater. I try not to think about how it felt to grip them, his hands holding me close, the taste of his minty-green energy in my skin. Why does he have to be so freaking good-looking? Why couldn't my first real kiss have been a skinny nerd instead of him? How am I ever going to follow that up?

His features shift like he spotted someone, a fierce look filling his face as he glares at a woman walking toward him. She comes into view, stopping at his side. I can only see the back of her head, but I know right away who it is with that long golden braid curling over her shoulder.

Astrid.

My gut sinks, watching them connect. Even though he's looking at her like she murdered his dog, I know it takes a lot of history to make that kind of animosity grow between two people.

He says something sharp to her and then turns to walk away, but she touches his arm, stopping him.

His features soften as his eyes fall on her again, and my nerves spark. *Don't give in, Faelan!*

He listens to her for a few seconds, and I can't believe it, but he nods. What could he possibly be agreeing to with that woman? Could he really be dumb enough to buy anything she says?

"Predictable," I mutter.

"What is?" comes a smooth voice behind me.

I gasp and jerk back as I turn. Kieran is cast in shadow, close enough to touch me. He moves into the light, attempting to see who I was looking at. "Spying, are we?"

I try to swallow but my throat is a desert. The torchlight flickers over his face, softening his features. It casts gold into his hair and makes his silver eyes almost glow.

"Your protector seems preoccupied," he says. His gaze moves to me. "He's left you unattended."

I press my back into the tree. I don't trust myself to open my mouth to speak. I might scream at him.

"Don't be afraid, little doe. What happened last night won't repeat itself." He steps closer, saying in a low voice, "I truly am sorry to have frightened you. Perhaps I should have approached things differently."

"You killed me," I manage to say.

He searches my face and then glances down to my hand. "I see you're still holding my tribute. Would you let me put it on for you?"

My insides quiver. I shake my head.

He reaches out and gently slides his finger across my knuckle. "It can give you peace. Won't you trust me, just a little?"

"Never," I say, but the word seems to float away, meaning nothing, so I add, "Leave me alone."

"But I can't. I'm yours and you are mine. There's no running from that." He leans closer, nudging my fingers open. "I think you feel it too. I sense your need. I have it inside me as well." He pulls the velvet sack from my grip. "And yet I know you despise me. So let me help you."

I just shake my head. "You want revenge," I say. "My sister killed your brother, and you want to drive me crazy for it."

He studies my face, conflict in his features. He doesn't deny it.

"You killed me," I choke out again, mostly to remind myself.

"No. I set you free," he whispers. And he pulls the necklace from the sack, holding the bronze medallion in front of my face. "Let me do it again."

I stare at him, seeing care and determination but no threat. Why don't I see the threat I know is there? Why won't he tell me what he wants?

He places the necklace on my chest and reaches around slowly, gently setting the clasp into place. His fingers brush my nape, sending a rush of cold through me. But strangely it's not an unpleasant feeling. It tingles in my lungs and throat. Then he steps back, giving me space.

And in an instant, my fear and my helplessness all shift to rage in my gut. As he pulls away, I get the urge to lunge at him, kick him in the balls, claw his face. Warmth fills my chest, and I stop cringing away, standing firm. In total control again.

"Next time you touch me without permission," I growl, "I break your fingers."

A new grin lifts his lips as he moves back a little more, like he's admiring me. "Well, well, there she is. Stunning. I hoped it would be this way with you. As soon as I felt you blossom in the night three months ago, I was sure of our connection."

I blink, confused. "What are you talking about? I have absolutely *no* connection to you." But my mind betrays me as his familiar gaze stares back at me, the memory of those silver eyes looking down on me still vivid. Once again, I see the need, the hunger, as our bodies moved together, as I melted into him, into the clover underneath me, wanting it all to last forever . . .

Heat pulses in my skin, my heart thumping like mad against my ribs.

He smirks, motioning to my body. "Of course, if you say so."

I look down and—

Flames slink over my arms, the same as earlier today with Faelan. Warm and comforting. And empowering.

"It's lovely," he says, moving into the shadows a little, the glow of my fire blinding me. "It's exactly as I hoped it would be. And it wants

231

me burned to a crisp." A smile lights his eyes, making them glow in the dark. "I knew you had the sun inside you."

The flames pulse lower, fading into my skin as my fear and confusion rise.

He turns to focus on the crowd like he heard something. "Your protector approaches," he says. "Looking very disagreeable. That's my cue to leave." Before I realize what he's doing, he reaches out, brushing a finger over the scar he gave me. "We'll continue this later." And then he's gone, leaving black smoke curling in the air in front of me.

TWENTY-EIGHT

FAELAN

I was hoping she'd leave well enough alone, but Astrid has always been the most stubborn woman I know. So I'm not surprised when she slips away from Duncan's side and approaches me.

I am surprised, though, that she'd let people see her speaking to me.

"Can we talk?" she asks. "Perhaps we can find a quiet spot, just for a moment."

When I first saw her at the club last night, I was shocked. But after seeing her with my brothers, the way she lets them lord over her, the old anger has bubbled up, the wound she left tearing open a little.

"You don't want to talk to me," I say. "And I certainly don't want to talk to you."

Her brow pinches. "I know that I hurt you—"

"You betrayed me. There's a difference."

"I know," she says. "There's just so much you don't understand."

I'm shocked she'd make excuses. To me, of all people. Is she really so clueless that she doesn't realize how low she sank? There's a reason I'm an outcast. "I understood a lot more than I bloody wanted to sitting in that dungeon, Astrid. For seven years."

"But it was all so long ago," she says. "Much time has passed. And your brothers are sorry they caused you pain."

I glare at her, wondering what underhanded thing she's playing with. "They've said nothing to me."

"They speak to me," she says, then she pauses, searching my face. "And they wish to ask you . . . they'd like for you to return home once your time with the newblood has passed. I would wish for that as well."

I want to laugh. It's too much to swallow, with everything else. And now here this woman is with the lies, the manipulation. I'd forgotten how good she is. But I don't have to listen.

I turn to walk away. She places her hand on my arm, stopping me.

"Please, Faelan." Her voice breaks on my name, and when I look at her, there are tears in her eyes.

My gut clenches, and a part of me cracks inside. I used to be swayed by those tears. Once, long ago, I'd have wiped them from her face and kissed her. Now I watch, frustrated, knowing she's merely using them for her own ends.

"I'm not doing this with you, Astrid," I say, attempting to be gentle.

She nods and brushes a glittering tear from her cheek. "I thought you'd wish to make peace, regain standing. Forgive me if I overstepped."

Regain standing? How can she not know that I never cared about that? It's as if she's forgotten the reason I wanted to leave my father's House to begin with. But even so, why come to me for reconciliation now, after being silent for so long?

And why would Finbar send my old lover if he really meant to make amends? He knows how she betrayed me, how she used me in the end. He knows I'd never trust her. It makes no sense.

My brothers are up to something. Or Astrid is.

Either way, I'm not playing. "Go back to forgetting about me," I say. "And tell my brothers to do the same. I won't return to the House of Cernunnos. Ever."

"I wish you'd at least hear me out. They have—"

An arrow of pain spikes my temple, shutting out her words. I clench my eyes and cradle my head, trying to push back at the pulse. It subsides nearly as quickly as it came, only a slight throb lingering.

I catch my breath and rub my temple. What the mangy hell was that?

"Are you all right?" Astrid moves closer and looks around us, her eyes wary.

Then I remember. I'm no longer simply me anymore. "I'm fine," I say absently, searching the crowd. Where the feck is Sage?

"Faelan, I—"

"Enough," I bite out.

And I walk away through the crowd.

I study all the faces, the figures I pass, not seeing her. I should be feeling her location if the connection is solid enough to spike me. It should be drawing me toward her. But I don't sense any tug. I might be too pissed right now to feel it.

I make my way among the bodies, not worrying about the turning heads or the whispers. I need to get a tighter rein on this link so that—

I spot her red hair and the panic fades a little. She's in the shadows, standing by one of the trees and—Kieran is reaching out to her. He's . . . he's bloody touching her neck. If he hurts her again, I'll fucking rip his bastard lungs out.

I move fast, but he's smoke before I get three yards away.

"Are you all right?" I ask as I come to her side. I turn her to face me, looking over her neck, her shoulders. She's lit with a fading glow at the center of her chest. She manifested? I urge her deeper into the shadows. "What's happened? Your power—did he hurt you?" If Kieran tried to attack her again . . .

She shakes her head, looking confused. "He put this on, and everything suddenly shifted."

"What shifted, what do you mean?" But then I see it, the ancient torque resting on her chest, lying over the one I placed on her. Queen Lily's torque. "You put it on?"

She shakes her head violently. "He did. And I didn't stop him—what's wrong with me, Faelan?"

"*He* placed it?" I can't help the disbelief in my voice. That's really not good. Why would she let him do that?

"I'm all wrong," she says. "I can't think when I'm around him. It's like I'm not in control."

"We need to go. We'll figure this out."

Relief fills her eyes. "Okay."

"Stay close until we're out of here, though." I was an idiot to let Aelia and her coven whisk her off in the first place.

She nods and moves closer to me. The smell of her spice fills my head, and without meaning to I lean toward her, breathing it in. The memory floats through me of our kiss only a few hours ago, the feel of her in my hands, and I absently reach out, about to touch her, to try and comfort her.

Thankfully, a pixie comes forward, saving me.

I bloody well need to get myself past this.

But then I realize it's Brea, the gift from the House of Lyr.

"I have the poultice," she says, bowing slightly as she blocks our path, holding up a small glass bowl. "I will place it on her temples, and then she can feed from me."

Sage shrinks back, repulsed. "Oh, God, no."

"You aren't needed," I say, trying to keep my voice even. I'm fairly sure she's more likely a spy for the House of Lyr than any sort of loyal servant. "You can return to your previous mistress and tell her the tribute isn't accepted."

Brea gasps loudly, and several heads turn our way.

"Is this true?" she asks Sage.

"Well, yes," Sage says.

Brea opens her mouth to protest, but I cut her off. "You heard what the princess said. Now, go." And then I nudge Sage past, not wanting there to be any more of a scene.

But I might be too late. We've collected quite a few onlookers. I put my hand on Sage's back and steer her along the path, heading for the exit.

"You didn't need to be mean," Sage says under her breath.

"I thought you didn't want her." I watch her fiddle with the medallion on her new torque. "Was I wrong?"

She shakes her head. "No. It all just sucks."

I have to agree.

"I need to get the hell out of here," she says, her voice trembling.

It's past time. After a few tense seconds of weaving our way out of the crowd, I ask, "Are you sure you're okay?"

"No," she whispers as we walk across the grass to the main building.

"The pixie will be fine, Sage. She was just a spy, anyway—"

"What? No, it's not that." She pauses. "The girl was a spy? I should've guessed."

"What is it, then?" I ask.

Several seconds pass before she says, so quietly I almost miss it, "It's like I know him."

"Who?"

"Kieran." Fear is clear in her voice.

"What? What do you mean?"

"I felt like I had no free will around him until he put on this necklace. He looks at me with those eyes, and crazy thoughts wash over me, like memories. What's wrong with me? Why haven't I just kicked him in the crotch like I would any other prick who pushed me like that?"

Those eyes? Could he be strong enough to glamour her? I can't imagine—demis don't get tricked by mirages. But then, Sage is still young in her powers. "What sort of memories are you having?"

She shakes her head violently. "I can't say it; it's just too crazy. And *wrong.*"

I put a hand to her arm, stopping her forward momentum. "You can't let him wear you down, Sage. That's what he does—he gets in your head and torments you. You have to say it. What do you see?"

She looks up at me, her expression tortured. Her breath quivers as she whispers, "We're, you know . . . having sex."

The impact of her words fills the space between us. I have no idea what to say. How could she have a memory of having sex with Kieran? Unless he really has managed to glamour her somehow, giving her false images in her head that she's confusing with memories. It's obvious neither of the torques are working properly on her, that something about her energy is different or . . . gods, could it be malformed, like Kieran said in the alley the other night? But she seemed to be finding balance in the greenhouse this afternoon.

"See?" she chokes out, mistaking my silence for disgust. "It's horrible. The guy's a monster, and some sick part of me wants to have sex with him, or thinks I've had sex with him, or something. I've never even *had* sex before."

Someone behind us clears their throat, and we turn.

Finbar, Duncan, and Astrid are standing in a small alcove around a table with Kieran, Mara, and several druids. The House of Cernunnos and the House of Morrígan are probably doing the usual business of contracts and deals that would occur at any tribunal, making arrangements for their holdings or firming up territory lines. I hadn't even remembered the alcove was there. Bloody fucking brilliant. I wonder how much they heard.

My brothers look on with twin frowns. Astrid is blushing, turned away a little, as if she doesn't want to snoop. Or doesn't want to see my face.

Kieran smirks, and I get the urge to cut his throat. It's becoming a familiar feeling.

"Is everything all right with our newblood, hunter?" Princess Mara asks in her silky voice.

But I barely hear her because the scent of death fills my nostrils. My gaze moves lower.

Horror fills me as I realize what I'm smelling. Her pet shade is hunched over what looks like one of the human waitstaff, just under the table. The flesh is torn too much to see if it's a male or female victim. Blood is pooled on the tiles and smeared on the wall behind them, the evidence of the shade's massacred meal everywhere.

Sage makes a choking sound and brings her hand to her mouth.

Mara is studying Sage with her sharp silver-blue eyes, still casually holding the red silk leash. "You should send the girl to us," she says to me. "My brother would be pleased to teach her, tame her, as the King of Ravens tamed her sister." A slow smile crawls up her face.

I take Sage by the arm and lead her away.

TWENTY-NINE

SAGE

I'm more than a little relieved when we pull up in front of the Cottages. Neither of us said a word the whole way home. The silence was heavy with horror and unspoken questions.

I just saw my first official dead body. And the worst part is, I'm numb now.

Maybe I'm in shock.

When I realized what I was seeing under that table—the moment my mind registered the human hand, the clothes, the torn flesh—my heart stopped and everything slowed. My mind couldn't understand what I was seeing, the pieces . . . bile filled my mouth and I wanted to cry, to scream.

But then Faelan pulled me away, and icy awareness hit me; nothing would happen because of it. No investigation, no arrests. Nothing. No one would ever know what became of that person.

The body was probably one of many in that place. And Kieran was standing right beside it as if it was a piece of dropped meat.

On the street, you get used to injustice. The shadows are full of bastards who get away with all kinds of sickening things. If a person is murdered in cold blood, though, you could tell yourself that someone might at least *try* to punish the people responsible. But in this world, human life is expendable, a means to an end. Food. This kind of viciousness is *normal* to these people. And now I'm one of them.

I swallow hard, not wanting to cry.

We pause as we come to the waterfall near the steps that lead to the cottages. Neither of us seems sure of what comes next. Seconds tick by, and the sound of water splashing into the lagoon pool surrounds us. An owl hoots from one of the taller trees.

"I'm sorry you had to see that," he finally says, "especially on the night of your Introduction to our world. And after everything that's happened . . ."

I don't really have anything to say in response. Would there have been a better time to see it?

"Does that happen a lot," I ask, "the . . . killing?"

He stares at the dark surface of the water. "Less than it used to." After a few seconds, he adds, "They have to be more careful now."

The way he says *they*, like he doesn't include himself in their world, strikes me as odd, but a trickle of relief comes. He doesn't think of himself as one of them.

I watch his profile in the moonlight, and the memory of how he called himself an outcast comes back to me. How he said he left his family. I find myself wondering about his life, what his story is. How did he become this, a servant and hunter, claiming he'd take a knife to the heart for me, a girl he barely knows?

"I'm sorry you got stuck with me," I say.

He turns and studies me, his eyes tracing the lines of my face. "I'm not sorry," he finally says. But confusion pinches his brow, like he's surprised at himself.

I can't help thinking of the way he tried to teach me to control my powers tonight, even a little bit, so I wouldn't hurt someone. And then he kissed me . . . an all-consuming kiss that rocked everything under me. I want so badly for it not to have been a lie. I need it to be true after what happened with Kieran tonight.

I reach up and touch the bronze medallion on my chest, wondering about my sister, this queen named Lily. Everyone acts as if she was so powerful, so strong. A killer, yes, but strong. What would she have done tonight? Would she have destroyed Kieran? Would she have let herself fall for Faelan? Or would she have run, like I want to do right now?

"I should take off the other torque," Faelan says, breaking through my thoughts. "It's useless now since the older, stronger one will take over."

A twinge of fear uncurls in my chest. "Will this one be safe?" I can't imagine it would be if Kieran gave it to me. But then, when he put it on me, the shift wasn't in his favor. I felt like I could finally breathe again and fight him off. It doesn't make sense. Why would he place a torque on me that gives me freedom to push him away?

"A torque isn't safe or dangerous," Faelan says. "It just is."

"So this one will be okay?"

"It was your sister's, gifted to her for her Bonding ceremony by her mother. It's rumored that it had to be very strong to combat Lily's powers."

"Does that mean I'm not dangerous with this one on?" I ask.

He shakes his head slowly. "No way to tell. A torque is meant to be shaped for a single spirit. So it likely won't work on you very well in the long run. Unless Kieran was somehow able to get a druid to reshape the bloodspell on it specifically for you. He would've needed some of your blood, though, to do that."

Back to square one, then.

He comes around behind me and gently unclasps the weaker torque. "We'll see how well it works tomorrow."

I turn to face him as he pulls the necklace off, my heart beating harder as I search his face. A yearning fills me. To push aside this fear, to feel the same rush of wonder he made me feel earlier, when he held me and kissed me and consumed me.

"Faelan," I whisper, stepping closer.

He goes still, muscles tensing, fear sparking in his eyes.

And an ache blossoms in my gut.

The owl hoots again in the trees above, and a smaller bird sings in answer. I take in a breath of the cool evening air, the scent of night jasmine filling my head, and wish I could sort out everything that I'm feeling.

I wish it had been a different kind of night.

"Thank you for bringing me home," I say softly. I give him a weak smile before walking away and heading for my cottage.

~

I sit on the couch, staring down at the coffee table. I've never felt more trapped in my entire life, not even when I was in that Catholic group home, or when my mom's next-door neighbor, Mrs. Randall, locked me in her broom closet when she babysat me. I can't run. I can't run from any of this—my powers, or Kieran, or my sister's past.

The only person I don't want to run from is Faelan. But I'm not even sure I can have him.

How could he kiss me like that if he didn't mean it?

My eyes fall on the scroll he gave me this afternoon—the scroll that supposedly has the stories about my sister in it.

My pulse picks up a little. The truth of what's happening to me could be in there. But I'm starting to wonder if I want to know what I might become.

The dark princess's words come back to me: *My brother would be pleased to teach her, tame her, as the King of Ravens tamed her sister.*

Like the king *tamed* my sister? Is that what Kieran wants to do to me? What does that even mean?

The king was their brother, and my sister was married to him, and then somewhere in there she murdered him and tried to destroy the whole world. And either Kieran thinks in his twisted mind that he and I should be together, or he thinks that he should torment me until I get thrown into goddess hell along with my sister.

I wish I knew what he wanted from me. Because however much I want to deny it, however much it sickens me, I do feel drawn to him. Like a part of me wants him too.

And I need to figure out why.

I pick up the scroll and set it in my lap. I hesitate for a second, and then I take the leap, gently pulling it open.

The script is delicate and decorative. Some of the letters are painted with colored designs: a bird or a horse or some other animal. It's definitely old, but the ink is only faded a little, the thick paper slightly discolored.

I find the spot where a new section starts and look over the unrecognizable language. I pick up the adder stone and bring it to my face, peering through the hole.

The script shifts, the ink re-forming in the weave of the paper. Familiar words begin to appear: *forgotten, punishment* . . . until it's all in English.

> Seven hundred and fifty-three, anno Domini, the third earth-child born of Our Holy Goddess Brighid, first of the female line, occurred within the short summer of the lily: born, Líle Ó Braonáin, of a human male. Named for the sorrow of her days to come, and the promise of a rebirth within the ashes. She is Daughter of Fire, Queen of Spark and Sorrow. Ever shall she burn.

A chill works over me as I absorb the words.

My sister's title was Queen of Spark and Sorrow. The name sends a twist of sadness through me for some reason. I push it away and keep reading. I shouldn't feel bad for a murderer.

In which the life of Líle Ó Braonáin begins on earth: An envoy of the Holy Goddess Brighid brought across, from the Otherworld, the first female child of fire and gave the newblood as a changeling to a smyth's widow in the south, a rare practice as it were. The babe held back the woman's sorrow for a time, but it soon came to the widow's attention that her daughter had many oddities, and she feared that her true child's soul had been taken by a sprite. The human woman became aware of the glamour placed on the child, seeing the truth of what had been done to her.

And so, in the long summer of wyne, the babe was abandoned within the Caledonian wood by the widow, for she hoped that the fae would take back their trickster gift and that the gods would be appeased. But no wolf or beast consumed the child. It lay, surrounded by the arms of ash and birch, and soon was found by a humble monk of unknown title to be raised in seclusion until her twelfth year, when her Emergence began.

Three years of the demi's life are marked here as void.

(Note here: As a matter of suspect, we believe the goddess collected her and kept her in the Otherworld for a time, but the reasons are unknown.)

It was upon her fifteenth year that the demi reappeared on the moors, near starving. She was taken in by the Church, found to be a girl of rebellious nature and stubborn of will. Many times she was chastised, to no avail. Soon she was sent by the Cast to live in a nunnery. There she would pass her most fearsome days, until she could be taught the value of balance.

(Note here: It was during this time that the first of the Great Breaking occurred.)

The demi lived in seclusion within the southern cloister for five seasons. On her eighteenth Beltane, it is thought she met with the human boy, the son of an earthly king within the southern realms. A Bond was formed in secret between the Daughter of Fire and this boy. And so it was upon the full moon of the summer solstice that the inevitable occurred; she fed from the human prince in her vicious rebellion many times but eventually lost control of the fire, killing him in a most conspicuous way. And so, to solidify her sin, in her ignorance she confessed it to the priest of those lands, allowing for the earthly king to learn a part of the truth, the most dreadful of all mistakes made in the name of love.

A punishment was established, and she was Bonded to a more powerful soul, in agreement with both deity creators, in order to contain her. Though it was a first in occurrence, the joining of two separate Houses and powers, it was deemed necessary. (Note here: See also v. VII, ch. III, within these Painted Annals.)

We know from the accounting of this first daughter, and her inability to keep her powers hidden, why the first human factions of the Church split with the Cast soon after this. Many druids were burned at the stake and disemboweled at this time, and the Christian priests only grew in strength, destroying more of our ranks. We must see and recognize here how the first crack was borne upon us. And we must understand, above all, that what was done next in the Bonding of the Morrigan and Brighid bloodlines did not end the destruction this Daughter of Fire would bring.

Instead, we brought this retribution of impurity upon ourselves. Her eventual descent into that most horrifying madness was inevitable, considering what we allowed to occur.

It seems we are eternally trapped within the culture of human weakness we helped to shape.

(Note here: See a more detailed account of the first Daughter of Fire within v. XVI, ch. V, of these Painted Annals. See also "The Visions of Bartious Lucius," in which a priest recounts her confession, and the tales of "The Vicious Flight," though a more unreliable source, still worthy of comparison. If the collections of Time Scrolls are within access, seek those out as well, v. XII, ch. VI, of the Black Years to Come.)

I sit back, lowering the scroll to my lap. There's more, but I'm not sure I can digest it. My heart is racing. The words read like something out of an old textbook, not like anything I'd usually be swept up in. It's silly to let myself get so engrossed.

But it feels very real.

And I guess it is. She accidentally killed her lover when she was young, was forced to marry Kieran's brother because of it, and eventually, if Faelan's right, she killed that man too. And went mad? And then birthed the Black Death.

Reading it in this dry accounting twists the knife of the revelations even deeper. There's a deep callousness there, and it makes me sympathize with the girl that my sister was. Could this happen to me?

I never thought I'd relate to someone accused of being a killer. But after what I did to Ben and nearly did to Faelan, after everything I felt with Kieran, I barely know who or what I am anymore. Am I evil or righteous?

My attention turns back to the scroll. I need to understand as much of this as I can. I need the truth, wherever it leads.

I take a deep breath and dive back in. I read until my eyes burn and my vision blurs. I devour every word, every odd story in the scroll, until I drift off, falling into a dream.

~

Fionn opens his wings, taking flight from his perch on my arm. He's small for a full-grown owl but no less fierce. I lower my gloved hand and watch him disappear into the trees, masked by the white flurry of snow.

The black steed shifts under me, his muscles flexing. I reach down and pet his regal neck, his shiny onyx coat striking in the white surroundings. "It's all right, Spark. He'll return to us. Hopefully he'll catch some of those mice plaguing my greenhouse."

The air is crisp with new snow, the bite of the cold lessened a little by the storm. I'm surprised that I can sense the slight shift in temperature at all; apparently, I've been here in this frozen land far too long—nearly six moons now. By my calculations it should be nearly Samhain, summer beginning to blur into autumn back home. And yet on this mountain, it's still ice and rock, the trees bare, only the ghosts of ash and birch standing as sentinels.

My blood is crying for the vivid green of home. I'm losing my mind among all of this death.

I've made my decision to leave, if only for a little while. I know my king will bring me back, like an escaped prisoner, but I must see my woods again. And so tonight, when he is on his hunt, I'll slip away.

The sound of snow crunching underfoot comes from the path behind me. A rider moves up beside me. It's the demon himself, clad in heavy black fur, his large raven perched on his shoulder.

I rode ahead of him on the pathway, needing a second to breathe without his silver eyes on me. Since I lost the child three moons ago, he's been watching me like a hawk. I've barely had a moment's peace except when he leaves me at my bedroom door at night.

There's an unspoken urgency in the air between us now. I haven't been able to bring myself to do as my mother said and surrender to him. If anything, my iron will to stay out of his sheets has only grown stronger. I could never love this beast.

Lailoken believes I should obey, but he says that I'll know when the time is right and not to rush. He's a monk, however, so what he knows of the bed and the heart is all of nothing.

The king is silent as he watches the sky. His raven, Bran, lifts off his shoulder to settle on a high branch, and the rush of his horse's breath curls around us. The gray steed is a beast—like its master. His speckled wolf pads past us, wandering ahead on the path, looking for hare or mice.

The only sounds around us are of crackling ice and branches creaking under the weight of the snow. Soon Fionn reappears overhead, emerging from the trees. I hold out my arm, and he lands heavily, a vole crushed in his beak. "Well done," I whisper to him, scratching his puffed-out chest.

"You've trained him well," the king finally says. "He's very loyal."

Fionn lifts off again, finding a branch ahead so he can consume his meal.

We nudge our rides forward at a meandering pace, side by side. I decide to speak freely since our ruse of being civil to one another will likely be broken by tonight when I take flight myself.

"Do you believe you're training me?" I ask.

He keeps his eyes forward, responding casually. "Is that what you'd prefer? To be trained like a falcon or an owl?"

"I'd prefer to be free," I say.

He's silent. Then he asks, "What would you do if you were, as you say, free?" He says the last word as if it tastes bitter on his tongue.

I didn't expect him to match my challenge. It takes me a moment to think about an answer. In the end, I simply say, "Everything."

Laughter rumbles from his chest. "Yes, you would, I'm sure. You are a true child of fire. Adventure and risk are in the blood."

Warmth fills my cheeks at his familiar tone. "And what is in the blood of a child of death?"

His smile turns wry. "Many dark things, if allowed." He turns his head to look at me. "But death can also be painfully beautiful, Lily."

I shiver at the sound of my human name coming from his lips. The last person who called me Lily, I loved. And then destroyed.

My thoughts are broken by a sudden screech of pain. My head snaps forward, recognizing the cry of my friend.

"Fionn!" I shout, kicking Spark onward, urgency filling me. We gallop a ways before I find my friend splayed out in blood-speckled snow, just off the path. An arrow pierces the owl's chest.

I slide from my mount and scramble over to the bird. Its wing is at an off angle, perhaps broken from the fall. It's still as death.

I hold back tears, reaching out, but then I hesitate. I could hurt it more with my touch. It's foolish to have grown so attached to a simple owl. But this is the only soul in this place that doesn't make me wish for horrible things.

"It's dead," the king says, coming up on foot behind me. "A hunter's shot. Perhaps it went for the intended prey." He glances back at the trees, watching for the hunter.

The tears on my cheeks turn to steam and anger fills me, melting the snow beneath me. "Be silent," I snap. "You have no idea what you're talking about."

He kneels down beside me. "You feel so much for the creature?" he asks, his tone curious.

"Of course, he's my friend."

The king turns his attention to the bird. "So you have come to love my gift."

I nod, my chest aching. It seems everything I care for turns to ashes.

The king shifts, then reaches out, pulling the arrow shaft from the flesh with a swift yank.

I choke out a sob at the violent movement, grabbing his arm. "Don't touch him!" No doubt the beast would pull apart my bird right in front of me.

He grips my wrist, moving it away, then places his other palm over the owl's body and closes his eyes, muttering under his breath in the ancient tongue: "Broken vessel, weave back into place, the thing that was taken . . ." His voice is a low hum.

I go still, listening in wonder, realizing what he's doing. He's calling the spirit back to the bird. A thin silver fog lifts from his arm and wraps around the owl, and I watch the tear in its breast fold back into place as he heals the flesh with his own ability to heal himself.

Several feathers regrow. The smell of rich earth and warmth fills the air, steam rising in a hiss from Fionn's form. The snow melts around the bird.

Its wings twitch, its talons flex. And suddenly the bird is twisting back upright, flying up into the branches. I cover my mouth, saying through my fingers, "Holy Mother. What have you done?"

The king hunches over, obviously depleted. "I stopped death for you, my love." And then he collapses into a heap in the snow.

THIRTY

FAELAN

It's late into the morning and Sage hasn't emerged from her cottage yet. Marius hasn't come by to see how she's doing yet either. Which is maybe a good thing. I feel like I need to talk to her first before I tell him my concerns about Kieran and the new torque. Before I confess what I've already kept from him, like the fire, and that kiss.

I knock on her cottage door around ten. No answer.

I sniff the air for smoke, but I don't smell anything except the overcast day—the morning dampness of the plants, the crisp water from the lagoon pool. I search for her power, for the connection I should have with her after the ceremony last night, but I don't sense anything. I'm not sure how to feel about that. I know it's working to a point, since I felt her anxiety at the tribunal, but I still can't tell how solid the connection is. It's possible her power is rejecting it.

I turn the knob, and the door clicks open as I call into the entrance, "Sage?" I step inside, looking around. The dim sunlight gives a gray tone to the room. I walk toward her bedroom door, deciding I should just wake her. But as I move through the small living room, I hear her breathing.

She's there, sitting on the floor, legs curled under her, head resting on the coffee table. Sound asleep.

I move closer and see she's lying on top of the scroll that I gave her. Her hand is resting beside a half-full cup of coffee.

I crouch at her side and touch her shoulder. "Sage, wake up."

She sighs but doesn't open her eyes.

"Sage." I brush her hair from her forehead and see she's drooling on the ancient script. Good thing it's protected by magic. I grip her shoulder and shake it gently. "Wake up, Sage."

She gasps, "Lailoken!" and sits straight up, eyes wild. "I need your help, Lailoken, I . . ." She pauses her panicked words and blinks, looking around. "What happened?" Her eyes find me, and she squints, reaching up to wipe the drool from her lip. "Faelan?"

Shock fills me. How could she possibly know that name, *Lailoken*?

She covers her brow with her hand and moans. "What the hell?" She sits back against the couch. "That was nuts. I dreamed . . . I think I was dreaming—what was it?"

A dream about an old monk she's never met? Could she have a memory of the other night when I took her to the Caledonian wood?

"Can you tell me anything about it?" I ask carefully.

She squints again. "I was . . . well, oh wow, I can't remember. Damn. I was definitely freaked out, though. My heart's racing." She puts her palm to her chest and picks up the coffee, then cringes and sets it back down. "Ugh, I'm so tired. Whatever it was, it was probably because of everything I read in this scroll. I was up all night." She yawns. "The part about her killing that guy and being put in the nunnery had me messed up in the head."

"You don't remember any of the dream? You said the name Lailoken."

"Perfect. I'm making up gibberish names in my sleep?"

"He's a monk." A hidden monk that only certain people would know. Her eyes grow. "A real one? How . . . how would I know his name?"

A very good question. "He's the one who brought you back after Kieran killed you. Maybe you remember some of that night? I took you into the woods, we went to his home. He lives in a tree."

She shakes her head, a lost look on her face.

It's all so strange. How in the name of the goddess could she know that name if she doesn't remember that night? Unless . . . "You said you had memories of Kieran," I say as a thought comes to me.

Pink fills her cheeks. "I hope they're not memories. I think they're a trick."

"But what you see is detailed?" I ask, ignoring her embarrassment. "They seem familiar, right? Do you think we could try something?"

A gold mist of fear filters from her chest. "Like what?"

"I think we should put you to sleep and have Aelia enter your dreams. Then we'll be able to tell better how Kieran is messing with you." The dark prince meddles in dreams. He could have sent visions to Sage, making her think she's living things that she isn't. It will be clear very quickly if her sleep is being messed with.

She chokes out a laugh. "Uh, no." And then she adds, "On second thought, make that a hell no."

"It's painless."

"For you, maybe. Aelia is the last person in the world that I want rooting around in my subconscious."

I move to the chair across from her and sit, leaning forward on my knees. I don't want to push her, but this is important. There's a reason her power can't be held by a torque, a reason she's feeling drawn to Kieran. If I'm going to help her through the transition—do my job— we have to clear this up. "You only have ten days until the Emergence, Sage. That's ridiculously soon. And choosing a House is the most important choice you'll ever make in this world. Don't you want to find out what's going on with Kieran before you have to make it?"

"No," she says quickly. She blows out a puff of air and adds, "But yes. You're right, I need to figure out what's going on. It's why I stayed up until my eyes bled reading those scrolls." She cradles her head in her hands.

"What did you find?"

She sighs, leaning back. "A whole lot of sad. My sister had a bummer of a life. She killed her first boyfriend by accident, then ended up basically sold into a prison marriage, and I'm guessing she killed Kieran's brother because he was some horrifying dickhead. It doesn't say much about the Black Death or the murder, though."

"She was Bonded to the king for several hundred years."

"Seriously? The scrolls only went to the first year in her slave marriage."

"Some believe they were madly in love."

"And then she killed him? That's even worse." She stands and shuffles over to the kitchen, then sets her cup down. "I want to sympathize with her, you know. It feels like I'm condemning myself when I judge her, like I could turn into a psychopathic murderer myself."

"I doubt that." But then I remember the Queen Lily I knew as a boy, how gentle she was, how kind to me. It was impossible to believe she was capable of what she did too.

"You barely know me," she says, walking over to her bedroom door. "But we'll worry about Homicidal Sage after I'm clean and coffeed. You check with Aelia about the dream thing—God, I can't believe I just said that."

She slips into the other room, and I sit for a minute, listening to the shower turn on, staring at the scroll, half rolled out on the coffee table. I lean over to see what part she was reading when she fell asleep. My pulse picks up, and a vision of Kieran and Sage under the tree last night pops into my head as I read:

And so eventually she succumbed to him. In the season of Samhain, the settling began. It wasn't clear what broke her, but what was clear was that she had given in fully. And once her power and his began to mingle within their Bond, the hope we had for our salvation instead became our doom.

THIRTY-ONE

SAGE

"Daddy won't like this, Faelan," Aelia says, folding her arms across her chest. "A dream spell can totally backfire. She could get stuck in there."

At first I wasn't really on board with this idea of Faelan's—I don't trust Aelia and don't want her help with *anything*. But then I realized I was being stubborn. If I can get this Kieran weirdness off the table, then all I have to think about is learning to control my fire. And that'll free me from this mental prison I've suddenly found myself in. Whatever Aelia does or doesn't do to me in the meantime won't matter anymore. I only have ten more days until the Emergence; I'm going to use every second of it to get free of this world—and learn how to live free without endangering myself or anyone else—before the hammer falls.

"In spite of your distracting obsession with fashion, Aelia," Faelan says, "you're an excellent druid. Even better than your sisters. I know you can do this and make it work."

Her features soften. "You're just bribing me with flattery."

"He is," I say, my voice tired. "But we need your help. I'll be honest, I don't like you, and I don't believe in you one bit. So, how 'bout you prove me wrong."

Faelan closes his eyes, a pained look on his face.

But Aelia straightens and gives me a nod, her teal eyes sparkling. "Challenge accepted, bitch."

~

By late afternoon they have me lying down in Faelan's nest while Aelia makes her potion in his kitchenette. The air smells like salad dressing and snappy greens.

Aelia seems to be thriving on being in charge. She's been ordering Faelan around for the last half hour, telling him what ingredients she needs, reading out loud from her spellbook in some other language.

"So," Aelia says loudly from the kitchen, "your part is pretty self-explanatory, Sage. You drink the potion and go to sleep. The important thing will be making sure your dreamworld is kept partially in the here and now so you don't float away and turn into Rapunzel."

"You're worried I'll grow super-long hair?" I ask, pretty sure that's not the faerie tale she's thinking of.

"I meant the sleeping one," she says, annoyed.

"That's Sleeping Beauty," I say dryly, then mutter, "Really not instilling confidence."

She just humphs and continues with whatever she's doing.

"You're not going to let that happen," Faelan says from somewhere down below, "are you, Aelia?"

"Nope," she says. "Because we're going to use a tether."

"You're planning on tying me to the bed now?" I ask.

"Nope." Her tone grows a mischievous edge. "I'm going to link your consciousness to Faelan's."

The snark evaporates from my tongue. I sit up, and Faelan and I say in unison, "What?"

I glance over at him from my perch in the nest. He's leaning on a tree branch near the kitchenette. He doesn't appear as worried as I feel. "What's that even mean?" I ask.

"It means I'll go into the dream with you," Faelan says, his voice tense. He doesn't look at me. "But I'll only be observing, so I can pull you out if it gets too deep."

The idea of Faelan joining me in a dream sends a wave of vulnerability through me. What if I dream about *him*? Or worse, Kieran?

Heat fills my cheeks. "I don't think that's a good idea."

"It'll be fun!" Aelia says. It's like she can tell there's a possibility it'll all end in my personal humiliation.

"Can't I just go in without a tether or whatever?"

"Nope," Aelia says, sounding joyous.

Faelan stays quiet, maybe sensing my unease, knowing full well why I'm not thrilled with him joining me in dreamland.

"I'm almost ready," Aelia announces. "Get your sexy butt up there, Faelan. The tether has to touch the subject during the spell."

He runs a hand through his hair, pausing before moving to comply. My heart pounds as he climbs up and over the edge. After he settles in to lie beside me, we both just stare up at the vines and branches that coat the ceiling. He clears his throat and shifts a little so his hip isn't brushing mine. "Sorry," he mutters.

"This is a bad idea," I whisper.

"I know."

"All cozy up there?" Aelia asks from below.

"So why are we doing it?" I ask through my teeth.

"You already decided we need to dig deeper—this is the best way I can see to do it," he says. "I'm your protector; it's my task to keep you from being lost. It might show us something, it might not, but I think it's worth a shot. It's your call, though, since this is your mind we'll be riffling through."

I squeeze my eyes shut, biting back a grumble. He's right, yet again. Maybe we won't see anything helpful, but it's worth it if we can. And a little embarrassment with Faelan isn't going to kill me. It's not as if this *thing* I feel between us can ever really go anywhere.

I ignore the pang in my chest when the thought comes. Because it sucks, but it's true. This can't go anywhere, whatever it is or isn't. No matter how attracted I am to him. Nothing in my world lasts. And I really don't want him to be another item on my long list of broken things.

Aelia appears over the edge of the nest, bowl in her hand. She sets it down beside me, the red liquid sloshing. "Three big gulps each, alternating, don't skimp." She disappears over the side again.

Faelan and I sit up, looking down at the bowl.

"Once I lock in," Aelia says, "I won't feel what you guys feel, but I should see glimpses of imagery if it works right. You can explain anything I miss when you reemerge—oh, and you should remember the dream really clearly once you're conscious again. I'm going to begin the chanting for the casting as soon as you each take your first drink. So tell me when."

I pick up the bowl, cradling it in both hands. My pulse thunders in my head, my nerves raw. All I want is to get away from this crazy. But it looks like the only way to do that is to walk right through it.

"Bottoms up," I mumble. And I take the first big swig.

The bitter taste of something like raw beets and the tang of vinegar mingle in my mouth. My stomach rises, but I manage to swallow it all. I gag as I pass the bowl over.

Faelan takes his drink and Aelia starts her chanting. We pass it back and forth, and by the third gulp things are becoming a green blur, the nest tipping under me, my heartbeat a slow whooshing in my head. I lie back. And the warmth of Faelan settles in beside me.

We turn to face each other, and his slow breath brushes my face. We blink in unison for a few seconds, sinking into the moment.

My eyes slide closed, his fingers gliding down my arm to settle on my wrist. As everything goes still.

And we drift into sleep.

~

Three days have passed, and the king still hasn't woken from hibernation. His raven, Bran, perches on the headboard, and his wolf is curled at the foot of the bed, both guarding their master. I sit close by, either beside the king's bed or near the fire, warring with myself, seeing my chance to run. But for some unfathomable reason, I'm unable to make myself leave his side as he sleeps.

His shade, Eric, a large Norseman who came in with the first invasions and died in battle, stays with me at all times, never leaving me alone with his master. He insists that the king hasn't ever been down this long after a healing, but he also mentioned that the king's feedings have decreased these last three months, so perhaps he's just weakened.

"Why has the king cut back?" I ask.

Eric merely looks at me.

"Shouldn't he have been paired with a shade for hibernation then?" I ask, a helplessness weaving through me. I'm not sure how the children of the Morrígan pair for hibernation, but my guess is it's bloody. I can't think how else he'll rejuvenate if he's alone and hungry, though.

Eric shifts his feet, looking uncomfortable.

"Speak, fool!" I bark.

The raven echoes my annoyance with a screech.

Eric clears his throat. "He wouldn't wish for me to speak of it with you, mistress."

"So you'll watch him sleep as eternity passes us by? Don't be ridiculous."

"My king is trying to please you," he says, as if he's accusing me of something. "His desire for you consumes him. He starves himself, believing he can learn to control his hunger, his power, more effectively. So that when you become his in truth, he won't feed from you or harm you in any way."

My pulse quickens. "What?"

I look over to the king, his hands folded over his chest, skin gray, lips violet, as if he were carved from solid death. He's denying himself so that he won't accidentally harm me? The idea doesn't fit with what I know of him, of his cruelty. It doesn't match the monster I faced during the Bonding ceremony.

"He wishes to please you," Eric says again.

"Well, he shouldn't," I mutter, rising to my feet and walking over to the hearth. I pull a pinch of lavender from the pouch tied to my skirts and toss it into the flames. It sizzles for a moment, the smoke lightening. "Mother Goddess, hear me," I say to the flames. "My Bonded sleeps and cannot be woken. Please give me guidance. How can I help him?"

The logs shift and sizzle immediately, as if my mother knows the urgency I feel. But when the words come, my heart sinks. Surrender . . . the flames whisper again, drawing out the sound with a hiss. The fire born within you shall bring rebirth. Surrender, child. Do not delay.

I turn away, turmoil brewing in my gut. I hardly know what that means now. How can I surrender to a force that's asleep?

"What did she answer?" Eric asks.

"Nothing," I say. "She said nothing." I walk away from the hearth and return to the bedside. "I need you to send a message. I need you to call for the monk Lailoken to attend me. Tell him his ward is in need of him."

Eric gives me a frustrated look, but then he reluctantly bows his head, saying, "If I must, mistress." He slips out of the room, leaving me alone for the first time in days.

I stare down at my king and wonder what the mother goddess could possibly want from me. To surrender to this beast? Truly? The image of him placing his hand on Fionn's breast to heal him surfaces again. It's the reason he's in this bed, silent. Helpless. He did that to himself to save a foolish girl's bird.

Lailoken arrives at the keep as evening falls. Eric begrudgingly lets me know of his presence in the gallery, but then stands by the door, resuming his position of guard.

"Bring him up," I say.

He looks back and forth between his master lying in the bed and me, as if the king could give an order for him to stop listening to me.

"Please, Eric," I add, attempting to put strength behind the words. I'm tired from lack of sleep, weakened from lack of food. I haven't truly fed for months. I'm practically human right now. Eric could deny me and have me locked in my rooms if he wanted. Of the two of us, he's the stronger at this point.

"He is a Christian monk," Eric says, bitterness on his tongue. He flexes his wide shoulders as if to intimidate me. "He'd see me damned to his hell."

"He understands the old ways and respects the goddess."

"Both of them?"

"Are we going to debate religion or seek help where it can be found?"

He seems to consider and then miraculously mutters, "Very well, mistress," turning to walk out. He returns with Lailoken in his grasp. The usually tidy old man is tousled from head to toe like he's been searched for weapons. His dark woolen robes are torn at the hem, and his cross is missing from his belt. There is a smudge of blood on his chin, his lip swelling.

Eric drags him forward and tosses him to the floor in a heap before the hearth.

I rush to the monk's side, praying none of his bones were broken. "What have you done?" I snap at Eric. I help Lailoken into my chair and turn on the shade. "You dare to touch my watcher? I should have you tossed in the dungeon. Foolish leech!"

Eric resumes his place as guard and stares at me, daring me to act.

Lailoken waves a hand. "It's all very well, Lily." He dabs his lip with his sleeve. "I'm still in one piece. No harm done."

"You're bleeding," I say, still glaring a hole through Eric. The shade scowls right back.

"It's nothing," Lailoken says. He takes my hand, patting it between his. "Now, tell my why you've called me here."

I reluctantly pull my gaze from the Norseman and focus on my friend. I kneel in front of him and study the cut on his lip, anger boiling up. I needed an ally and he came. Even though he likely knew this would be the consequence. I was a fool to think he'd be treated well by the king's men. There's a reason he stays in the caves.

He makes a small sound of pain as he shifts to face the bed. "Is your king ill? What's happened, child?"

"He brought Fionn's spirit back, and this is the result. Is he being punished? What can I do?"

Lailoken frowns and leans forward, studying the still form of my Bonded. Ice crystals are beginning to grow slowly around the king's mouth and at his temples now.

"Have you called on your mother?" Lailoken asks.

I nod.

"Well?"

"She said the same as before." I glance at Eric.

Lailoken furrows his brow, concern flickering over his features. "She did, did she?"

"Yes, but it's impossible now . . . Why do you look so glum? I don't understand."

"It seems obvious to me, child."

"What?"

He scoots closer, whispering, "She wishes for you to allow him to feed."

My pulse skips. "On me?"

He gives me a dubious look.

I rise to my feet. "I can't. I won't." Panic fills me. I thought she wanted me to allow him into my bed, not my spirit. "This whole thing is madness."

He releases a tired sigh. "I will pray, then."

Eric steps forward. "What is all this whispering? What goes on?"

"Nothing," I say. How can I let the king feed from me? He could consume me altogether, leave nothing.

Of course, in that case, I'd finally be free.

I look back to his still form. I am grateful for what he did, how he healed my Fionn. But it doesn't change what he is, what his power could do to me. My choice appears to be to let him languish or to sacrifice myself. My inclination leans toward the former. What good will it do anyone to have both high royal children of the two great goddesses become useless?

But something deep inside won't allow me to just let this go. The same force that has kept me at his bedside these last three nights is tugging at me, urging me to give in. It draws me to him. It makes me yearn for the most terrifying things.

"You are considering," Lailoken says, reading me as he always does.

"I don't know."

"I think your mother will protect you, child," he says.

"What?" Eric asks. "What are you considering?"

I meet his eyes. "I wonder if I should attempt to feed myself to him."

Eric's body stiffens. "You would do such a thing?"

"I wouldn't want him to suffer," I say, surprised that I mean it. "I would do what I can." And I am trying to be obedient. I am. I don't wish to hurt anyone else. Not again. "Sitting here isn't doing any good."

"He wouldn't wish for you to be harmed," Eric says, but he watches his master with concern, like he's considering helping me, anyway. He doesn't care for me, but he does care about the king.

I decide to play that to my advantage. "We'll tell him that I forced you. Your king won't have to know you helped me."

Eric studies the stone floor, his brow creased in concern. But then he nods. "What do you need?"

"I need you to ensure my friend is given food and supplies, then safely escort him back to his cave," I say. "You'll leave me here alone with the king and not return until one of us walks through that door."

"How do I know you're not planning to feed from him yourself and sap him further?" he asks.

I hold his gaze, hoping he'll see the truth in my eyes. "Because I'd rather die than feed from this beast."

He blinks like I struck him, but he gives another nod, then waves Lailoken forward. "Come, monk. I'll escort you myself. No harm will come to you."

Lailoken takes my hand in his again, gripping me tight. "I fear for you, daughter."

I kiss his cheek. "I'll come to you at sunrise tomorrow. Either in spirit or in body. But I'll see you one last time, I promise." I give him a small smile. "We'll see if my mother is as wise as they say."

Fear overwhelms me for a moment as I watch him go, and I have to dig my nails into my palms to keep my power from surfacing. I shiver and turn to the king. The cold is suddenly a sting in my bones. But if I plan to do this, I need to get it over with.

I move to stoke the fire, trying to bring more heat into the room. Then I steel myself, letting my woolen shawl fall to the ground. I reach up and pull the string on my dress, loosening the neck, letting the fabric fall past my shoulders until it hangs at my waist. My shift covers my breasts. I can't bring myself to strip naked for him, but I need to allow for as much skin as I can.

The bed is soft under me as I move my way across to lie at his side.

This is my Bonded. I won't need herbs to encourage his connection. I won't need spells. That's all been done already. What I'll need is skin, his and mine, and a willing spirit on the other side of the connection.

His shades have already removed his leathers—only his thin linen tunic remains. I tentatively reach out and unfold his hands, pulling them from his torso. I gather the fire in my fingers and run them softly along his arms and chest, burning the fabric enough so that it all falls away.

My body shakes, teeth chattering, nerves raw. I nestle in, pressing my body into his side, laying my arm over his pale chest. Resting my cheek in the crook of his shoulder. There are salty tears on my lips.

"You may feed from me if you wish," I whisper.

I hope he can hear me.

What am I thinking? Am I wishing myself into oblivion?

"Goddess, help me."

I almost don't notice the first pull, it's so subtle. A slight ache in my cheek, my palm. I'm half-relieved, half-terrified when it comes. I focus on breathing and ready myself for the inevitable pain, knowing very little of what might be coming, knowing only that it is death.

Again, the ache surfaces, stronger. And a chill blossoms next, small prickles left in its wake.

I watch in confusion as ice crystals crawl from his chest, over my fingers, up my forearm, to my elbow.

Fear washes over me, but I don't pull away.

A moan rumbles from his throat, vibrating in my skin.

And the pain flares, at last, my whole body lighting with the burst, the ache growing jagged edges, sharpening into agony in mere seconds, blinding me. Talons and teeth claw at my insides, in a frantic swarm, tearing, writhing, like a riot of birds trying to burst from my bones.

I can't move, I can't breathe, I can't hear anything except my thundering heartbeat.

But just as quickly as the agony comes, it washes away like a tide fading out.

I gasp and convulse, trying to get air into my lungs as I scramble away from the monster trying to rip me in two.

Fingers grip my wrist, and the king rises, his body looming over mine. His silver eyes burn blue. "What've you done?" he growls, his voice scraping against my skin. "Fool woman."

I try to squirm away, but I'm weak, my limbs useless. "Please," I rasp from shivering lips. "Please." It's all I can say, my mind blurring in and out of focus.

"I've hurt you," he says more gently. As if he were ashamed.

He gathers me up, his fingers delicately caressing my face, almost unsure. I hardly know how to interpret his touch.

"Listen to my voice," he says, "and focus on my face."

His features are tight with worry. Still, his fingers brush carefully at my cheek, my neck, lulling me.

"It wasn't for you to do this," he says. "I would have returned to you. I always will."

"Couldn't leave you alone," I whisper. No matter how much I wanted to. I don't have my own will any longer. This Bond holds me captive to him, beyond my control. It's suddenly clear to me now.

He goes still, as if stunned by my words. He studies me, fingers playing in my hair.

And then he leans in, kissing me gently on the lips.

The scent of him surrounds me, sweet roses and rich wine, the tang of it on my tongue so stunning I nearly gasp. Heat spills from my core, filling my skin, my power seeking, hungry as it reaches out, as it responds in a heartbeat, wanting him.

But I struggle with it, pushing it back, then tuck it away as I always do.

"Don't resist," he says. "Let it do what it wants. Let me feel you, Lily."

His lips touch mine again, this time with a need of his own, his hands gripping me, pulling me close. Everything in me sparks to life, bright and vivid in a vibration of urgency. His body and mine cling to each other, natural as magnets. My hunger seeking, nudging, needing.

And I answer. Surrendering.

THIRTY-TWO

FAELAN

My eyes snap open. I gasp for air, feeling like I haven't breathed in decades. The chill of the stone room shifts to the warmth of my cottage; the bed melds into my nest; the smell of snow turns to the smell of green life.

What did I just see . . . feel? That wasn't Sage in that vision. It wasn't Sage.

And with sudden clarity I know why Sage feels a connection to Kieran, what memories she's sensing when she's with him. It must be one of these dreams. One of Lily's memories of the king.

Because that was Queen Lily. I can barely believe it. Sage was living her sister's memories in her sleep. A striking, vivid dream of a real moment from long ago. How is that even possible?

It's *not* possible. Unless . . .

Unless Sage was given the blood memories by someone.

No. That's not—it can't be. Who would do that? And how would I have missed it? It takes a fairly complex spell, and whoever did it would have had to store the memories for centuries. Not to mention the fact that Queen Lily isn't *dead*, so she wouldn't have released her memories yet. They'd still be inside of her, and she's in the Pit.

What I just saw is . . . impossible. You can't have memories from a spirit that's still among the living—even if they are in hell. I'd believe Sage's mind had made it all up if it wasn't for the striking accuracy of details she could never know—of Lailoken, how and where he lived at that time. The knowledge of how to contact the goddess. How the King of Ravens would have fed.

None of that would have been in the annals, even if she'd read them all.

The repercussions of what I just witnessed are unfathomable—for Sage, and for the House of Brighid. Sage carries the memories inside her, the truth of what happened between Lily and the king. Marius needs to know. Right away.

Sage sighs, shifting in her sleep. Her hand moves to my thigh and her fingers twitch. The sting of her pull shoots through my leg.

I snatch up her wrist, returning her hand to her side.

"Aelia?" My voice comes out more like a croak. Like I've been asleep for years instead of minutes—or hours? How long have we been under? "Aelia, are you here?" I ask.

Only silence answers back. Of course.

Sage releases a sudden gasp, her back arching a little. And then her eyes flutter open, locking on me.

Pink fills her cheeks, and she goes still. "Faelan?"

"You okay?" I ask quietly.

She starts to prop herself on her elbows, nodding, but then she shakes her head. "I don't know." She licks her lips and coughs.

"Let me get you something to drink." My stiff body moves slowly, but I climb down from the nest and fetch her a bottle of water from the fridge, then make my way back up beside her.

Her hand shakes as she reaches to take the offering. Her gaze stays trained on the grass between us.

She drinks a few sips, then asks, "How long have you been awake?"

"A few seconds before you."

She lifts her thumb to her mouth and begins to chew on the nail.

The silence stretches out. I realize she's not going to say anything, so I go first. "I saw everything," I say. "And felt it. I was there with Queen Lily in the castle—it was a memory. And you were Lily."

She nods and takes another sip of water.

"How long do you think you've been dreaming her memories?" I ask.

"Not sure," she says. "But a bunch of moments flooded in just before I opened my eyes. I remember so much—it's all mixed up, like it's my own life. Burning the boy I loved—I mean who *she* loved. There was a ceremony with blood and chanting and . . . well, it was the Bonding, I think." She shakes her head. "I remember this beautiful owl that I had—I mean . . . you know what I mean. His name was Fionn; he was white. But it doesn't make any sense. Why? Why is all of this spilling into my head?" She finally looks at me, adding, "Why do you have that expression on your face?"

I shake my head. "We really need to talk to Marius."

She searches my face like she's trying to figure out what I'm not saying. But I'm fresh out of explanations. Marius will need to handle it from here, especially if Sage is confusing Lily's experiences with her own. After everything that we just saw, everything that happened between Sage and me last night at the Introduction, the kiss, the moment with Kieran . . . I need a clear head to make sure I can see it all straight.

"Why don't you get cleaned up, and I'll call him to see if we can go to the office." I'm not sure we should wait until dinner for this.

"Okay," she says, not sounding too sure. Then she adds, "You seem worried. This is bad, isn't it?"

I decide to be honest. "I have no idea. But I know we did the right thing, opening up the dreams. It could be the answer to everything."

I leave her in my cottage and step outside to call Marius. His secretary, Dana, tells me he's indisposed, which is code for feeding, so I let her know I'll be coming by the office in an hour or so. I hang up, feeling unsure. I need to tell Marius everything. But I know he'll be seriously pissed at what I've kept from him about Sage and her shortfalls. I'm not eager to experience his wrath.

I spot Aelia sitting by the pool, sunbathing. "Did we bore you with all our sleeping?" I ask. "Way to keep your eye on the ball, Lia."

"Oh please, you should thank me." She rolls over onto her stomach. "Once I felt all the steam, I was out. I wasn't about to be the third wheel on that ride."

"How much did you see?"

"Enough. It's obviously some kind of memory implant."

"Seems so."

"But how's that possible, with Queen Lily still alive?"

I shake my head.

"I called Daddy and left a message about twenty minutes ago telling him we had an update on the newblood. I thought he'd want to know. Are you going over to the office?"

"Yeah, Sage is getting cleaned up."

"You know she's even more of a walking treasure now, right?" she says.

"What's that supposed to mean?"

She rolls back over and sits up. "Once word gets out that she's a vault of intel on King and Queen Tragedy, this Emergence will get even more nuts, Faelan—everyone will want her. And you still haven't gotten this locked down. You should see what tributes came today: Lyr dropped off a race horse, which is still in the front yard; your brothers sent over a Tiffany lamp; and I peeked in an envelope the House of Morrígan left, and there were keys to his vineyard in Spain." She laughs. "Oh, and Kieran sent an invite to his house in the hills tomorrow evening—some swanky party." She waves at a black envelope on the glass table beside her. "He was nice enough to invite you. And me." A sly grin tips her mouth.

"This isn't a game, Lia."

"Everything's a game, Faelan."

~

The drive to Marius's office is slow, traffic on the 10 not cooperating. Sage has been silent the entire ride. I should talk to her about everything that happened during the dream and find out how she's processing it all. We should at least be talking about her powers to see if she's had any slips since her manifestation last night with Kieran. There's a myriad of things we should be working through, but I have no idea where to start. She seems content to stare out the car window at the city passing by, so I leave it at that.

The big question right now is how these imprinted blood memories got spelled into her. And, almost as important, how will she deal with it? Because blood memories can become completely overwhelming over time, and we have no idea how long they've been bubbling up in her sleep. I'd heard that the visions feel strong, as if you've lived the moment yourself, and now I've felt firsthand how accurate that is. One druid from the fifteen hundreds was addicted to the process. He stole blood memories from the Cast's collectors several times, absorbing them into his consciousness through the holy ritual, before he was caught and executed for it.

Whoever did this to Sage took a very serious chance at getting their own head removed. Only the Cast sanctions blood memory removal, and only the House sanctions when they're passed on.

Why would someone take such a risk? The dreams were bound to be discovered.

We pull into the parking garage and leave the car with the valet. When we get in the elevator, Sage leans on the rail and hugs herself like she's cold. "What do you think Marius will say?" she asks.

"About what?"

"My brain reliving my homicidal sister's life."

"Hopefully he'll be able to help us figure out why the memories are there."

She releases a breath. "It's obvious something's wrong with me."

"Sage—"

"The first torque didn't work, and I burned down the cottage in my sleep. I've somehow attracted the most manipulative guy in this whole freaky world into stalking me. And now I have this new torque on that only he can take off."

Damn, I forgot—I have to break the news to Marius about that too.

She continues, "And we don't even know if this torque works either."

Gods, another thing. "We should test it," I say, pressing the button for the floor just below Marius's. He'll want to know whether this torque is effective, no matter how mad he might be that Kieran is the one who placed it. I should've thought to test it last night.

The elevator dings, and the doors open to the empty floor. I step out, and she follows me hesitantly. She looks around at the bare drywall and steel beams of the unfinished offices.

"The floors above and below Marius's offices are empty," I explain. "He owns the building so he doesn't lease them out. This floor is glamoured to look like an ad agency to the humans, I think." I pick up a scrap piece of cardboard from where it leans against the wall and place it in the middle of an open area. "Okay, you're going to try and light this on fire."

"What if I can't?"

"It's not a can or can't. It'll be what you feel inside when you try." I turn to face her, wondering how best to spark her power. Unfortunately, the most effective stimulations are pain or passion—not things I want to ignite in her. "There are a couple of ways we could do this," I start, not sure how to put it. "We could use force, like pain from a cut on your arm." I tap the sheath on my side. "Or I could . . . we could . . . touch."

She blinks up at me. "Like, I could try to feed from you again?"

I nod.

"Or you could cut me?"

"Yeah."

"Wow, both sound so great," she says dryly. "I barely know what to pick."

"It's your call. We could also wait and let Marius do this."

Her feet shift, and she shakes her head. "No, let's just cut my arm."

My chest constricts with disappointment, surprising me. She'd rather cut herself than have a repeat of last night—so what? Why the bloody hell am I bummed she doesn't want to feed from me?

She must see my conflict because she adds, "I don't want to hurt you by accident. At least this way it's just me."

I nod, not commenting, then pull out my dagger and hand it to her by the hilt.

She takes it and starts to point it at her arm, but then pauses and holds it out to me again. "Sorry, can you just do it? Apparently I'm a horrible masochist along with everything else."

I take the blade back, but I hesitate. My body refuses to move. "I'm not sure I can," I say, literally unable to do it. It's as if I couldn't hurt her even if I wanted to. And then I remember the protector spell. Of course I can't.

I stare at her, overwhelmed by my need to shield her. I've never felt this way for anyone. Even Astrid. But . . . if it is just the protector spell, then why am I noticing how her pale lashes frame her eyes and highlight the gold specks in her irises? Why does the slight upturn of her nose make me want to pull her closer . . . and kiss her?

Being in that dream reminded me of something I can never have again—the joining of soul and body with someone, the feel of connecting, caring, worshipping. And in this moment, I realize it's her I want that forbidden thing with.

It's her.

THIRTY-THREE

SAGE

"The protector spell won't let me hurt you," he says, his voice tense as he passes the knife back.

I take it from him for the second time, the smooth hilt cool against my palm.

"Okay," I say. "I'll just do a quick cut then—where's the best spot?" I wave the blade over my forearm.

His hands go in his pocket. "Your palm. And you should hurry. I feel like I'm going to come out of my skin if I don't stop you."

"Right." Without thinking about it, I press the blade's edge to the soft flesh of my palm as hard as I can and slice with a quick swipe.

I hiss in a breath, my hand throbbing instantly. It's a good cut, blood pearling up, sliding in a thick coat over my palm, dripping from my fingers to the floor. "Now what?" I ask through my teeth.

"You'll still heal with the torque on, maybe a bit slower, but you shouldn't be able to release the energy in its element form." He directs my attention from my bloody hand to the cardboard. "Focus on the pain. Try to push it into the cardboard. Remember yesterday afternoon, how the energy felt when it rose."

I have no trouble focusing on the pain. I stare down at the cardboard and try to sense that part of myself I'm just getting to know, the spark of heat in my blood.

The sting pulses over my arm and up my shoulder, and something stirs. My belly is growing warm, and my chest is heating.

"I feel it," I say.

"Now attempt to push it outward, like the sensation is your weapon, your punch at something trying to hurt you."

I stare at the cardboard and try to get a grip on the stirring. I breathe in slowly through my nose. And I shove outward.

The energy surges, growing hotter in a nanosecond. My hand coats with orange light, small tongues of fire licking over the wound as it closes. But there's a sudden pushback, the heat dulling as quickly as it flared.

The cardboard smokes at my feet.

"Good," Faelan says. "I felt the block, did you?"

"I think so."

"It's working."

I release a shaky breath and touch the medallion, tracing the amber-encased moth with my fingertip. "It worked." I can't help the huge smile that fills my face as relief washes over me. "Oh my God, that was awesome. I felt it. Like, *really* felt the thing inside me that time."

"Good, Sage," he says, answering with his own smile.

The sight of his dimple sends tingles down my legs. "I'm going to be able to control it," I say, giddy.

"You are."

The realization of what that means hits me. I won't hurt anyone now. I'm free. I could actually leave if I wanted to.

But as soon as the thought rises, my excitement twists, turning sour. *And where will you go, Sage? You'll be totally alone out there.*

"You all right?" Faelan asks, bringing me back.

"Yeah, totally," I lie. "I'm super relieved."

"Well, let's go talk to Marius," he says, studying me like he knows I'm faking my smile now. "We still have a lot of ground to cover."

THIRTY-FOUR

FAELAN

Sage and I walk down the hall to the red door. It opens before my knuckles hit the wood to knock. Gerald, Marius's selkie assistant, is there, looking at us with his white eyes. "The master will be out in a moment. Please wait for him there." He points to the two seats facing the desk.

When Sage sits, she grips the arms of the chair, her knuckles turning white. I'm not sure why she's so tense. It seemed like she was relieved for a second about the torque—for good reason. Her energy being contained will help her have a smoother transition. And it'll allow for a clearer head when she chooses her House. She'll still have to deal with the memories, but I'm hoping Marius will have a solution to that, maybe speeding up the process so they'll fade faster.

It doesn't take long for Marius to emerge from his feeding room. His chest is bare, a towel is wrapped around his neck, and there are drops of water falling from his damp silver hair. The scars from his years as a child slave in Rome are apparent. I glance at Sage to see how she reacts. She's not really looking at him, though. She's biting her nails and staring past him at the feeding room door where Marius's selkie concubine, Paris, can be seen climbing from the feeding tub, naked.

My eyes move to the floor, and my stomach clenches as I realize Sage will think all the wrong things about what she's seeing.

Marius shuts the door and walks over to us, drying his hair with the towel. "What's the urgency?" he asks. "I was planning to come to the house in an hour or so. Is everything all right?"

I stand. "Yes, sir—I mean, we're not sure. Sorry to interrupt you. I just wasn't sure this was something that I should wait on."

"Sit, Faelan." He goes to the other side of the desk, pulls a white cotton T-shirt from a drawer, and puts it on. He folds his towel and sets it aside. "Did something happen last night after I left?"

"In a way," I say. Sage is silent as Marius focuses on her. "It's come to my attention," I continue, deciding to get right to the point, "that she's having dreams of Queen Lily. Blood memories, to be exact."

Marius looks between us. "I don't understand. How do you know this?"

"We did a dream spell," I say. "And I went in with her as the tether."

His features tense. "What pushed you to do such a thing?"

I hesitate.

Sage breaks in. "I was feeling connected to Kieran, like I knew him or something, and it scared me. Faelan was trying to help me figure out why."

"And when we went into the dream under the spell," I say, "it was clear that Sage was dreaming as Lily. Like a blood memory."

"Blood memories show themselves when the person is awake," Marius says, his eyes narrowing. "Not asleep. This is very odd, Faelan. You know how these things work. We would've been aware if such an invasion of her mind had happened. We've watched her. No druid has had access to her. And even so, the ceremony takes hours, and the memories don't *hide* themselves."

"Yes, sir," I say, trying to gather my thoughts and figure out how to explain it better. "But she has knowledge of Lailoken, the wise man.

And she knows about the King of Ravens and how he fed, how he looked. How would she know those things?"

"It was foolish to follow this." He shakes his head, frustrated. "This could confuse matters even more."

"But, sir, something was wrong. She'd had a slipup with her energy in her sleep, even with her torque on. At one point, she wouldn't heal. And then this strong connection she was feeling with Kieran . . . we were trying to figure out what was going on."

"It seems a lot has gone on," Marius says.

"Yes, sir," I say. "I'm sorry, I wouldn't have bothered you with this either, but I'm not sure how to help her now."

"Don't apologize, Faelan," he says. He turns his attention to Sage. "Come here and stand in front of me, child."

She glances at me, then stands and moves around the desk to the other side, in front of Marius.

He examines her face, focusing on her eyes. "Your energy seems very clear. I can sense the torque working with—" His eyes fall to her torque, and he steps back. "Where did you get that, child?" His head turns to me as he points at the medallion. "Where did this come from, Faelan?"

I didn't expect him to react so strongly to the ancient torque. If anything, I thought he'd be relieved that it was found after it went missing so long ago. But now my nerves turn raw at the anger in his eyes. I feel him begin to stir his energy in the air, my muscles twitching, my veins aching, as he manipulates the water around him—including inside me.

"It's my fault that I'm wearing it," Sage says, her tone worried, like she can sense Marius's simmering rage. "Kieran gave it as his gift last night at the Introduction. Faelan had nothing to do with it."

Marius turns his attention back to her. "And you placed it yourself? Take it off."

I start to explain. "Sir—" But he waves his hand and a sharp sting fills my skin, my gut twisting with his manipulation. I grunt, hunching in pain and clutching my stomach.

Sage's eyes widen and she steps back. "Don't hurt him—"

"Take it off," Marius repeats coldly.

Sage shakes her head, reaching up to clutch the medallion in her fist. "I can't. Kieran put it on me," she says, her voice shaking.

"Kieran?" Marius says through his teeth. He turns back to me. "You allowed the Prince of Shadows to place the most powerful torque in existence on the newblood he wishes to control, Faelan?"

"Faelan wasn't there," Sage says quickly. "I slipped away from him even though he told me to stay put. It was my fault. When he found me, I already had it on."

Why would she lie? It doesn't matter if I was there or not. I was meant to be watching everything, to be guarding. And I failed.

The tension of Marius's power releases from my body, the pain fading a little.

He studies her. "You protect him with your lies," he says, his voice softening. "You have loyalty, young one. This is good. I'm very relieved." He moves to his desk and unlocks a hidden drawer underneath, then pulls out a small scroll. He glances at me. "I saw last night that you were becoming attached to this newblood, Faelan. But I was unsure about her. I see now that we may be able to trust her."

He holds the scroll out to Sage in offering. Once she takes it, he continues, focusing on me again. "I knew Kieran and Mara had possession of the torque. Someone from the House of Morrígan stole it several hundred years ago, believing it belonged with their House. I suspected that it would emerge with the arrival of our young Sage— though I had no idea it would happen so quickly, which is why I was surprised to see it. But I knew Kieran would have made sure he was the one who placed it when the time came." He looks at Sage. "He has designs on you, princess. He thinks their House can re-create the past, control all the cards in this. What are your thoughts about him?"

When she doesn't respond, he adds, "You are afraid of your feelings, I see. And this is why you allowed Faelan into your dreams?"

She nods.

"The blood memories are causing a problem," I say, trying to clarify. "Do you think Kieran is responsible for them being implanted?"

Marius shakes his head. "I doubt he'd have the foresight. Kieran knows a lot of details about the Bond between his brother and Queen Lily, and I'm sure he's built it up in his head as his birthright to own Sage's powers as the King of Ravens owned Lily's. But it's all fantasy. The boy is deluded."

"What can we do about it, though?" I ask. I don't want to ask the question roiling in my head: *What if he wins her over?* I can't voice that concern in front of Sage and make her think I don't have faith in her. But I know Kieran.

"There is a spell in the scroll that can help," Marius says. "It will aid in the assimilation of the memories and allow for the implant—if there is one—to fade faster."

"How long?" Sage asks.

"Months rather than years."

She looks down, turning the small scroll in her fingers. I know she's thinking of the dreams, of living all those moments of Lily's struggle, the pain, the sorrow. And eventually the madness. Thinking she'll be overwhelmed by it for months.

"I'll check in by phone tonight," Marius says. "I need updates every day, Faelan. This new revelation needs to be monitored. Keep her safe from it."

"Yes, sir."

He turns to Sage, reaching out to gently touch her slumped shoulder. "Don't lose heart, young Sage. You have much to contribute to our world. You could find a home here with us, a family, someone to trust. If you wish."

THIRTY-FIVE

SAGE

I really don't want to go back to the Cottages. The closer we get, the harder it is to breathe.

I should be relaxing into the idea of finding a way out of this now. My problems are all solved: my power is contained, I won't hurt anyone, the dreams will eventually be gone. Yes, I'll have to deal with them for a while, but I can do that anywhere. There's no reason to stay and be tortured by this crazy Emergence choice anymore—because how does a person choose their *destiny* in one week? That's ridiculous.

And I could get free from it tomorrow if I wanted. Be back to depending on myself again. Simple.

But deep inside, I know that I won't. I won't leave this time. I won't run.

The old me is seriously pissed, and confused. I can't understand why I'm not willing to leave this behind all of a sudden.

"What's going on, Sage?" Faelan asks as we leave the 10 freeway and merge onto PCH.

I'd like to know the answer to that myself. I watch the silver blue of the Pacific appear beside him and swallow the rock in my throat.

We pass shops, beaches, houses, and I can't find a way to say what I'm feeling.

"What, Sage?" Faelan asks again, his tone growing tense.

I shake my head. "Can we stop?"

"What?"

"The car."

"Why?"

"Stop the car!" I snap, shocking myself. And him.

He steers the Audi to the side of the road, pulling off at a vista point and parking so we face the ocean. He turns off the engine. Then he watches me cautiously as several seconds of silence pass. When I can't take it anymore, I open the door and get out, walking to the edge of the bluff and trying to get oxygen into my lungs. I gulp the sea air and swallow my rising tears.

The crunch of rocks and dirt underfoot sounds behind me.

The ocean rages below, and the salty mist clings to my skin as the breeze carries it past.

"I don't want this," I whisper, to the sea, to Faelan, to my goddess mother, wherever she is. "I don't want to be this."

Faelan stays quiet beside me, staring out at the water, the wind tousling his hair.

"I've been wanting to run away," I confess. He doesn't respond, so I add, "I was pretty much out of here as soon as I learned to get my powers under control." Shame fills me, and I have no idea why.

Maybe because I'm a coward.

"Where do you plan to go?" he asks, surprising me.

I shrug.

"You know they'll find you, right?" he says. "Next time it'll be Kieran who takes you under his wing." He turns from the water to face me. "Is that what you want?"

"No!" I say quickly.

"Then what do you want, Sage?"

I can only shake my head as my throat goes tight. Because I don't know. What Marius said before we left his office hit me hard. My whole life all I've wanted is a home, peace, safety. I want to be able to trust someone.

But I don't even think I'd know how to do that. How can I ever be sure it's real?

Faelan touches my wrist, and I look down as his fingers slide over my palm and weave through mine. I stare at our joined hands, and everything inside me settles. I look back out at the water and take in a shaky breath. Release it.

Then I lean over, resting my head on his shoulder. Together we watch the ocean churn.

~

The sun is setting in bright orange and violet by the time we get back to the house. We part ways silently, Faelan going to his cottage, me to mine. We haven't said anything more, but nothing needs to be said. Marius put the offer on the table, an offer for a family, for a home. Faelan echoed it in his own way. Now I just have to decide what to do with it.

I set the small scroll on the coffee table next to the one that Faelan gave me. And I notice something sitting beside the ring left from my morning cup of coffee. A black velvet bag.

I stare at it, not wanting to touch it. I know with sharp clarity why it's there and who it's from.

I shouldn't know so definitively, but I do.

The bag is sitting on a black envelope with a silver seal. It's tied with a satin strap, diamonds on the ends. I pull the envelope out from under it and turn the square over in my hands. The seal is pressed with a complex design of Celtic knotting, a bird at the center: a raven. I bend it and it makes a satisfying snap.

A silver ribbon spills out of the envelope, a large rusty key tied to the end. When I tug on it, the paper contents pull smoothly from the envelope. I study the key as I unfold the black paper; it looks Victorian, like something out of a Brontë novel. But then I swallow a gasp as I realize the paper's not just paper. Small silhouettes of birds and trees and swirls are cut out in an intricate piece of artwork to create a frame coated in gold leaf.

At the center, in proud silver script, it says:

> *My Love,*
> *A small token from the House of Morrigan: a villa in Spain, fully stocked and ready for your pleasure. The steward will contact you in a day or so with the paperwork. Whatever you choose for your future, it's yours with our affection.*
> *The sunrise is breathtaking over the vineyard.*
> *Additionally, this bag attached carries a personal gift, a small token from me. I hope to have a chance to explain its meaning soon.*
> *K.*

My heartbeat thunders in my head. I pick up the velvet bag, pulling off the satin ties with shaking hands. Then I tip the sack over.

A smooth white figure tumbles out into my palm. A delicate milky-glass owl.

My throat tightens.

I touch the cool surface tentatively with the tip of my finger, almost expecting it to move, it looks so real. So like the owl in my dreams.

"Fionn," I whisper, an ache filling my chest, missing him.

Missing a bird I've never known in real life.

It's three inches tall, each speckled feather painted with intricate detail, a shadowed spot on the breast where the arrow struck. The head is tipped to the side, as if in curiosity. The large black eyes glitter knowingly.

It's stunning. And I want to ask Kieran why, why would he give this to me? How does he know about my Fionn? *No, not my Fionn. Lily's Fionn.*

But it's no use. I felt the bird's soft feathers; its talons gripped my gloved arm. I loved Fionn. Somewhere inside me, I loved him.

The memory rises of the king touching the bird's still form, drawing it back from death. I watched his warrior form collapse into the snow, my heart stopping in terror. I sat beside his bed. I prayed for him, for help from the goddess. I gave myself to him. I gave everything.

And it was horrifyingly beautiful.

~

Something caresses my cheek, lifting me from sleep. It slides down my neck and makes a circle on my bare chest, a rush of remembered heat flowing through my bones.

I open my eyes slowly, almost afraid of what I'll see when I face him again.

He's lying beside me, playing with a white feather, turning it in his fingers, holding it up to the rising sunlight spilling through the casement. When he realizes I'm awake, he turns his head and a slow smile tips his mouth.

I blink at him, my pulse skipping as I look into those silver eyes, remembering what was woven between us in this bed.

He stays silent, rolling close, kissing my lips delicately. His hair brushes at my cheek, his fingers caressing my jaw.

I remain still, unsure, searching his features as he moves away.

So many questions are gathered in my head, too many doubts, fears.

I barely know what to feel.

"My sun," he whispers, kissing the tip of my nose, "my fire. Don't be afraid."

"You're well?" I ask, thinking of my desperation to bring him back only a few hours ago and how I took from him. How I haven't taken for so long, and never from someone so full of rich power.

"I am well." His thumb slides over my collarbone. "But I hunger for more." His eyes meet mine. "Do you?"

The memory of his icy energy filling me, coating my insides as we made love, as I fed, sends a shiver through me. Of course I wish for more. My skin aches with longing at the thought. But I shake my head, needing control right now. Needing to understand what's happened.

My whole world shifted in a moment. I need my feet under me again to make sense of it all.

"I would have a bath," I say, sitting up. "And perhaps some quail eggs." I move to the edge of the bed, but his fingers trap my wrist, stopping me.

"Why do you run, my love?" he asks. "Am I still so repulsive to you?"

"I wish to be alone," I say, trying to keep the tremble from my voice.

He releases my wrist, and a traitorous part of me aches with the loss.

But I shove it aside and gather my clothes, clutching them to my chest as I slip from the room.

THIRTY-SIX

SAGE

I open my eyes to an unfamiliar world. Then the sound of the waterfall drifts into the room, and I realize this is reality. I rise slowly, uneasy, an odd feeling of disassociation hovering over me. The sensation of the king's grip on my wrist still lingers, the conflict inside, wanting something I despise. But it was just a dream.

I touch the bedspread, making sure the soft yellow cotton is real.

Sunlight fills the room. I wonder what time it is.

I slide from bed, my muscles protesting as I walk into the front room. The clock on the microwave says it's ten. Faelan should've come to get me by now. But I'm not complaining. I make myself some breakfast, oatmeal and a banana, and then wander into the living room and sit on the couch. I eat the warm oats and stare down at the glass owl next to the black envelope on the coffee table.

I know Kieran isn't the king, and I know I'm not Lily, but all of this is seriously messing with my head. I have this tangle of emotions coiling in me, and I have no idea what to do with it. Since I'm not going to run, I'll have to walk right into it and hope I survive.

A knock sounds on the door.

"Come in," I say, setting the oatmeal down. I snatch up the owl and hide it in the pocket of my pajama pants.

Why did I just do that?

Before I can take it back out, Faelan comes in. He studies me as he steps into the living room. "How did you sleep?"

"Fine."

He hesitates, but then asks, "Dreams?"

I shrug. I don't want to talk about it with him, not right now.

He takes the hint and moves to the couch, looking down at the coffee table. He picks up the smaller scroll, turning it in his hand. "I asked Aelia to help us with this spell after lunch. We can do some training until then."

I keep quiet, unsure how to feel, and take my oatmeal bowl into the kitchen.

"Also," he says, his voice hesitant, "there's a gathering tonight for the House of Morrígan that you were invited to."

I set the bowl in the sink with a clang. "Are you kidding? No way."

"You know that I don't want you to be around Kieran, but it would be good for you to mingle with others, test your will. Marius would want you to go."

"Which I couldn't care less about."

He nods, not arguing. "So, are you up for practice?"

All I want to do is sit around in my pajamas and disappear into a book, pretending there's nothing going on with me. As if I didn't feel like I barely know where I belong, or who I am right now.

"Sure," I say. "Just give me a second."

"Wear a bathing suit."

I go into my room and shut the door. As soon as it clicks behind me, I pull the owl from my pocket. My thumb slides over the smooth surface and my head aches.

I move to the bed and slip it under my pillow. Then I go to get dressed.

~

Practice, as he calls it, turns out to be more like swim training. First he makes me do a million laps. Then he has me tread water as he yells from the edge of the pool, reciting the names of the Houses and their leaders, like I don't already know.

I realize that my knowledge has increased, and I wonder if it's because of the dreams. I don't say that, though. I let him talk and repeat things back to him, until he finally lets me stand in the shallow end.

"Why don't you have to sweat?" I ask, trying to catch my breath.

"I'm the boss." He smirks. "I tell, you do."

"Is that right?" I walk to the edge of the pool, my hands on my hips. I notice him glance at my body, but then his eyes quickly shift to my nose. "Seems very totalitarian."

"Welcome to the Otherworld."

Eventually he's in the water with me, and we're competing to see how long we can hold our breath. But then he surprises me, dragging me down to the deep end and showing me how he breathes underwater. Cheater. I marvel as I watch his chest rise and fall, the pool water rushing in and out of his lungs like it's nothing, but I have to swim to the surface, my own lungs aching.

"The best way to learn is by force," he says. "It's not natural the first time."

"News flash." I cough as we move to sit on the steps. "It's never natural."

"I could help you," he says, like he thinks I might want to try. He settles in next to me.

"Uh, no." I release a nervous laugh.

"One of my brother's concubines taught me when I was fourteen," he says, and I find myself wondering if she taught him other things too. But I'm not sure why that matters.

"What was her name?" I find myself asking. I know nothing about him. I feel the need to fill in the blanks.

"Genevieve," he says, recalling easily. The memory makes his gaze go distant with what looks like sadness. "She was kind to me when I first came into my brothers' House. Things were difficult for me."

I study his profile, fascinated by his sudden openness. "Why?"

He shakes his head, wiping water from his face. "I didn't . . . fit. I was very young. And I missed my mother terribly."

I wait as he works through something, and I know. "She died?"

He nods. And his eyes meet mine. "The river took her," he whispers.

A sharp pain pierces my throat. I start to reach out to him, to put my hand on his arm, but I stop myself.

He slowly shifts to face me, leaning closer like he's going to whisper a secret. My heart thunders in my chest, as I wonder what he's going to say.

The sound of approaching footsteps breaks into the odd moment, and I find myself exhaling deeply.

Aelia's voice comes down the pathway from the house. "Do you guys want to do the spell now?" she calls.

Faelan moves away, putting a few feet between us as she comes through the trees.

THIRTY-SEVEN

FAELAN

Aelia gets everything set up in the living room in the main house for the new spell. The freshly mopped marble floor glistens. She had the servants rearrange the couches to make more space and created her circle on the floor out of a mixture of salt and chalk dust, rose petals sprinkled around the rim for an extra guard. One of the side tables is set up as an altar, and she's arranged bird bones and marlstones in a lunar pattern for the gravity of the spell to hold, all around a rye candle to center the energy more effectively.

Aelia may be a flake in most things, but in her magic a spark of genius shines through.

She has the small scroll laid out on the couch, the tiny Gaelic script covering every inch of the vellum. She refers to it, and then motions to me. "You can't be in the area of the spell, Faelan. Your energy will muck with the weaving. Go stand over there." She points to the French doors near the kitchen.

I do as she says, standing in a spot where I can still watch everything that happens in case something goes wrong.

Aelia arranges Sage at the center of the circle and asks her to focus on the memories, to think of the last remnant of what she saw and hold it in her mind. She reads over the scroll before moving to light the candle.

She takes a match out of the box. "Close your eyes and imagine the last moment where you experienced a memory," she says to Sage. "Be a part of it again, and repeat what I say in your head."

Sage closes her eyes and takes in a shaking breath. Her brow pinches like she's in pain.

"Okay, I'll begin." Aelia strikes the match, flame flaring to life. She whispers in Gaelic: *"This bond must tear. All threads snapped, frayed, severed, upon the transfer of light. Let the weaving come undone once this claiming is complete."* She lowers the match to the candle.

"Wait!" Sage says, her voice full of fear.

Aelia moves the match away from the wick. "What? What's wrong?"

Sage shakes her head. "I can't do this."

I step forward. "What are you saying?"

"I can't do this." She turns to me, looking lost. "I don't know what I'm feeling. I just know this is wrong. I can't."

Aelia waves the match in the air to put it out and turns to me. "I think the memories have already threaded too deep."

No, that can't be right. "It's too soon for her to be that far gone."

"She's clearly protecting them," Aelia says, motioning to Sage.

"No, she's not," I snap.

Sage steps from the circle. "Yes, I am. And don't talk about me like I'm not here."

I run a hand through my hair, trying to figure out what's going on. Yesterday all she wanted was to get away from this. "But, Sage, you can't be serious—"

"I can, Faelan. And I am."

"She sure seems serious," Aelia adds, not being helpful at all.

"You're getting too wrapped up in it," I say, urgency filling me. "You're just confused—the memories can trick you. They merge emotions and personalities. It's very dangerous."

"No kidding," she says. "As if I don't know that."

"Why not be free of them then?" I ask.

She folds her arms across her chest. "Look, I get how recalling all these vivid memories, or whatever, could screw with my head. That's become very clear to me. But there's something about what's happening that feels right. It's a part of me—I can't explain it." She starts to pace, the slap of her flip-flops the only sound in the room. Aelia and I watch her for several seconds until she finally continues. "I need to know everything. I can't reject information. I'm a part of this story."

"She's making sense," Aelia says.

But to me it sounds like Kieran's manipulation is finally sinking in, and the blood memories are taking hold. This can only go one way if she lets it in and allows it to become a part of her. Aelia has no idea the damage this could do to our House if Sage ends up turning to the Morrígan.

I meet her pleading gaze, knowing she's completely wrong in her thinking. But how do I convince her? Until this moment, I've never wished to be like my brothers, but I could use a little of Finbar's conniving spirit right now.

As it is, I can only hold in my fury and speak the truth.

"It's a mistake not to do the spell," I say. "You're wrong, Sage."

She just shakes her head, determined.

Tension looms in the air as Aelia cleans things up. Sage helps her, believing she's right in her decision not to do the spell. I move the couches back, then walk out, having said my piece. Once I'm back at my cottage, I hesitate at the door, wondering if I should even stay here right now—my emotions are far too raw. I'm more angry than I've been in a long time. I'm going to do something foolish if I leave, though. And I can't abandon her.

I'm so wrapped up in my thoughts that I don't hear her come up behind me until she says, "I need to stop running, Faelan. From everything."

I release a breath and rub my face. Then I turn to her.

She's a few feet away, cautious. "I'm tired of being afraid of everything," she says, her voice wavering. "My whole life, I've always thought I was so tough, but really I'm a coward. I only look for an out, a way to escape. I never face anything." Her eyes glisten in the sunlight. "I need to face this."

I want to shake her. She's so far from a coward, she has no idea.

"Don't be angry with me," she says.

"I'm not sure I can watch you fall, Sage," I whisper, my voice nearly breaking.

She blinks.

I step closer, reaching out to brush a copper strand of hair from her eyes. "I care about you." I let the words sink in, into me, into her. And then I say, "Whatever you choose, promise me you'll be careful."

She nods, tears filling her eyes.

I turn away and shut myself in my cottage.

THIRTY-EIGHT

SAGE

My mind races back and forth, back and forth, trying to figure out what happened when Aelia was doing that spell. As soon as she started speaking in the strange language, I couldn't get out of that circle fast enough.

Okay, if I'm being honest with myself, from the second Marius handed me the scroll, I felt odd about the spell. Still, it was the right thing, the safest thing. And I wanted to be free of it.

I did.

But now . . . out of nowhere . . . I'm unsure about pushing these memories away. I think something shifted inside me last night when I held that glass owl. I want to understand what it is.

Which terrifies me. Because what if Faelan's right? What if I really am being tricked?

We still don't know who put these memories inside me, or why. What if it was Kieran? What if it's supposed to make me choose something that could destroy me?

That doesn't feel true, though.

All I have to go on right now is my gut. And for the first time in my life, I don't want to run away. To me, that means something. And if

I'm going to chase this down, I just need to go for it. No more hiding. From now on, I walk into the fire—literally—I don't back away from it.

Which means that, as much as it pains me, I need to go to that dumb party of Kieran's tonight. If I'm not going to leave this place, then I need to find out where I belong.

I leave my cottage and find Aelia in her room. I plop down on her bed, hug one of her narcissistic pillows, and ask if she can help me find something to wear. You'd think I asked her to be my wedding planner for my marriage to Channing Tatum or something, with all the clapping and squealing that bursts forth.

She drags me into her closet and starts flinging dresses around. "You can't fall back on your baggy-shirt-grunge-girl theme tonight," she says. "This is serious if you want to make Kieran sweat."

"I don't want to make Kieran do anything," I say. Except maybe leave me alone.

"Oh, come on, the game is half the fun." She pulls out a dress made of nothing and, fortunately, tosses it aside. "You make him think he has a chance so that when you crush him and choose the House of Brighid, it's that much more yummy."

"I don't play games, Aelia. I just want to learn as much as I can about this world."

"Oh, honey." She clucks her tongue. "Lesson one: this world is *all* about the games."

No kidding. I'm not up for it yet, though. "Well, for tonight I'm only going to observe the lunacy."

She snorts out a laugh. "You know this party is for you, right?"

"What?"

"Kieran is throwing this little soiree for you, girl." She tosses a dress at me and I catch it.

I don't bother to see what it looks like. I'm now second-guessing everything, my determination flittering away. "No, no, no."

"Yes, yes, yes." She tosses shoes at my feet: bright red heels.

I think I'm going to throw up. "Oh, God."

"You better get used to it. You're a hot commodity."

I groan.

"Don't worry, you're going to kill it." She goes to a drawer and pulls out a long strand of glittering diamonds. "They won't know what hit 'em."

~

Within an hour, the three of us are in the back of a limo. Faelan barely looks at me as we make our way to Kieran's house in the hills. Apparently, this is just *one* of his California houses.

Faelan's expression darkens as Aelia goes on about how many properties Kieran and his sister own all over the world. This morning, Faelan acted like he wanted me to come to this thing, but I can tell he's still angry about this afternoon—angry about anything to do with Kieran. And I don't blame him. I don't care how many houses Kieran has, he's still . . . Kieran.

When we arrive, a valet opens the limo door. I try to get Faelan's attention before we go inside, but Aelia hooks her arm in mine and pulls me away, heading for the sprawling house. Well, more like mansion.

It's absolutely stunning. Tall lamps light the yard, casting flickering shadows as the sun disappears into the hills behind us. A cobblestone walkway weaves through mossy ground cover, leading to the entrance, all framed with a rose-covered trellis.

The house itself is a stone beast with ivy climbing up the face and sleeping morning glories trailing along the edges. The only hints that we didn't step from the limo into the nineteenth century are the two large bouncers flanking the huge oak door.

Faelan walks behind us, silent, as Aelia talks my ear off about how the house was brought here from France and had been owned by an English duke or something.

The bouncer on the left opens the door as the one on the right touches his earpiece and says, "Princess Sage has arrived," like he's Secret Service. I want to laugh, it's so cheesy. Are they going to give me a code name next, like the Albatross?

But the laughter dies in my throat as we walk inside. The soaring ceiling is vaulted three floors above us; I can see people milling about on the landing of the next floor. A wide staircase winds up and splits in two directions. The only light is coming from thousands of candles along the floor, lined up to create a pathway. Huge tapestries hang on the gray stone walls. They're woven in bright colors, images of peaceful pastoral scenes, bloody battles, and entwined lovers.

Aelia walks ahead, but I pause, my eyes catching a tapestry with a woman resting in a forest. She's sitting beside a river, and a smaller figure that looks like a water faerie is perched on a rock, weaving yellow flowers into the woman's curly auburn hair.

"She's so lovely," I say to Faelan, who stands beside me.

"That's your sister, Queen Lily."

My stomach flutters. My sister . . . I look closer, studying her features, the high cheekbones, the large golden eyes, how her hand rests delicately on her cheek. "She looks peaceful." That's not how I recall her feeling in any of my dreams, but maybe there was a time when she was.

"It's from a story," Faelan says, "'The River Queen,' about a young woman who fell in love with a water wysp only to have it kill her, drowning her in her own tears. It's silly, really. And an insult to Queen Lily's legacy to be pictured in it." He sounds sad.

I turn to him, about to ask him if he's going to be all right, but his features shift to anger as he spots someone over my shoulder and a voice comes from behind me.

"Welcome, my love."

A chill works up my spine.

Kieran.

He moves to stand in front of me, his gaze scraping over me in a way that has heat climbing my neck and cheeks. "I'm breathless," he says. "You are a sight." And without turning to look at Faelan, he directs his next words to him. "She's going to be the death of us both, isn't she, bastard? This one is true fire in the flesh. It's too bad you'll never taste her."

My pulse skips at his insinuation.

"Fuck right off, prick," Faelan growls.

Kieran just laughs softly. Deadly. "Poor castoff. You have certainly gotten yourself in trouble this time, haven't you? You're completely taken."

Faelan steps up to loom over him.

They size each other up, and the more Kieran stares at Faelan, the harder his features become.

I wave a hand between them. "Hey, I'm right here."

Kieran turns to me, and I step back at the stone in his eyes. "He apparently feels something more for you than a simple protector bond. Does he have reason to?"

"What?" I ask, trying to play dumb. "What do you mean?"

"His spirit is tuned to yours," Kieran says as he looks me over. "And yours to his."

I release a nervous laugh, crossing my arms over my chest. I'm pretty sure it will be really bad if he thinks there's something between Faelan and me. So I lie. "The guy can't stand me. And I'm not exactly a fan of his either. He's a huge downer." I shrug. "He thinks I'm gonna go bonkers and become some kind of killer."

Kieran glances at Faelan, who's frowning at me, his jaw working.

"But you know, it's a party, so . . ." I wave my hand aimlessly at the crowd upstairs. "Have fun measuring dicks, boys." I step back, then I turn and say over my shoulder, trying to sound unaffected, "I'm off to find the bar." As I walk away, I focus on breathing, praying it's not obvious that every inch of me is shaking.

~

I wander aimlessly through the crowd for a while and am relieved when no one seems to know or care who I am. I get a few second glances from a group of men around a smoky pool table, but I walk past them and head into a long hall where the milling people thin out. The shadows grow and the light dims as I work my way along. The people I see are either making out or talking on their phones, not paying attention to me.

I was supposed to be getting to know this place, this world, but here I am hiding like my old self. Maybe I'm not ready for this. After that moment downstairs, I realize I've got no clue how to keep from falling into a trap—and everything's a trap.

I find a door at the far end and knock, going halfway in when there's no answer. It takes me a second to realize I'm not alone in the room; the sound of rustling makes me freeze. It's too dark to see, though.

"Hello?" I say, backing out. Could Kieran have made it past me when I wasn't looking?

I put my hand on the handle and push the door open more.

Light from the hall casts into the room, falling on something on the far side, in the corner.

A bird.

I spot the light switch and flick it. A dim glow comes from a chandelier above.

It's a black bird. A raven, perched on a stack of books.

I step into the room again and study the creature. As I look around, I realize I'm in a library.

Oh wow. It's huge, two stories high, bookshelves floor to ceiling, full to the brim.

The raven squawks.

I walk into the center of the room. As I get closer to the bird, I realize it's huge, almost unnaturally so. There's an odd patch of silver feathers on the right side of its neck. It tips its head and eyes me sideways, like it's making sure I'm allowed to be in here, then it hops closer and opens its shiny beak, releasing a low caw. It keeps staring at me as if it has something to say, and all I can do is stare back and wonder if it's really just a bird. In this place, who can tell?

"What a party, huh?" I say.

It tips its head again. If I didn't know any better, I'd swear it's keying in on my boobs, but that's just—

A flash of yellow light reflects on the wall behind the raven, and I realize it's a reflection from my medallion. It must've caught the bird's eye.

The creature screeches again, then flies up and perches on the edge of a higher shelf. The sound of wings continues, though, and I swear I smell roses . . . smell ice . . .

The ground tilts, tingles washing over me—

"You shouldn't be in here," a clipped female voice says from behind me.

I spin and see Princess Mara standing in the doorway. She's glaring at me like she's completely offended that I'm in this library with her pet bird instead of out mingling.

She glances up at the raven. I could swear fear flashes across her features for a second. "This room stays locked. How did you even get in?"

I shake my head and point at the door. "I knocked," I say stupidly.

She considers me for a second and then looks back at the bird. "This isn't a safe place for a newblood princess."

It's a library.

"You need to go back to your party," she adds.

I almost say, "Yes, ma'am," like I've been scolded by a teacher for not having a hall pass. Instead, I just nod and back out of the room. What was I thinking wandering around this place alone? The door slams in my face, even though Princess Mara's hands stay clenched at her sides.

~

It's official: everyone's having fun at my party except me. Well, or Faelan. I'm pretty sure that wherever the guy is, he's miserable too.

I find Aelia and her coven laughing and cooing in a room full of young men. One of the girls, Victoria, is doing a magic trick, floating playing cards around her hips. Each time a card flies out, one of the guys catches it. If it's hearts, she kisses them. Long, slobbery kisses. I gag and walk away after the third guy. I'm pretty sure she was flicking the kissing cards on purpose, like a rigged Spin the Bottle.

I wander outside and wish I could just drive myself home. As I settle on a patio chair, a shadow falls over me. I know right away that it's Faelan.

"Where've you been?" I ask.

"Following you," he says. "Watching Kieran."

"Sounds thrilling."

"You're miserable."

"I am." I glance up at him. "Your world is sorta boring if you're not into drinking countless cocktails, gossiping, or playing tonsil hockey with strangers."

He sits across from me, ignoring my snark. "Did you notice that Kieran's been avoiding you?"

I did wonder why the dark prince hadn't accosted me again. I just shrug.

He rests his elbows on his knees. "I spotted him going into the room you came out of, almost the second you left. He's still in there." He runs his fingers through his hair, and it falls over his left eye. "He's up to something."

"And? What am I supposed to do about it?"

"Do you feel anything . . . odd? Like, in your mind or spirit?"

"What? No—what are you talking about? Be more specific."

"At first I thought he'd brought you here to show off for you, but when he came over to us and acted so . . . un-Kieran . . ."

"He was a prick, how is that un-Kieran?"

He lowers his voice. "He was jealous. Kieran has everything, he needs nothing. And he never shows weakness."

I frown at him, not sure where he's going with this.

"I have a hunch he may have brought you here for a different reason. Like a spell."

THIRTY-NINE

FAELAN

"You're sure you don't feel anything weird?" I ask, looking her over more closely. I try to ignore my body's reaction to the scattering of freckles on the soft skin of her bare shoulders, the shape of her legs in those heels. Kieran's a prick, but he's right; she's going to be the death of me.

"I'm fine," she says. "Bored to tears, but fine. What do you mean, a spell?"

"I think we should leave." The faster we get out of here, the sooner I can relax. Something's up with Kieran. After Sage left us, he leaned over and told me I shouldn't have brought her. When I asked him why, he just growled at me to be better at my job as he walked away.

"Fine with me," she says. "The sooner we get out of here, the better. Shouldn't we find Aelia, though?"

"I'll text her. She can get a ride with one of the girls in her coven."

We stand and make our way back through the party, heading for the entrance. I watch the crowd, looking for a hint of why things feel so off. Then it hits me. How did I miss it? They're almost all human, only a few Others mingling in the herd. Too many mortals all in one place for a demi party.

I grab Sage's arm and pull her back through the people and down a hall, looking in each room and seeing shades, druids, pixies, but no humans. The Otherborn are all separated out for some reason.

As we come to the last door, I spot Aelia and her coven making out with a bunch of shades. "Lia!" I bark.

She removes her face from some guy and sits up quick. "What? I didn't do it!"

"We're going. Now."

She slumps, pouting. "Why?"

I step into the room and yank the shade that was groping her from the couch, tossing him. He hits the opposite wall with a crack and falls to the floor, limp. "Now!"

She stands in a rush, teetering. Everyone else is sitting up, gaping at me.

"You're such a downer, Faelan," Aelia mutters, her words slurred. "Gods." She wobbles a little as she comes closer. I can smell alcohol on her breath.

"What did you drink?" I ask, grabbing her by the arm, looking in her eyes to see if she's been dosed with anything.

"Vodka. Calm down."

"What's going on, Faelan?" Sage asks from the doorway.

"This party is a trick," I say loud enough for the drunk druids to get the clue. "It's probably a fucking bloodworking or something."

Aelia frowns and presses a finger to my mouth. "Shhh . . . your face is too loud."

Victoria sits up, all focus now. "What kind of bloodworking?"

"Hell if I know," I say, "but you probably don't want to be here when that room full of humans out there gets ripped to shreds by the half dozen drunk shades in this room."

"Hey," one of the shades says, like he's offended. "I only drink bagged blood, never take from the tap. I'm clean."

"Sure you are, skippy." I pull Aelia from the room, leading her down the hall, Sage close behind. I say over my shoulder, "Don't stop for anything. We head straight for the doors."

We work through the crowd quickly. I soon see the entry and it's clear. No Kieran, no Princess Mara, no servant shade. Whatever they're up to, I need to get Sage as far away from them as possible.

Someone steps into my path, making me stop.

"Finbar," I say, shocked. What's he doing here? And then I see Duncan, Astrid on his arm, just behind my elder brother.

Finbar doesn't acknowledge me; he looks right past me to Sage. And then he bows deep. "Princess, you look stunning."

"We were just leaving," Sage says.

"So soon?" Finbar asks. "I hear there's to be sport."

My skin goes cold. "What sort of sport?"

Astrid smiles sweetly and says, "Well, the best kind, of course. How many are up there?" She cranes her neck to see the crowd above us. Then she reaches down and lifts her hem, showing off her thigh. Where her dagger is strapped. "I brought Talon."

My gut roils, the urgency I felt a moment ago turning into real panic at what Sage will witness if we stay. If this is a bloodworking, it's going to be done the hard way. The humans are to be hunted, probably released on the property like drugged game. I haven't heard of a party hunt in over sixty years. The Cast outlawed them because it was becoming too difficult to hide the mass killings.

Leave it to the House of Morrígan to get away with breaking such a concrete rule. I know now why my brother Finbar is here, blood-thirsty wretch that he is. But why invite Sage? Especially if the House of Morrígan truly wants to court her favor. It's crazy. Unless they're so blind they can't even see how their own twisted nature would look to someone like her.

"Well, I'm taking Princess Sage home," I say, making sure to direct my words to Finbar.

"You must stay," Finbar says to Sage. "It's going to be brilliant."

She stares at him, her gaze hard. "Are you deaf? Your brother's taking me home. If you'll excuse us." She brushes past them, heading for the door.

When we get into the limo, Aelia is laughing, trying—and failing—to drunk high-five Sage. "That was an epic asshole takedown, bitch!"

Victoria climbs into the limo behind Aelia. "Now I know why Mom said not to go to Morrígan parties without protection." She reaches into her bra and pulls out a small sack: a charm. "This thing shielded me from whatever was in the drinks." She points at Aelia, who's now slumped over my lap.

"What the hell was all that?" Sage asks, trying to scoot away from Victoria. "What is going on, Faelan?"

"I'm pretty sure they were about to have a hunt and kill a few dozen people."

Sage gapes at me, speechless.

Aelia sits up straight in a rush, holding up a finger, declaring, "That's illegal!" And then she slumps back down, this time choosing Sage's lap.

Sage ignores her. "Why in the hell would that be part of *my* party? Do they think I'm demented? We have to help those people!"

I can only shake my head. I pull out my phone and call my contact line for the Cast's envoy, leaving a message about the hunt, hoping they can stop it before too many people are butchered.

When I get off the phone, Sage picks up Aelia, moving her out of the way, and scoots closer to me. "Why would they do that, Faelan? What were they trying to prove?"

"I don't know. It doesn't make sense." I just wish I knew if Kieran wanted Sage or if he wanted her *dead*. It would make this so much easier. I'll just have to keep her away until after the Emergence.

We drop off Victoria and make it back to the Cottages around midnight. I carry Aelia through the yard, into the back of the main house, and up to her bedroom. I lay her out on the pink blankets, and Sage pulls down her hiked skirt and takes off her shoes, then sits on the other side of the bed.

"Do you think she'll be okay?" she asks.

"It'll wear off with sleep, I'm sure. Druids have pretty solid metabolisms."

We sit for a while, both just watching Aelia sleep, not sure what to say. Eventually Sage stands and we leave the room, heading down the stairs and out through the backyard. When we come to our cottages, she pauses and turns to me, like she wants to say something but she's unsure. Her eyes search my face for a couple of tense seconds. I know I should turn away, but I can't manage it.

"Thank you," she finally says quietly.

But I can't accept her gratitude. "I'm sorry I let you go in the first place. Anything could've happened."

She shakes her head. "You were being supportive." She shifts her feet, and then asks, "How many more days until this Emergence thing?"

"Seven."

"So we'll lay low," she says, determination in her voice, like we're making a plan.

"That's what I was thinking." I let myself step a little closer, wanting her to know I mean what I say. "But I don't want to keep you shut in if it's going to make you feel overwhelmed."

She surprises me, resting her palm on my chest. "I'm not going anywhere. I want to see this through. I need to know." A thin ache blossoms where her fingers graze my sternum, and I realize she's taking from me, unaware, even through the torque. It's not enough to harm me, though. And a part of me is strangely comforted by it. As if it's what I was meant to do.

My heartbeat picks up, and I wonder if she can feel it in her skin as my energy slinks into her.

She rises to her toes and brushes her lips against my cheek.

I stay still as she kisses me, and I let her pull away, rooting my feet to the spot, holding myself back from touching her.

Because I know that if I allow myself to reach out in this moment . . .

I won't stop.

FORTY

SAGE

I close my cottage door and sigh, feeling lighter than I have in forever. In spite of everything, he was there. Again. He had my back. I think I've totally let myself fall for the guy.

It's so dumb.

I peel off my dress, wash my face, and pull on a pair of stretch pants with skulls on them and a baggy Nirvana shirt. I smile to myself, thinking of how I felt his breath catch when I kissed his cheek. I climb into bed, curling onto my side, hugging my pillow, and marvel at his steadfastness.

Then my fingers touch something cold.

And I remember.

I pull the glass owl out from under my pillow, and all thoughts of Faelan slip away as I roll onto my back, holding it up, studying it in the bright moonlight that's coming through the window. *My little Fionn.*

Thoughts of the evening float away as I run my fingers over the bird's face, tracing its features, its speckled feathers. And then I grip it in my hand, pressing it to my chest. Thinking of the comfort of a cold mountain keep, the comfort of a king. Knowing I'll be with him soon.

Very soon.

~

I would say that our world on this icy mountain has returned to how it was before my surrender, but that would be said only to comfort myself. Because I . . .

I am not the same.

However much he is.

Every evening after supper, he still walks me to my bedroom door, telling me that I am his, and then he leaves me without protest when I push his advances away. As before, he doesn't force his will. He never touches me without invitation. And I still don't know if I should give such a thing again.

However much my body longs for it.

Every night after I crawl into bed, I lie wide awake for hours, arguing with myself, contemplating sneaking through the back passage to his room and climbing into his arms where this hunger can be satiated.

I have wished many times that I was another girl, one who could embrace this cage. Then I could settle into the cold in the arms of this beast. But the child of fire in me resists; it yearns for green life and struggles with the idea of giving itself over.

Still, the strangest thoughts come to me now, about him, about the two of us together. As if this were more than a physical hunger I'm feeling. Like how I miss the sound of his whistling when he doesn't come out with me on my daily ride, or how comforting it is to smell his leathers when he arrives home after a long day in the village.

And how I miss the feel of his arms gripping me tight . . . even though it happened only that one magical time.

The thought has come to me that I could be happy in this life.

I cast it away and remain in between. Forcing my hopes into submission.

Because I will be free of this one day. I will. I'll return to the green of my wood with Lailoken, and I'll be home again.

And this will be nothing but an icy memory.

~

My eyes open slowly as I surface from the dream, the emotions in me still raw, the chill of the snow still lingering in my bones. The sun is shining in soft beams across the bed, the morning light filtering through the gauzy yellow curtains.

I stare at the dust motes in the air and sift through the dream as I emerge from it. So much turmoil and resistance. Fighting the hunger, the yearning. Yearning not to be alone. And I wonder why.

Why am I pushing the king away?

My nerves spark, realizing my mistake.

No—it's *Lily*. Not me. I'm not doing anything.

A shiver works through me as I realize how deep I'm getting. The dreams are too vivid right now, lingering in the morning air, lingering inside me.

Even as I try to bury it, it sticks to my bones.

I have to focus on the present. Only the present. I can't let the dreams, the emotions, sink in too deep and mess with me. No matter how much I want to cling to it. It's not real.

It's dreams. Dreams of the dead.

~

The next few days roll by in a steady rhythm of late-morning "power practice," as I call it, with Faelan, then afternoon laziness by the pool with Aelia and whichever friend she's let tag along, ending with dinner with Marius and ditzy Barb.

But in the night, I shift. I become another soul, living in the cold, my best friend a monk, my lover my enemy.

I don't want to admit it, but with each morning that comes, I'm starting to think that there's a part of me that *is* Lily now. I feel her as she sits on the fringes during the daylight, waiting to be set free. I know

I should keep her at arm's length; I should be trying to keep the dreams separate. But I can't.

Yesterday, I started to ask Faelan where my favorite glass combs had gone. But I don't have any glass combs. And then I remembered: in my dream the night before, the king had gifted stained-glass combs to Lily and they were missing. She'd asked him if he knew where they were. Just like I almost asked Faelan.

The mistake nagged at me the whole day. I decided I couldn't keep pretending the dreams were helping. I wasn't finding out anything new about what happened to the king, or how he died, or why Lily went crazy. I was just letting her play around in my head.

I went looking for Aelia to talk to her about doing the spell, the one I'd walked away from a few days ago. But when I found her, I changed my mind again.

I really should just tell Faelan what I'm feeling, but he'll worry. And lecture me.

Anyway, he probably knows. He keeps watching me like I might grow horns. I feel like I already have.

I just want to pretend it'll all be okay. I don't yearn for Kieran anymore. I don't care when his gifts come. In fact, I haven't opened any of the tributes from any of the Houses since my murder party.

Aelia, of course, tells me every day what shows up for me, but I blot the list of gifts out of my head, letting the sound of the pool waterfall muffle her words as much as I can. Apparently, I now have a couple of houses, three cars, and a ton of bags full of things like electronics, soaps, oils, candles, towels, and robes—I could open my own Bed Bath & Beyond about now. I asked her to donate the gifts to a local homeless shelter. What am I going to do with twelve robes, one in every natural fabric known to modern man?

I've been invited to several private clubs, VIP rooms, concerts, concertos, plays, sporting events, and even a picnic in Paris by Finbar.

I now have box seats at the Met in New York City, season tickets to the Hollywood Bowl, and a regular table at the House of Blues in Vegas.

But I couldn't care less about any of it. The only thing I feel is the ticking forward of time, shoving me closer and closer to the Emergence. Only two days left. Pressure is building in the house, in Faelan, and in me.

There's an unspoken shadow over us all with these dreams. Everyone knows they're affecting me. Marius is the only one who asks me about them, but I'm trying with everything in me to keep them separate, so I usually give half answers.

They all watch me like a doomsday switch is about to go off in my head.

All I want is to get past it and move on. I have no idea what I'll do when the moment of my Emergence comes, and whenever I try to wrap my mind around it, I just want to get to the after.

This night of destiny can't come fast enough.

FORTY-ONE

FAELAN

Only two more days. Two more days and she'll decide. I wish I could say for sure that she'll choose to stay with her blood House, but I can feel a piece of her holding back, as if it's waiting. I just wish I knew what she needed.

She hasn't seen Kieran since the hunting party, and she doesn't seem to care about it. So that's a relief. I was sure these dreams would somehow draw the two of them together, but only his gifts arriving every morning say he's still in the game—there've been no personal appearances.

The sun is a quarter of the way across the sky by the time she emerges from her cottage. I'm finishing up my morning swim. I climb out of the pool and grab a towel, hiding a smile as I look at her T-shirt.

It says "A druid is my homey" and has a picture of Aelia's face on it.

Sage sees me noticing. "My tribute from Lia," she says with a stiff grin. "Don't judge, it's really soft cotton."

She follows me into my cottage and settles under one of the trees next to the nest as I go into the closet and throw on a T-shirt and dry shorts. When I come back out, she's staring blankly into the ferns and chewing on her thumbnail.

"What's wrong?" I ask.

She lowers her hand to her lap. "Nothing."

I give her a disbelieving look. She's been more absentminded the last couple days, and during training she keeps losing focus. It could be stress from the approaching Emergence—we're all feeling that—but it could also be the dreams. I've allowed Marius to take over on that subject—he talks about it with her in the evenings at dinner—but I can see something happening, a distance growing. A part of me is terrified that she's slowly slipping away.

"You can talk to me about it, Sage."

She shrugs. "I think I just want to talk about the after-the-day-of-doom stuff. It'll help me. Like, will I be a high executive? Will I get a plane?" Her snarky smile appears, and the knot in my chest loosens a bit.

"All right." I wave her into the greenhouse, and we settle in our usual spot under the wisteria. "There are some tests you'll take after the final ceremony that will help you choose a path. I borrowed the books Aelia used to study for them."

Sage frowns. "So . . . it's exactly like being a human. It sounds like college entrance exams. Blech."

"If college exams are about moving objects with your mind, or making plants grow in seconds."

She snorts. "Well, I can't do either of those things. What do *you* think I'd be good at?"

I've actually been considering this quite a bit. It's my job to make a recommendation at the ceremony, and I knew almost immediately which path would suit her best.

"You'd make a very good tutor and mentor for the younger Otherborn," I say, watching for her reaction. "Some are brought in at very delicate ages. You could help them feel less alone, to get acclimated in a healthier way, even protect them. It can be a very dangerous time for a newblood. And the long process can be difficult for the more vulnerable." A reality I know all too well. "You've retained your kindness in spite of your difficult childhood. And you have a wildness that draws spirits in and makes them feel safe. It's a magic all its own."

She chews on her lip, staring at the ground for several seconds before she looks up at me again. "You really see me like that?"

I hesitate, realizing by the tremble in her voice how much my words mean to her. "Yes," I say, holding her gaze. "I do."

~

She leaves in a bit of a daze, pensive and distant again, so I'm surprised when an hour later she calls me out to join her in the pool, sounding playful. I make excuses for a bit—I've been trying to avoid being with her when she's out there in her bathing suit—but she's extremely persistent.

Before leaving the cottage, I slide my palm over a cluster of ivy climbing up the wall beside me and steady myself as I pull the buzz of green life into my skin. I need some strength.

I step outside and spot her sliding into the clear water of the pool.

My throat tightens as my eyes take in the sight of her in a white bikini. I'm an idiot. I should've known it'd be impossible to pretend she doesn't affect me.

I have to force myself to keep walking forward and turn my focus to the ground instead of her. But the image of her is squarely under my skin. After only a couple of feedings from me, she's become a woman. Her curves are supple, her muscles shaped to perfection. The bright copper waves of her hair, grown just past her shoulders now, reflect the sunlight in golden streaks. Her skin is a perfect peach, scattered with freckles, only the scar on her neck from Kieran marring the smooth surface.

It was inevitable that she would blossom once she was able to feed properly and use her powers. I should've known that what I saw that first night was because her demi side had been starving for so long. Now she's exquisite.

Aelia comes down the path through the trees just as I start to back away, heading for my cottage again.

She spots me and points. "Faelan's here for *fun*? I didn't think that was possible."

Niamh and James trail behind her. James grabs Niamh, picking her up with a hoot and surging forward, leaping into the water as she squeals in protest. Niamh comes up sputtering and scolding as she makes her way back to the edge of the pool.

James gives me a nod while the girls aren't looking, like he's making sure it's all right that he's around. I nod back. I could not care less if he hangs with Aelia, sleeps with her, even if he's feeding from her, as long as it's consensual. The rules against underlings being equals with druids and demis have seemed archaic to me since the industrial revolution.

Niamh climbs out of the water and grabs a towel from one of the chairs, pouting. "You totally messed up my hair, James."

James leans on the edge and rolls his eyes dramatically. "Oy, pixie, leave it at the gates, will ya. We're not on show."

Aelia scoffs, "Silly, James, you're always on show."

James just laughs and works his way over to Sage. "Hello, love," he says, his grin wide, fangs showing. "How's the ascendance going today?"

"Horrible, as always," she smirks, sinking into the water.

James turns to me. "You joining the fun, mickey? Or you just gonna loiter?"

"Come on, coach," Sage teases, splashing me. "Come show us how to breathe underwater." I want to feel relief at her playfulness, but something about it feels forced.

"Okay, you guys, I have news!" Aelia says, working her way down the pool steps. She holds out her hands, like she's preparing us all for something big. "So, last night I was at the Dark Circle club, and there was this girl there who's a shade concubine for Kieran, and she said that our Prince of Shadows hasn't been seen all *week*."

I glance at Sage in time to see her face fall.

"He hasn't been seen at all?" I ask, not sure I'm buying it.

"Nope. The dark prince is totally missing," Aelia says, sounding very sure. "No one's seen him since his freaky party."

"Why're you listening to a concubine, Lia?" James asks. "You know they gossip like church ladies at a potluck."

"Hey," Niamh says from her chair, offended.

"You know it's true, dear," James says.

Aelia continues, "This girl is completely trustworthy. She's a super-solid part of his House. She said he left that night—the night of the murder party. Since then, he hasn't popped up anywhere, not even the European compound. And he didn't go back to New York with Princess Mara."

"Very mysterious," James says in a conspiratorial tone.

Sage stays silent and swims over to the far edge. A stone sinks in my gut. She seems concerned about Kieran.

A maid appears down the pathway, looking a bit lost. "Excuse me, mistresses." She's holding a black velvet bag out in front of her like she's a little afraid of it. "A messenger dropped this off for the princess. They say it's very important. It shouldn't wait with the other tributes, they say."

"Who is 'they'?" Aelia asks her.

The maid just gets a lost look on her face. Whoever *they* were, they wiped her memory.

I walk over and take the bag from her. "Thank you, Martha." She scampers away, back to the house.

"Open it, Faelan," Aelia says, swimming to the edge. She gets more excited than Sage does about this stuff. Sage isn't even paying attention. She's still several feet away, staring at the surface of the water.

"We'll let Sage do it later," I say. "I'll put it in her cottage."

Aelia sticks out her bottom lip, but James kisses it, and she seems to forget about presents for a second.

"I can set it inside," Niamh says, reaching out. I hand the bag to her and she smiles, curling her fingers around it possessively. Pixies. She's probably hoping it's something shiny; she's sure to open it once she's in the cottage.

She turns and starts to walk away, saying over her shoulder, "I need to get this water out of my hair or it'll turn purple again. Can I use your bathroom, princess?"

Sage doesn't answer.

Aelia unhooks her lips from James. "Yoo-hoo, Sage! She's talking to you."

"Oh," Sage says absently. "Sure. Whatever." Then she swims over to the waterfall and glides behind it, perching on the ledge there. She stares at the water and moves her legs back and forth, her mind lost now, all sense of playfulness evaporated.

And for the hundredth time, I want to slit Kieran's throat.

FORTY-TWO

SAGE

I listen to the splashing of the water and watch it swirl in small eddies in front of me, lost in a sudden rush of anxiety. As soon as Aelia mentioned that Kieran hasn't been seen since the party, my gut sank. A very real fear for him bubbled up, and I have no idea what to do with it.

How can I feel any sort of worry for Kieran?

"You good?" Faelan says.

I turn toward his voice. He's treading water two feet away, hair slicked back. Sunlight bounces off the water, glittering around him, shimmering in his green eyes, the water thickening his lashes.

This is the guy I want. Not Kieran. I should be glad for the dark prince to disappear.

"Uh, yeah," I say, absently. "It's all good."

He squints at me like he's trying to figure me out. "You sure?" he says. "I could get you something to eat—"

"No," I say quickly, not wanting him to worry about me. "I'm just tired, that's all."

I step out of the pool and walk over to grab one of the towels folded on the chair.

"I know something's wrong, Sage," he says.

I don't turn around. "I'm fine. Just let it go, Faelan." I dry my face, but when I hear him getting out of the water, I add, "I'm going to try and get some sleep," and then I walk away, heading for the cottage.

I open the door and go inside, nearly colliding with Niamh. I'd totally forgotten she was in here. She turns, dropping the black velvet bag in surprise. She raises her hand up in front of me, like she's trying to show me something. And then she goes perfectly still.

Her skin becomes waxy and pale.

Blood runs from her nose in a slow, thin drip.

Crimson pools in her large eyes.

She moans like she's about to cry, and red tears spill down her cheeks.

I gape at her, not sure what I'm seeing.

"I'm sorry," she says, her voice turning into gurgles. "I just wanted to try it on." Then she coughs.

Blood splatters my face and I stumble back, a cry of horror bursting from my lungs as she collapses.

Faelan rushes in behind me. "What happened?" He takes me by the arms, looking me over frantically. "You're bleeding."

I shake my head and point down at Niamh, not able to form the words. She's writhing on the floor, choking, drowning, blood bubbling from her mouth in a frothy pink mess.

"Holy Danu," he says, kneeling at her side as she goes still again.

In seconds the blood is everywhere, coating her face, her neck, pooling under her. He tries to lift her head, but it's like she's melting, her body crumpling in on itself.

I sob, covering my mouth, and fall to my knees. I squeeze my eyes shut. My stomach rises. My chest throbs. I want to scream until I go deaf so I don't have to hear the gurgling.

More voices enter the room—James's and Aelia's. Someone's shouting, and the smell of green grass fills the air. Nothing makes sense. When silence falls, I dare to open my eyes again.

Aelia, James, and Faelan are all kneeling around Niamh's body. Or what's left of it. Part of her skull is caved in, and her right hand and part of her right arm have melted into a gooey liquid. There are dark purple veins showing through what's left of her skin, and her eyes are completely gone.

I keep my hands over my mouth, but I can't hold in the groan that spills out. How can this be real?

"What was she thinking?" Aelia shakes her head, tears filling her eyes. James reaches out for something, but she smacks his hand hard, shouting, "Don't touch it!"

"The ring's poisoned," Faelan says. He glances at me. "It was meant for Sage."

"Goddess below," Aelia breathes, her voice shaking. "Oh, Niamh. You stupid, stupid pixie."

"What . . . what happened?" I choke out.

Aelia wipes the tears from her cheek. "She must've opened your tribute from the House of Morrígan." She motions to something in the pool of liquid that was Niamh's hand and arm. "She put it on."

A ring sits where Niamh's hand was. A ring with a large ruby. The stone catches the light, glinting red over the walls, like the cottage is bleeding too.

I stare at it, confused. "I don't understand, why . . . how could a ring do this?" *Niamh is dead. She's in my living room and she's melted, dead.*

Faelan sits back, rubbing his forehead. "It looks like *Sagitta Anathema*." Fear is thick in his voice, and it sets my pulse racing. "It's poison. Undetectable and very effective." He stands quickly and walks away, heading for the kitchen. "Kieran is an evil bastard, but I had no idea he'd go this far." He pulls a pair of tongs from a drawer and comes back, kneels down, and uses them to pick up the ring.

"I don't get it," Aelia says. "He wants Sage for his House, doesn't he?"

"Did Kieran do this?" *It was meant for me . . .* I was the one who was supposed to put on that ring. I should be lying there, not Niamh.

Faelan picks up the discarded bag from beside Niamh's body and drops the ring back inside. "We can't know for sure, but the Cast could decide to claim the property. Since it happened at the master's personal home and it was an attack against his guest."

"Shit," Aelia says, standing in a rush. She waves her hand at the air, and a lamp flies across the room, crashing into the far wall. "Shitshitshit!"

Faelan ignores her and turns to James. "I need you to call my underground contact." He looks down at the body again. "We need to get this cleaned up fast. No one outside this room, besides Marius, can hear about it. Niamh doesn't have family, so it'll be a while until anyone realizes she's missing, and by then Sage's Emergence will be over."

My gut twists, the reality, the horror of the world I'm becoming a part of hitting me all over again.

"We can't hide this," Aelia says, sounding nervous now. "We need to at least tell the Cast. If this was Kieran, he should be held accountable."

"Are you kidding me?" Faelan says, his words dripping with bitterness. "The Cast couldn't give a shit about the life of this pixie. You were at that party; you know what they planned to do, and those were humans. Where is the Cast's justice for that? They've done nothing, not even a slap on the wrist. They're only worried about the Balance. Princess Mara has them in her pocket. And Sage is too monumental to delay the Emergence with an inquiry. They'll just take away your father's leadership in the House instead, pretending to do their job, saying he's weak."

"Why would Kieran want to kill me?" I ask, unable to accept it.

"The poison wouldn't have killed you," Faelan says. "Niamh is an underling, so it was . . . detrimental to her. It wouldn't have done this to you, a demi. It would've poisoned your blood and made you sick for a very long time. You'd likely have wished you were dead, but you'd have been plunged into a comatose state, so you wouldn't have been able to say a thing about it." He shakes his head. "But I don't get why Kieran would do this."

"I need to call my dad," Aelia says, resignation threading through her voice now.

"I can do it, Lia," Faelan says gently.

She shakes her head. "No, I want to tell him."

James stands and wanders over to the kitchen with Aelia, like he wants to stay close to her. He taps on his own phone, puts it to his ear, then reaches out and rubs her back. She leans into him a little. I look away, feeling like I'm intruding.

My eyes skip back to Niamh's body.

Pain spikes my throat. I rise to my feet and head for the door, unable to look at the death anymore. I need air.

The sunlight hits me, but I still feel the image of her, of poor Niamh, sticking to my skin. Over and over, I see her crying bloody tears, saying she's sorry.

My throat closes, and I gasp for breath. I have her blood on me. I need to get clean. I need to wash my mind of the vision of horror flashing in my head.

I stumble toward the pool and splash into the water, tears welling up. The water closes over my head, and I swim for the deep end, my belly scraping the bottom. I rub my hands on my face to get the blood off, and scream and scream and scream until I feel like I've pushed every ounce of shock and horror from my bones.

Until all that's left behind is an empty vessel.

I don't want to rise to the surface again. I want to stay here in the silent nothingness and not have to face this madness.

But in the end, when I can't hold my breath anymore, I float up. I emerge and see Faelan standing in the water near the steps. He watches as I make my way toward him. His concern is obvious, the tension making his shoulders flex.

A new sort of madness fills me when my eyes meet his. I find myself propelled, needing to feel something else in my skin. Needing to feel anything but this darkness, this confusion.

He grips the edge of the pool as I come up to him, but he doesn't move away.

So I reach out. I touch him, the water from my fingers dripping down his bare chest.

I can't say out loud what I'm thinking, that I need him to touch me back, that I want him to kiss me again like he did that night by the fountain. This storm inside won't let me speak. But it's like he hears me, anyway. He moves to take hold of me, to pull me closer into a hug. His arms wrap around me, his hand gripping the back of my neck, his chin resting on the top of my head.

I press myself against his chest, feeling his warmth. I plead with this thing in me not to hurt him or take from him. Because I need this. I need to feel him.

After several heartbeats, he pulls back a little, tipping my chin so our eyes meet. His thumb slides back and forth over my jaw, his brow pinching like he's in pain.

"Am I hurting you?" I whisper.

He shakes his head slowly, his hair falling in his eyes.

I reach out and brush at a dark strand, then trail my fingers to his jaw, his neck, and down across his clavicle, his skin soft against mine. I let myself look at him, soaking in his beauty. Wondering about the scar above his eye. Studying the perfect shape of his mouth. Then I rise up on my toes.

And touch my lips to his.

He breathes me in. His arms wrap tighter around me, strong and unyielding. I twist my fingers in his hair, falling into him until he's leaning against the edge of the pool. Everything in me tingles and buzzes with his body so close, his hands sliding down my bare back, gripping my hips, pulling me closer. And the storm of confusion inside me calms, a new whirl of emotion rising as he presses into me, his breath becoming mine. I cling to him and kiss him and taste him, blocking out the whole world for as long as I can, getting lost in the urgency, in the frantic touch.

Memories mingle, twisting in my mind, the water growing cold, Faelan becoming the king, me becoming Lily, and then shifting back again. I'm surrounded by water, clutching at Faelan's damp body, but then I'm surrounded by cold stone, wrapped in the king's arms.

I'm desperate and hungry, and I don't want to pull away anymore. I don't want to lose him. I can't lose him.

I'm so lost that the warmth growing in my skin doesn't register. Even as the familiar smell of Faelan's green energy fills my head, and the taste of mint trickles into my throat.

The buzz of it all trails around me, through me, the heat blossoming in my chest.

And I realize where I am, and that I'm feeding from him. The one Sage cares about. *Faelan.*

Panic falls over me in a rush.

I pull away, breathless. "Stop," I hiss at myself.

I watch as steam rises from his arms, his face. A rush of relief fills me when I don't see any burns.

"I think I was feeding," I say, feeling ill.

He shakes his head. "I'm all right. The torque held most of it back."

I move to the steps and slowly sit, cold fear creeping through me. "I hate this." What's happening to me? I was completely lost. I'm going crazy.

"It's okay, Sage." He sinks down to sit beside me.

I shake my head. No. No, it's not.

FORTY-THREE

FAELAN

I can't believe that I let it happen again. I kissed her, I touched her, I let myself want her more than I've wanted anything. And it's no longer under my control. If it wasn't for the torque, I probably would've let her consume me as she fed. That's how far I've let myself fall.

Something changed when I saw Niamh's mutilated body. Something twisted in my gut, shifting reality for a moment. And it was Sage I saw, broken and bloodied. But unlike the last time I thought we'd lost her, this time I was only thinking about myself instead of my master. I was thinking how I wouldn't get to hold her again. How that smile in her eyes would flash out.

And I knew I'd be lost if that happened. It's more than the protector bond now, more than duty. Somewhere in all the madness my heart's become hers.

"Niamh's dead because of me," she says, breaking into my stunned thoughts. Torment fills her words.

"You can't blame yourself for this, Sage."

"But—"

"No." I take hold of her arm and gently turn her to face me. "You are not responsible. You won't go down that road, do you hear me?"

She nods, tears filling her eyes.

"Whoever did this, we'll make sure they feel it," I say, knowing she needs to believe justice is possible, even if it's not. "The bastard will go down, Sage."

Something crackles on the other side of the pool, and a loud pop fills the air. Water sprays from the fountain in a sudden burst, and Marius emerges. He walks quickly toward us on the surface of the water.

"What's happened?" he asks. "Where's Aelia? She called me and said Niamh was poisoned."

I rise and step out of the pool. "In Sage's cottage."

He's heading in before I can catch up. Sage stays behind, probably not wanting to see Niamh again. James took off when I wasn't looking, thankfully; as a shade, he wouldn't want to stick around for the master's arrival. Aelia is in Sage's cottage alone, sitting on the couch, looking down at her friend's body.

"In my own house," Marius growls, staring at the mess.

I pick up the black velvet bag and hold it out to him. "It's a ring. Appears to be from the House of Morrígan as a tribute to Sage."

He takes it from me, then steps closer to Niamh's body, crouching to see her wounds. "Kieran's been missing for several days, which is concerning. And I can see him wanting Sage pliable before the Emergence. But why did he wait so long? He had several chances to use his trickery on her, and he barely scratched the surface."

"It really could be anyone," I say, thinking of my brother Finbar. This smells like something he'd do. And he hasn't had much access to Sage, which would make him desperate.

"The only thing to do is investigate the poisoned ring. Magic might reveal who created it, or at the very least where it was made. That would point us in a direction."

"I'll do it," Aelia says, surprising me.

Marius stands again and looks at his daughter. "It's too much for you, little Lia."

Aelia sniffs and wipes her cheeks. "I'm not a baby anymore, Daddy. I can do this. She was my friend. Pixie or not, I loved the stupid girl."

Marius nods and takes her hand, urging her to stand. Then he says gently, "Tell me what you need."

I leave them to their father-daughter moment and go to get dressed, preparing my head for the hunt.

I'm back in my cottage, pulling on a shirt, when Sage comes through the ferns behind me. "What did Marius say?" she asks.

She's staying a good distance away, like she's wary of me. Or maybe she's just wary of us. Like I am. I don't turn to her. I don't think I can take the sight of her sad eyes after having had my hands on her just a few minutes ago. I'll only want to comfort her again. "Marius and Aelia are going to see if they can get a hint of where the poison was made," I say, "and I'm going to go threaten people until I find the killer."

"I want to go threaten people."

Now I look at her. "Right bloody no."

"Why not? I can't just sit here."

"Did you miss the part where someone was trying to put you in a coma, Sage?"

"Exactly," she says. "Which means I'm not any safer here than I am out hunting for the guy." She steps forward, pointing at the door. "I know you don't want me to feel guilty, but we both know that girl out there would still be alive if it wasn't for me. Let me at least try to make this better."

I study her determined features, the flash of life in her eyes, and like a fool I want to kiss her again. I turn away, grumbling curses under my breath as I grab my knife belt. Then I head for the bathroom and say over my shoulder, "Get dressed. We're leaving as soon as Aelia has a direction."

FORTY-FOUR

SAGE

I've just finished showering and dressing when Faelan calls from outside my cottage. "If you're coming, Sage, I'm leaving right now. Meet me out front."

I hurry outside, trailing him to the car.

"Where are we going?" I ask as we pull down the driveway onto the main road.

"Romania," he says. Because that's completely normal.

"Like, the country?"

It turns out that the poison was made in Romania of all places. Faelan explains that Marius knows a guy in Bucharest who we can contact. Apparently, he's the only druid in the area who makes that specific species of poison. When I ask how we're going to fly to eastern Europe and back in a day, since I'm guessing he doesn't want me to miss my own Emergence ceremony, he says we're not flying.

"Swimming takes a lot longer than a day," I say. "What. Are we teleporting?" Not much more could surprise me at this point.

"In a manner of speaking."

And there you go.

"It's a passageway," he continues. "There are different passages that go different distances. We can't use the one at the Cottages because it doesn't have enough juice. It only works for local spots."

Of course there's a teleportation thingy back at the Cottages. "Where is there a passageway, or whatever, at the house?"

He glances sideways at me. "The backyard. The waterfall. You watched Marius come through."

I decide I'm not going to fully comprehend half this stuff, and go back to why we're looking for one of these passages in the first place. "So what're you planning on doing once you find this druid who made the poison?" I ask.

"Convince him it's in his best interest to tell me who bought it from him."

"What makes you think he'll tell you anything if it'll get him in trouble?"

"I'll persuade him." I can tell by his tone he's planning on doing it through pain, and at this point I'm pretty okay with that.

I can't think why any of these Otherborn would want to poison me. They all seem more interested in showering me with ridiculous gifts than hurting me—well, except for the whole Kieran-slicing-my-neck-open thing. Which was apparently a mistake? This place is all upside down, so who can tell.

"Could this druid be the one who wants to hurt me?" I ask. That seems too easy, though.

"A druid rarely does anything so huge—especially something like attacking a high-ranking demi—without backing. The Cast would make sure his head rolled without blinking. He probably wouldn't even get a trial. Having the backing of a House covers his actions. The reality is, there are probably layers and layers of messengers involved. We may not find the killer before the Emergence. But we need to try."

We leave Malibu and drive through the Valley. Finally we're pulling off the highway and heading down a frontage road. When we turn onto the next street, I have to do a double take to be sure I'm seeing right. "Are you taking me to a graveyard, Faelan?"

"There's a passage here and I know it works. I used it to take you to Lailoken the night Kieran killed you."

"It's in a graveyard?"

"Yes." He gives me a tired look, apparently not up for all my newbie questions.

I just shake my head.

He parks on top of a rise, farther back in the cemetery, and gets out, pointing at a crypt in the distance. "It's right there."

I follow him along the headstones toward an overgrown part of the graveyard. Large hydrangeas crowd around a fence with weeds poking through, and up ahead is an old stone structure with a broken metal gate.

"So the demigods use cemeteries as public transportation. Huh." This isn't something I would've guessed in a million years.

"A majority of the time we use average human transport, since gateway travel can be depleting, but . . . well, yeah."

"Did this dead person give you permission to use their resting place as a subway station?"

"It's an old gate, so the family's—" He stops abruptly.

"What's wro—"

He covers my mouth with his hand and puts a finger to his lips. He points at a dark spot a few yards ahead, just outside the crypt, like a puddle in the weeds. A black oily puddle.

A wraith.

I stumble back and turn to run.

Faelan tries to grab me. "Wait. Don't!"

Black smoke fills the air three feet in front of me, shifting and forming into a man. Faelan yanks me back as Kieran takes shape.

A hiss and a slurp come from the ground behind us, the wraith emerging, growing, its shadow falling over us as it rises from the ground, floating in a dripping mass.

Hundreds of birds burst from the surrounding trees, taking flight in a cacophony of screeches. They swarm in a mass, swooping up, then turning. At first I think Kieran is sending them out, but then I remember the birds coming after me in Faelan's cottage that first day. And when I glance at my protector, his features are pinched in focus.

The birds come around in a dark cloud, heading straight for us. I duck as the shrieking mass dives in a sharp slice at the air.

And cuts right through Kieran.

He bursts into black smoke again, the birds flying out in a chaotic disarray.

Kieran re-forms, a bored look on his face. "Let's not play this game, bastard."

"What do you want?" Faelan growls. The birds turn in a wide swooping movement and splat right into the wraith. The oozing creature screeches in rage, breaking apart. Several birds flop to the ground, dead, but the wraith is gone. "Tell your creatures to stand down," he says.

I look around and see two more wraiths on either side of us, one on top of a swaying bush, the other hovering above the ground in a weird crouched position. Their sucking sound fills the air, and their hollow eyes are turned on me.

"I heard from a little bird that you're looking for answers," Kieran says. "I'm seeking some as well, and I'd like to talk to our princess in private." He bows his head to me. "With your permission, of course, my love."

"Feck off," Faelan says.

"Can't she speak for herself?" he asks.

I search his face for a clue, any clue, that might tell me what he's up to. "Feck off," I repeat, trying to sound sure. But as I study his familiar features, the assurance in his tall frame, the sly glint in his silver eyes, I can't stop my legs from shaking. A part of me wants to walk toward him; it craves his touch. It wants . . . him.

But it's not *him* that the traitorous part of me wants. That man is gone. Lost.

"You're of one mind, I see," Kieran says. "But I still need to speak with you, princess. One way or another. So you'll come with me now."

"No way," I say, stepping back. My pulse picks up. I'm suddenly very sure that if he touches me, I won't be able to stop myself from surrendering.

Kieran looks sideways at Faelan. "If you allow me to take her without trouble, hunter, I'll make it worth your while. More riches, more power, than Marius could ever give you."

Faelan just glares.

"No?" Kieran says. "I thought it was worth a try. If I have to rip off your head, our princess won't be pleased with me. No one else will miss you, though."

At the vision of Faelan being torn in two, warmth rises into my skin, buzzing in my chest.

I step in front of Kieran, blocking his path to Faelan. "What do you want?"

His gaze moves to me. "You."

My heart stutters. I shake my head.

"Come with me, little doe," he says. "It's urgent that we discuss what I've discovered. I'll allow you to bring your protector if you wish. Or I can pull his entrails out here and now. And I think you know that I will. He doesn't have to die; he can merely be quartered a bit."

"You're a monster," I say, meaning it.

"Yes." A smile fills his lips.

"He can do whatever he bloody wants to do to me, Sage," Faelan says. "I don't give a shit. But if you give in to him, he won't let you go in the end." Faelan puts his hand on my arm protectively.

Kieran's muscles tense, readying to strike.

"Don't, Kieran," I say. I know he'll hurt Faelan. He'll do worse. And he won't stop until I give in. I can see it in the sharp set of his jaw, the slight rise of the shoulders as his muscles tense. He has the same look of deadly determination that my king wore. An unbreakable will. He'll get what he wants.

He's suddenly as familiar to me as if I've known him my whole life. And it's terrifying.

"I'll talk to you," I say, my voice weak. Shame fills me, but I don't see any other way. I can't let him hurt Faelan to get to me. "I'll go."

"No, Sage!" Faelan growls, grabbing me hard. "You can't."

Kieran's eyes lock on Faelan's grip. And then he's shifting, smoke, until he's suddenly re-forming inches away.

He takes Faelan's head in his hands and turns it with a quick snap, breaking his neck.

The sound jars through my bones. Faelan collapses to the ground, lifeless. But before I can scream, before I can move, Kieran's got me by the throat.

"Hush now," he hisses, lips against my cheek.

He turns to the wraiths and their shadows begin to move, darkness crowding around me. My vision clouds, dimming, my mind slipping. I squirm, trying to pull back, urgency screaming in my blood to get away. My power rises, glowing in my skin.

But Kieran's fingers around my neck are stone. He knows the torque will keep him safe from my fire.

"You have chosen," he whispers in my ear. "Let go now, my love."

The words slink over me, coiling around my heart as if they're coming from the past, coming from my king . . .

I try to find the truth, the light, but I can't. I can only feel *him*.

And so I obey. I let the darkness take me.

~

"You should let go, my love," the king says. "The wolf won't relent, that is sure."

I yank harder on the velvet shawl, but the king's wolf merely growls, setting its jaw, its teeth firmly gripping the fabric.

The king opens his book again, saying dryly, "You shouldn't have left it on the floor." Then he returns to ignoring me as he always does now during his evening read.

"And a wolf shouldn't be inside," I snap back. "So the world is topsy-turvy." I direct my next words to the beast. "Let go, you mongrel, or you'll be fed to the crows." The wolf's brow moves as if it doubts my threat.

So I tug again. The sound of rending fabric fills the air, a hole appearing in the weave. The garment is ruined.

I growl in frustration and release my end. As soon as it falls to the floor, the king's wolf drops it as well. The creature looks up at me, tongue lolling, mouth open in a toothy grin. Traitor.

"Take it, then," I say, collapsing back into the chair, too tired to fight any longer.

The king looks up, catching my gaze with his. "And that is why the wolf will always win."

I give him a questioning tilt of my brow.

He leans forward, resting his elbow on his knee. "Don't you see? He's willing to destroy everything you hold dear to claim what he wants."

The back of my neck prickles.

He closes his book, setting it aside. "And the wolf is very patient." He stands and walks across the floor to where I sit. He looms over me for a moment, watching, and then he leans forward, gripping the arms of the chair, caging me in. "Once the beast has tasted what he craves, he will hold on to it forever. He has no choice. He won't let it go."

I don't let myself look away or cower from him. I cannot give him any ground. "What do you want from me?"

"You aren't foolish," he whispers. "You know."

I shake my head.

"Oh, but I know you wish for it too, my love. I hear your quick breath in the night; I feel your need through the walls."

My heart falters.

"Yes," he says, moving closer. "But it isn't only your body I crave. I need more, I need loyalty." He studies me for a moment, his silver eyes softening. He kneels to my level and says gently, "I seek love, Lily."

A sharp pain hits the center of my chest. I search his face as disbelief trickles in. Surely he can't mean it.

"We are both alone," he says. His fingers move to brush my knuckles. "Why do you resist the hand wishing to hold you?"

My throat tightens. I have no answer.

His touch grazes my cheek, coming away damp with tears that I hadn't felt fall. He leans in and gently kisses my brow. His lips are chilled as he kisses a trail to my temple, the tip of my nose, my salty cheeks. "Let me hold you for a time, Lily," he whispers into my skin. "Take what you wish from me, I won't harm you. I could never harm my own heart—"

I stop his words with my lips, reaching out to take his tunic in my fists and pull him closer. And as his arms wrap around me, his hands gripping me, his strength lifting me, I rise . . .

Days and nights merge together . . . Time slips past.

It holds. It builds. As the days weave minds together, a partnership in all things emerging, the nights weave spirits together into one.

Death merged with flame.

In the joining of my essence with his, I am blinded, thinking our growing power can allow for no enemies. That our secrets will never be known.

But I am wrong . . . An enemy already lurks among us. She seeks me out to destroy me. To destroy my king. She despises us with an iron will. And she won't be satiated until we are ripped from each other.

She won't relent until all the power is hers.

FORTY-FIVE

SAGE

I open my eyes. The smell of smoke lingers in the air. The familiar dark canopy of my bed hangs above me, curtains a sheer red. I turn toward the king. But the bed is empty.

He was just here. Wasn't he? I sit up, disoriented.

A trickle of unease fills my chest.

Where is he?

"Hello?" I ask the silence.

But wait. When I fell asleep, I wasn't here; I wasn't in the keep. I was with the king in the wood, under the rowan tree. I was . . . why can't I remember?

Something was wrong before I closed my eyes. The king had called to me, drawing me into the wood, and I'd found him resting under the rowan tree. He said there was something we could do to hide ourselves, hide our secret. Something that would save us from her. We argued because his plan was terrible, it was horrifying what I would have to do . . . but . . .

Confusion rolls over me again. *Why can't I remember?*

I rise from the bed, wandering over to the fire. The embers have faded to nearly nothing. I snap my fingers, sending out my spark into the dying blaze.

The energy slinks over my skin but goes no further. The embers stay as they were. I blink at the coals and try again.

Still nothing.

Something is very wrong.

I reach for my pouch of lavender, to call my mother—

Where is it?

I look down. What . . . what is this? Am I wearing trousers? I pat myself and realize how strange my clothing is. And I'm wearing my torque—why would that be? It was taken off me soon after the Bonding. Am I a prisoner?

My heart begins to race as I look around again. And then I spot the painting over the hearth. It's not the painting that was there before. It's a portrait of me now. I stand on an icy bank, Fionn perched on my arm, ready for flight.

Fionn.

"It's lovely, isn't it?" a voice says from behind me.

I turn, nearly stumbling into the fireplace.

The young man grabs me by the upper arm, tugging me away from the flames, closer to him. "Take care," he says. "You could catch your clothes on fire, and we wouldn't want that, would we?"

I gape at him, lost. "Who are you?"

He smirks, his silver eyes full of mischief. "We're not here to be coy, little doe." He pulls me to the chair and releases me into it.

As I watch him begin to pace, confusion fills me again. He's familiar, he's so like the king. But I don't know him.

Kieran whispers in my head. The name of my king's brother . . . but he was just a boy the last time I saw him, fourteen winters old. This is a man.

The ground tips. A memory of this young man's face, how he broke someone's neck. The violent moment flashes in my head, and I grip the arms of the chair, panic hitting.

Faelan!

No.

Wait . . . who's Faelan?

Pain shoots through my head, and I groan, squeezing my eyes shut. I pinch the bridge of my nose.

"Are you well?" the silver-eyed young man asks, urgency filling his voice.

"Where is my king?" I mutter.

"Sage?" Someone shakes my shoulders. "Sage, are you all right? Look at me!"

Sage . . .

No . . . it's wrong. It's all wrong . . . My stomach shivers, everything swirling inside of me, bones aching, chest tingling . . . *What's happening—*

My eyes fly open, and I gasp, my lungs stinging. I grip his arms as a lifeline. "Kieran!" I gulp in air like I was drowning a second ago. I was. Who was I? What just happened? "Oh my God, Kieran."

His face comes clear in front of me, fear in his eyes. "That was her, wasn't it?" he asks.

I nod my head, not even caring how he knows. It all totally took me over. I couldn't even have my own thoughts. I was just . . . gone.

His hand becomes a fist at his side as tension fills his body. "It's too soon," he whispers. "I was sure the torque would hold this in."

"You what?"

"It was her torque—Queen Lily's. It should have held her spirit down. That's what the damn monk said."

I blink at him. He knows Lailoken? "You know what that was." It's not a question. I can see he's fully aware.

He nods, his eyes going distant.

"How much do you know? About me."

"A lot more than I like." He moves to the fire, staring into the embers.

"Tell me. What just happened?" I look back to the bed, all the memories and emotions of Lily swirling in the background of my mind like a mist trying to press in again.

"She surfaced," he says, his voice tense. "Her spirit took over your body."

Dread soaks into my bones. "How's that even possible?" Her spirit? In me? My body begins to shake. This has gotten totally out of control. "Am I possessed or something?" I nearly choke on the words.

"No," he says, and then he adds, "And yes." He releases a long breath as my lungs stop working. "The truth is," he continues, "I've known for a long time that Queen Lily pulled all of her power—her spirit—from her blood, leaving her body an empty vessel, before the Cast came to drag her into the Pit. It was her way of escape. I kept her secret. Because all of this time I assumed she'd simply had her essence placed into her owl, that she'd remained in the wood. But when I went to the old monk, he said that the owl had died centuries ago."

The realization of what he's implying begins to sink in. "She needed a vessel," I say under my breath.

"When I read your spirit that night in the alley, it didn't make sense," he says, still caught up in his thoughts. He starts to pace again. "Something was wrong. You were merely supposed to be a second daughter, lesser, not a being to be reckoned with, not carrying the power I felt inside you as I looked deeper. It was as if you were something . . . more. Extra. I assumed that I wasn't sensing right, especially when you didn't defend yourself, then bled out so swiftly. But . . ." He pauses, looking oddly unsure, not like himself at all. "Then I learned more of the truth of what Queen Lily did to my brother, what they had both done to force the hand of fate, and I knew with sudden clarity that it was Lily's spirit hidden inside you that I was sensing."

The stone floor seems to shift under my feet. And the truth looms like a specter, clouding my vision. All I can see is the painting of her above the mantle. Of a woman dressed in pure white, cloaked in furs, wild copper hair a stark contrast to the icy surroundings.

It's nuts. It's crazy. These visions, these dreams, they aren't just memories. They're actually *her*. Queen Lily.

Her spirit is inside me.

A shiver runs through me. That's why it's been so overwhelming, why I've felt like someone else at times. And just a minute ago she was able to take me over so completely.

God help me. It's getting worse.

And now I'm with Kieran. Who I'm not even sure I can trust.

"How do you know all of this?" I ask.

His voice drops so that I can barely hear him. "My brother." I open my mouth to ask what he could possibly mean—the king is dead—but he cuts me off, saying, "I'll explain, I swear, but first we need to hide you from the creature trying to poison you."

I thought that was him.

"Faelan is being brought up momentarily," he adds. Then he tips his head, giving me a curious look. "But you don't seem to be terribly worried about him."

"Oh, God. Faelan!" I can't believe I forgot for even a second.

"I assumed you'd accost me the moment I came into the room. I should have known something was amiss when you didn't."

I shake my head, overwhelmed, confused by his shift to semicongeniality. This isn't a side of Kieran I've seen before; I have to wonder if it's real. I'd be stupid to buy into anything he says. But right now my mind is exhausted from the shock of what just happened. All my guards are down.

"I know you don't trust me," he says, like he can see the turmoil on my face. "That's fair. I'm not known for my subtlety."

"You slit my throat," I say to remind myself yet again. But my voice is weak, so I add, "And broke Faelan's neck."

"Whatever you think of me," he says, a defensive bite in his tone, "the moment in the alley was necessary. I needed to see why your energy was off—any weakness in you could have been exploited by others. It was better you die than become a weapon. So I had to be sure you were truly a second Daughter of Fire. We have seen that you are." He motions to me, like my presence proves his point. "I was hoping you'd come to trust me in time."

"So you made sure that you controlled my ability to use my *own* power?" I say, reaching up to touch my torque. "How is that supposed to make me trust you?"

"It needed to be me to place the torque—so that no one could manipulate you."

"You mean, like you have? Killing me, taking my free will, and kidnapping me."

"I kidnapped you to help you."

"Said every serial killer ever."

"There are eyes watching," he says, his tone getting tense, "creatures listening. I needed to speak with you away from all the spies—are you telling me you'd have come willingly?"

"You didn't have to break Faelan's *neck*!"

He pauses and then smirks as he says, "Snapping that plant-eating bastard's spine was just a bonus."

I rise from the chair in a rush. "You're a snake and a liar!"

He tsks at me. "Manners, princess. I may be a snake but I've never lied to you. I've only been completely honest." He pauses as a knock sounds on the door, then adds, "Unlike others in your life." He holds my gaze as he waves his hand, opening the door from across the room. "Speaking of the hunter . . ."

A tall man drags Faelan in and drops his limp body in the middle of the floor before walking back out, slamming the door behind him.

I rush to Faelan's side and roll him onto his back. His face is swollen, nearly unrecognizable. A giant torque is around his neck, like the one he put on me that first night, and I know that's what's kept him from healing completely. He's breathing, though. He's alive.

"Can you hear me, Faelan?" I reach out to pull the torque off. A burst of pain runs through my arm as it sizzles against my skin.

I stumble back, cradling my hand to my chest.

"It's locked," Kieran says behind me. "Only I can take it off, since I placed it there."

"Then get it off him," I say through my teeth.

"Very well," Kieran says, sounding disappointed but giving up far more easily than I thought he would.

He kneels behind Faelan and draws a dagger from his boot, then pricks his thumb with it.

Blood pearls at the tip of his finger, and he slides it over the edge of the torque, smearing red on the metal with a hiss. It unlatches with a clink and falls to the side.

Faelan's features immediately begin to return to normal as the swelling goes down. Several bruises remain, though, and a cut on his cheek doesn't fully heal. He must need to feed. He probably used most of his energy to heal his spine before Kieran put the torque on him.

He opens his eyes. "Sage?"

"Are you okay?" I ask, brushing the hair from his forehead.

He begins to sit up, his features clenched in pain. And then he spots Kieran only a foot away from me. He goes still. "Get back, Sage," he says, his voice deadly.

"Now, now," Kieran says, his haughty tone returning in full force. "Can't we be civil?"

"Civility went out the window when you kidnapped us," I say.

He gives me a tired look. "Haven't we been over this? I've told you why I brought you here."

I help Faelan to the chair, and then I turn on Kieran, sick of his games. "What the hell do you really want from me, Kieran?"

His head pulls back. "I'm protecting you, obviously."

I release a derisive laugh.

"Or did you miss the dead pixie in your cottage?" he asks.

I gape at him.

"How do you know about Niamh?" Faelan asks, his voice thick with warning.

But I don't care how he knows. "You know who did it," I say, suddenly very sure. "Spit it out."

He goes over to the hearth, pulling out the poker and nudging the embers with it. He turns and swings the poker as if it were a sword. "I'm fairly sure it was my sister," he says.

Wait, what?

"I thought Princess Mara wanted Sage for your House," Faelan says, echoing my confusion. "Why would she hurt her?"

"Mara is . . . shall we say, a complex creature," Kieran says. "She's insecure and has always been jealous of anything her brothers aren't cruel to." He looks at me. "She does want the power you can bring, Sage. She was going to draw you in, control you, in order to get it. But she grew impatient when she saw how attached you were to this hunter. She sees you the same way she saw Queen Lily: as a threat. So she sent the poison, wanting you to be as pliable as possible when the Emergence came around."

"Does she know about Lily and me?" I ask, my nerves turning raw as I realize what I'm up against.

Kieran shakes his head. "And she can never discover it."

"Know what?" Faelan asks.

But I'm not ready to explain it all to him yet. I can't even imagine how he'd look at me if he knew that I'm a ticking time bomb. So I stay focused on Kieran. "She killed Aelia's friend, Kieran. Why didn't you stop her? You had to have known she was going to try something."

"Mara is a force, Sage," he says. "You need to understand, she may not be more powerful than I am, but she's far more insane, which makes her dangerous. There's nothing she wouldn't do." He looks over to Faelan. "That party you brought Sage to the other night? That was meant to be a bloodworking to manipulate Sage into killing you."

I lower myself into the chair opposite Faelan, feeling sick at the thought.

"She assumed that she could drive you mad, Sage. She thought it would be easy, that you were weak from living in the human world for too long. It's why I made sure to put the torque on you right away, why I warned Faelan to get you out of the party."

"That was a fucked-up warning," Faelan says, his voice angry.

I add, "You could've just called and told us your sister was a homicidal maniac."

"Every Otherborn left on earth is aware of that," Kieran says. "And if I had contacted you, she would have known I was working against her. She watches me like a hawk. It's why I had to slip away. I told her I was going off to lick my wounds from your rejection of me, and she said she'd take care of it, that she'd be sure you became hers. So I watched."

A thought comes to me, a memory of the dream I had a few minutes ago, just before I woke up, how Lily was thinking of *her*, and how this unnamed woman in Lily's mind wouldn't *relent until the power was hers*. "Kieran, did your sister do something to my sister?"

He nods, unsaid things in his eyes.

"What did she do?" It suddenly seems very important.

"You'll have to ask Lily," he says.

But that's the last thing I want to do. There's one other source I could ask, though. Even if it terrifies me. I know that I can call to her—I've felt myself do it several times. And if a connection is made, it could answer everything.

FORTY-SIX

SAGE

"I need lavender," I say, stepping up to the fireplace.

"You don't have to do this, Sage," Faelan says, his voice unsteady.

He's afraid. His goddess has been silent for hundreds of years—most of his life. And now I'm going to draw her closer.

I hope. There's so much that I need to know, that I need to understand.

The old me of two weeks ago would be baffled by what I'm about to try, but in this moment I have a deep assurance. As a Daughter of Fire, this is what I would do. And I want to feel this. I want to understand. To know why . . . why she just abandoned me to that horror of a life.

Kieran holds out a bowl of lavender buds as if he'd known I would need them. "Is this all you need?" he asks.

I nod, taking some between my fingers.

"Marius should be here," Faelan says. "As leader of the House of Brighid."

"He'll understand," I say, even though I'm not sure of that. "It may not even work."

"It'll work," Kieran says, very sure. When I glance at him, he adds, "Why do you think Brighid has been silent since Lily's fall?"

"She only speaks to her daughters," Faelan says, clarifying.

I'm filled with a sense of purpose as the realization hits: I'm *the* link to the goddess. It's a stunning thought. I scoop some more lavender into my palm, my hand shaking as I turn to the fire.

"I'm ready. But I need the torque off, Kieran."

After a moment, his fingers brush the back of my neck, and the necklace loosens. As it falls away, everything inside me seems to grow lighter, like I'm floating from the ground, a hum filling my chest. Warmth stirs in my belly, but I try to dampen it, not wanting it to spill out. I still don't know how strong this power is. If Lily really is inside me, then I have a feeling the energy could be monumental.

I focus on my pulse, like Faelan taught me. On the blood weaving through me, the buzzing energy threading into my muscles.

Then I let a small trickle emerge into my fingers, and I toss the lavender into the fire.

The flames spark and shiver. I breathe slowly and try to speak. "Mother Brighid, hear me," I say, my voice barely a whisper. *Please hear me.* "I must speak with you. It's your daughter L—Sage."

Remember me? The one you abandoned?

"I need your help," I continue, listening to the same thing I always hear—*touch, feed, control*—coming through the flames. "There's an imbalance," I say. "I'm not sure what to do."

"Ask her how we can stop my sister," Kieran says. "We need to somehow block her from watching us or—"

"I got it," I say, agitated. "Now be quiet so I can hear."

I take in another deep breath and release it, then say one more time, "Mother Brighid, hear me, please. I need to talk to you about so many things. What do we do about Mara? What do we do about me and . . . Lily?" I watch the dancing light, the flames sliding over the charred logs. I listen to the snapping wood. But I don't hear any new voices. Just fire.

Then something pops with a spark. The logs hiss.

My daughter . . .

I blink, not sure I really heard it. I keep staring at the flames, straining to listen.

And the whispers come again, like a soft wind: *You are more than most.*

"Mother," I breathe, my voice breaking. I move closer, falling to my knees on the hearth.

I reach out to the light. My fingers brush the fire, the blaze encompassing my hand, the flames sliding over the surface of my palm. The heat fills me like a caress. And no pain comes.

Forgive me, daughter, the snapping logs say. *I didn't mean for you to be alone for so long.*

An arrow of pain spikes my throat.

I loved you both. My own flesh. I was weak—I couldn't choose between you and my Lily.

"What is she saying?" Faelan asks.

I ignore him, desperate to stay locked into the connection. "We're in danger, Lily and I," I say. "Mara is trying to hurt us. We need your help to stop her, to understand."

The light flares, and I feel the goddess's urgency in my gut. *Poison. My sister's daughter is poison. She is chaos, she is destruction, and her weapon will strike true. You must hurry—you must keep him safe.*

"Who?" I ask. "Keep who safe?"

Two will be lost. Only one can be saved.

My nerves prickle. "What do you mean? What do I do?"

One made of water who leads my flock. Another a true friend in the wood who gave all and asked for nothing in return. Hold one to you, or the other will be lost.

Dread fills me. The flames dim, returning to embers. And I sense her fade away.

I know who she means. *The one made of water who leads*—that's Marius. And the second, *a true friend*—as soon as I heard the words,

Lily's memories of the wood, of his gentleness, his kindness, all filled my head.

"We have to go to Lailoken," I say, urgency filling my bones, thinking of him being hurt. My friend. He was my only friend for a time—*Lily's only friend.*

"Why?" Kieran and Faelan ask at the same time.

"Brighid says that two people will be in danger, but only one can be saved." I hesitate, knowing what Faelan will do, but I decide to tell them everything. "It's Lailoken and Marius."

"Marius?" Faelan stands. "Where is he? How is he in danger?"

"She said poison, but that's all I know." And if it's anything like what happened to Niamh, there's no time to waste.

Faelan blanches. "We need to go. Now." He starts for the door.

"I'm not going with you, Faelan," I say.

"What? What do you mean?" He frowns. "Marius is your master; he's mine. We have a loyalty to him."

"You do," I say. "I don't."

Conflict fills Faelan's eyes.

I move closer to him, hoping he hears me. "I have to go to Lailoken, Faelan. I know it doesn't make sense, but to this thing deep inside me, he's my truest friend. I can't let anything happen to him."

Faelan nods. But then he shifts his feet, torn. "I can't allow you to be harmed."

Kieran sets the iron poker back in the rack. "I know this old monk well enough. I'll take her to him. You go to your master, hunter."

"No fucking way," Faelan says. "She's not going anywhere with you."

"Faelan." I give him a look, not wanting to argue in front of Kieran. I understand where Faelan's coming from, but he has to loosen the leash. "I can take care of myself now, remember. Thanks to you."

Kieran looks back and forth between us.

Faelan runs a hand through his hair, then releases a growl and kicks the chair with a crack of wood. He nods, saying through his teeth, "Fine." He steps over to Kieran, getting close and pointing a finger at his neck. "You let anything happen to her, I'll rip your throat out."

Kieran smirks. "And here I thought we were becoming friends."

~

I fall to my knees in the clover, stomach heaving. I have a vague awareness of trees around me, but I'm focused on the spasms of pain racking my body.

"Apparently you've never traveled like this before?" I hear Kieran saying over me. "It can be a shock the first time."

"I'm fine," I lie. Another surge rips through me, forcing me to vomit.

Kieran crouches nearby. "You have to breathe deep when the initial vibrations hit." He mimics slow breathing. "In and out, three times. Long and steady. Focus on a single spot on the ground while you do it. Like you're convincing your body you've arrived."

I nod, breathing in through my nose like he is.

"Yes, then out."

I release the shaky breath slowly, focusing on a single blade of grass near my hand, and my stomach actually settles. Another spasm ripples through me, but it's smaller and I don't throw up this time. I breathe in and out again, pacing myself, then I try to stand. I stumble.

Kieran takes me by the arm to steady me. "You're good," he says.

I lean on him, and reality hits me. I almost burst out laughing. How did I get here, being propped up by the freaking dark prince? This guy pretty much murdered me in an alley only a week ago. His sister is apparently trying to torment me and control me, and maybe did the same to my sister. But somehow I've ended up walking through a magical doorway beside him.

What the hell is wrong with my head?

"What did Brighid say about Mara?" he asks.

"That she's poison." I brush leaves from my pants. "And chaos. And destruction—my mother's not a fan."

He considers that for a minute as we begin to walk. "The goddess isn't wrong."

I shrug, not wanting to talk with him like I would with Faelan. I decide to ask my own questions. "So you figured out Lily's spirit was inside me. Do you know how that happened?"

He shakes his head. "That I don't know. I only knew she'd be within a new vessel that could eventually help her hide for a time."

And now she's stealing my body? That's extremely creepy. "Why did you say that you had some kind of rights to me then? Was that just because of your brother marrying my sister?"

"When she was free, Lily told me her sister would belong to me."

"Excuse me?" *Belong?* "How did she even know she'd have a sister? That would've been long before I got here."

"I don't know. But I trusted her. She was good to me, even though I was a boy, young and annoying. All I knew of her was how happy she made my brother."

So he's been waiting this whole time, thinking I'd show up and be his? And instead I hate him.

Maybe if he wasn't such an asshole . . .

"What are your powers?" I ask. "Besides being a weirdo raven man, I mean."

He gives me a crooked smile. "Why do you wish to know?"

"For self-defense reasons, obviously."

"Well, in that case," he says, clearing his throat, "as a son of Morrígan, my element is spirit, so that is what I manipulate. I can walk into dreams, change emotions, and take away a person's will."

My pulse speeds up as he rattles off the list.

"Oh, and I can be a weirdo raven man," he adds. He moves a branch out of the way and allows me to pass first. When he follows, he says, "This also means I can see through the eyes of other ravens. Which is how I followed you most of the time."

My feet stumble in the moss. "Followed me?"

"Before you came to us, when you lived on the street, I was watching. And then once you were at Marius's house, I kept my birds close." He looks at me. "I saw many things."

His words hang in the air. I don't want to think about what "many things" might mean. But that must be how he knew about Niamh.

"So what're we going to do about your sister?" I ask, trying not to think about the pixie she killed, the horrifying death. Instead I need to focus on how to get revenge.

Kieran is quiet for a few seconds like he's thinking. "I was only going to hide you from her. I'm not sure how to destroy her. And the Cast is behind her, always."

"I can't hide forever, Kieran. We have to do something."

"Lily assumed something could be done," he says, his voice full of sadness. "She was wrong."

"Your sister hurt her—is that why Lily went crazy and killed your brother?"

"In a way," he says.

"If you know what happened to them, tell me."

"It's not my story to tell."

I stop walking and turn to glare at him. "Really? You're gonna be coy? People have died."

"Some stories kill as well. Even a demi." He moves ahead on the path, and I hear him say quietly, "And I won't be the one to put you in the crosshairs of that mess."

I watch him go and then follow a few paces behind. He's impossible to understand. And he's obviously not going to tell me anything. But if

Lily's really a part of me, I need to know what she knew about Princess Mara. I need to understand where everything went wrong, why Lily killed the king.

"Did your brother and sister get along?" I ask.

"No, never," Kieran says. "My brother felt my sister's way of living, of feeding, was undignified. He never allowed her to be a part of the court. At the time I felt he was unfair to her. Now I understand why."

"And now she's in charge," I say. How convenient. "How do the children of Morrígan . . . feed?" I ask. When the king fed from me in the dream, it felt like I was being ripped to bits from the inside.

His shoulders stiffen and at first he doesn't answer. Then he says quietly, "We pull spirits from their bodies."

Chills rake over me.

"A bit at a time." He sounds tired saying it. "It can be very painful."

I remember.

"As a fire demi, what you take from a body is related to their molecular structure; it's physical. The Morrígan children take the essence of a person's spirit," he continues. "It can be messy if it's not tightly controlled, and pieces of the spirit itself can peel off in the feeding. That's why most of my younger siblings have shade consorts—they're already dead in the important sense of the word, only threads of spirit left behind. You can't usually pull those threads from a shade by accident, so they're more likely to survive."

I let all of that soak in. Then I ask, "Do you kill every time you feed?"

"Not anymore."

The pathway narrows and the trees become thicker. I'm wondering if we're ever going to get there, when Kieran says, "It's just up ahead."

We pick our way through a section of dense ferns followed by some pretty crazy brambles, pushing forward. And just when I think he's lying and we'll be walking in an endless loop for an eternity, we stumble out.

Right into a huge field of purple and yellow flowers.

I gasp, taken off guard by the beauty in front of me. And I immediately recognize it as the place Lily wanted to return to, the woods of Caledonia, a field of bluebells and daffodils.

A rush of elation washes over me. "Oh wow, it's barely changed at all." I search the other side of the clearing for the juniper tree. It has twisty limbs, I remember—

My gaze catches on an overgrown area on the far side of the clearing. A branch sticking out looks familiar, so I head toward it.

FORTY-SEVEN

FAELAN

I burst through the French doors of Marius's house. Screams fill the air around me, coming from upstairs. Two females, from the sound of it.

I take the stairs two at a time, pulling out my dagger. When I get to the landing, I slow, trying to catch a scent in the air that might tell me what I'm walking into. But I don't sense anything odd or off. There's soap and old perfume. One of the females is Aelia, I think. The other is a human, likely the mother, but it could be one of the servants.

I move along the hallway, aware now that the arguing is coming from Aelia's room. I pause outside the door, peek through the crack, and push the door open while trying to stay back.

My thundering heart stops.

Marius is on his hands and knees on the floor, the hilt of a dagger sticking out of his back. He's gasping, gagging, trying to reach out for someone, trying to speak, but he can't. Blood is coming from his ears, his nose, his lips, dripping onto the wood floor.

Aelia is shoving a woman against the wall—the wife, Barbara. She sobs, then screams in her mother's face. "What the fuck have you done?"

The human looks confused. She's shaking her head, but she's not fighting back. "It was to help him," she says. "He was sick. I was told to put the medicine in him."

"It wasn't medicine, bitch! It was a poisoned dagger!" Aelia shoves her hard and turns to her father, crumpling beside him. "Oh, gods, oh, Daddy, what do I do, goddess help me."

I rush in as she's reaching to touch the hilt. I pull her hand away. "No," I say, "it's cursed, like the ring." I watch my mentor struggling to move, to speak, my mind frozen in horror. His eyes find mine, and tears spill from them.

"What's happening, Faelan?" Aelia grips me. "Stop it, please make it stop."

"I can't," I whisper. Rage unfurls in my gut as she clings to me, shaking, desperate. I should've moved faster. Only minutes earlier and I could've stopped it, seconds faster and he'd have been spared. "We'll fix this. Don't be afraid." I hold her to me as we watch him convulse, his features contorting.

The poison is filling his skin now, spreading out, weaving its black web through his veins. He goes still, black ooze slipping from his mouth in a thin string. He collapses to the side, eyes wide, face contorted in pain—*am I truly seeing this?*

Aelia clutches me as we watch her father disappear inside himself.

Barbara just keeps talking, telling us that it'll help in a second. It's got medicine on it, the dagger, she was told it would fix him. She's obviously been severely glamoured—she's in some kind of trance, barely aware that her husband is on the floor in front of her.

After a moment, I grab a scarf off one of the mirrors and gag her. Then I pull her to the closet and shove her in, blocking the door with a chair from the vanity.

It's either that or I cut out her heart. The way I feel right now, I'm barely sane enough not to kill her. Even though I don't think she knew what she was doing.

Aelia sniffs, like she's trying to collect herself. "We can't just leave him here," she says. "What do we do?"

"He'll need to be put somewhere until we can get the antidote."

"Maybe his study? It has a view of the lagoon. I think he'd like that best." She looks up at me, her cheeks glistening with tears. "I can't take the knife out. Will you do it?"

"Yeah," I say, but the word barely emerges. I stare down at my mentor, not sure what to do exactly. As if I were a newblood all over again. "We need to call Cias. Hopefully, he can start making the antidote right away." Marius will be in excruciating agony as long as he is under.

I kneel beside him, pull off my shirt, and use it to grip the dagger's hilt. I slide it out, my gut rising, thinking of who this is, how strong he is, how helpless he's become, in seconds.

I should have been here to stop it.

I wrap the dagger in my shirt. Aelia helps me move Marius into his study and lay him out on the long window seat. She sits beside her dad, taking his hand in hers, and I go to the safe, locking away the cursed dagger.

Looking at them tears me in two, knowing I can't stay. I have to get back to Sage. But how can I leave Aelia alone like this?

I step into the hall and pull out my phone, tapping in James's number.

"Everything okay?" he asks, his voice tense.

"I need you to come back to the Cottages right away. Aelia needs you."

"What is it?"

I don't know how to say it. "Just come."

Back in the room, Aelia is still sitting beside her father, both of them framed by the picture window. "I have to go," I say.

Aelia turns slowly, her eyes lost. "What?"

"I have to leave, I'm so sorry. Sage needs me." I can barely utter the words. Marius is my master. He's my keeper. He saved me and took me in when everyone rejected me, when they betrayed me. He's the only true friend I've ever had. And I should be with him, at his side, taking care of every detail to bring him back. But I can't help it. I have to go.

I keep seeing Sage in danger, and I'm not by her side. I'm not but Kieran is. An irrational fear is coiling in my chest as I realize I could lose her, lose something that was never meant to be mine to begin with.

FORTY-EIGHT

SAGE

"Do you hear that?" Kieran whispers as we cross the field.

My feet slow a little, anxiety trickling through me. I scan the trees, seeing only shadows.

Before I can tell him no, one of the shadows moves. A large one. Just slightly.

I freeze.

Kieran grabs me, pulling me to the side, ducking under a fallen tree. "Stay here, don't move." He brushes his fingers along the scar on my neck. "And trust that I'll be watching you." Then he poofs away.

Seriously?

I peek over the tree, searching for the spot where I saw the movement, but I can't see anything now. It's all a thick wall of tree limbs and ivy. I don't even know if what I saw move was a threat. For all I know, it could've been an animal. Like a really big raccoon or something. Are there raccoons in this forest? Bears? We're in Scotland, right? What sort of animals run around in the land of plaid? There aren't monkeys, obviously, but maybe—

"What are we hiding from?" whispers a voice beside me.

I twist to look, nearly falling over.

An old man is crouched behind the log, staring at me with wide, curious eyes. "Is it a Norseman?" A squirrel appears over his shoulder, peeking at me too.

I stare at them both. The smell of him wafts around me, a thick, barnlike scent. His eyes are a piercing blue, framed by the bushiest eyebrows I've ever seen. His hair is a tangle of silver gray and his hat looks like—well, I think it's a bird's nest. There are leaves and vines woven into his long thick robes, and his hand is gripping a tall walking stick. He looks like he just popped out of a children's story.

Something brushes my foot, and I bite back a gasp of surprise as I look down.

It's only a rabbit. Its ears twitch back like it's annoyed that I'm not petting it.

"I hope it's not a Saxon," the old man says with a snort. "They smell like the underside of a horse. Very disagreeable. Whoever they are, they bring bad apples."

I don't quite know what to say. Or do. But I think this is Lailoken. He doesn't look the same, not even a little. But he's familiar.

He sinks lower and asks me in a conspiratorial voice, "Did you come here by way of sky or sea?"

"I walked?" I say, like a question. I should tell him why I'm here, that he's in danger, but I'm at a total loss for words. Suddenly my memories are no help at all.

"Oh!" he says in wonder, brow going up. "Well, that is exciting."

"Um"—I look down at the rabbit by my foot—"I came to warn you."

"You did?" He adjusts the nest on his head.

"Yeah, there's someone who's trying to—"

He places a dirty finger to his lips to hush me. Then he points to something behind me in the field, whispering, "The tale begins, my child." Giddiness fills his features, and he motions for me to look. "I've been waiting so very long."

I turn.

Faelan is emerging from the woods. He pauses at the edge, searching the opposite tree line, his body tense.

Relief washes over me, and I start to stand, lifting a hand to wave. But I'm grabbed from behind, the old man yanking on my shirt. "No, no," he hisses. "You're interrupting. Hush now and sit still."

I open my mouth to scold him, and he puts a finger to his mouth again. My throat clenches. I can't speak.

"No more foolishness, Lily. This is what we've waited for." He motions at me to watch.

Fear threads through me, my skin turning clammy. What is he talking about?

He called me Lily.

I turn to Faelan, but when I open my mouth to call to him, nothing comes out. I try to get up, to move, but it's like my feet are stuck, my legs useless.

Fear becomes dread. I stare at Faelan, helplessly watching him cross the clearing, his body crouched low to the ground, his eyes watchful. He won't see me here; he's focused on the trees across from us. He moves steadily. And when he passes us, he's forty yards or so away.

He pauses halfway across the field, pulling a dagger from his waist like he heard something. He studies the trees ahead, then turns to look behind him.

An object sings through the air. And a dull thwack echoes around the clearing.

Faelan flies back, an arrow protruding from his chest.

A cry fills me, horror burning in my limbs, but I can't move, I can't speak. I'm frozen, useless. Held captive by a crazy old man.

Lailoken touches my shoulder like he's consoling me as we watch. He leans over, whispering, "He is a brilliant boy, Mr. Winter. I hope he brought his heart with him. He shall need it."

Another snapping of twigs nearby and someone else emerges from the forest. I blink, not sure I'm seeing right. I think I recognize him. He's in old-fashioned black leathers, a bow held in his hand, a quiver on his back. His hair is dark brown, cut close to his head, and his skin is tan.

Ben. The shade from the Halloween party where all of this began.

"You got him," he yells to someone behind him. "That should hold him for a minute, maybe two. Hurry up and get the bigger torque."

Someone else yells back from the cover of the trees, a female voice, but I can't hear it clearly.

"No way, not without the torque. I'm not getting paid enough to be gutted by your lover."

There's silence, and the man is joined by a second figure, a tall female. She emerges into the clearing like a Viking princess, her perfect body clad in tight, ancient-looking leathers, a thick iron shackle in her fist.

A white-blond braid curls over her shoulder.

Astrid.

What is she doing here? I expected to see Mara, but this . . . it doesn't make sense.

I watch her and Ben walk toward Faelan's body. They slow as they get closer, both pulling out daggers. Astrid says something quietly, and Ben goes around in a wider circle, to the other side. Then he kneels and grabs Faelan, pushing him into a limp sitting position.

Faelan looks completely out of it, his chin on his chest, his dark hair curtained over his face. A huge arrow is sticking out of his chest.

My own chest aches and tears fill my eyes. I want to run out there, to rip that bitch's braid out by the roots. What the hell are they doing to him?

"Now they shall see, Lily," Lailoken whispers. "It will come as quite a shock, but they shall see."

Astrid leans over and places the torque around Faelan's neck. Then she nods at Ben, who hoists him up and starts dragging Faelan's body across the clearing into the trees. Astrid follows, slipping her dagger casually back into her belt, a satisfied grin on her face.

"Well, let's go!" Lailoken says, sounding excited. He snaps his fingers and my throat warms, the lock on my limbs easing. "It's almost your cue, princess. The boy needs us to save him." He grabs me by the arm, yanking me to my feet and tugging me through a raspberry bush like he's as strong as a twenty-year-old.

I stumble forward, getting pricked and snagged on the thorns as I'm pulled.

"Let go!" I hiss, trying to get away, but he's gripping me too tightly, dragging me through brush and past branches, hurriedly weaving through the trees.

"No," he says. "No more letting go. I've missed you too long." The rabbit follows at our feet, and several more pop up from the bushes, joining the herd. The squirrel rides on the monk's shoulder, clinging with its tiny claws. It glares at me with its beady eyes, like I've offended it.

"What is going on?" I ask, desperate.

"You're going to complete the circle, of course. As your mother planned."

I growl in frustration. That makes no sense.

"I know," he says, like he actually pities me. "You're mixed up in your belly. It's how it had to be done. No other way to hide. But don't worry, child. It's all blossoming now!"

His words strike me—he knows why this is all happening. I open my mouth to ask him the millions of questions crowding my head, but he yanks me again, pulling me forward faster.

"Not now," he says. "No time for questions." Like he's reading my mind.

We come to a sparser part of the forest, and he pauses, looking around frantically. He whistles, and a huge bird swoops down from an upper branch, landing on a root nearby. Lailoken leans over like he's listening to the creature.

I stare at the owl. The perfectly soft white and tan feathers. The black eyes reflecting the forest around us.

"Fionn," I say in amazement. Kieran said the bird was dead!

"He whispers that Mr. Winter is this way," Lailoken says, pointing through the shadowed trees.

I don't look away from the owl. No, this can't possibly be the same bird. It just can't, not so many years later.

Of course, I'm apparently talking to this guy, who was alive back then too, so . . .

The bird takes off, disappearing into the limbs above.

"Was that Fionn?" I dare to ask.

Lailoken uses his long staff to move the curling arm of a fern off the path. "It's a maybe and a most definitely. It isn't my place to say what spirit returns to me now and then."

The vision of the bird splits me in two again. I feel the familiarity of the trees around me and the cool, damp air—Lily's longing for it all—but this time I don't push her back. I want to believe that Fionn was three feet away from me just now, that he's still alive. It makes the magic in this world seem less horrible, after all the manipulation and dead bodies.

We come to a denser part of the forest again, and Lailoken slows, tapping his staff on a tree with a hollow thunk, thunk, thunk, like he's knocking to be let in.

Another squirrel scuttles from above and begins to chatter, its tail ticking and swishing.

"They come this way," Lailoken says to me, waving at the trees ahead. "Hiding is necessary, I believe. We should choose our moment wisely." He tugs on my sleeve, urging me back behind a rock, and presses me into a bush. I search the trees ahead expectantly. When we hear the crunching of brush and pine needles underfoot, I duck lower behind the rock.

"I think we should take the arrow out," I hear Ben say. "It's tearing his lung. It could make a mess, and he's bleeding an awful lot. I didn't think we were planning on killing him."

"Enough sympathy, Ben," Astrid says in a silky voice. "I know what the demi hunter can take."

My gut clenches hearing them talk about Faelan, his wounds. And when I see the pair of them emerge from the trees, Faelan in tow, I nearly lunge forward. His hands are tied behind his back, the thick torque keeping him powerless. His blue shirt is coated in slick red, and his skin is ashen.

Lailoken grabs me by the arm, shaking his head. "Choose wisely," he mouths.

Ben sets Faelan on the moss, leaning him against a tree. "How long, then? We could be wandering in this place for a fortnight at this rate. We're not going to find the old bastard. He's flown the coop."

"We'll worry about the monk after we catch the princess. Now that we have her protector she'll sense it, and she'll come. Any minute. The stupid bitch is in heat. You should've seen her mooning over him at the Introduction. She has no idea." Astrid crouches beside Faelan. "Does she, lover?"

He opens his eyes slowly, grunting. "Bitch," he mutters, blood glistening on his bottom lip.

She grabs the shaft of the arrow, staring at him. Then she leans close, kissing him full on the mouth, and yanks the arrow out in a swift jerk, laughing as she pulls it away.

He squirms. "What've you done, Astrid, you've gone too far—"

She kisses him again, swallowing his words. When she pulls away the second time, he glowers at her.

"You remember how to play our game, lover?" she asks softly, running a finger down his blood-soaked shirt to the waist of his pants.

His blood is on her lips and smeared on her chin. "We'd play for hours under the willow. Skin and clover and sweat."

My nails scrape against the rock.

"Go fuck yourself," he says through his teeth.

A dark smile slinks up her lips, and she tugs on the waist of his pants, straddling him. "I will do it," she says, "you know I will." She reaches over to her boot and pulls out a smaller knife. She points it at his face, then aims down, cutting the collar of his shirt before ripping it and baring his chest.

He grunts in pain from the sudden movement.

My bones ache watching it. Lailoken takes my arm, like he wants to hold me back from stopping them. I have no idea what I'm waiting for. I can access all my power now. My torque is still in my pocket from when Kieran took it off earlier.

But a part of me knows I still don't have total control over the fire, and I'm terrified of hurting Faelan.

Astrid trails the blade of the knife along his clavicle. "I'll force you to break your vow," she says. "Right here against this tree, with Ben to bear witness—your body never fails to respond to mine, does it? Then you'll be forced to return to your brother. You'll have no choice any longer."

His vow. Could it somehow be keeping him free of his father's House? But how? I thought he was an outcast.

"How could you?" he chokes out. "After everything, you've done *this*? You've sided with Mara, killed a pixie, cursed Marius, chased away an old human—and for what? Just to get me imprisoned again by my brothers, held by your manipulations, after all these centuries?"

She laughs. "Please, you're amazing, but not enough to risk the Pit for. This isn't about you at all; your punishment for leaving me alone is just a bonus." She rests the blade of the knife against his cheek and leans forward. "This is about the newblood. I made a deal, you see. Your precious firebird is going to be worked on by the Princess of Bones.

She's going to drive your pupil completely mad. And then she's going to siphon all that power from her, leaving her a dried-up husk."

Faelan jerks, and the blade breaks his skin, cutting into his face. Blood runs down, slicking his jaw and neck.

Astrid grins as he squirms. "She'll probably look like she did the night you dragged her from the gutter. And all will be complete." She moves the tip of the blade in a circle on his shoulder. "I know you thought I'd changed my mind about leaving your brothers. But I never actually planned to go with you. I couldn't believe you were serious. I'd hoped you'd challenge your brother and take over as master. But I should've known—always so noble. So I waited patiently, and my opportunity finally came. And now I get what I want by upgrading to Kieran, and Princess Mara will get to play her freaky games. I'm excited to watch the bitch you're infatuated with live a horrifying eternity in the princess's claws. It's a win-win for me, really."

A chill works through me as Faelan goes completely still.

Then a burst of noise comes from above, the sound of hundreds of birds filling the trees.

Astrid's smile fades, and she yells into the forest, "You should come out now, Sage. Or I'll make you watch me do more than cut him. Olly, olly, oxen free!"

Lailoken lets go of my arm, whispering, "Go play, Lily."

FORTY-NINE

SAGE

"There she is." Astrid smiles as I move away from the rock. "I thought I smelled you, newblood. How did you like the show?"

"A bit melodramatic," I say, hoping my voice isn't shaking.

"Sage," Faelan says, sounding helpless. He shakes his head. "Just run."

"Oh, she can't leave her crush," Astrid says. "She'd ruin the story."

I give her a plastic grin. "I'm so going to hurt you, bitch," I say. "Lots of pain." And I mean every word. I've never in my life wanted to strangle someone so badly. I think this is what it feels like to be willing to kill. I'd be very okay with her not making it out of here alive.

"Aren't you precious," she scoffs. But her lip twitches like she's bluffing. "It's so good of you to join us."

"Get your ass off him," I say. "Now."

"Are you going to smite me, fire whore?" Her eyes fall to my chest.

"No torque," I say. "You picked the wrong day to mess with me, bitch."

But she laughs, like she's got the upper hand. And then she places her palm on the ground.

"Run, Sage!" Faelan shouts.

A thick vine bursts out of the ground near my foot, scraping up my leg, curling around my hips, my waist, cutting into my sides in seconds. I try to jerk away, to pull free, but the vine holds, cuts into my skin. The growth branches off, capturing my wrists. And I'm stuck.

"Oops," Astrid says, laughing again. She slides off Faelan's lap and stands, then walks over to me.

My energy stirs in my chest, heating, but I hesitate. I'm not sure I know how to focus it yet. And she's still too close to Faelan. I could kill him right along with her. If I can just burn away the vine—

A metal shackle clicks around my neck, latching from behind me. My energy presses at my skin, trapped. And Ben comes up beside me, giving me a shrug.

Astrid's smile stiffens. "Double oops." She's a foot taller than I am, athletic, her striking features heightened by the glow of her white-blond hair.

I want to rip her perfect face off.

"I know you're fond of your protector," she says, her voice dripping with pity. "Such a shame. You realize that it's never going to happen with him, right?" She looks me over, then glances at Faelan. "She's barely a woman, my love. You weren't seriously entertaining her childish infatuation, were you?"

She steps closer, holding up her hand and moving it around me like she's feeling the air. She breathes out a derisive laugh. "The girl's a virgin. How much will you wager you were her first kiss, lover?"

"Enough with the messing around, Astrid," Ben says, sounding annoyed. "Let's just get out of here. This place gives me the creeps."

"We still need the wizard," she says.

"You already stabbed the crazy bastard. And we were running in circles looking for him for more than an hour before these idiots showed up."

Stabbed? Lailoken didn't look stabbed.

"His scent isn't right," Astrid says. "He's probably masking it." But she's still looking me over, like she's searching for a weakness.

"We don't need him," Ben says, "we've got the girl."

"The monk has to die," she snaps. "Princess Mara was very clear on that."

"Why?" he asks, sounding done with it all. She shouldn't have picked a twentysomething frat-boy shade for a sidekick.

"Just get the ivory bowl out of the pack," she says, ignoring him. "Stop being such a child."

Ben grumbles, then walks past me and starts digging in a bag by his foot.

I twist my wrists, trying to see how tight the vines are. There's a little give, but not much.

Ben pulls a bone-white bowl out of the bag and walks it over to Astrid. "Can't we just do this when we get back?"

She snatches the bowl from him. "I'm not traveling with him linked to her, dumbass."

My mind races, trying to figure out what she means.

She steps over to Faelan and squats down, holding the bowl against his chest. She turns to look at me with stony eyes. "You better hope he fed before he came running for you. This takes a lot of blood." She lifts the blade of her knife to his neck. "And he's not like you, Daughter of Fire. He's been cast off from his power source. So if this boy loses too much, he can die."

Real panic hits me then, and I jerk against the vines holding me captive. "No! Don't you dare!"

Her lips twist in a horrible smile.

She swipes with a quick flick of her wrist, like she's finishing off an animal.

Faelan's mouth opens, his throat moves, and his eyes widen. But he's silent. His blood flows into the bowl, soon spilling over the edge.

My heartbeat thunders inside me. Fury beginning a storm.

A storm that can't go anywhere.

Except . . . something tickles behind my eyes. And I smell sulfur. It's not fire; it's not the same as my other energy. It's dark and horrible.

"Thank you, lover," she whispers to Faelan. Then she moves away and turns to me, the bowl of Faelan's blood cupped in her palm. There's blood all over her hands and arms too. She looks like a crazy Serial Killer Barbie. "I was going to do this once Mara put you under," she says to me, "but now you'll have to be wide awake."

From behind her, Faelan gasps for air. But I can't take my eyes off her bloody hands. Faelan's blood. Rage scrapes inside my skull. I want to rip her heart from her chest.

She raises the knife and puts the blade to my neck, just under the torque; it's still warm. Her green eyes lock on mine. "And it really, really hurts to get a protector bond torn out." Satisfaction fills her gaze as she looks into me. But then something catches her eye, and she focuses on my hands.

She cringes. "What . . . is that?"

Ben goes still, looking at me. "That's not right."

I turn to try and see what they're looking at and spot threads of black smoke leaking from my fingertips. What the hell?

"That's not supposed to happen," Ben says. "She's a fire demi."

"Get this thing off me," I growl.

They both jerk back like the sound of my voice physically hit them.

"Her eyes," Astrid whispers. "They're gold."

Ben just shakes his head, seemingly terrified by something in my gaze. "We should hurry and bleed her."

Astrid steps back in front of me, pressing the blade to my throat again.

I stare at her stupid flawless face and snarl, "I'm going to ki—"

She swipes the blade. Pressure fills my head, my eyes widening, my throat closing.

My heartbeat thunders. I can't hear Faelan's labored breathing anymore. All I hear is my hammering pulse and a raven crying in the distance. Everything else is going dim. I barely feel the cut, the loss of blood. Pain doesn't exist.

My mind goes still, and a buzz starts in my hands. The stirring behind my eyes prickles again, more determined. The blood running over my shoulder, sliding down my chest, it doesn't feel right. It isn't warm.

It's cold.

Astrid is standing several feet away now. She's watching me with terror on her face.

"Take . . . it . . . off," I choke out, straining at my bonds.

"How is this happening?" Ben asks, his voice quivering.

"She's manifesting like a Morrígan," Astrid says. "But her eyes . . ."

"She's an abomination." Ben steps closer, pulling out a large dagger. "We need to get her head off."

"Don't touch her!" Astrid rushes forward, reaching out to stop him.

But it's too late. He grips my hair, tipping my head a little, readying the blade to cut.

And the black smoke seeping from my hands slides in his direction, curling around his neck in quick threads.

He stiffens, the knife falling from his fist. His mouth opens in a silent scream, eyes widening as ice crawls across his gaping face, spreading from where the smoke touches, the crystals growing, clouding his wide eyes. The buzzing in my hands radiates into my arms, my chest, shaking my bones as red mist drifts from Ben's mouth into the air, on a hiss of breath.

The body crumples in on itself, wilting like a dying flower, collapsing to the forest floor with a crackle of frozen flesh. I stare down at his broken body, feeling nothing.

The torque that he locked around my neck strains, then snaps with a loud clink.

Instantly the chill in my blood sinks away, the strange dark threads of energy dissipating.

My skin warms, then heats, the torn flesh on my neck shifting and tightening. Healing. The familiar pulse of my power fills my chest, then spills out, coating my skin. Fire flickers at my fingertips. The yellow and orange flames move over my torso, down my arms, snapping at the air with a steady hiss, turning the vines holding me to ash. As I step free, the fire slinks over the ground to Ben, and crawls up his legs, the dead body of the shade becoming a blaze.

Astrid is shaking her head in disbelief, backing away.

I barely believe it myself.

Something moves in the shadows beside her. A raven.

"Danu, save us," Astrid whispers. And then she turns in a rush, grabbing her bow and running toward the trees. Running right into Kieran. His shoulders still seep black smoke from his transformation.

He grabs her by the neck before she can get past him. "Leaving so soon?"

"She's an abomination!" Astrid gasps. "She broke the torque, manifested—there was smoke, black veins. She has Princess Lily's eyes!"

"I know," he says, like she's dense. And then he drags her back to stand in front of me, gripping her neck.

I struggle to focus myself, trying to calm my nerves, trying to pull the fire back. It settles and sinks into my skin again, but the heat keeps swirling with my anger. "Where have you been?" I demand. "If you hadn't noticed, we could've used help."

"I've been watching," he says. He admires me for a second, like he's enjoying all of this. "I've been in the trees, my love, waiting for my moment. You're doing a brilliant job, by the way." He turns back to Astrid and says, "Now, explain to the princess why you're attempting to destroy her."

As soon as he lets go, she crumples to her knees. "I wouldn't hurt her! Please, mistress," she says, suddenly contrite. "Have mercy. I'm a simple servant, an underling of no consequence."

I ignore her pleading and hurry to Faelan's side. I take in the hole in his chest, skin streaked with blood, his hair matted with it, the gaping wound on his neck . . . His eyes are closed, his lips pressed together, as if he's holding in a scream.

"Oh, God, please no," I whisper, trying to untie the rope binding his wrists. "You're okay, Faelan, you'll be okay now." But the knot won't come undone. "Kieran, get the torque unlocked!" I yell. "Hurry!"

He squats on the other side of Faelan, then swipes some blood onto the rim of the torque. It falls away, and Kieran tosses it aside, pulls out his knife, and cuts the bonds. He frowns, watching me warily as I cup Faelan's cheek, touch his forehead.

"Can you hear me, Faelan?" I ask. "Come on, wake up. I'm right here. Please." I study his chest, his neck, but nothing happens. I turn to Kieran. "Why isn't he waking up?"

Kieran just looks at me.

"What do we do?" I shake Faelan's arm. Why is he so cold?

"He's not strong enough," Kieran says, his voice flat.

"What? No. Of course he is." I grip his shoulder. He's fine. He has to be. "Faelan, come back. Wake up!"

"He's not going to wake up, Sage," Kieran says.

"Shut up!" I scream, my voice cracking with pain. And then I go back to shaking Faelan's arm. He'll wake up. He has to wake up. He's a demigod, like me. Astrid was lying when she said he could die, she was trying to scare me. Now Kieran's just being evil. This is *his* fault, anyway—if he'd helped instead of watching . . .

No, it's my fault. I should've just used my power, but I hesitated. I hesitated. And now . . .

No. "Come on, Faelan," I whisper, resting my head on his shoulder.

"You care for him deeply," Kieran says, his voice tight.

I don't say anything. I can't believe this is real.

He seems to be considering something. And then he shifts, slipping his knife into his boot. "Move away," he says, his tone stiff.

But I can't. I can't move. "Please wake up, Faelan."

"Sage," Kieran says. "You must move if I'm to draw his spirit back."

I sit up, staring at him, wondering if I heard him right. His features blur, becoming the familiar face of my king, the green of our surroundings fading to white. Tears streak my cheeks, and I smell ice. But the air around me is warm. It's a dream filtering through. "What are you saying?"

He ignores my question and says again, "Move away, Sage. There is a time limit to this."

I blink, and he's Kieran, surrounded by green, his features tight. He nudges me back from Faelan's side. "You can't touch me, or him, as I do this. And I'm going to need to feed when it's done." He glances behind me to Astrid. "Speak up if you have any ideas on a victim," he says.

I obey, moving back.

He closes his eyes and rests his hand over Faelan's heart.

My pulse stutters as the silver and black smoke lifts from Kieran's chest, swirling and trailing down his arm. The scent of roses fills the space between us just before the familiar snap of mint bites at the air. The moss and grass around us shift from rich green to brown.

Faelan's hand twitches, and the flesh on his neck begins to move, sliding back into place as his wounds seal.

I look over at Kieran, opening my mouth to thank him but the words die in my throat. His pale skin is violet and dark circles rim his eyes. He mutters something I can't hear and then goes limp, collapsing beside Faelan.

"Kieran!" I lunge forward.

"Feed," he whispers.

"Okay, take from me." I move so that he can hold my arm or something, get his hands on bare skin.

He shakes his head. He moves his hand a little, like he's trying to point, and I know he's directing me to Astrid.

"You'll kill her, Kieran."

"Good."

While I was all for it a few minutes ago, I'm not sure I can kill her now that she's pleading for her life.

Before I can wrap my head around what to do, Astrid is suddenly scrambling up, taking off, running for the shadow of the trees as she sees her chance to escape with Kieran weakened.

Shit.

But before I can even stand to chase after her, she crumples in the ferns.

Kieran releases a low chuckle beside me. "Tethered her spirit to mine."

The snap and crack of bending and breaking branches rises into the clearing. Astrid's screeches of protest follow as the grass and ferns shift, and Astrid is dragged back by an invisible hand, kicking and flailing through the trees until she's sliding up to Kieran's side.

As soon as his fingers catch her ankle, Astrid chokes on her screams. Kieran pulls himself up, crawling over her like a beast, straddling her, gripping her neck. He leans in, getting almost nose to nose with her as thick black smoke threads from his arms.

"You," he growls. "You shouldn't have touched her." The black smoke coming from him thickens, coating her body, wrapping around her arms and her chest like a spider's trap as she gapes at his pale face.

Then he sucks in a quick breath, and a strangled gasp pulls from Astrid's throat. Her body jerks, back arching, eyes wide, mouth wide.

A red mist bursts from her skin where the black touches. Ice forms at her neck, crawling up her jaw with a crackle, the same as it did to Ben. She stills, her body settling back into the moss, breath continuing to hiss from her lungs.

Kieran moves off her, his own chest heaving. I can't take my eyes off the red dots of Astrid's blood speckling his face.

FIFTY

Faelan

"I *died*?" I ask, the shock from Sage's words rolling through me.

I woke up in Lailoken's tree, Sage at my side. I didn't even get a word out before she was tackling me and hugging me, sputtering out everything that happened after I passed out. Saying that Astrid killed me, let me bleed out—the one thing that would ensure I wouldn't come back, since all I have left from my father is the power in my blood.

Lailoken comes into view behind Sage. "Oh, it was amazing to watch! So much tension and knots in the stomach." His brows go up and down. "And then you were totally kaput!" He throws his hand in the air. "Who would've thought Mr. Shadow would be so quick to help Mr. Winter? But our tale even surprises me at times." His smile becomes whimsical.

I'm at a loss. I sit up and give Sage a questioning look.

"Kieran brought you back." She motions to someone across the room.

I turn my head, and a shadowed Kieran is leaning on the far wall, arms crossed over his chest, foot propped on the tree behind him. My muscles tense, my nerves buzzing again. *He* brought me back? Not Lailoken?

"You're welcome," Kieran says, his voice flat. "And I ate your ex-lover as well."

My hands flex involuntarily, gripping the moss under me. "Astrid. You fed off—?"

"Killed her, actually," he finishes for me, a satisfied glint in his eyes. "She was a bit more broccoli than I like, though."

Sage glares at him. "Seriously, Kieran."

His gaze falls on her, and his expression softens.

My pulse skips seeing him look at her like that. As if he has a heart to care for her.

"I should go," he says. "This forest is protected from my sister's eyes, but she'll be missing me if I'm unseen for too long. We wouldn't want her getting suspicious." He pushes off the wall. "Thank you for the potion, monk."

"Yes, yes, my boy," Lailoken says. "I hope it helps settle him."

"I'm sure it will." He glances at Sage once more, like he's hesitant to go. But then he slips out into the woods.

"What a nice young man," Lailoken says.

Obviously they haven't properly met.

"So now that Mr. Winter is awake, let's get started on young Lily here." He motions for me to sit on a bench at the table.

My legs wobble as I rise, and I have to lean on Sage as she helps me to the seat. I struggle with my emotions, watching her move back to sit beside Lailoken on the dry brown moss where I was lying.

Because I failed. In the end it was Kieran who did the protecting. Of me.

"What's going to happen?" Sage asks the monk. "Will the spell fix the confusion with the memories?"

"Are you removing the dreams?" I ask, trying to shift my thoughts.

"No, no, there's no helping the truth of the past," Lailoken says. He starts plucking pieces of mint from a bush at the edge of the room and tossing them into a bowl. He turns back to Sage. "But this *will* allow you to accept things inside, to balance the spirits, so the tug-of-war can settle. For now, the two within must come to an understanding. This way you can serve your purpose. You can become your true self."

Her tense shoulders relax.

"What does that mean?" I ask. There's still so much we don't understand. If this is about Sage's problem with the blood memories, I need to be sure that what the monk is doing is safe. "All you have to do is take out the implant and help her with the dreams."

Lailoken sighs. "There is much to say about that, much. I will tell you in the best way I can, and maybe you'll understand better." He sets down the bowl of mint and pulls the nest from his head, making an attempt to straighten his hair. "It was long ago. And I have much clouding the nut. But I will try." He taps a finger at his temple. Then he clears his throat and takes a deep breath, closing his eyes for a second. When he opens them, they seem clearer, more . . . human. "I was the queen's watcher, you know," he says, directing his words to Sage.

She nods, sadness filling her eyes.

"She was so young," he continues, "only a child when I stumbled upon her. Father Caelus at the monastery had taught us of the other things that roamed the woods, at times wolves, at times gods that masked themselves as wolves. So when I found her, I knew what she was, though I had no real knowledge of how powerful she'd become." He stares into the small flames dancing in the trough, his eyes going distant. "The goddess came to me that first night."

He looks up at me, then back to Sage, and it's like he's pleading with us to believe him, like he's letting go of something he's held tight for too long. "Brighid came to me in the flames—me, a lowly monk. It was a miracle." He shakes his head like he has trouble believing it himself. "She told me who the child Lily was, told me how vital she was, and asked me to keep her daughter close. And so I did." He releases a shaky breath. "Until the very end, I stayed with her. And when she was taken from me, when the Cast put her in that place they call the

Pit, I thought I would finally die at last. I had been here on this earth so long, surely it was time to bid farewell." He shakes his head again, looking weary.

"But I waited. I made my home deeper in the wood. And still I stayed.

"Before my Lily had been taken, we did a spell that bound her power, bound her energy and her spirit and her memories, into an owl's egg. And then we burned it, turning it into ashes that I was to spread in the field once Lily was taken by the Cast—we knew they were coming. It was Lily's way of being free, even as she was trapped in the Pit. Her sorrow could remain behind. She'd go forward as a mere shell, and feel nothing." A tear slips down his weathered cheek.

"I was ashamed of what we'd done." His voice wavers. "Her eyes were dead the day they came for her, nothing real left behind. I felt as if I'd destroyed her, and it was for nothing." He pauses, swallowing hard. "She had become ashes in a field of bluebells. But after a moon had passed, the goddess Brighid came to me again, this time in the figure of a horned owl. She told me that she'd brought me her second daughter to care for. She told me she had another spell for me to do. And she left me with a golden-and-black egg the size of a melon, along with a lock of brown hair."

An egg the size of a melon? The words poke at my insides and a chill runs down my spine.

Sage—but that was so long ago.

"That was me," Sage says, wonder in her voice. "I was born from an egg?"

"You were, child," Lailoken says. "All children of a goddess are born from an egg." He stands and walks over, pulling a small box from a nook in the wall of the tree. He brings it over to me and opens it, showing me the contents.

Sitting inside are three large pieces of what look like a broken porcelain bowl, the inside shiny sky blue, the outer swirled in black and gold—the remnants of Sage's shell. And beside the pieces of shell is a curl of light brown hair, tied with a piece of vine. I frown at the contents, not understanding.

"You gave this bit of hair to my Lily," he says to me. "Yes?"

"I don't—" I'm about to say I don't know what he's talking about, but then I remember, the silver coin. Queen Lily had asked for a lock of my hair in exchange for a silver coin three nights before she was taken by the Cast. "Yes, I gave her my hair." And then I thought nothing of it.

"The goddess placed this and the large egg at my feet that night, and she told me to lay one over the other, to cast protection and loyalty between them. I was to give the sturdiness and loyalty of the winter wolf to the source of the hair and the determination and passion of the flame to the life within the egg. I was to speak it over them for as long as they were in my care. And make them into two sides of a coin."

"How long ago was that?" Sage asks.

He looks to the side, like he's trying to remember. "I counted the moons, one, two, three . . . the years, one, two, three . . . and the decades, one, two, three . . . and on and on. I moved deeper and deeper into the wood, hiding and keeping it all to ourselves, lost and forgotten. Finally, she hatched. Eighteen years ago." He shrugs, tipping his head at Sage.

Sage swallows, her eyes turning glassy.

"Your tiny pale body was so delicate," he continues. "If not for the owls bringing milk and shiny baubles to me from far away, I don't know how I'd have cared for you. You were such a fragile doll." He smiles at her softly and reaches out, taking her hand.

A tear slips down her cheek. "But I don't understand. How did I end up with Lauren?"

"I was told not to keep you past your third year. I didn't understand, you see, what to do." Guilt fills his eyes, and he gives her a pleading look. "But when I went into the world again, to find your path for you, I was overwhelmed. It was all a big noise. So many things hurt my eyes, my ears. And I got confused." He leans forward, like he needs Sage to understand. "I was to follow a trail of gold, that's what the goddess had said. The gold energy led me to a most horrible place. But I didn't know. If I'd known what that woman was, I wouldn't have obeyed, I don't think." He looks away, his eyes haunted. "I found the dead child in the green box full of trash down the road. But I'd already left my treasure—you—in its place. When I went back to the woman, she was holding my little fire-haired girl and singing her a song, crying quietly. I thought perhaps . . . perhaps you'd be all right." He shakes his head, his shoulders sinking. "Perhaps . . . I am so sorry, child. I should not have obeyed." He dares to look at Sage again. "I went back many times to search for you. But I'd forgotten where I put you. I'd forgotten where the road was. I looked for days and days, finding only sadness and pain."

Tears streak Sage's face. She just nods. But she grips his hand back now, like she's trying to reassure him.

He sniffs and wipes his nose with his wide sleeve. "But all was not lost, as I thought," he says, his voice brightening. "A sennight ago, this boy brought you to me." A smile grows on his face. "And in that moment, when I realized who you were, my despair washed away. Things cleared in my mind that had been muddy for so long. I'd nearly forgotten my task, you see. Now I understand what the goddess meant."

I lean forward. "So you knew who Sage was that day? Why didn't you tell me all of this before I left with her?"

"And what?" he scoffs. "Reveal the truth before the tale had even begun?" He rises and goes back to plucking mint. "No, no, boy. I marked her with my protection before you left again, so that most would stay out of the way. It was all taken care of. She would be safe, see."

"Wait, it was *you* who marked me?" Sage says.

"Of course!" he says. "I wouldn't dare allow you to be lost from me again."

"But I don't understand," I say. "Why did she stay hidden for so long with the humans?"

"The goddess cloaked her—cloaked her power, her name, her birthright." He grinds his pestle into the bowl, mixing the ingredients. "She needed to keep her Lily safe."

"Wait, how is that related to Sage?" I ask, not sure the dots are connecting. Because what I'm thinking can't really be right.

He pauses his potion making, setting the bowl down again. He scoops some of the contents into her palm. "Sage's power is her own, but it's Lily's too, you see." He shows me what's in his hand, pieces of mint leaves and lavender, mixed with what looks like cinder. "The ashes I spread into the earth kept the spirit, the energy, the memories safe. Brighid pressed them into her new daughter, hoping to join them together and allow her first to have a voice again."

Two sources, Sage and Lily, joined together. Holy Danu, that's a lot of power in one vessel. I've never heard of such a thing.

He spits in the bowl of mint and then turns to me. "I hate to ask, but this requires more blood from you, Mr. Winter."

"Why do you keep calling me that?" I ask.

He squints at me. "You are Mr. Winter, are you not? The protector? The gray wolf?"

I don't see how any of it connects. "I'm Sage's protector, but—"

"Well, then." He raises his brow at me and holds out a blade and a bowl. "I need blood."

I sigh. "What for?" I eye the contents of the bowl warily. There's been too much spellwork in this mess already.

"I wish to ease her struggle," he says. "The two spirits need to come to an understanding. Your blood will be key in that, since you are her balance, the ice to her flame. You see?" His eyes brighten like he's just revealed the key to the whole story. But I'm still lost.

I pull out my dagger anyway. "How much do you need?"

FIFTY-ONE

SAGE

A wash of affection rolls over me as we say goodbye. I smile and kiss Lailoken's wrinkled forehead. I feel more connected to him than I have to anyone in my life, and even though he knows me, I've really only just met him. But he raised me for a time, he cared for me. I can't hold it against him that he left me with Lauren. He couldn't have known what she was. "Thank you, friend," I whisper.

Color rises in his cheeks. He grabs the nest from the table and plops it back on his head.

"Don't fret," he says. "The boy will bring you back to me for more adventures. Won't you, boy?"

"Yes, sir," Faelan says. He hesitates and then asks, "I wonder . . . do you happen to have an antidote for *Sagitta Anathema*?"

"Oh my. A sharp dart, that one." He frowns, then looks through the bottles on his table. "I think some of this." He hands Faelan a blue bottle. "Mixed with this, equal parts." He hands him a milky bottle too. "Along with three pixie tears, a pickled robin's egg, and fennel. Maybe an onion, if you like."

Faelan gives him a doubtful look. "Fennel and onion?"

"Helps with the smell." The old man shrugs. "But be sure to give it when the moon is highest or it won't work."

"Thank you," Faelan says, hope filling his voice. He tucks the bottles into his pocket. "I'll be waiting for you outside, Sage." He slips out the door, into the green, leaving me with the old monk.

He must be able to see that I'm not quite ready to say goodbye. There's so much still inside me.

"Thank you for everything," I say once the door closes. When I was a kid, I always wondered how it felt to have that person, the one soul who cared where you were late at night, or wanted you to get good grades in school. The person who gave a damn. I never thought I'd have that. But he's been here the whole time, waiting and wondering where I'd gone. And a tiny piece of my heart has locked back into place. "I'm really glad you finally found me."

He nods, tears glistening in his eyes.

"I'll come visit after the Emergence," I say. A twinge fills my chest as I realize how close I am to the moment, so I add, "I'm going to be okay." It's almost a question, but I need to speak it and make it true. Like a spell.

"You'll shock them all," he says, a mischievous smile growing on his face.

"Thank you," I say again as I step toward the door. "Really."

"No more of that now," he says, shooing me. "You'll have my head as big as a pumpkin."

"Just take care of yourself. And that squirrel."

"Yes, yes." He pats my arm. "And don't forget to eat your vegetables. And be careful playing in the hedges."

Outside, I find Faelan waiting a few feet away in a patch of bluebells, watching bees gather pollen.

I stand beside him and look out at the meadow. "It sure is pretty here." I see why Lily longed to come back.

"It is," he says absently, but when I glance at him, he's looking at me and not at the woods.

"Are you all right?" I ask, sensing he's conflicted about something. I don't like seeing that shadow in his eyes.

He watches the forest ahead, staying silent until we've left the field of flowers behind and entered the trees. But when he speaks, his words aren't what I expect.

"I was ten years old when my mother died," he says so quietly I almost don't hear him over the crunching of our steps in the underbrush. I'm unsure why he said it. But there's a determined quality to his voice, as if he needs to speak the words, so I don't ask questions. He continues. "They told me she'd fallen into the river and drowned. But later, after—a long time after—I asked the river for the truth and learned that it wasn't an accident. She'd killed herself, placed rocks in her skirts and tied a stone to her ankle."

My throat tightens in pain. "I'm so sorry," I say, his childhood sorrow very real to me. He was a boy alone in a difficult world. I understand that life better than anyone.

"It was Astrid who taught me how to hear the river," he says, pushing aside a branch and letting me duck under. "Later, after I understood what the water's current was telling me, it was Astrid who helped me heal. At least for a little while." He looks at me like he needs me to understand. "It's why I forgave her so much all those years."

I nod, unsure what to say.

There's a weight on him as we walk, his body tense like he still feels the pain of the past in his skin. "My mother drowned herself because she was ashamed," he says. His voice falters and his pace slows. He stares out at some distant point, a lost look in his eyes. "She was ashamed of how I was conceived." He turns to me again. "I wasn't born of an encounter made of love or lust, but of violence, Sage. My father, a god of virility who could have enticed most any woman, saw what he wanted in my mother and chose to take it from her by force."

Chills rake over me. "Oh, God."

"I was born of that sickness. It's a part of me."

Urgency fills me at the tormented sound of his voice. "Faelan . . . that's not true."

But he doesn't seem to hear me. "After I learned the truth, I was overwhelmed by the lie my life had become. So I abandoned my House—I broke the vow I'd made at my Emergence. I couldn't be loyal to a father who would be so vile. I couldn't stay under my brother's rule—I'd quickly realized that his nature was as debased as our father's. And I was terrified I would become just like them."

I can only shake my head, disgusted, words failing me.

He stares at the ground, like he's ashamed. I want to touch him, to comfort him, but I know he'll push me away.

So instead I say, "You're nothing like that, Faelan."

"I made sure I never would be," he says, his voice tight. "In order to leave, there was a payment to be made. A demi doesn't just break a vow on a whim. I had to give things up, to sacrifice. So I severed the link to my father, allowing for a majority of my power to return to the gods, keeping only my secondary gift and locking away my healing ability in my blood so that I wouldn't have immortality anymore." His brow pinches. "But I also forged a soul vow with the Cast to remain celibate, to sever that part of my life. And if I break my vow, I'll be forced to return to my brother. It was the easiest choice in the world when I made it. Until . . ." He turns to me, searching my face. "I find myself regretting my choice now."

His words settle in the air between us like a question.

The forest around us creaks, waiting.

"I find myself wishing for another man's life when I'm near you," he says. "I feel a hundred things for you that I can't feel."

I let his words sink in. And I understand, finally. He hasn't been keeping his distance for the reasons I assumed. He's been tormented, broken, in ways I could never imagine. He's had to face more sorrow than I could ever carry. And yet he still sees me as I am, and cares about me, cares for me. It feels like it's too much.

I move in front of him, unable to hold back from comforting him now. I want to take away that haunted look in his eyes. I want to say a million things, anything to help him carry the burden of those horrors, let him know that I'll never think of him as a monster, that it doesn't matter what he can give me; I'll take it.

Instead I reach out and slide my fingers through his, then ask under my breath, "What about this? Is this against the rules?"

He studies me, his features softening. "No," he says.

I could tell him that I feel sorrow for him, that I want to relieve him of his pain—but I'd rather just push the darkness back. I need him to understand that I don't see him like his nightmare. Not even a little.

So I step closer. "Because this is nice," I say, "standing with you in the trees." He seems relieved at my words. The scent of his energy envelops me, fresh mint tingling in my throat like he's seeking me out. I feel my power stir in response, but I hold it steady—easily, the control second nature now. And I let myself whisper, "I think I'd like to kiss you. Is that all right?"

He nods slowly, brushing his fingers over my jaw as the space between us shrinks. "You're an amazing one, fiery Sage," he says.

"Too true."

I smile, rising as he bends, and our lips touch, gentle and delicate. I take in the smell of his skin, the taste of his breath, fresh and alive, then we pull away and continue walking, his fingers still woven through mine, as we listen to the life in the trees, the song of the birds and the rustle of the leaves. Leaving behind the weight of what came before.

After a while I say, "Astrid was right about one thing, you know."

He frowns, giving me a sideways look.

I grin at him. "You were my first kiss."

~

I find my king in a small thicket, resting under a rowan tree. His head leans on the dark, twisted trunk, eyes closed, the limbs above him heavy with red berries. His raven, Bran, announces my arrival with a screech as I come through the ferns. He hushes the bird with a cluck of his tongue.

"Why did you draw me here, my love?" I ask, kneeling beside him in the clover. "I thought you were in Constantinople."

He reaches out, brushing his calloused fingers along my jaw. "I wanted you here in this moment, to be home where you feel safe."

The pained look in his eyes stills me. Something's wrong. "What's happened?"

"My sister."

"Mara again? What of her?" His sister is always a nuisance, trying to pull his strings, to manipulate me as well. But what could she have done to create that torment in his eyes? There's never been any true danger from her.

"She's done the unthinkable, Lilybird." He takes my hand, weaving our fingers together. "She's set to destroy you, to steal your heart, your soul if need be. And I'm afraid she's come too close this time. We weren't wary enough of her."

"What do you mean?"

He reaches into his pocket and pulls something free. "I am poisoned."

I go cold, the warm summer air of the wood no longer soothing my skin. "Poison? But you . . . what are you saying?" It doesn't make sense.

"I had to be sure," he says. "I felt the effects of something, but I didn't realize what it was. I discovered her trickery last night." His palm opens, and I see my torque cradled in his fingers.

I look at it, trying to understand why he's showing it to me. "I haven't worn that in centuries."

"I tucked it away long ago, when you first came to me, and now I carry it with me when I'm away from you, so that it's always near my heart." I reach out to take it, but he closes his fingers, hiding it in his fist again. "She

somehow had it soaked in an insidious poison. It's very powerful. I've never felt anything like this. I'll be lost to it soon."

A sharp pain pierces my chest. "No," I say, very sure, "you can't be seeing this right. It can't be true." My love cannot be lost from me. Not my king. He is death. He is forever.

"I've asked your monk, and he's revealed the truth for me," he says. "It appears to be a poison from a Chaldean sect. I have little time before it eats away at my mind. I'll be useless within a fortnight, and there's no antidote. Not even your monk knows of one."

"No," I say again. His words won't settle in me. This can't be real. I saw him last moon before he left on his journey to the east; he was well, strong.

"It's why I called you to this wood," he says, ignoring my protest, "where my sister's eyes can't penetrate. We must act now or it'll be too late. I won't be able to instruct you on how to destroy me."

"Stop," I say, rising to my feet. "Enough. You're talking nonsense. I'll speak to Lailoken, he'll know what we can do. We should have your younger sister call on your mother—"

"Silence," he growls, struggling to his feet, leaning on the tree. "Hear me, Lily. I'm telling you, there is only one thing to do if we're to salvage this and protect what we've created."

I stare at him, shocked by his weakness, even as I feel his wrath filling the trees. The raven screeches, then spreads its huge wings, lifting off the ground to settle on a branch above.

"It is a very old magic," he says, his voice shaking now. "It is very delicate. But it will allow us to hide, to bide our time." He coughs and blood stains his lips; he wipes it with his sleeve as if it were nothing. "We will create a story. It will go before us, and when we're able to complete the circle, we can find our way back. It's the only way."

Fear crawls through me. "What magic is this?"

"We sever our spirits," he says, "leave our vessels behind us." When I only stare at him, he continues, "You will hide yourself in Fionn, and

I will hide in Bran." He glances at his raven, determination in his eyes. *"We'll ensure that your demi body is preserved for a while so that you can come back first, when the time is right. My body will need to be destroyed, however, because of the poison—and it must happen tonight before we leave this wood. I trust you will find a way to pull me from Bran and place me in a proper vessel soon after your own rebirth."*

It's impossible to breathe. My whole body shivers as I listen to him, my fire stirring in my skin. Tonight? He will be lost to me after tonight?

I can only shake my head.

"Once Mara believes we're lost forever, we'll be free to find our window to destroy her." He leans back against the tree and stares up into the branches. *"When I have my strength again, I'll gleefully rip her spine from her body with my bare hands."*

"Goddess be with us," I whisper, tears stinging my eyes. My teeth chatter as my insides quake.

He reaches out to me, pulling me closer, into his embrace. *"You mustn't allow her the victory of your tears. Be strong, Lilybird."*

"I won't be anyone when you're gone from me."

"Nonsense," he says, kissing my brow. *"You are the Daughter of Fire. No man or woman will touch you and come away whole."*

We sink down, resting in each other's arms beneath the tree, the roots and moss cradling us.

"Mother has spoken of a sister for me," I say, thinking of my prayers last night. *"A new daughter will come into the fold. Perhaps, in time, she'll aid us."*

"I've left a message for Kieran to find once he's ready," the king says.

I clutch him tighter, burying my face in his neck, unable to consider letting go.

"I will find you, Lily," he says, his chest vibrating against my temple. *"I will always find you."* He pulls back, tipping my chin to meet his gaze. *"Look at me and see the truth. I am yours and you are mine."* His silver

eyes search my own. "Nothing will destroy that. Neither time nor death will sever us."

He leans in, his lips brushing my cheek, kissing away my tears, as he whispers promises into my skin that I cling to. His hands grip me tight, holding me to him, bruising me, pulling me down beside him, insistent, urgent. Until we're cradled in the roots, twisted together in the clover, clutching, grasping for an escape. Moving to the sound of our breath. To the beat of our hearts.

Saying goodbye.

FIFTY-TWO

SAGE

I sit under the trees by the pool and watch the sun rise on the day of my Emergence. The sky is silver as the birds begin to stir. It shifts to pale blue, then a wash of pink emerges as the first rays of sunlight hit the ocean. The dew clings to my skin.

The dream from the night before lingers, and an ache has settled in my rib cage since I opened my eyes. Now I know how it ended. Lily didn't kill the king, not really. I have no idea what to do about it. Especially today of all days.

Today I choose my path. Last night I packed a bag, in case the path I choose to follow is not to pick one of the Houses at all but to walk away altogether. To become a child of a goddess in hiding.

When I packed the bag, I wanted that option in front of me. But once I woke up, the vision of my king's death vivid in my mind, I realized I couldn't go anywhere.

I look down at my hands, knowing they're not Lily's. But I feel like I can still see the blood of my lover on them . . . so much blood . . . He showed her how to aid him in pulling his spirit free, in destroying his vessel, placing him temporarily in the large raven, Bran. Poor Lily obeyed down to the last horrible detail.

Until she was a shivering mess, like a crimson-stained ghost in the clover.

My first instinct after waking was to grab a steak knife and find Mara to cut her head off. But that isn't a plan I pull off in one piece. She's way too powerful. And it's clear that she'll ensure others get ripped to bits along with me.

I have to think of something else.

I hear Faelan's cottage door open and close, and I turn as he appears on the pathway.

"Good morning," he says tentatively, like he can sense my mood.

I smile up at him, my insides heating as my energy stirs in spite of my torment. "How'd you sleep?"

"I didn't," he says. "I was making sure the antidote really worked for Marius as well as we thought."

"How's he feeling?" We gave the cure to him yesterday morning. By evening he was downstairs making pancakes.

"He seems . . . amazingly unaffected. Back to his old self. You can't talk to him today, though, until this Emergence is over—no demi contact from the Houses until after the ceremony. I don't count, since I'm your shadow." His voice becomes unsure at the end. He settles in to sit next to me and his eyes go to the sunrise. "Are you all right?"

I nod, lying.

He turns his attention to the rocks and moss between us. "My job ends today."

I reach out and touch his arm, moving my thumb back and forth. I want to tell him he'll always be my protector, but I don't know that. I don't know what my life will look like after today. I do know one thing, though. "You're the one I want beside me," I say.

He searches my face. A small smile lifts the corner of his mouth.

I lean in to him, resting my head on his shoulder, and hope I can hold on to this feeling—of home.

~

I stand alone in the shadow of the large stones and watch the representatives of the five Houses walk onto the stage. My heart races as they take their places on the large pentagram painted in the center of the courtyard. Marius of Brighid first, stepping onto the point of fire. Then Gwyn of Lyr, walking forward to stand on water. Beatrix of Arwen next, moving to the point of air. Finbar of Cernunnos, stepping up to earth. And last, Princess Mara, the creature who destroyed my sister and would like to do the same to me, slinks over to her place on the point of spirit, a vision of pale skin, long dark hair, and deadly beauty.

A few hours ago, a very stiff alfar named Ira, according to the badge on his shirt, explained where I'm supposed to stand and what the order of things will be. For such a huge deal, it seems to be a fairly simple process.

Faelan stands off to the side, waiting for me to enter the courtyard before he joins me. The moment is supposed to represent my entrance into the world alone, according to Ira.

The crowd on the other side of the courtyard appears to be large, but it's difficult to tell from where I'm standing. I know Kieran is out there somewhere. And Aelia, who was very annoyed that the priests chose to use the ancient wardrobe for this ceremony rather than a modern one. She couldn't help me accessorize because I was only allowed to wear my torque, so she helped me get this toga thing to look a little less awkward by tying it with a golden cord.

A hum begins in the distance, and five robed druids, male and female, walk forward, holding torches aloft, a wordless song droning from them. They weave through the crowd, their voices rising and falling, sending the eerie vibration through the courtyard. Once they enter the stage, each takes their spot behind a House on the pentagram.

The envoy to the Cast steps forward onto a raised platform off to the side. He's clothed in robes similar to the priests' but his are pure white, unmarked by stitching or design. "We gather to welcome a new spirit to the fold," he says to the onlookers. "The second Daughter of Fire will raise the level of the House she claims. She will be a gem for the one who holds her." He turns toward my place in the shadows. "Daughter of Fire, come forward. It is time for your naming."

My pulse picks up. My feet are stuck.

Just one step at a time, Sage.

I move, my whole body shivering as I walk into the moonlight and enter the courtyard.

The crowd stirs, and I stand straighter, lifting my chin as I step onto the raised platform beside the envoy.

"Kneel, fire child," he says.

I obey, trying to ready myself for what he'll say.

"The Cast that watches over you has chosen a title for their new ward." He places his palm on my head. A surge of heat washes over me, and my skin shimmers, gold light pulsing up my arms. He continues, "You are to be Princess of Hope and Morning, your life symbolizing rebirth for us all. As fire destroys, it also cleanses and readies the earth for new growth. So it shall be with you."

My breath catches at his words as they hit me, soaking in. And the weight in my bones from the last two weeks—the last eighteen years of my life—seems to lift off me.

"Now you choose, child," he says. And he holds out his arm, ushering me forward.

I breathe in and step off the platform, walking toward the circle. Faelan joins me as I approach. But I pause for a moment, coming to the edge of the painted blood circle. I look to Marius, and he bows his head slightly. I give him a small nod in return.

I think of my choice, how much it will mean to so many. How I don't want to hurt anyone. I want to do the thing that'll hold the most value. But as much as I feel like I'm a part of this new world now, the core of who I am is simple: I'm a girl who's looked her whole life for one thing.

Just one.

I reach out for Faelan's hand, and he offers it easily.

This. This is what my heart wants more than anything: family and trust. And now that I've found it, I'll protect it. I'll protect it with my life, my heart, even my soul.

I give Faelan a small smile and squeeze his hand, wishing I could say out loud what I'm feeling. Then I look across the circle at Princess Mara, and our eyes meet. My smile grows as hers fades.

Because I see it now. She's afraid.

Of me.

And with sudden understanding, I know how to make her pay.

I let Faelan's fingers slip from mine and step into the circle, staring straight at her, feeling Lily surface, my sister's rage and my rage mingling, sending a sheen of fire across my palms. So much was stolen. So much . . .

But I can claim it all back, everything—the lost years, the lost blood. I'll rip it from her bony fingers.

I watch her unease from across the circle, and my own thirst for justice grows. My need to stop her, to protect what I've found here.

I know what she loves. I know what I can steal. And I know I'm not alone once I begin this.

So I step toward her, keeping my eyes locked with hers. As loudly as I can, I announce, "I claim Morrígan." Then I smile and whisper sweetly so that only my new princess can hear: "You hurt my family, bitch. Your crown is about to be mine."

EPILOGUE

KIERAN

What was she thinking? Fool girl.

I hurry down the hall toward the library, breaking the lock and opening the door with a wave of my hand when I'm still several yards away. Mara will return any minute with her entourage in tow, feeling vindicated, thinking she's won. I'll need to take precautions, begin to change my plans—to what, I have no clue. But I certainly can't start a war in the House now, not with Sage in the crosshairs.

I'm going to throttle that bastard Faelan for giving the girl so much bloody free will.

Once I'm in the library, I shut the door behind me and call out, "She's gone and done the unthinkable, brother."

The raven swoops down from above, landing on the desk lamp. It screeches and pecks in my direction. I know my brother is in there somewhere behind those black eyes. I haven't managed to find a way to understand him since Mara found him three months ago and held him here, but I'm hoping he'll finally understand me.

"I broke the spirit tether," I say as I move to the stained-glass window, opening it and revealing the night sky. "The counter spell will only last a minute or two, so you need to go. Now. Time's run out, no more foolishness. Mara will be on a tear." I've tried to get him to fly away several times, but he remains in this room, imprisoned by our sister. I don't understand it. No matter how many times I've found him an escape, he stays.

A foolish part of me wonders if he's protecting me from her wrath—if he escapes, she'll know I'm the one who released him. But the realist in me is fairly sure that my brother is no longer capable of thought like that. After living inside the raven for so long, his thoughts are those of a bird, rarely more complex than the need for a meal or a shiny bauble.

I'm not sure how Mara discovered him after all of this time—or why she hasn't destroyed him. I've known what happened since the day I found Lily in the glade, surrounded by the pieces of his body. My brother had tucked a note to me in my favorite map, explaining that his raven would house his spirit until he could find another vessel, and Lily would be inside Fionn—though that turned out different than he thought. But I never saw the raven again, until three months ago when Mara brought him to me, triumphant at her discovery. He's been stuck in those hollow bones and onyx feathers for nearly seven horrible centuries.

Horrible for me, that is. By putting Mara on the throne, he left me without a protector. While he's been flying around, living out this twisted fae tale, I've been in hell.

Bran squawks again and hops down onto the desk, pecking at a stack of paper.

"Please, brother," I say. "You need to go. I won't be able to protect both of you. Lily will be lost if Sage is consumed by our sister. You should at least care about that." I step closer to the bird, hands turning to fists at my side to keep myself from reaching out and wringing its bloody neck. "Hear me, dammit."

Bran pecks at the papers again, even more insistent. And this time I notice a symbol on the top paper in the stack.

It's a flame knot in a circle. Burned in. Was that there before?

The raven pecks again, and I watch, stunned, as a second knot burns in beside the first, the paper sizzling as an unseen brand stamps the symbol for spirit on it.

The bird created the mark. But it doesn't make sense.

"What am I meant to do?" I ask, sensing my brother may be instructing me on how to fight back against Mara. But I've been fighting against my sister in secret for all these centuries, and what good has it done? She only gets stronger by the day.

The raven pecks again below the two circles. And the Gaelic word for vase—or is it jar?—appears.

No, *vessel*.

Realization dawns on me. "You wish for me to find you a vessel?" I've looked already, with no success. It would take a very powerful demi to filter my brother's magic once he begins to allow his power to flow through the blood again. "A new link could fail," I explain. "I haven't—"

My brother tap, tap, taps harder on the paper with his beak. A new word appears, and my chest constricts as it forms in hissing embers.

Kieran.

I stare at my name. Then at the bird.

Cold understanding filters through me then, as I see where this has always been leading. What my brother, the king, must've considered long ago.

Me. My brother wants me as his vessel.

ACKNOWLEDGMENTS

Every story has its own process. And along the road there are countless angels to help a tale find its way. This novel certainly had its fair share of heroes.

I'm so very grateful to my agent, badass Rena Rossner, who reminded me more times than I could count that I could do this. You're a fighter and a miracle worker, lady! And I'm beyond thankful to have you walking alongside me on this perilous journey of publishing.

To the team at Skyscape, who make this publishing thing seem painless and work hard to let it be the great adventure I always dreamed it would be. To Adrienne—I'm so thrilled that you believed in this one, and I'm really hoping it'll make you proud. To Marianna—you're a visionary, lady! Thank you so much for bringing clarity to the crazy that I send you.

A million hugs and boxes of chocolates to my writer friends, Merrie, Becky, Paul, and Mike, for your ready ears and red pens. Panera memories are the best memories. We'll still be meeting in a booth when we get to Paradise.

To my weekly savior and plotting guru, Catherine—what, in the name of pants, would this book have been without your amazingly helpful imagination? I don't even want to know. Thank you for all the emergency chats! And for not laughing hysterically when I told you my silly idea.

A big venti-sized hug to Angie for all our Starbucks chats and for helping me understand the goddess a little better through your eyes.

Thank you to the Lit Bitches for your constant encouragement and acceptance. And to all my Codexian pals, I'm so very thankful we're in the trenches together. You guys inspire me every day. I seriously can't believe you still let me hang out with your talented selves.

To the best bestie that ever was or will be, Cayse Day—you're always willing to listen to my venting and feed me amazing food and fab wine when things look dim, then pour me more wine when they look great. Thank you for letting Dave ignore chores to read my books and give me his awesome feedback!

To my mom—I'd buy you all of the KitKats on planet Earth and Mars if I could afford it. Thanks for putting up with me and my weird brain—of course, it's kind of your own fault, so . . .

To my amazing kiddos—there are no words for how grateful I am to you for all the slack you give me. You deserve a way better and more smarter mommy, but I know you're okay with this crazy lady who would watch *Friends* reruns with you into eternity. Anyway, it's a "moo point"—a cow's opinion, that is—because you're stuck with me.

To my husband, my partner in crime, my lover, and my best friend—you made this nutty dream of mine possible, believing in me when I didn't believe in myself, and challenging me not to give up when everything seemed hopeless. Even when it meant you had to be annoyed late into the night by the light from my computer screen. The waves in Heaven are gonna be awesome, sweetie, just for you.

And, as always, I give you the glory, *El Elyon*, God of gods, and keeper of my heart. I rest beneath your wings . . .

ABOUT THE AUTHOR

Rachel A. Marks is an award-winning writer, a professional artist, and a cancer survivor. She is the author of the Dark Cycle series, which includes *Darkness Brutal*, *Darkness Fair*, and *Darkness Savage*, and of the novella *Winter Rose*. Her art can be found on the covers of several *New York Times* and *USA Today* best-selling novels. She lives in Southern California with her husband, four kids, three chickens, two precocious pups, and a cat. You can find out more about her weird life on her website at www.RachelAnneMarks.com.